DESCENT INTO DARKNESS

BOOK TWO

A THREE MOONS REALM NOVEL

JAMES R. VERNON

JUST A FEW PEOPLE THAT DESERVE A SPECIAL THANKS.

My immediate family for supporting all of the time and effort I've put into this story.

My excellent beta reader, C.D. Verhoff, for helping me shake off the bad habits of a new writer. I am becoming an adequate adverb killer and plot streamliner thanks to her help.

My amazing and patient editor, Josephine Hao from Sound Copy Editing.

My cover artist, Mominur Rahman, for the amazing work he creates that helps draw both my readers and myself into my world.

And certainly those that backed me in a big way to get this book whipped into shape;

Jim and Frances Vernon
James and Kim Logan
Caitlin G.
Charlie and Amy Metz
Angela Q.
Mary Elizabeth Gaige
George Windsor
James E.
Linda Aben-Kralowetz

DESCENT INTO DARKNESS

CHAPTER 1

EAN OPENED HIMSELF UP to as much of the energy from the Abyss as he could. It rushed into him, more than he had ever held before. He felt like a jar trying to contain a flood as it swirled about inside of him. The glove on his right hand, as well as most of his sleeve, seemed to burn away as the tattoos encircling his arm blazed to life. Even the grass beneath him withered from the intensity of the power flowing through his arm. He grasped her arms tight as she sat on top of him.

The female creature straddling his body stared down at the glowing tattoo in wonder. The brightness from the tattoos on his arm illuminated her pale, blue skin and put a spark in her pupil-less red eyes. Her violet, bat-like wings stopped their flutter. Unfortunately, the light only distracted her for a few moments. The beautiful woman shook her head and tried to free herself from his grasp again. Tried and failed.

She pulled and yanked her arms in multiple directions trying to get free, but Ean held on tight. They thrashed about on the forest floor, kicking up dirt and leaves. The power raged through him, giving him the strength to keep her from going after his friends. From his position pinned beneath her, he watched as the creature's

1

expression changed from surprise to annoyance and ended on anger. She sneered down at him, her dark red eyes seeming to glow as she struggled against him.

Eventually she slowed, a blank expression washing over her face as she looked down at him. Was she giving up? Ean had no idea how fast she could run or fly, but he hoped that he had given Jaslen and Bran enough time to get away. As for himself, he had no idea what he was going to do about this creature straddling his body.

As her struggling eventually ceased, she continued to stare down at Ean, her blank face masking whatever emotions she was feeling towards him. After what felt like an eternity of silence, she finally spoke.

"You're an...interesting...human. What's your name?"

"Ean."

"Just Ean? How simple." That sly smile had returned, and her arms relaxed in his grip. "My name is Azalea, Ean the human. There seems to be a little more to you than I originally thought. I find you quite...intriguing."

Her voice had taken on a more sultry tone at the end, and she leaned down a bit so that her face was closer to his. Ean had no idea what to do. He still kept a solid grip on her upper arms, but she seemed much calmer now. Had she accepted that the other two were gone? He watched her as she gazed right back into his eyes. Her lip twitched slightly as she smiled down at him. It was then that he realized the position they were in and could feel his cheeks reddening.

"Well," he said breaking the silence. His voice warbling slightly, causing him to wince before continuing on. "If you think you can handle not killing anyone for a few moments, I'll let you get up."

"Who says I want to get up?" Her fingers curled into his shirt. Using the grip, she slowly pulled Ean up to the point where their faces were practically touching. "I said I found you interesting, Ean. Maybe I want to have some fun with you."

Her tongue darted out, brushing his lips for only a moment before disappearing back into her mouth. Ean knew his face must be red by this point; it felt like it was on fire. His hands relaxed slightly around her wrists as he tried his best to speak.

"I'm...uh, glad that you have calmed down. It was--"

"Shhh," she quieted him with the sound, but even more so with how she did it, lightly touching her lips to his. He felt his jaw drop slightly but didn't care. "Time for talking is over."

Leaning back, she gave him a seductive stare that melted his resolve. He let the energy from the Abyss flow out of him slowly until it was completely gone. As his hands slipped from her wrists, she let out a short laugh as that sly grin returned.

"Oh, little one, whatever am I to do with you?"

Before he could ask what she meant, she pulled him up slightly higher...and then brought her forehead crashing down into his.

All Ean felt was a sharp pain as she struck, but dropped into unconsciousness before his body even hit the ground.

FLOATING IN DARKNESS, EAN struggled against the weight of unconsciousness. As the darkness slowly receded, voices seemed to drift through his thoughts. Although barely audible, the female voice with its impatient tone was loud and clear.

"...better know what you're doing, imp. I have no intention of..."

"...trust me. In the long run, things will work out well for you, you just..."

"...and you're sure that he..."

"...looks young, but has..."

"...better not betray me..."

The snap of a twig to his left made him sit up. His vision returned, but the cobwebs weaving his mind made it hard to remember where he was and how he had gotten there. Instant nausea hit. Trying to blink away the darkness, he peered into the dark shadows of the trees. His hands grasped at the earth and leaves beneath his fingers. Then that familiar tingling feeling, like pins-and-needles lightly jabbing his skin, caught his attention.

"Zin." Although the imp only went up to his knee, he resonated a distinct and noticeable presence through Ean's connection to Abysmal energy. "Is she still here?"

He struggled to his feet. His stomach churned, and it felt like something was crushing his head, but he kept it together. If only he could clear the cobwebs from his mind and focus.

Zin's presence moved a bit closer and then stopped. When the imp spoke, his voice was low, and Ean detected a hint of annoyance.

"We're still lost in the woods, in what little moons' light can break through the trees, and your 'friends' have left you, taking the food with them. There are plenty of squirrels and rodents for me to snack on, but I doubt I could catch enough to keep you fed. And then of course, there is our new companion..."

"New companion? What are you--"

"Aww," a new voice said in the dark. "I hope you're not holding a grudge for the little tap I gave you on the head, little one."

That womanly voice, a mixture of playful and sultry, brought everything back. The fight with Bran and Jaslen. Summoning the beautiful creature. The struggle. Receiving a head butt, then the blackness. Finding her by sight was impossible, but then he felt her, felt the Abyss covering her like a thick blanket, and turned his head towards the sensation.

"Can this human see in the dark like us?" Her voice sounded surprised, and a little impressed. "I wouldn't think his hearing was that well developed he could find us by sound."

"No, no," Zin's voice said from the darkness. "Apparently he can feel things connected to the Abyss. It's something new and makes games of hide-and-seek incredibly unfair."

"Interesting." He felt the woman rise and start to move towards him. Ean tried to climb to his feet, but dizziness overwhelmed him and he sat back down. Feeling around in the dark, he tried to find something he could use to defend himself.

"You don't need to worry about her, Ean." The imp said. "She's agreed to join us. Whether or not that's a good or bad thing is up for debate, but at least she promised not to kill us. And trust me, that's a pretty big deal for her kind."

Ean listened, trying his best to comprehend what was going on, but a fog still clouded his thoughts. And she was still moving closer. If only he could start a fire or had a candle he could light, anything that would let him see...

With a thought, he opened himself up to the energies of the Abyss, letting the power flood through him. The tattoos on his arm lit up, basking the trees of Rensen forest in their blue light. A flurry of movement signaled creatures fleeing deeper into the woods from the light. When he caught sight of the blue-skinned woman, sitting cross-legged with her leathery wings folded against her back, the name Azalea flashed into his mind. She flinched at the light and held up a slender blue hand to shield her eyes.

"Dim your light, little one," she requested. "Or are you trying to punish me for what I did?"

"Maybe I am."

"Aw, don't be that way. You started it, after all. You got me all worked up over a good meal and then denied me of it. Can you really fault me for being angry? If it makes you feel better, I didn't go after your friends, although that boy's angst and jealousy tasted absolutely delicious."

"You only left them alone because I showed up, Yulari," Zin said with a grunt. Ean could see the imp clearly now. His beady yellow eyes were locked on the woman. A fresh scratch adorned one of his pointed ears. There were scratches all over his brown skin, and his clawed feet and hands were covered in dirt. "I had come back to check on Ean and found him unconscious on the forest floor while you were about to head out into the woods. It took me a bit to 'convince' you to stick around."

The woman shrugged, not bothering to deny it.

"Wait," Ean said, placing a hand on his head. The energy from the Abyss had eased the pain, but putting thoughts together was like trying to carry water in a sieve. "I thought your name was Azalea. Why did Zin just call you Yulari?"

"Azalea is her name," Zin cut in. "Not that you can believe anything she says. Yulari is the name of her race. I figured a healer of your intelligence would have known what you were bringing out of the Abyss before you had the bright idea of summoning her."

Zin paused to give Ean a snide eye roll. "If you recall, I warned you to never summon a Yulari. So imagine my surprise when I saw Azalea standing over you, about to leave you for wild animals to snack on. I had half the mind to leave you there, too. It would serve you right if a wolf came and had a little snack of your foot. Maybe then you would finally learn to listen to me."

"You let your pet imp talk to you like that?" Surprise touched Azalea's voice.

"He isn't my pet. He's, well, he's my friend."

She let out a laugh, then took a closer look at Ean and grew serious. "You mean that, don't you? You actually consider this little worm a friend. How curious. I think I am starting to understand why--"

"I'm standing right here you know, life sucker," Zin cut in. "You could at least wait until I wasn't around to insult me to the boy."

"Life sucker?!" Anger flashed across her face for a moment, and then was gone, replaced by her playful smile. "Little imp, if you're smart enough to be able to talk, you should know better than to call any of my kind that name. You're lucky we have this little arrangement, otherwise I would rip each of your limbs off and beat you with them."

"Enough!" Ean was letting things get out of control again, but this time he would stop it. "What do you mean, 'arrangement'? What have you two been discussing while I've been...sleeping?"

He made a point of staring directly at Azalea and was surprised when she looked away quickly.

"Well, we had quite the lengthy discussion," Zin said, a hint of amusement in his voice. "And to sum things up, she's agreed to help us and follow your orders--" Azalea coughed loudly, cutting the imp off. He looked at her with a frown before continuing. "Agreed to try and follow your orders whenever possible."

Ean looked over at the Yulari and this time received a nod and that same smirk that seemed to be a permanent fixture on her face. Shaking his head, he turned back to Zin.

"And how exactly can she help us?"

"The better question," the Yulari said, a hint of annoyance to her voice, "is what <u>can't</u> I do. Or more importantly, what can't you do, little one. Obviously you know very little about the Abyss and how to use that energy coursing through your body. You're also a horrible warrior, so I can handle any fights you get into. Unless, of course, that would hurt your ego too much, having a girl fight your battles."

She stared at him, expecting an answer, but Ean refused to play her games. Returning her gaze, Ean plastered on a blank expression. Realizing she wasn't going to get a rise out of him, she sniffed indignantly and continued on.

"Well, if none of that sounds appealing, there is one last thing I can do that you cannot."

Without warning, she extended her wings and pushed off into the air. The light from Ean's tattoos silhouetted her in the darkness; the shadows created only seemed to add to her beauty. She hovered for a few moments slightly off the ground, her leathery wings beating just fast enough to keep her aloft. Then, with a wink at Ean, her wings tripled in speed and she shot into the air. Branches rained down as she dived through the canopy above and disappeared. Moments later she came crashing back down, dislodging even more twigs and leaves from above, before landing in front of Ean.

"So, little one," she said mockingly. "Which way do you have to go in order to get out of this forest?"

His supplies were gone. His friends, well, ex-friends, would be almost impossible to find, and he wasn't sure that he wanted to find them. And even if he did want to and eventually found them, they still would have no idea which way to go. Azalea was his only hope now. The fact that Zin seemed to support the idea of having her along cemented his decision.

Ean searched her eyes for any sign of treachery. He saw mockery and arrogance reflected in those blood-red eyes, but no treachery. Trusting his gut, he relented with a defeated sigh. She meant him no harm...at the moment. He extended a hand in her direction.

"You swear to follow my orders and not ignore them when you think they're inconvenient?"

She gave his hand a puzzled glance and then gripped it firmly, her nails digging into the skin of his hand.

"I promise, little one, that as soon as you make my presence in this world more permanent, I will aid you to the best of my ability."

"It's a deal then," Ean said, pulling his hand away. He grimaced a bit as he noticed small pinpricks of blood where her nails had dug in. "And the first thing you need to do, after telling me which direction to go, is to stop calling me 'little one.'"

"Fair enough, child," she said with a smirk.

Wonderful. Another person that teased him about looking young. Ean was eighteen-years-old, but due to his thin build, smooth complexion, dimpled cheeks, and scraggly black hair, people often mistook him for much younger. He found it demeaning when strangers referred to him as a boy, but a child was even worse.

"Now make my visit here a bit more permanent." Ignoring Ean's scowl, Azalea turned and walked over to a pile of leaves. Brushing them out of the way, her summoning circle came into view. It still glowed faintly with the power that kept her tied to this world.

Ean took a few deep breaths to compose himself before moving over to join her. Making her time in the realm more permanent meant transferring the summoning rune to something he owned, just as he had carved Zin's rune into the pendant around his neck. It had to be something that he could keep close as well, just in case she got out of control and he had to send her back to the Abyss. It would be much easier to break the rune if it was inscribed on a physical object anyway.

Ean spied a small, flat piece of bark resting on the forest floor. It was about half the size of his palm--thin enough to tuck into a pocket, with a large enough surface on which to draw the intricate summoning rune. Picking up the wood, Ean was about to open up his Pocket to retrieve his carving knife when a thought struck him.

Well, it wasn't so much a thought as it was a feeling. Taking the bark in his right hand, he placed his left one down on the summoning circle. Closing his eyes, he pictured the rune on the ground transferring onto the bark. A chill washed over his body, moving from his left hand to his right, and sure enough when he opened his eyes, the summoning rune that had been on the ground was now perfectly inscribed on the piece of wood.

He glanced up to catch Azalea's red eyes studying him carefully. When their eyes met, she broke their gaze and turned to walk away, mumbling under his breathe. "He could have at least bound me to this world by something more flattering than a scrap of wood."

Ean was about to call her out, but she spoke again, louder this time.

"If you want to get out of the forest, you need to head that way." She pointed off in a direction opposite the one he would have chosen. "I could fly to the edge of the forest in barely any time at all, but since I'm supposed to follow you two geniuses around, it will probably take us a day or two on foot. Unless you are as weak as you look of course, then I would say three to four days."

"Leave now? I can barely see anything," objected Ean.

"Well then, I suppose I'll have to lead you by the nose, and then you and your ugly little imp will be out of the woods in no time."

"Unless you enjoy being called soul-sucking hag, I would stop with the insults and call me by my name," Zin retorted.

"Fine, fine, can we go now?" Azalea was staring at Ean, her hands now on her hips with one foot tapping impatiently on the ground. Ean returned her stare, drinking in Azalea's form. White leather hugged her curves. Thick purple hair hung to her shoulders, framing a face with petite features. Any normal man would consider her beautiful...if they could ignore the bat-like wings spread out behind her.

Ean knew better. As alluring and almost hypnotizing as her beauty was, deep down she was no ordinary woman. She was just another denizen from the Abyss. A creature of darkness. If Zin hadn't made a deal with her, she would have killed them both by now.

"Yes, we can leave. There's nothing left to pack. So if you're ready to go, then so am I."

Without another word, the Yulari walked off into the dense forest. Zin and Ean hurried to catch up. The threesome walked single file through the forest, with the light of the moons barely breaking through the canopy and creating dappled shadows on the leafy ground. Azalea took the lead position, while Zin and Ean walked a few paces behind.

Zin had been the one to support the decision of keeping Azalea around after all. It was confusing now to see him frown in her direction. Ean couldn't exactly ask the imp what the problem was with Azalea only a few steps ahead of them. So, all three of them walked on in silence until tiny rays of light began poking through the canopy above, signaling the beginning of a new day.

CHAPTER 2

OUT OF THE WOODS

THEY WALKED ON THROUGH most of the morning. Every now and then, Azalea would tell them to stop and then fly off into the air. When she returned, she would always point them in a different direction than the one they had been going in. It was surprising for Ean to see how off track they could get when he believed they were going straight. It made him wonder if she was purposely misleading them. He wouldn't put it past the creature to keep them lost longer than necessary to make herself seem more useful. Every time Azalea altered their course, he glanced over at Zin to raise a questioning eyebrow. The normally cautious imp didn't seem concerned, so Ean decided he had no choice but to go along with whatever the Yulari said.

"Not too much further now," Azalea said after her sixth check of their position. "You've been keeping up a better pace than I gave you credit for, and I'm very surprised that the imp's little legs have been able to keep up as well. Guess I underestimated you both."

"These legs don't feel so little when they're kicking things, Yulari," the imp responded. "Keep that in mind."

"Such big threats from such a little creature," the Yulari retorted, her expression that of mock concern. "Good thing I have Ean to keep you from hurting me. Oh wait, it's the other way around. It's a good thing you have Ean to keep me from hurting you. But don't think the fact that I can't kill you because of our partnership doesn't mean I can't hurt you. So watch your tone when you address me."

With a sigh, Ean decided to step in before things got worse.

"Azalea, once we're out of the woods, we'll run into other people, which will certainly be a problem with how you look. When they catch sight of your blue skin, red eyes, and wings, I'm afraid they're going to come after you with sticks and stones. And when they are done, I'll be next just for being with you."

"Oh, by the Abyss." Azalea's voice was a mixture of sadness and condescending. "Don't you know anything about Yulari? Well, you are going to learn something today."

Stopping, she turned around to face him. Once she was set, her wings lowered and folded about her body, underneath her arms. Then her entire body seemed to shimmer, blurring the image of her entire body until Ean was barely able to make her out. Then, just as suddenly as it had appeared, the blur was gone and Ean's jaw dropped.

Standing in front of him now was a woman slightly smaller than himself, short blonde hair framing a petite face, her body covered in what appeared to be a thick cloth robe. The woman's features resembled Azalea's but were slightly muted, the thin nose a bit more rounded out, the mouth smaller but with lips just as full, her eyes slightly slanted and of a dark green color with actual pupils. Her hair was cut the same, but was a dirty blond color. Her skin had taken on a lightly tanned tone, like someone that spent most of their life out in the fields but had just spent the Chill season indoors.

But there was something else. That shimmering effect was still slightly there, although it didn't blur her appearance any longer. It was the same effect Ean saw on Zin any time he became invisible.

"Well?" Azalea asked, lifting her arms up and slowly spinning around. "Will I pass for human?"

"Yes, absolutely, unless normal people can see that shimmering effect as well."

She stopped spinning abruptly and turned to face him. "What shimmering effect?"

"I think I can see the spell or whatever it is that changes your appearance. The same thing happens when Zin tries to turn invisible."

"Oh really? How peculiar." Shrugging, the Yulari spun one last time with a laugh before dropping her arms. "Well, I'm sure it won't be a problem."

Raising her arms again, the shimmering effect washed over her once more and in an instant, she had returned to her pale blue skinned self. "All that spinning made me forget which way we need to go. I'll be right back."

Taking off into the air once more, Azalea was only gone for a moment before fluttering back to the dirt and mud of the forest. With a casual wave of her hand she motioned for Zin and Ean to follow. The three of them walked on in silence again, with Zin shooting daggers with his eyes at the Yulari while Ean pretended not to notice.

"Here you are," she said, spreading her arms wide. "Delivered from despair and starvation by your wonderful Yulari guide. Just a little bit further and we'll be out of these woods and hopefully to more populated areas." She flashed Ean a smile and patted him on the head. "Not that I've found your presence boring, of course. It's just that you stink of depression, and it leaves a sour taste in my mouth."

Ean dodged another head pat from the Yulari and returned a furious scowl. "Quit patting my head like I'm your puppy. And I'm not depressed. If I'm not exactly cheerful, it's only because it's been a rough journey, and I'm tired. That's all."

"You sure?" Tilting her head, Azalea gave him a quizzical look. "I'm pretty sure I've been smelling depression wafting off of someone, and it certainly isn't the imp."

"How do you know it isn't Zin?"

She flashed Zin a wide grin. "The only emotion that I've been smelling from him is distaste, and I'm sure it is directed at me."

Returning her grin, the imp began making his way towards the end of the forest. "Finally, something we agree on."

Ean jogged to catch up with Azalea, who was trailing after Zin, and in no time they were walking three abreast out of the forest into a clear stretch of land. Hills of green grass rolled into the northern horizons, a refreshing change from the brown dirt of his village. To the west he could see the Skyfall Mountains, not that far off in the distance. It was what he saw to the east, though, that made his eyes go wide.

A huge stone wall trailing north to south towered over the land. It stretched up into the clouds and out of sight and seemed to travel into the horizon without end.

His mind reeled from the sight of such a massive creation. Who could have built such a wonder? Did it protect them from something worse than the Abyss on the other side? How had no one from his village ever mentioned something so wondrous and intimidating? When Ean was finally able to shake away his shock, he turned to his companions.

"What in the world is that?"

Azalea shrugged, as if something as grand as the giant wall was commonplace for her. Zin shrugged as well, but moved closer to Ean's side to speak.

"The wall was here the last time I lived in your realm, but no one seemed to know who built it or why, and that was a long time ago. At this point, the gods are probably the only ones who know its purpose."

Ean nodded and returned his gaze to the wall. Maybe he would be able to see it up close. Not today though. He needed to spend what was left of the afternoon traveling towards the capitol of Lurthalan.

By the low position of the sun over the mountains, Ean knew dusk was on its way. That meant if they wanted to make good time, they would be relying on the three moons to light their path.

"Well, let's move on," he said. "We have no idea where we came out from or how long it will take to reach the city. My best guess is that if we head northeast, we should eventually reach Lurthalan or at least a road that heads there."

"Sounds like as good a plan as any," the Yulari replied. The shimmering effect washed over her again and the vision of an ordinary girl returned. "Just in case we meet anyone out here."

She walked past him, giving his shoulder a playful shove. Or at least Ean thought it had meant to be playful. He stumbled away a few paces and almost ended up on his back. Either Azalea forgot her own strength sometimes or she was messing with him again. Regaining his balance, he marched off after her with Zin following behind.

It was nice to have open space all around him. Even at home he had been used to having the mountains surrounding his village, so to have nothing but the open plains in front of him was pleasant.

Ean wasn't sure how long they had walked, but eventually Azalea had put some distance between herself and the two of them. She paused at the top of the hill and shielded her eyes as she looked out over the next horizon. After a few moments, she called back to them.

"If you two are done crawling along, there are buildings up ahead."

Sure enough, when Ean and Zin reached the top of the hill, spread out before them was a farm. A large field full of some kind of plant taller than any of them spread out at the bottom of the hill.

Ean knew a good deal about plants that were useful for medicine, but he knew little about any kind of edible plant outside of the bean plants that were grown in his village. At the opposite side of the field, a barn and small wooden house sat with a few chickens grazing outside.

"I think we've been spotted," Azalea said, pointing towards where a figure was exiting the house. The person took a few steps in their direction and then waved.

"Zin, you better--" Ean began to say, but cut off as he realized the imp had already turned invisible. "Alright, let's go down and say hello."

As they made their way down the hill, the figure began making his way through the field towards them. By the time Ean and Azalea had reached the field, the figure was coming out of it.

The man that stood before them was average in every way possible. He stood about as tall as Ean, wearing a simple, brown short-sleeved shirt and matching pants. The wrinkles in his face and his scraggly white beard made Ean put his age at over fifty, and the way he was slightly bent over made Ean think he was possibly older than that. The man's dark, sunken brown eyes looked at Ean first, then lingered on Azalea's face quite a bit longer before he spoke.

"You two lost?" His voice mirrored his appearance, the words coming out of his mouth slow and sounding coarse. "I don't get no visitors from the south. None, actually. Nothing but forest that way. Nobody's got no reason to visit an old man living smack in-between Halyquain and Lurthalan."

He paused for a moment to reach out a hand in Ean's direction. "Name's Dotain, by the way. Dotain Frelyn."

Ean gripped it, surprised to find a strong grip. Maybe he wasn't as old as he seemed, or at least not as frail as Ean had imagined. Must have been the years toiling the fields under the hot sun that had withered his skin and made him appear much older.

"My name is Ean, and this is Azalea. It's nice to meet you, Dotain. As for how we got here, we were coming from Rensen on our way to Lurthalan and got lost in the forest. Thankfully, we made it out and wound up here."

"I see, I see," Dotain said, one hand rubbing at his chin. "You must have gone off the road. Very foolish. And lucky to have made it out. You two related?"

The question caught Ean off guard. His mouth worked but nothing came out as he tried to think of an answer.

"Yes, we're brother and sister." Azalea said before Ean could get two words together. "Ean is my older brother, but I'm the wiser one out of the two of us."

"Brother and sister, that's good." The man mumbled, then shook his head. "Well, it will be getting dark soon. Nothing else nearby, so why don't cha spend the night. I was about to put on some dinner."

"My brother and I would appreciate that. Plus a conversation with a real man like yourself, rather than my slow-witted brother, would certainly be a pleasant change."

The old man grinned ear to ear, but his eyes took on a hunger, as if someone had just passed a freshly cooked steak underneath his nose.

Ean shot Azalea a dark look, more for her flirtations with the old man than for the insult. The Yulari looked young, especially in her human form, and Ean would have put her around his age in her early twenties. He had no idea how a Yulari aged, but the farmer was clearly double that if not more. Yet she batted her eyelashes at him and playfully placed a hand on his shoulder. The woman had no shame.

The old man either didn't see Ean glaring at Azalea or chose to ignore it. He returned Azalea's smile, showing off a mouth that was missing a good deal of teeth. "That's good, very good. Why don't you two follow me and I'll show you where you will be sleeping. Then I'll get to making us some dinner."

The old man started to make his way back through the field. Azalea winked at Ean, then followed after the man. Ean stared after her in frustration until she disappeared into the tall plant stalks. The way they were laughing as if they were old pals, made the pair easy to trail. Ean caught up to them just as they were exiting the field, standing in front of a rickety white barn with peeling paint.

"I only have the one bedroom, so you two will have to sleep in the barn." Waving a hand at Ean, the old man motioned him inside. "Why don't you take your things inside and find a nice place for the two of you to sleep. Your sister can accompany me inside while I get dinner started."

"We don't really have much to--" Ean began, but Azalea cut him off.

"That sounds like an excellent plan, and it will let Dotain and I get better acquainted." Turning towards Ean, her voice became more drawn out and serious. "You go ahead Ean and find a good spot. You can take your time. I'm sure Dotain will be pleasant company."

"But..."

"Run along now and we'll see you inside a little later," she said, her voice stressing the end of the sentence. All Ean could do was stand there and watch as the two of them headed into the house.

"Don't forget that I'm your big brother," Ean called out to her in warning. "And I have more power in my one arm than you do in your whole body. Don't try to eat anything I'd disapprove of or we'll have a serious problem."

"He's so over-protective," Azalea said with a chuckle and linked arms with Dotain. "Of course, I can't blame him. I have been known to break a few rules every now and then."

Dotain joined in with her laughter. Ean fumed.

"And that's why you can never completely trust a Yulari. They always have their own agendas."

Ean almost jumped out of his skin. He had completely forgotten about the imp. "Is that wise," he growled at the now visible Zin. "He could come back out here any second."

Laughing, Zin shook his head. "I doubt that. That man's full attention is on Azalea. The only way he would come back out here is if she told him to, and from the looks of it, that girl wanted some time alone with him. Probably wants to feed off of the lust the man was feeling towards her."

"What? If she feeds off of him, won't that kill him?"

"No, no, I doubt she would do what she tried with Bran," the imp said, raising his hands in a soothing gesture. "Yulari can feed off of emotions without killing a person, without even touching them actually, although they enjoy direct contact more. Think of it this way. When you smell something delicious being cooked, it makes you hungry right? But you're not truly satisfied until you actually get to eat the food. It's similar for Yulari. They can survive off the emotions that creatures put out, but they are much more satisfied drawing them directly out of a body. It's just unfortunate for the victim that having them drawn out usually kills them."

"You're sure she won't kill him?"

"No, I never said that. I just said she didn't need to kill him."

"Oh, that makes me feel much better." Dismissing the other questions he had for Zin about their new companion, Ean decided it would be best if he got into the house as fast as possible. Moving into the barn he found a spot that suited their needs, dropped his things, and was back outside before Zin had even taken a step inside.

"Come on," he said to the imp. "Let's make sure she doesn't get us into trouble."

"No thanks. I'm going to look around for my own dinner. Good luck, though."

Ean frowned as the imp turned invisible and disappeared around the edge of the barn. Mumbling to himself, Ean walked into the house.

The front door brought Ean to a narrow hallway. To his left was a sitting room with a chair and a barren fireplace. A little way down the hall on the right was a staircase that led to the upper floor. The first thing Ean noticed as he entered the house was how run-down the inside was compared to the outside. A thick coat of dust covered the furniture, most of which had seen better days. The paint was filthy, with thick strips curling away from the walls. Save for one large window that let in a swath of natural light, the shades were drawn and the house was dim. Overall the place barely seemed lived in. Judging by the light and sound of voices coming from behind a door at the end of the hall, the kitchen and his Yulari were in the back.

The second thing he noticed as he walked towards what he believed was the kitchen was the smell. It wasn't a putrid smell or anything too offensive, but the place did smell musky. Like wet clothes left too long to sit in the dark. That combined with the general disrepair of the entire house was starting to make Ean feel a bit uneasy. He moved at a brisk pace to the end of the hall, not bothering to pause and announce himself as he pushed open the door.

Stepping into the next room, he sighed with relief at what he found. The room was indeed the kitchen and it was in much better shape than the rest of the house. Candles were lit and a large open window looked out onto the plains, allowing a great deal of light into the room. A table, in much better condition than the rest of the furniture in the house, sat in the middle of the room surrounded by five equally well put-together chairs. Against the far wall was a stove; the door opened showing off the fire inside. On top sat a pot, steam and the smells of meat and vegetables wafting out of it. Both Azalea and Dotain were standing in front of the stove, speaking loudly over the crackle of the fire.

They stopped speaking when Ean entered and turned to face him.

"Well, you moved a lot faster than I thought you would, brother," Azalea said through a tight-lipped smile. "I was hoping to get a little more time alone to talk to this pleasant man."

"No worries," the old man said quickly, "I'm sure after dinner your brother will want to catch up on some sleep. We could continue our conversation then."

"I'm not sure that's--"

"An excellent suggestion!" Azalea said, cutting Ean off. "My brother has been pushing himself a great deal and could use the rest."

The look Azalea directed towards Ean sent a chill through his body.

"You're right, of course, sister. A little extra rest will be good for me. Especially knowing that the two of you will be safely inside."

He tried to put as much emphasis on the word 'safely' as he could. Azalea had agreed to listen to him, and she was smart enough to understand what his words really meant. The smug grin that his words earned from Azalea did nothing, though, to ease his worries. Ean shook his head, the realization that he might not get much sleep that night souring his mood even more.

"Take a seat." Dotain stirred the pot as he spoke. "Tell me your story. I want to know why anyone with a lick of sense would stray from the main road through the forest."

"I didn't want to leave the road," Azalea said, sending Ean a glare. "You see, my brother means well. I love him to death, but he's a headstrong fool like our father. May the gods give me the patience to continue to travel with him on our way to the city."

"What my sister isn't mentioning is that we ran into some bandits on the road and had to abandon most of our supplies to get away from them." Ean flashed Azalea a self-satisfied smirk. He could lie just as well as she could.

A slight movement out of the corner of his eye made Ean turn towards the old man. Ean caught him glancing over his shoulder at the two of them but as soon as their eyes met, the old man quickly turned back to his cooking.

"Bandits, you say?" His attention on stirring his stew, the old man's voice sounded disinterested. "The traders that buy my crops have been talking a lot more about bandits. They say whole packs of them roam the land now, some even setting up camps in the forest somewhere. I don't much worry about that though. Only people I see out here are the traders. And now you, I suppose."

The old man leveled a hungry look at Azalea, and she returned an encouraging smile. Ean's stomach churned. He wondered if anyone would blame him if he hurled all over the table. The old man had no shame either.

Turning back to his pot, the old man continued on. "Off to the capitol you said, right? I haven't been there in years. No need to really. Too busy for my tastes, all them people running around doing who knows what. That city can be as dangerous as the woods. You two are better off finding a nice place in the country. You know, I could always use another hand around here, boy, and I'm sure we could find something for your sister to do."

"That sounds lov--" Azalea began, as she moved to take a seat across from Ean.

"That's a generous offer, but we have to go to the city. We've got business for our village that we have to take care of."

"Well, your sister could always stay here while you--"

"Again, a generous offer, but my sister will be staying with me." Ean had tried to keep his voice civil, but he must have missed the mark as a look of anger flashed across the old man's face. Ean watched as Dotain reached at his side, grasping for something that was not there.

A sharp pain struck Ean's left shin, and he bent over in his chair to rub at it. Looking up he caught Azalea frowning at him and shaking her head. She had kicked him! Ean sat fuming, rubbing at his leg while Azalea spoke.

"Excuse my brother. He gets a bit over protective. He often forgets that he's just a poor village boy while I've had much more experience out in the world. I've been trying to teach him to respect his elders, but as I've said, he is quite the hardhead."

Waving her off, the old man returned to his stew. "It's nothing. That's good that your brother is protective." Then Ean heard him say under his breath, "And even better that you don't listen to him."

Ean was done. If the fool man wanted to try and "take advantage" of his sister, let him try. It would serve him right if she drained every last drop of his life...

Flashes of his nightmares ran through his mind. Torture, corruption, murder...

He couldn't let her kill him, regardless of how little he thought of the man. He would not even entertain the thought. Ean would just have to have a talk with Azalea before anything happened. She had promised to listen to him after all.

"All ready!" Dotain said, interrupting Ean's thoughts. "I'm sure you'll like it. It's a family recipe. A rabbit stew with a few secret ingredients."

Grasping the pot with a towel, the old man carried it over and set it down in the middle of the table. Producing three bowls and a set of spoons from a nearby cupboard, he distributed the utensils and began dishing out the stew.

Ean's mouth watered as Dotain poured some stew into a bowl in front of him. He had been so worried about what Azalea might do that he hadn't realized how hungry he really was. Stirring around the contents with his spoon, it was easy to pick out the bits of rabbit meat, and the potatoes were a staple food in his village of Rottwealth. While his stomach growled he studied the flecks of oniony greens as they floated at the top. Not many people knew that onions could thin the blood; he had used them as a remedy often enough on sick patients. The peppery black herbs smelled similar to Balalur, an herb useful for fighting off colds. He had never thought to add it as seasoning to a stew before.

"This smells wonderful!" Azalea said, clapping her hands together excitedly. "I've never had rabbit stew before."

Ean couldn't help but laugh. "I know soup isn't your usual meal. Are you sure you can handle it?"

The look she shot him could have curdled milk.

"I don't understand where the sarcasm is coming from, brother. Why, only just this morning you were harping on me to try new things. Would you prefer that I go back to my usual menu? It would be a simple matter of..."

"No," Ean said vigorously. "My apologies. Go ahead and fill up on the stew. Lots and lots of stew. Only the stew."

Azalea's green eyes scrunched in merriment as her lips curled back in victory. It annoyed him the way she took such pleasure in seeing him squirm.

"Yes," Dotain encouraged, the real meaning of their conversation lost to the man. "Eat up. Plenty here. Enjoy."

Dotain pulled his own bowl closer and sprinkled something into it. He stirred the contents around before bringing a spoonful to his mouth. He took two more mouthfuls before he noticed Ean and Azalea staring at him. "What?" he mumbled.

Ean spoke first, more curious than anything else. "What did you put in your stew?"

"Just some spices, nothing special, just adds a little kick to the flavor is all." Keeping his eyes down, Dotain continued to shovel spoonfuls of stew into his mouth.

Moving closer to the man, Azalea reached over to put a hand on his arm. "I like a little kick in my food as well. Can I have some spices to put in mine?"

"No!"

Both Azalea and Ean were taken back a bit by the sudden outburst. Dotain had an annoyed expression as he looked at Azalea, but it quickly turned into one of embarrassment.

"Sorry, I...that was the last of my spices. I'm sure you wouldn't have liked them anyway. Just give the food a try, I promise it tastes good just the way it is."

Shrugging, Azalea pulled her bowl close and began to eat. She shoveled the food into her mouth and seemed to be enjoying it, but Ean couldn't tell if her expressions were sincere or just a part of her act. His rumbling stomach interrupted his thoughts and told him to get to eating. The stew did smell extremely appetizing, especially after a day without eating. Filling his spoon with stew, Ean took a tentative slurp.

The stew was as good as Dotain had said! Ean began to scoop spoonful after spoonful into his mouth. He could understand now why the man had said they wouldn't need extra spices. The broth had a little kick to it that was starting to numb his tongue. It wasn't enough to make him stop eating though, and he continued to scoop large spoonfuls into his mouth.

Looking over in between gulps, he noticed Azalea had slowed down a bit. She only took little sips as she watched Dotain eat. Her expression was peculiar, but Ean dismissed it as just another quirk. Probably some way she was trying to seduce their host. It was obvious that Dotain was already picturing the two of them together by the way he was openly looking at her now. Shaking his head, Ean focused on eating.

Whew! Whatever was in the stew was really starting to get to him. His tongue was almost completely numb now and he felt a little flushed. Tired too, probably the days of traveling finally taking its toll on his body. He had to pause from eating for a moment to wipe some sweat from his forehead, but only for a moment. He could handle being a little warm, the stew was that good. He continued to scoop more and more of it into his mouth...

...and then dropped his spoon.

His fingers suddenly felt very heavy, as if something was pushing down on them. Had the past couple of days worn him out that much? Reaching over to where the spoon had landed on the table, he tried to pick it up, but his hand had gotten too heavy, and he had trouble working his fingers. Frowning, he tried to lift it again but had no luck. It was becoming quite frustrating as he wanted to eat more! Maybe his other hand...no, that was hanging limply at his side. His thoughts were fuzzy, more so than if he was just tired, like he was trying to think while...uh...doing something that made it hard to think.

A dull pain washed across the side of his face. At first he thought he had been slapped, but realized that his head had dropped down onto the table. From his vantage point he could see both Dotain and Azalea looking at him. The man was wearing a grin that did not instill a good feeling in Ean's fuddled brain. Azalea on the other hand was looking at him with chagrin, shaking her head as she slowly pushed her own bowl away. She was always judging him. He was just tired...so tired...

CHAPTER 3

A QUESTION OF CHARACTER

THE FIRST THING EAN noticed was that he was face down on a wooden floor covered with brownish-red splotches. Years of being a healer had made him familiar with stains like those--blood. His tongue felt stiff and dry like it was coated with dirt. He licked his lips trying to push away the nastiness with his own saliva. And that's when he noticed it. A pale face with lifeless eyes staring right at him--well, no, more like through him. As if the eyes were looking past this world and into the next.

Giving a yelp, he scrambled backwards on the floor until his back hit the wall. He struggled to make sense of what had happened. Dotain was dead. A chill went down his spine. What had happened? The man had been so hospitable...

"Don't look so upset," a woman's voice cut through the haze of his mind. His eyes found Azalea leaning back in her chair, her wings tight against her back and her pale blue feet up on the table. She was picking at her teeth with a long, blue fingernail. "The fool man tried to drug us."

"He...what?"

"Drugged us. Planned on killing us. Well, kill you then do some things to me most would find unpleasant. You should have seen the look on his face when he realized I was unaffected. Of course that paled in comparison to the look he had when I revealed my true form."

"So you killed him!?"

A look of surprise crossed her face for a moment and then was gone. "That surprises you? He tried to kill us. Well," pausing for a moment, she tapped her cheek with one long fingernail. "Drugged you, at least. Whatever he put into that stew didn't seem to have much effect on me."

"If it didn't affect you, you could have stopped him from doing anything to me. You're certainly strong enough to handle one man. You didn't have to kill him."

Azalea threw her hands into the air. "I don't get you, Ean. This creep wanted to have his way with me and then kill us both. He as much as said those exact words while I was feeding off of him. He said a lot of things, wouldn't shut up actually. What if I told you he had done this before? That this wasn't even his farm? He killed the family that owned it and has been using it mostly to do to random strangers what he was about to do to us. Does that make it okay that I killed him?"

"Now you're making things up to justify feeding off of him. There is no way you could have learned all of that from him."

"You're an idiot." Rising, Azalea's face couldn't have looked more disgusted. She moved towards the door, kicking the lifeless body of Dotain as she left. Once she was out of the room and into the hall, Ean heard her yell back, "I don't know what that stupid imp sees in you, but you two fools belong together."

Ean sat there, not knowing if he should go after her or not. She was probably right, but he couldn't justify killing the man. There had to be some kind of law in the area or at least in Lurthalan. And Azalea could have easily handled Dotain. On the other hand, if every despicable thing about him was true, maybe he did deserve death.

Ean spread his arms over the table and laid his spinning head on top of them. Sure, a healer's job involved decisions about life and death, but innocence and guilt was out of his domain. Dontain might have deserved it, but that wasn't for Azalea to decide on a whim.

The energy of the Abyss twinged in his chest, alerting him that someone tied to its power was approaching. He sighed in relief when he saw it was Zin, not Azalea. The little imp's brown skin was covered with small scratches.

"What did you do to anger the Yulari?"

"We had a slight disagreement about her feeding habits and she stormed out."

"Well, YOU upset her and she decided to take it out on ME. It's really a bad idea to push a Yulari too far you know. She might decide that getting sent back to the Abyss will be worth killing us both. They can be very emotional creatures."

"All I said was that she didn't have to kill the man, and I don't think I even said it that harshly."

"Oh." The imp glanced at the corpse spread out on the kitchen floor. "She saved your life and you lectured her for it. I have to say, I'm glad you are ok, but you really can be an idiot sometimes."

Climbing up onto the table, Zin sat down in front of Ean and shook his head.

"You have to keep in mind that life in the Abyss is much different than it is in your world. Down there it's kill or be killed, and there is always someone stronger than you trying to take what's yours. Azalea saw that killing that man, and more importantly keeping him from killing you, as a huge show of generosity. In the Abyss, no one and I mean no one, would offer aid to another unless they were getting something out of it in return."

"Is it really that bad?" Ean could feel his anger faltering.

"Worse than you can imagine. I have no idea how old she is, but since her wings look fully grown, I would put her at least over fifty.

That's fifty years in the Abyss where I can guarantee that she has been bullied, used, or hurt hundreds of times in her life."

Now Ean felt bad. Not so much because of how angry he had been at Azalea. He still didn't want her going around killing people, especially once they got to a highly populated city like the capitol. But he could have thanked her for saving him, and he certainly could show her a bit more understanding. He knew almost nothing about her kind, and it would probably take her a while to get used to living in his realm and not the Abyss.

"I will go apologize then. Maybe if I explain why I got so angry, she will understand and hopefully not resort to killing someone as her first option."

"Nope, you shouldn't do that. That's a bad idea."

The way the imp said it, so matter-of-factly, just confused Ean even more. "And why not?"

"If Azalea is ever going to respect you--"

"She doesn't already?"

"If she ever is going to respect you, you can't go back on your decisions. If you get angry, yell, scold, or take any kind of stand, you absolutely cannot back down whenever she throws a little tantrum. If you start giving in to her moods, she'll simply try to get away with more and more. That's just how Yulari behave. Best to stay strong. She'll get over it eventually."

"Even if it means she takes out her anger on you?"

Shrugging, Zin climbed to his feet. "I can handle it. She may be strong, but I'm still much quicker. For the future, if you know you're going to get her angry, give me a little heads up first, hmm?"

Flashing him a toothy smile, Zin leapt off the table. Hitting the ground softly, he moved towards the door.

"Come on," Zin said, waving Ean after him. "I found a supply of jerky in the shed out back, so we can eat and get back out on the road. After your little village and Rensen, I'm looking forward to seeing what passes as a major city in this world nowadays. Plus, that body is starting to smell a little ripe, and not in a good way."

The imp was certainly right; the room was starting to smell a bit foul. Ean's stomach was growling as well. What little stew he had eaten before passing out had not been very filling. Climbing to his feet, he took a quick last look at the dead man and left the room. He really shouldn't feel bad about his death; the human had tried to poison and probably kill him after all.

Human.

That was strange, why did he call the man human? Of course the man was a human, but it was strange that he thought of him that way. Why not "the man" or Dotain? It probably had to do with all the time he was spending with the imp and the Yulari. No need to overthink it.

Making his way down the hall, Ean left the house. By the position of the sun, it was sometime between mid-morning and midday. No wonder he was hungry, he had been knocked out for almost a whole day. Crossing the front yard, Ean opened the barn door and had to duck quickly as something small, brown and with flailing arms and legs flew past his head.

"And I didn't ask you to talk to him for me!"

Azalea sounded even angrier than before. She stood on the other side of the barn, her hands on her hips and a look of fury on her face. Her wings were spread out behind her, the leathery appendages quivering slightly. Ean's immediate reaction was to turn right around, but he remembered what Zin had said about not backing down.

Zin, who unless he had recently grown wings of his own, had been thrown out of the barn by the angry Yulari. The same angry Yulari that was now glaring at him from the other side of the barn. Steeling his resolve, and filling himself with the energies of the Abyss as a precaution, Ean strode right toward Azalea.

"You can't go around taking out your anger on Zin."

Azalea started moving as well, lifting slightly into the air with a few beats of her wings and meeting Ean about half way into the barn. "Oh, here to issue more orders, are you? I think I might have been too hasty agreeing to follow you. If I have to spend all of my time keeping you out of trouble, while you whine at me, I might be better off in the Abyss."

"Did you not promise to follow my orders?" Ean tried to make his voice as hard as steel and let the energy of the Abyss flow into him. It helped to make his voice sound cold. Azalea's eyes dropped for a moment, but she quickly regained eye contact with him.

"Yes, I did say that I--"

"Good. Promises might be worth next to nothing down in the Abyss, but in my world they weigh more than gold. I will not have someone with me who breaks her promises whenever it becomes convenient for her. You will follow my orders or I will send you back to the Abyss. It is as simple as that. Do I make myself clear?"

For a moment Ean thought that he had gone too far. Azalea's dark red, pupil-less eyes seemed to come ablaze as they narrowed and met his gaze. Her wings fluttered about behind her as her hands clenched into fists. The image of the last time Ean had tried to send her back to the Abyss appeared in his mind and he almost faltered.

Almost. Ean kept her tied to this world by a summoning rune inscribed on a fragile piece of bark. If he needed to, it would be easy to snap the bark, breaking the rune and send her back to the Abyss. Ean hoped it wouldn't come to that.

After a few tense moments, Azalea relaxed. Weary resignation settled on her pretty face and she let her hands drop to her sides, her wings following suit and drooping dejectedly behind her. Her head dropped slightly as well, and she stared at the ground to Ean's right.

"Fine," she said. Ean didn't believe it could really be that easy, so he decided to keep pushing.

"You will no longer kill anyone without my permission, whether it's to feed or to protect any of us?"

"Yes."

"You will make sure that if you find or figure something out that might put any of us in danger, you will immediately tell me."

Azalea kicked at the ground. "Yes."

"You will treat Zin with respect and not like your little punching doll whenever you get upset or angry."

"Yes."

That last 'yes' came through clenched teeth, but she said it without hesitation. A movement behind Ean caught both his and Azalea's attention. Standing in the doorway was Zin, a few new cuts and bruises on his body. The imp was smiling though.

"That's right. You'll treat me with respect from here on in!" Zin shouted, waving a fist in her direction. "I'm not like one of those thousands of imps in the Abyss that you can boss around and take your frustrations out on!"

Ean expected the Yulari to lash out, but instead she looked more dejected. Feeling a little guilty about coming down so hard on her, he tried to offer her back some dignity.

"I do want to thank you, though, for saving my life. Without you there, I'm sure that man would have slit my throat from ear to ear while I was unconscious. Your strength and ability to read people will certainly be an asset while we travel."

Her mood didn't seem to lighten, so Ean decided to throw her one more bone.

"And I will listen to any advice you might have, as long as you accept that the final decision is mine. Parts of this world are just as new to me as they are to you. I'm sure however many years you've spent surviving in the Abyss has given you some insight on how to deal with some of the less savory characters we are sure to run into in the city."

Ean heard a slapping sound behind him and turned just in time to see Zin removing his palm from his forehead. The look he directed towards Ean was less than pleased. Turning his attention back towards Azalea, he barely caught her usual smirk leaving her face, quickly replaced by a look of innocence.

"Now, just because I said--" he began, but she cut him off.

"I understand, no killing without your orders, no mistreating the imp, and I should offer my advice when you're heading into something dangerous. I can handle that, Master."

"Well, it's not that cut and dry, and you don't have to call me Master, Ean is fine, and..." His words were running together as he tried to keep up and recover at the same time, but she was good. With a pat on his cheek with one hand, she stuck a stick of jerky into his open mouth with the other.

"You should eat up then, Master, I mean Ean." Her tone had returned to its usual playful self, as if she had neither been angry or ashamed moments earlier. "I don't know about you, but I'm excited to get somewhere with more people."

She strode past him towards the exit. As she moved, her wings dipped, wrapping around her body and by the time she had reached the door, she had returned to looking human once more. Passing Zin, she reached down as if to pat him on the head, but the imp ducked past her and moved into the barn. Azalea just laughed and made to walk outside, but stopped and turned.

"Do hurry up and fetch our things. Like I said, we should be off to try and find the main road as soon as possible." She winked at Ean then and stepped out into the light.

Ean gaped, the piece of jerky hanging from his mouth. He felt like he had just been caught in a windstorm. Zin, on the other hand, looked ready to do murder as he stormed towards Ean.

"For a moment when I walked in," the imp growled through pointed teeth, "I thought you had actually listened to my advice and were taking charge. And then you go and throw it all away. You do realize she manipulated you there?"

"Mmhmm," was all Ean could say, finally closing his mouth around the jerky and beginning to chew.

"So, you realize that she in no way felt bad about what she had done or the fact that she had disappointed you?"

"Mmhmm." It seemed like the safest answer at the moment.

"AND you realize that instead of limiting her say in the group, you actually gave her more leverage to speak her mind?"

"Mmhmm."

"So then you realize you're an idiot?"

"Mmhmm... hey!" Spitting out a chunk of jerky, Ean glared at the imp. "I'm not used to dealing with manipulative people. Usually when someone wanted something from me, they would just bully me into doing it."

"I'm sure her beauty had nothing to do with your slacking on discipline either?"

Actually it hadn't. She was certainly beautiful, but Ean didn't really think about Azalea that way. Maybe it was the fact she was from the Abyss. Or more likely, maybe it was the fact that she was incredibly deadly. Whatever the reason, his letting up on her had nothing to do with her looks.

"What's done is done, Zin. No point dwelling on it. I'm sure she'll give me plenty of opportunities to dress her down." The imp looked less than convinced. He stalked out of the barn, leaving Ean standing alone.

Knowing he would never understand women, or imps for that matter, Ean headed to the stall alone. The few supplies they had left were stored there--a bag of spare clothes, medicinal herbs, the jerky the man had left, along with a few skins of water. After shoving everything into one bag, he slung it over his back and headed outside to find his companions.

He found Zin and Azalea, both avoiding looking at each other. As he exited, they both took a step towards him, saw the other mirroring their movement, and stopped, turning away from each other again. The next few days were going to be painful with those two.

"So which one of you has an idea which direction we should head to reach the main road?"

Wearing a smug expression, Azalea stepped forward. "I've scouted it out already. We just walk straight in the direction away from the back of the house. There is a tiny path worn out of the grass that should lead to the road. From there we just follow it east to the city."

"Sounds like a good enough plan to me. Let's go."

Azalea turned and stuck her tongue out at Zin. To the imp's credit, he pretended not to see it, although his face did darken slightly. Trying to ignore the exchange as well, Ean walked past both of them at a brisk pace and started off in the direction that Azalea had implied. The sooner they got to the capitol, the better.

Ean was ready to find some answers. Find out more about what he had done to himself. Most importantly, Ean was ready to get some direction back into his life.

CHAPTER 4

YULARI AND HAWKPURSES

AZALEA TOOK THE LEAD in front of Ean while Zin trailed behind as they left the farm. The path Azalea had mentioned was barely noticeable and seemed rarely used. Clearly the man had not felt the need to leave too often. The land on this side of the forest consisted of grassy mounds, so the three often found themselves trudging uphill or stumbling downhill. By the time they crested the fifth hill, the farm was gone from view.

It took them the rest of the day to climb up and down the hills, but as the sun started its decent, they had found the main road the older man had mentioned.

Ean had been expecting to find a road cut into the dirt by wagon wheels and the passage of time, just like what he was used to back in Rensen, but instead he found square slabs of white stone. A single slab was larger than a wagon rig. The spaces between them were filled with yellow sand. As his eyes watched the road stretch into the horizon, it looked more fitting for a giant then the average human.

After he got over his initial amazement of the construction of the road, Ean decided it was a good point in the day to stop and set up camp for the night. The sun was still between the halfway point in the sky and the mountains to the west, but they had kept up a fast pace as they traveled, not taking a single break, and Ean was fairly tired. And hungry too, certainly hungry. They picked a flat spot a bit off the road and settled in.

For a while, they sat in silence, simply letting their bodies rest from the long journey. Ean had gotten out a few pieces of jerky and offered them to his companions. Zin had taken one with a grin, wasting no time in biting off a large piece easily with his sharp teeth. Azalea declined, but did smile slightly at the offer. It was a small smile, but it was something. Maybe Ean could figure her out yet. He chose a particularly large piece of jerky that fit the size of his hunger and sat back chewing slowly, occasionally taking a swig from one of their water skins to relieve his thirst.

Ean found the entire experience to be quite peaceful. His companions seemed to be lost in their own thoughts, which was fine with him since it meant they weren't shooting daggers at each other with their eyes. The day had been warm, but a slight breeze moved through the hills, strong enough to keep Ean cool. He watched the grass around him constantly change direction with the wind. All around him, besides the road, was green as far as the eye could see. It was all a pleasant change from the dampness of his home and the darkness of the forest.

It wasn't until the sun was just beginning to touch the peaks of the mountains to the west and the wind began to have a bit of a bite to it, that Azalea broke the silence.

"We really should come up with a plan of what we're going to do once we reach the city. I'm sure it's going to be difficult to find any kind of record of Zin's former master, and even more so about the location of where he called home."

"What?" Ean was sure he hadn't heard correctly. "The reason that we're going to the city is to find a way to kill the creature that has made its home in the mines of my village. What does Zin's former master have anything to do with that?"

He directed the question at both the imp and Yulari, but his eyes were on Zin. The imp looked at the ground, flicking at a pebble with one clawed finger. Azalea of course grinned at the imp's discomfort before continuing to speak.

"Oh, the imp didn't tell you, my mistake. I thought he had. Zin seems to think that it would be a smart idea to travel to his former master's lair."

"What? How could that be a good idea?"

"Well...the way I see it, if you were to gain even a fraction of the powers my former master had, you would have no trouble killing that creature in Rottwealth."

"You mean the same powers that made him into a power hungry tyrant? The ones that led him to try to enslave the entire world?"

"Yes, those powers, but only enough so that you could better control the creatures you summon."

"I certainly like the sound of enslaving the world," Azalea cut in. "You never mentioned that part before, Zin. If you were hoping to leave that tidbit out of our little arrangement, you've made a big mistake. I would be quite content to follow this one if that was the plan all along."

"No, it's certainly not the plan," Zin replied, while Ean responded just as quickly,

"I would never want to be that kind of a monster!"

"Mmhmm, I see," was the only answer they both got from the Yulari. She was looking at Ean now the same way Zin looked at a fat rat. It sent a shiver down Ean's spine.

"My plan," Zin said, "was just to find out how he could control so many creatures from the Abyss. Ean could use that to summon a handful of Hounds or other minor creatures to take down the beast terrorizing his village. That's it. I have no intention of turning him into anything remotely resembling my former master."

Shrugging, Azalea leaned back onto her elbows and looked off into the distance, as if no longer interested in the conversation. But if Ean had learnt anything about the Yulari in the few days they had been together, he was sure she hadn't let the idea drop from her mind.

"That's good to hear, Zin, because I certainly have no intention of becoming any kind of tyrant." Ean said, directing his words at Zin while at the same time staring at Azalea, hoping that she got the point. For his troubles, he got a small smile and a wink as she looked at him for a moment before turning her gaze back to the countryside.

"Good, that's exactly what I wanted to hear." Zin tore his worried gaze from Azalea to address Ean. "We both want the same thing--to enjoy our lives in peace and comfort--so trust me when I say that the last thing I want you to do is repeat the mistakes of my former master."

"Good, because a peaceful life IS exactly what I want. A simple healer's life. Up until I helped the wounded in Rensen, I looked at healing as a way to make money. But now I know I can get so much more from it. Being a healer gives me a purpose. All I want to do is set up a healer's shop of my own."

"That's all well and good," Azalea cut in. "But you should know we're about to have company. And a lot of it."

Raising a hand to shield his eyes, it took Ean a few moments to follow Azalea's gaze to the west to see what she was talking about.

He spied five, large horse-drawn covered wagons, each a different color, approaching from the west. Following behind the wagons were teams of oxen hitched to open bed wagons stacked with various goods. One was heaping full of gray roundish balls. Another was hauling blocks made from the same material as the balls. There seemed to be no end to the slow-moving convoy. By the time the last one crested the hill, Ean had counted twenty-six wagons in all.

"Zin, you should certainly disappear," Ean said, but the tell-tale shimmering of the already invisible imp was the only thing Ean could see. Azalea was walking towards the road.

"Wait a second!" Ean chased after her. "Maybe we should hide and just wait for them to pass."

"It's a bit late for that," she said, slowing down just enough for him to catch up. "Do you have any idea what they are up to?"

"No. I would guess that they are traders, but I've never seen a group this large. Besides maybe the one that was camped next to Rensen."

"Well, we have traders in the Abyss, and they are usually a sneaky lot. Best if you let me do all of the talking. Otherwise they might trick you out of what little supplies we have left."

Ean was about to object, but then changed his mind. He had been caught by surprise by the bandit at the farm. Maybe it would be better if he let her take the lead in this situation.

"Alright. Just try not to get us into any trouble."

"I would never dream of it." The smirk that touched her lips, though, said otherwise.

The two of them moved to the side of the road and waited for the wagons. The sun was halfway behind the mountains by the time the first wagon reached them. A man on the front wagon raised a single hand, and the entire caravan came to a stop. Leaping down, he walked over to them at a brisk pace, stopping right in front of the two of them and leaving little space.

Standing slightly taller than Ean, the man was as thick as Ean was lanky. He was covered from head to toe in leather and fur, which was strange for how warm it was, with the clothes sitting tight enough on his arms and body for Ean to be able to tell the man's bulk came from muscle and not fat. He wore a small hand ax at his side, the blade the same dark black color as his curly beard and short hair. A large, bulbous nose stuck out over his beard, and made his brown eyes seem sunken into his face. When he spoke, his voice sounded like rocks tumbling down the side of a mountain.

"You don't look like bandits," he said gruffly. "And I'm sure even if the two of you were, you wouldn't be stupid enough to attack a caravan the size of ours."

"No sir," Azalea replied. "We're not bandits, just simple travelers making our way to Lurthalan."

Her usual sensual and alluring voice was all innocence now with a touch of breathlessness that Ean often heard from the less intelligent girls in his village. The personality she had taken on matched her appearance, and even Ean had trouble keeping in mind that there was a Yulari underneath her illusion. He did his best to keep his face straight as she continued.

"We were traveling, and my brother got us lost in the forest to the south." Of course she would stick to that story. "We luckily made it out and found our way to the road."

"An unfortunate story," the man replied. "But thankfully you are only a three-days walk from the capitol. If you are short on supplies, I can happily trade you enough to get you there." He paused for a moment to scratch at his beard. "For the right price, of course."

"We have what I would assume are enough supplies in terms of food," Azalea said, her eyes wandering to the sky as she spoke. She really was playing up the part of a vapid hick. "But no money. What we really could use is a ride so we could rest our tired feet."

"A ride would be more expensive than the supplies, I'm afraid, lass, and you've already said you have no money. I can't see how you could go about paying for a ride on one of my wagons."

Ean watched as something about Azalea...changed. It was hard to pinpoint exactly. It wasn't anything in her appearance or the way she spoke. It was as if the air around her grew thicker, but even that wasn't a proper description of what he noticed.

"I'm sure a trader as rich and powerful as you, someone in charge of such a large group, could handle carrying us along without payment," Azalea said softly, her gaze lowering. To Ean's amazement, the man slowly began to nod as he scratched at his beard.

"I suppose for a few days journey, money wouldn't be necessary." The man's voice had changed now too. It was still rough, but the words seemed more drawn out as he spoke, like he was struggling to get them out. "You have your own supplies as you said, after all, so you won't be costing me anything. I'm sure some room can be made amongst some of the workers."

"Oh, that's ever so kind of you, but we couldn't accept your hospitality without offering you something." Placing a hand on Ean's back, Ean couldn't help but cringe as that smirk appeared on Azalea's face for an instant before disappearing. "My brother will be happy to pay you back by providing free labor. Wouldn't you, Ean?"

Ean nodded dumbly although in his mind he pictured himself throttling her.

"Well, we can always use shovelers to keep the offal from the horses and bulls off the road. The temples take great pride in their roads, and it's a trader's responsibility to keep those roads clean of their own wastes."

"That sounds like an excellent job for my brother."

"Think nothing of it," the man said and then gave a shake of his head. Whatever had changed about Azalea was suddenly gone. When the man spoke again, his voice had returned to its normal speed. "My name is Trait, Trait Deepdweller, of the Deepdweller Hawkpurses."

The way he said the last part made it sound important, but Ean and Azalea just looked at him with confused expressions as they each took his hand in turn.

"Don't tell me you've never heard of the Deepdweller Hawkpurses?"

Azalea looked at Ean and he shook his head.

"No," Azalea said.

"Unbelievable! Everyone knows the Deepdweller family name. Especially since we are Hawkpurses."

"Hawkpurses?" Ean asked.

"You mean to tell me you don't even know what a Hawkpurse is? You truly must be from a tiny village." Waving at a man on one of the wagons, Trait turned back to address them. "Hawkpurses are families specifically chosen by the god, Drenks...you do know who Drenks is, yes?"

Azalea started to shake her head no, but Ean jumped in. "Yes, of course, Drenks the god of Wine and Fortune. We are familiar with the gods of course."

"As I was saying, we are one of a few families chosen by Drenks to control some aspect of trade in the land. My family is in charge of all of the major mining operations throughout Ven Khilada."

"Ven Khilada?" This was something new to Ean.

"Lad, don't tell me you've never even been taught the name of the land you live in. What village did you say you two were from?"

"Rottwealth," Ean replied without thinking, then immediately regretted it.

"Rottwealth?! And they let you out of there?"

"Of course they did, why wouldn't we be able to leave?" And the real question Ean wanted to know was why everyone outside of Rottwealth had such strange opinions about his home to begin with. But instead of asking, he waited for answer to the question he had asked.

"Not much really to say anyway, most people know very little about Rottwealth. More rumors and guesses than actual facts."

"Well, why don't you tell me what rumors you believe and what you think to be facts, and I'll tell you if you're right or not."

"Tell you what, let me get my caravan settled in for the night, the two of you settled in as well, and then we can talk about your home as we sit around a fire and have something decent to eat. Sound good?"

"Sure, that sounds great."

As the man walked away, shouting orders and waving his hands about, Azalea muttered under her breath.

"Next time you tell me to take the lead, let me take the lead. When he started talking about your village, it looked like you had the wind knocked out of you. As long as he is letting us hitch a ride, who cares what he thinks about Rottwealth. You almost ruined all of my hard work."

"You're hard work? What exactly did you do to him? I saw the air about you change and then all of the sudden he was much more agreeable."

"You could see that? Very curious."

"You didn't answer the question."

"Oh, well that was just one of my little tricks. It helps me keep my victims," she paused, raising her hands quickly as Ean's face darkened. "I mean, my unknowing participants, calm and more compliant. It's how I got your two little friends to just sit there why I tried to feed, although you put a stop to that."

"How many other 'little tricks' do you... ooffff!"

A sudden shove from the Yulari sent him tumbling backwards off the road and onto the ground.

"Sorry, brother, but the wagons were moving, and I didn't want you to get run over. Here," she extended a hand to him. "Let me help you up."

Looking at the hand as if it was a poisonous snake, Ean ignored it and pushed himself up. The action earned him a girlish laugh from the Yulari as she turned her attention to the parked caravan.

The six covered wagons left the road to form a tight circle in the middle of the meadow. As more wagons bumbled past them, they formed a concentric circle around the original six. Ean saw that what he had thought were gray balls in those wagons were actually rocks polished smooth. Other wagons contained rock slabs that were a bright white color or grey stone slabs that reminded Ean of larger versions of the stone blocks that made up the first floor of Old Cleff's house. Those wagons made up a third circle around the other two, but they weren't the last of the wagons.

The final four covered wagons finished off the large caravan, each one painted a brilliant yellow color and had large wooden steps coming off the back. Those wagons parked off to the west side of the outer circle. A few men filled out of the back of them, but it was what followed those men that made Ean's eyes widen in surprise.

People made of stone, as in dark gray boulders twice as tall as any man, stepped down from the wagon. Their heads were square blocks disproportionately small compared to their massive torsos. Small blue gems like topaz served as their eyes. When they walked, their joints made sounds like two slabs grating together, and all of their movements were rigid. The strength went out of his legs just to look at them. Once off the wagons, the stone men stopped in front of the human ones and stood still.

Seeing their rigid movements, Ean immediately thought back to the huge creature in the Rensen sawmill and the conversation he had had with the girl, Paige, about the creature. Vilathos, she had called them. He vaguely recalled her saying that the one in her village was one of a kind. These smaller versions must be more common place by the reaction of those around him. The workers moved around them just as calmly as they did the wagons.

As the members of the wagon train finished setting up their camp, Ean watched with rapt fascination as the Vilathos worked. Their task seemed to be setting up the thick wooden tent poles. Using their fists like hammers, they drove them into the ground as easily as a baker might stick a toothpick into a cake. Ean couldn't fathom that kind of strength.

A hand on his shoulder made him jump. Trait laughed and introduced the burly mustachioed man beside him. "This here is Gaiden Pul. He's a good man. I've asked him to help you and your sister get set up for the night."

"Pleasure," Gaiden said in a dry tone. "This way, please."

Gaiden began walking off in a different direction than Trait. When it was clear he wasn't going to slow down for them, Ean and Azalea hurried after him. They weaved quickly in-between wagons and tents as they moved. Tents had been set up on the outside of the wagons, as well as in between the two separate rings, with the workers' tents sitting outside the ring of open wagons and in-between the open and covered wagons. People of higher standing in the caravan seemed to have their tents all the way in the middle. A tent was waiting between the first and second ring of wagons.

"Here we are," Gaiden said, standing in front of a brown tent. It was bigger than any tent Ean had seen in Rottwealth, its peak sitting tall enough that Ean would barely have to duck to enter. Peering inside, he was pleased to see that a brown canvas lining divided the tent into two separate rooms.

"If that is all," Gaiden continued, "feel free to join any of the fires that the workers build in this area. I will ask you, though, not to enter the inner circle of wagons. That area is for Master Deepdweller, his caravan supervisors, and his guards."

"But Trait said that--"

Gaiden raised a hand, effectively silencing Ean. "First of all, you will call him by his title, Master Deepdweller or Sir Deepdweller. Second, Master Deepdweller is much too busy to spend time 'chatting' with whatever riff-raff we come upon in the road. Just consider yourselves lucky that he was gracious enough to offer you a ride to the capitol in the first place."

"Riff-raff!" Ean had never been called that before. "Hold on a second. Master Deepdweller said he would speak to me about--"

Gaiden cut him off with a cough. "Camp will be broken at first light, whether you're ready or not. You may ride in any of the open wagons as long as you do not bother the drivers. I suggest you try to meet one tonight so you know which wagon you will be riding tomorrow. Someone will fetch you when you are scheduled to work. Good evening."

Without waiting for a response, the man walked away, heading past the inner wagons and disappearing around one of the much larger tents inside. Ean took a few steps to go after him, but before he could even utter a word, a large man stepped out in front of him.

"You will turn around now." the burly man said, crossing his arms across an incredibly broad chest. His head was entirely bare of any hair but had plenty of scars all over it. The look he gave Ean made him stop dead in his tracks and quickly turn around. Ean cringed as the man laughed at his back as he slunk away. It looked like he wasn't going to get any answers about Rottwealth from Trait after all.

"You could have used some of your tricks there on that fool," Ean growled at Azalea. "I really wanted to talk to... hey, what's wrong with you?"

Azalea was standing straight, her eyes closed and her body swaying slightly back and forth. She wore a broad smile that seemed to lighten her face, or the illusion of the face she was currently showing. Ean touched her lightly on the arm, and getting no response, gave her a little shake as well.

"Wha..." she finally mumbled, her eyes remaining closed. "Go away. I need a second."

She shoved Ean away with one hand. Azalea had returned to her swaying, little shivers running down her body. All Ean could do was wait for the Yulari to return to her senses, which thankfully did not take much longer. When Azalea finally broke from her trance, her eyes were only half open. She wore a lazy grin on her face, similar to the one Zin wore after a night of stuffing himself with mice and rats. She took a step towards Ean, stumbled a bit and deciding against further steps, decided instead to stand in place.

"Oh, this caravan is wonderful," she purred, hugging her arms around her body. "So many emotions, many of them dark and hidden. Jealousy, hate, anger, resentment. They all taste exquisite. I've never been around this many people before... mmmmm...." Her eyes closed again, and Ean wasn't positive but he thought he saw a bit of drool escape the corner of her mouth.

"Azalea, focus a minute. You've been around people before? How?"

"Shhh...." Before he knew it, Azalea was right in front of him, placing a finger on his lips. "Don't ruin my fun with pointless questions. Just be happy that I'm feeding without killing anyone."

She had a point, and Ean decided against pressing the issue. After a moment, her finger slid from his lip and her hand dropped to her side. She began to sway, further and further to each side. Ean stood awkwardly next to her. He shrugged at a worker passing by who shot them a strange look.

"She is just tired. We've been on the road a while," Ean said, but the man didn't seem to care. Instead he picked up his pace and disappeared around the side of a wagon. Growing frustrated, Ean placed a hand on Azalea's shoulder and carefully gave her another shake. He tensed his body just in case she sent another shove his way.

Instead, Azalea collapsed into his arms, her body going limp. An occasional shiver ran up her body but other than that, she remained limp against him. Lifting her gently, Ean got her high enough so that he could get a look at her face. Sure enough, that lazy grin had widened. And the drool coming out of her mouth was easy to see this close. Barely awake and in her human form, Azalea almost looked innocent. Maybe she wasn't as bad as he feared. After all, she was feeding without killing. That was a step in the right direction.

Unless of course she was simply feeding this way because it was convenient.

"Even mostly asleep, little one," she said, her words slurred and cutting through his thoughts, "I will not kiss you. So get the thought out of your head..." Wrapping her arms around his neck, she pulled him close and lay her head down on his shoulder. "Now be a good boy and help me to our tent. I want to take a nap."

With a sigh, Ean half led, half dragged Azalea the couple of steps to their tent. Getting her down and inside was a bit more trouble, as she offered absolutely no help. Even with a cool breeze blowing through the campsite, Ean was sweating from the effort by the time he stood back up and tied the tent loosely closed. Looking around, Ean realized he would be on his own for a time while Azalea slept off her...feeding.

CHAPTER 5

FELLOW TRAVELERS

TAKING ONE LAST LOOK at the now snoring Azalea, Ean left the tent and walked out of the inner ring between the wagons. He was shocked to see how fast the workers had gotten fires going and were enjoying the evening. Some fires had one or two people gathered around them, those in the smaller groups focused on smoking a pipe or carving a chunk of wood. Others contained larger groups, with men singing, already deep into drink, or playing at some kind of dice game. All of the fires had cooking pots over them, creating a mixture of smells around the camp that made Ean's stomach growl.

Not accustomed to meeting new people, Ean tried the smaller fires first. He hoped they would be a bit more inviting then the larger groups. Instead, all he found were people that either gave him a cold stare as he approached or flat out ignored him until he left. One even went as far as to take out a knife and start to sharpen it while glaring at him until he walked away.

Ean found just as little friendliness at the first couple of larger groups he tried. The men playing at dice were quick to welcome him, until they found out he had no money. Then they laughed at him and sent him on his way. Those purely drinking usually had mixed reactions, with none of them being pleasant. Most grumbled at him and told him to find his own stuff to drink. Not wanting to have a repeat of his one bad night in Rensen, Ean tried to explain he wasn't interested in their drinks, but this only brought about more laughter and some choice words about his age and what he could be doing instead.

The whole experience was embarrassing, especially when a group would watch him go off to a different campfire and then laugh loudly as they saw him being turned away again. This continued until the sun had completely disappeared behind the mountains and the first moon was covering the camp with its green light. Ean was about to give up for the night when he noticed a man with a mug in one hand wave him over with the other one. Ean watched the man a few moments, not sure whether he was being genuine or wanted to join in the fun of messing with him, until the man started to frown. Not wanting to insult the only person that had shown him anything but a cold shoulder or ridicule, Ean hastily moved over to the man's campfire.

There were four other men sitting around the camp fire as Ean approached, and the man that had waved him over pointed to an open spot on the ground as he took a swig from his mug. Two of the men give him curt but friendly nods as he sat between them, while a third man offered him a drink. Ean was about to refuse until he saw that all that the mug contained was water.

"Thanks," he said, taking the mug and immediately draining half of it. As soon as the water touched his lips he realized how thirsty he had been.

"Not a problem." The man that spoke wasn't the one that had given him the mug but was instead the one that had waved him over. "We can spare a little food as well if you're hungry."

"Yes, thank you. I would appreciate it." Ean took a closer look at the man as he took another drink and saw nothing but openness on his clean, shaven face. For some reason, Ean found the positive attitude as slightly off putting. He knew it was just his own insecurities, but after a night of being ridiculed, he was finding it hard to accept someone being nice to him.

"Well," the friendly man said. "I guess introductions are in order. My name is Wil Asbury. The two on each side of ya are my brothers; the one sitting on your right is Lyde while the one on your left is Phil. This one," he said, waving over at the man that had given Ean the mug, "is trying his best to get us fired from this job."

"Hey!" the man said, looking embarrassed. "I kept the wagon from rolling down that hill. It's hard to get fired when you've never actually done anything wrong. I'm Baird Tulman, by the way. "

"What my soon-to-be son-in-law fails to mention," Wil said with a grimace, "is that the reason they almost tipped was because his attention was on writing a letter to my daughter when he should have been watching where our wagon was going. All it takes is one major mistake with a Hawkpurse family to find yourself not only without a job, but also unable to find a new one. And that's if they go easy on you. My one friend, Dade Trilman, lost a delivery for the Soushade family once and they--"

"There you go again," Baird cut in, "telling that same old story. No one has ever even heard of this so-called friend of yours. I think you just made up that story. If the all of the Hawkpurse families were as bad as you say, I doubt they would let you go on spreading rumors about them."

"They don't do anything because they are too powerful to worry about a simple man like me. And Dade was a real person, he lived down by..."

Ean felt a nudge at his side and turned to see Phil tapping him lightly with his elbow.

"They will be at this for a while, I think," Phil whispered. "Might as well get some of the stew and sit back and watch the show."

Leaning in, Lyde voiced his opinion as well. "This happens every night. My brother is a bit of a hot head and his future son-in-law is as stubborn as a rock. We don't let them drive the wagons together during the day, but we let them go at each other at night. It's great entertainment, and I think it lets them both relieve a little stress. Here," he said, passing a bowl and spoon to Ean, "help yourself to the stew."

Ean accepted the bowl and filled it with a warm, steaming broth from the pot over the fire. The stew contained bits of vegetables and meat, nothing special but certainly filling. He enjoyed it so much that he ate two more bowlfuls, all the while Wil and Baird argued over everything from how to properly catch fish in the pond in their village to how best to seal a roof. Ean couldn't keep track of how the topics changed so rapidly, but he did agree with Wil's brothers--it was certainly entertaining to watch the two.

The arguments stopped when they both realized that the stew was almost completely gone, and all five of them sat around talking about their families and homes. Except for Ean, of course. After seeing Trait's reaction when he had mentioned Rottwealth, he decided to make up a story about growing up in Rensen. It turned out the other four had never been there, so Ean was free to make up whatever suited him. After telling what he considered to be an excellent story, which concluded with his brush with the bandits that attacked the village, Ean deflected the attention back to the other men. It wasn't hard; all four of them seemed to love to talk.

They ended up talking well into the night. By the time they were all yawning more than speaking, all three moons hung high in the sky. Wil offered to give Ean and Azalea a ride the following morning and took a few moments to show him where their wagon was sitting. Thanking Wil for his hospitality, Ean made his way back to his tent.

To his surprise, he found Azalea missing from the tent and not asleep as he had hoped, but he should have known better. Focusing his attention, he could feel the stronger aura that Azalea's connection to the Abyss gave off but figured he would leave her be.

Azalea had promised to stay out of trouble after all, and if they were going to be traveling together, he had to start trusting her.

Zin, of course, was also nowhere to be found. It took a little more effort for Ean to feel the imp's much smaller presence. Ean eventually sensed him towards the other side of the camp, more along the edges of it actually. With a lack of rats or other small vermin about, the imp was probably stealing real food from the various camps. Ean silently wished him luck as he crawled into the tent. With the flaps tied closed behind him and a full stomach, the darkness of the tent helped Ean to drift right off to sleep.

CHAPTER 6

ANOTHER POINT OF VIEW

EAN KNEW RIGHT AWAY he was dreaming, but it felt different. He didn't have any control of his body, but all of his senses felt enhanced. It was like he was trapped in someone else's body, stuck watching what their eyes could see, feeling what their body felt, without the ability to control even the slightest movement. He also couldn't make himself wake up, which worried him the most. Unable to do anything other than hope for the best, Ean watched through eyes that were not his own as he exited a small, dark, stone room.

The body he was hitching a ride with raised a hand to shield his eyes as he exited the room, and that was the first indication that he wasn't human. When the hand pulled away Ean was looking at four fingers where there should have been five. The skin of the hand was a dark yellow and covered in ridges. Both the hand and his arm were covered in scars as well, some old and some new, but that didn't seem to bother his host as he took a look around.

He was in a circular stone room, similar to the one he had just exited, except much larger. The walls stretched up and out of sight in the darkness above him. On the other side of the room was another doorway, a large stone door--about the height of the creature he was inhabiting-- and was currently closed. The air felt heavy as his body breathed it in with short, controlled breaths. It also had a particularly nasty taste to it, but that in no way compared to the smell.

Ean had been around dead or rotting bodies before. It was part of his job after all as a Healer, well at least in Rottwealth where the Soulbearers never came. So he was used to the horrible smell that a body gave off a few days after death. The smell in this room, however, was like nothing he had ever experienced before. Being in a room with one dead body would be like sitting out in a field of flowers compared to the smell that assaulted his nose here.

There was the smell of death--that much was obvious--as if dozens of bodies had been left in the room to rot. The smell of feces and urine was mixed in as well, which overwhelmed even the smell of rotting flesh. That, and whatever other smells were in the room, made Ean want to vomit, but apparently whatever person or thing he inhabited had a much stronger stomach. Instead, the yellow-skinned creature walked further into the room with a confident stride, as if he had been here many times before.

As he moved, the gate across from him swung open, revealing a creature pulled straight from a nightmare. The monster looked like someone had pulled off the scariest pieces of every insect, jammed them together, and then increased its size to twice that of a man. It stepped out of the opposite room on two pairs of shelled black legs as long as a man's entire body, which ended in tiny points instead of feet. Those legs connected to a more humanoid body high above them, although it was covered in what appeared to be a dark violet carapace. Two tiny appendages similar to its legs came out of its sides just above the hips while a regular set of arms sat just above them. Instead of hands though, those arms ended in a large pair of pinchers almost as long as the creature's torso. At the top of the thick, shelled body sat a head that sent chill's through his body.

A round insect-like face with pinchers coming out of its mouth and eight tiny black eyes stared back at Ean, or whomever Ean was inhabiting in this dream. A word, Amalgagrim, popped into his mind. Looking through the eyes of someone else, Ean felt the first emotion from his host: fear.

"Let the entertainment begin!" boomed a coarse voice from somewhere high overhead. It was immediately followed by the sounds of cheering and yelling, most of the words lost in the din above. When Ean could pick out a particular voice from the mess, it was usually in a language that he didn't understand.

As the noise from above increased, the creature across from Ean began to move, slowly weaving to the left then right, as if it was impossible for the Amalgagrim to move in a straight line. In response, his host let out a primal roar and lifted his four arms into the air, spreading them wide.

That's when things started to click into place--the four fingers, yellowish skin, four arms...he was in a Cruxlum!

As Ean watched the creature across from him move slowly in his direction, a thought appeared in his head that he knew was not his own.

Testing me, to see if I will blindly rush in and attack.

The words came to him in the Cruxlum's language, but he understood them as if the thoughts had been in his own native tongue. Was it because of the dream, or was this more than a dream? As usual, Ean had multiple questions and absolutely no answers. He was forced to simply ride along in the body of the Cruxlum and see what happened.

"I need to be ready for it," the Cruxlum thought, its eyes locked on the other creature. "It's faster than the size of its body would imply. It will feint with its pinchers. Its usual attack is to try and skewer its victim's legs with the points of its own front legs. That is how it will attack first and will be my best chance to counter and kill it quick."

An image of the Cruxlum getting behind the other creature quickly flashed in Ean's mind. He pictured himself, the Cruxlum, grabbing the head of the monster with all four hands and twisting as sharply as possible. In the brief image, he saw that the Cruxlum would probably lose a finger or two to the Amalgagrim's powerful mandibles, but it would be an acceptable loss if it assured him a quick victory.

All Ean could do while the thoughts of the Cruxlum bounced around his head was silently wish it luck.

Without warning, the creature rushed straight at him, its four pointed legs making loud clicking sounds as their points struck the stone floor. As the Cruxlum expected, it was fast, closing the distance between them in an instant. Its left pincher struck out towards his right side.

The Cruxlum dodged the blow, moving just enough that the shelled appendage harmlessly brushed against his side. Then he rolled forward underneath the creature, narrowly dodging the creature's front right leg as it crashed down where the Cruxlum's left thigh had been only moments before.

Grunting, the Cruxlum let his momentum carry him underneath and completely past the Amalgagrim. He rolled to his feet, turning around and leaping back without looking, hoping the creature was still standing in the same place. When all he felt was air, both the Cruxlum and Ean knew that the plan had failed.

All the Cruxlum could do was watch as he sailed over the monster, which had spread its legs out wide and dropped low to the ground. Ean watched as well, his host's body twisted in the air and tried to dodge the pincher that reached up for him. It clamped down on the Cruxlum's ankle, sending a jolt of pain through his body. The pincher tried to crush through skin and bone, causing such an intense pain that Ean knew if it had been his body, he would easily have succumbed to unconsciousness.

The Cruxlum, however, stayed focused, even as the pincher stopped his momentum and slammed his body down to the ground. Ignored the pain, the Cruxlum was able to twist in the creature's grip so that he was on his back. This allowed him to get his two lower hands up just in time to catch the Amalgagrim's leg as it tried to slam down and impale his body.

The Cruxlum struggled with the leg while the pain of the creature's pincher slowly bit deeper into his ankle. That pain suddenly increased as the creature used its pincher to hold its own body up enough so that it could send the end of its other front leg straight towards the Cruxlum's face.

Again the Cruxlum was able to grab the creature's leg, this time with its upper set of hands. The creature tried one last attack, sending its free pincher towards the Cruxlum's head as well but was unable to get at an angle to either catch his head or his arms with it. At a stalemate, the Cruxlum and the creature stayed locked in their position, both struggling against the other to obtain some kind of advantage.

Trying his best to focus his own thoughts through the Cruxlum's pain, Ean knew the stalemate wouldn't last long. He could already feel the Cruxlum's strength waning as he was forced to hold the creature aloft by its front legs.

Soon, both of those legs started to lower, their pointed ends getting closer and closer to the Cruxlum's body as they flailed about above him.

The Cruxlum's upper arms nearly gave out, dropping the creature low enough that the point of its leg was able to slice into his right cheek and down to his chin. The pain and the blood dripping into his mouth brought on a second wind, or perhaps a surge of desperation, and the Cruxlum was able to slowly lift the creature back up into the air. But it would only be a matter of time before the last of his strength gave out and those pointed legs did real damage.

"There is no glory in death."

The Cruxlum's thought was like a shout in Ean's mind. If he had been in his own body, Ean would have shrunken back from the power of the thought as it cut through all the pain.

"There is no glory in death, unless that death comes as the price of victory."

Ean did not like the sound of that. He had no idea what was going on, if this was a dream or something more, but he certainly hoped the Cruxlum's death wouldn't lead to his own. Another image from the Cruxlum flashed across his mind, this time showing the right leg of the creature piercing the Cruxlum's stomach.

"No!" Ean shouted in his mind. He knew it was useless, but he continued to shout anyway. How would getting stabbed in the gut help him be victorious? As a sense of peace settled into the Cruxlum's body intertwining with the pain, Ean began shouting louder. The mad creature really was going to let it happen!

All four of the Cruxlum's arms began to lower slowly, allowing those pointed ends to get closer and closer to his skin. The creature, which had been quiet the entire battle, began to make excited chittering noises. It saw the end coming.

With one last push, the Cruxlum lifted both of the creature's legs slightly higher, then let his lower two hands slip off the creature's right front leg. Letting out a few more chitters and clacks, the creature drove its now free leg down.

An explosion of pain ripped through the Cruxlum's stomach, the sensation so strong, it made the pain Ean felt after a summoning feel like a stubbed toe.

The leg made a crunching sound as it traveled all the way through the Cruxlum's body and struck the stone floor underneath. The force and the momentum of the blow caused the creature to tip slightly to its right, forcing its left leg to move higher instead of crashing down to finish the Cruxlum off.

And that is when Ean, through all of the pain and anguish he was experiencing with his host, felt the Cruxlum's lips twist up into a smile.

With a strength and speed Ean did not think possible, his lower hands shot out and joined his upper hands in gripping the creature's front left leg. With a sudden jerk and twist of all four arms, the Cruxlum snapped the creature's leg in two places, and then yanked with all of his might.

The pain and surprise were clear in the creature's ugly face as it toppled to its side, clawed arms and legs flailing in every direction. It tried to catch itself with its destroyed leg as its pincher lost its grip on the Cruxlum's ankle, but the leg simply folded up at the places it was broken, and the creature rolled to its side. The momentum also pulled its right leg out from the Cruxlum's body as it fell, freeing Ean's host.

Pushing himself up on wobbly arms and legs, the Cruxlum seemed oblivious to the pain that Ean felt crippled by. He regained his feet, letting all four arms dangle at his side, and watched as the creature tried and failed to right itself.

With grim determination, the Cruxlum hobbled around the creature, staying out of reach of flailing pinchers and legs, until he was positioned behind it. Taking his time, he reached out with his four large hands and carefully gripped the creature's head, his patience allowing him to grip it in a way that didn't sacrifice any fingers to the creature's mandibles.

The creature began flailing about even more wildly as the Cruxlum's hands squeezed tighter and tighter, but its pinchers could not reach him. Gathering what little strength the Cruxlum had left, he closed his eyes for a moment, taking away Ean's only way of knowing what was happening. Ean felt one of the Crux's feet step on the back of the creature, and then the Crux took a deep breath.

With a surge of his muscles, he yanked backwards while pushing off his foot. In the darkness, Ean felt the resistance of the creature's body to the effort and then heard the sickening tearing sound as the strength of the Cruxlum won out and the creature's head was torn from his body.

The Cruxlum stumbled for a moment, and then stood still, his eyes closed and the creature's head in his hands. He took deep breaths, his nostrils catching the scent of both his own life seeping out of his wound, as well as the putridness of the creature's blood. There were erratic sounds of the creature flailing about, diminishing to a small rustling sound as the creature's body began to succumb to death. And over it all, over the pain and the agony, both Ean and the Cruxlum heard the thunderous cheers coming from above and all around them.

"Victory is mine," the Cruxlum thought, finally opening his eyes, pride and joy almost drowning out the pain and the noise for the briefest of moments. "The glory is mine."

As the thought drifted through his mind, the Cruxlum's legs finally gave out and he dropped to his knees. The creature's head tumbled from his grip, bouncing once off the stone floor and then rolling away. Numbness swept through his body, and Ean could feel the blood from the wound flowing down his side. It was then that the Cruxlum looked down at the wound, allowing Ean to see the damage as well.

A large hole, spilling blood, gaped on the right side of his abdomen. The hole was in a place that the Cruxlum knew did not hit any organs, but he pictured himself dying anyway. And yet somehow that knowledge seemed to bring Ean's host peace instead of fear, which was fine because Ean was feeling enough fear for the both of them. The Cruxlum might be ready to accept his own death, but Ean certainly wasn't in the same state of mind. Unfortunately, there seemed to be nothing that he could do.

"Well done! Well done!" The same gravelly voice that Ean had first heard high overhead was now coming from behind him. The voice soured the Crux's sense of pride at his victory.

"A truly spectacular battle, one worthy of my guests. You have served your Master well this day, and for that I will make sure that you live so that you can serve me just as well again."

While hearing that the voice was going to save the Cruxlum's life filled Ean with hope, it was despair that flowed from his host's mind. Despair and rage. With an energy that Ean didn't think the Cruxlum had left in him, he turned and rose in one shaky motion, then lunged in the direction of the speaker.

Before he had even completely turned around, blows struck him from every direction, forcing him back down to his knees. They continued to rain down on him, hitting his head, body, arms, legs, practically anywhere there was a spot to be hit, except on the wound in his side. The Cruxlum had his eyes closed again, which meant that Ean couldn't see where the blows were coming from. And then, just as quickly as they began, they stopped.

"Just because I treat you as a prized possession," the gravelly voice said, "does not mean I will let you get away with demonstrating a lack of respect. You can either be a well-kept slave or you can be a slave that must constantly be put in its place. Either works for me, as both require an equally small amount of effort and time. You decide."

The tensing of the Crux's muscles and grinding of its teeth told Ean exactly what his host was deciding. Inwardly sighing, Ean did what he could to brace his mind as the Crux pushed himself off the ground and lunged blindly in the direction of the voice again.

The pain was worse this time. It felt like a million needles piercing the Crux's skin over and over again. What little energy Ean's host had was drained instantly, and he fell to the ground. Without the energy to even catch himself on his four large hands, the Crux hit his face hard on the ground. He lay there struggling to get up while Ean screamed in his head for the Crux to just stay down. Eventually, the Crux stopped struggling as unconsciousness took him and Ean both.

CHAPTER 7

ROAD TO LURTHALAN

WHEN EAN WOKE, IT took him a few moments to remember where he was. It was dark, and he was on the ground, which for a moment made him think he was still in the dream. Or whatever it had been. Reaching out with a gloved, five-fingered hand, Ean felt the fabric of the tent give way slightly to his touch. He was still in the caravan's campsite, not some dank gladiator pit.

Ean wiped sweat from his brow. Whatever he had just experienced, it had affected him physically. He felt sore all over, as if it had been his body that had been receiving those blows. On top of the physical pain, he also felt a pang of guilt over the Crux's situation. To have to live a life like that, forced to fight and suffer for the amusement of something more powerful. If only there was some way to--

"Good, you're awake. I wanted to talk to you about--"

Startled by the unexpected sound, he spun around. His closed fist made contact with an invisible lump. Something bounced off the tent wall with an oompf.

"Zin, I'm so sorry! I just had the worst dream and it made me a little jumpy."

"A little jumpy?" the imp responded with a grunt. "I'm pretty good at dodging the occasional blow you send my way, but you reacted faster than I've ever seen you move... Wait a minute, what did you just say?"

"I said I had a bad dream."

In the darkness of the tent it was hard to make out the imp, although he could sense exactly where he was. He felt Azalea too. She wasn't close by, which made Ean nervous.

"Alright, Ean," the imp said slowly. "I want you to say that just one more time."

"Why are you acting so strange? All I said was..." His mouth froze as he listened to the words coming out of his mouth. They weren't human.

"Ean, you're speaking--"

"The Crux language, I know." And yet knowing didn't help him to switch back into human. "Zin, I don't know what's happening, I can't stop."

"Well, don't look at me. I have no idea how you all of the sudden know a completely new language, or why that's the only one you can speak."

"Zin, I can't go around speaking another race's language, especially one that comes from the Abyss. I'll stand out like..."

He trailed off as he realized he had switched back to the human tongue.

"I think I'm getting it under control." Still human.

"Especially if these words come out in Crux." And they had.

Ean couldn't help but clap his hands together in excitement. At least that horrible dream or whatever it was gave him something positive.

"Glad you're having fun," Zin said, "but can you try to explain what happened? I believe a dream was mentioned?"

"Yes, I dreamed that I was stuck in a Crux's mind. He was in some sort of arena and was forced to fight this ugly looking creature with pinchers and four pointed legs. He won, but then he rebelled and tried to fight his master and was knocked unconscious. That's when I woke up."

The imp had begun to pace as Ean told him his dream and didn't stop once Ean had finished.

"Mmm... mmm..." was all he mumbled for a time as he paced back and forth. Ean watched him move about until a sliver of light started to creep under the gap left by the tent flap.

"Well?" he said, not trying to hide the annoyance in his voice. "What do you think?"

"What you described sounds like a typical show that a Nar'Grim would put on to show off his power and influence."

"Zin, the same thing happened after I summoned the Hound. Do you know what it means?"

"I have no idea what it means." Shrugging, the imp sat down in front of Ean. "Could have something to do with the tattoos on your arm, or it could be you're somehow bonding a bit with the creatures you summon. Or it could be something completely unrelated to both. Who knows? Maybe you're just going crazy."

Ean took a swing at the imp. Zin rolled backward and avoided the blow, smiling a toothy grin back at him.

The imp certainly had given him a lot to think about it. Could his tattoos somehow be bonding him to the creatures he summoned? He hadn't had a dream about Zin yet, but on the same token, the last time he had summoned the imp had been before he had put the tattoo on his body. Did that mean he would eventually dream he was Azalea too?

Shaking his head, Ean tried to put those thoughts away for another time. Just as an experiment, he tried to switch his thinking to Crux. The words came easily and switched back to human just as fast. It was interesting to think in another language and would be useful if he ever did have to summon a Crux again.

A voice from outside cut through the silence. "Time to get up and get out, traveler. The tents are going to be put away, and I've been told you have morning clean up duty. Best get your stuff on a wagon and find a supervisor to get your shovel and assignment. Hurry now."

He had forgotten all about his "job." Azalea was to thank for that, of course. He would have to think of some way to pay her back. Fighting his sore muscles, Ean rose to his feet and gathered up his things, groaning each time he had to bend over. Zin chuckled at Ean's misery before turning invisible and leaving. The imp was probably going to find a good spot to watch Ean shovel animal turds all morning.

Exiting his tent, Ean was surprised to see most of the camp already cleaned up. The man certainly hadn't been joking about the caravan moving out soon. Most of the tents in the middle of the circle were already gone, and many of the wagons had their drivers up and ready to go. He found Wil's wagon easily enough, earning a wave from him and his family as Ean dropped off his things. He was about to climb up and have a quick chat with the man when a hand dropped heavily on his shoulder.

"I assumed you wouldn't seek out anyone to put you to work, so I figured I would have to hunt you down."

Ean did his best not to cringe at the sound of Gaiden's dry voice. The thin man wore an annoyed expression on his face.

"I find it quite interesting," the sour man continued, "that Master Deepdweller would offer you all of this hospitality and you would try to get out of the one duty you were assigned."

"I'm not trying to get out of my duties," Ean tried to keep his tone civil. "I was dropping off my things, as I was instructed, before going to find my assignment."

Gaiden sniffed loudly as he stared at Ean for a time. Clearly the man didn't believe him.

"Very well. Follow me."

The man stalked off, not waiting to see if Ean followed, which Ean did. He wasn't about to shirk away from responsibility. He followed Gaiden until they got to one of the covered wagons. Without a word, Gaiden signaled to a man inside and was tossed a shovel. Pushing the shovel into Ean's chest, Gaiden moved towards the outer ring of wagons, waving Ean to follow. Stopping behind a random wagon, Gaiden spun around to face Ean again.

"Following the order set down by the temples, the roads must be kept clear. You will follow behind this wagon, removing any offal left by the animals in front of you or missed by other shovelers. You are to remove as much of the offal from the road as possible before you fall three wagons behind. Whatever is left you can leave for the shovelers behind you."

Lifting a hand, the sour man jabbed a finger into Ean's chest. "And just so you know, shovelers take it very personally if they feel someone isn't pulling their weight. You leave too much for those behind you, and you might find what you've missed sitting outside your tent in the morning. Or perhaps in it. Understand?"

Removing his finger, Gaiden stalked away without another word. Ean hoped he didn't have to deal with the man every day. Starting tomorrow morning, as soon as he woke, he would seek out the supply wagon, get his shovel and get behind his assigned wagon before Gaiden could even find him. That would show the snotty little man.

Not long after Ean was assigned his wagon they all began to move, the circles of wagons unwinding like a snake and moving back onto the road. Ean's wagons were those in the middle that carried the huge blocks of stones. Ean had no idea who would want to buy such things or how much they would cost. Back home, the inn and Cleff's home were the only buildings made of stones, and those stones were much smaller than the ones on the wagons. Ean hadn't even seen a building in Rensen with stones the size of the ones in the wagon in front of him. Maybe they were easier to transport in larger pieces and would be broken down at their destination?

Ena's thoughts were interrupted as he stepped in a large pile of ox poo. Already? He couldn't believe that they were only a few steps down the road and they were already starting to go. Didn't they go at any point before they left?

Wiping off his boot, he jogged back and started to shovel away what he had stepped in. It took a few trips to carry it all to the side of the road, but he was finished before his second wagon had passed. Jogging back up to the rear of his first wagon, Ean decided it would be best not to get lost in his own thoughts too much.

The rest of the morning was uneventful. Ean's job turned out not to be as bad as he had originally thought. Not counting the smell, it was fairly easy to keep the roads clean. The shovelers in front of him must have been doing an excellent job as Ean never had to shovel more than one pile at a time, and there were long spans where he didn't have to shovel at all. He found the shoveling itself to be a nice little workout, and when he wasn't heaving dung around, he was able to walk along peacefully and enjoy the scenery.

Although there wasn't much to see, the broad expanse of grassy hills were a pleasant change from the dull browns of his village and the almost smothering closeness of the forest. Occasionally he would catch a glimpse of the edge of someone's farmland with its variety of crops as it interrupted the sea of grass that made up most of the area. Very few fields contained the large beanstalks that everyone grew back in Rottwealth. Considering himself an expert in plants, Ean was a bit taken back by the number of plant life he saw growing which he was unable to identify. He would have to remedy that--soon. If he was going to eventually head out on his own and maybe open up his own shop on the side, he would have to make sure he knew about what grew outside of his hometown of Rottwealth.

Azalea was nice enough to grace him with her presence as the sun approached the middle of the sky. She, of course, only came to taunt and tease him, but Ean didn't mind as much as it did give him someone to talk to for a time.

"Well, look at you," she said, standing off ahead of him as the caravan moved past her, "being all helpful and productive. I'm sure everyone throughout the land appreciates your hard work in keeping crap off of their roads."

Ean stayed silent until he reached the spot where she was standing. As soon as he reached her, she fell in at his side, all the while wearing her usual smirk. It always looked a little strange on her human face, as if her cover wasn't used to the expression. After a few steps, Ean decided to acknowledge her.

"At least one of us is doing some actual work. What have you been up to since I left you passed out last night?"

"Oh nothing special, just enjoying a few delicious snacks." She glanced at him, letting out a little laugh as his frown grew. "Oh don't worry. I didn't have any big meals. Plenty going on with this group that I can keep myself stuffed just being around them. Would you like to hear all of the funny things I've learned while being amongst these wonderful people?"

"Not particularly."

"Too bad. I'm going to tell you anyway." She placed an arm around him for a moment, then frowned and pulled it back. She looked confused for a moment but then shook her head and laughed as a pile of feces appeared ahead of them. Waiting patiently, she watched Ean clear the road before continuing.

"Anyway, as I was saying, the first person I came across was a delightful fellow who wanted to keep to himself at first. The smell of guilt wafting off of him was too good to ignore though, so I stayed until I won him over. Turns out he had killed his brother back in the town this caravan is coming from. Over a girl no less! Killed a member of his family out of lust for a girl! Isn't that delightful?"

Ean tried to keep his face as blank as possible. Maybe if he showed a complete lack of interest she would stop. The Yulari continued on anyway.

"Not interesting enough for you? I suppose not, maybe if he had killed the girl too, it would have made for a better story. Well, the next two men I met were a bit friendlier, especially after I let my robe open 'accidentally' and revealed a little leg. Those two stole a great deal of money from the wrong person and have been hiding out with this caravan for over a year. But that's not the most interesting part." She paused, obviously trying to add a little bit of suspense. "Can you guess what is?"

"No, and I don't care."

"Sure you do. Stop trying to ruin my fun." Her lips lowered in a pout but only for a second, and then she was laughing again. "The best part is, later in the night I found a man that only joined this caravan because he was sent to kill the other two men! Or kill one and torture the other in order to find out if they still have the money. I gave him a few suggestions."

"I don't want to hear about how you're helping someone murder two other men, regardless of what they did. I don't want to hear any more about how horrible people are, understand?"

Ean was hoping the anger that he let fill his voice would deter her from going on. He should have known better.

"Okay, okay, you didn't like my two stories about murder. It's not your thing and that's fine. But you should find this last story really entertaining."

Rolling his eyes, he turned his attention back on the road.

"The last person I found still up late last night was a boy a little younger than you. He joined the caravan in hopes of making enough money to buy his girl a home so they could start a life together. He was so in love with the girl I thought my teeth were going to simply rot from how sweet his emotions tasted. Isn't that something?"

Actually it was rather sweet, and not a story Ean would expect Azalea to enjoy. Maybe she did have a good side to her after all.

"I slept with him, of course."

Ean put a hand to his face and groaned. It smelled like what he had been shoveling all morning, but at this point he didn't care. Azalea just giggled.

"What? Obviously he must not like her that much if he was willing to bed down with me. I mean, sure he did cry the next morning when he realized what he had done, but I'm sure he'll be over it by the time he gets home to his girl. It's not like she'd know unless he told her right? No harm in that one."

"And I bet you didn't use any of your skills to get him to sleep with you?"

"Of course. He was a stubborn one, ignoring both my subtle hints and my more blatant moves. He would have wanted me eventually. I just got bored with having to try so hard, so I cheated a little. Either way would have ended with the same results."

A small pile of offal appeared ahead. Taking a firm hold of his shovel, Ean scooped out a large amount of the dung and turned to face Azalea. Her expression changed from mirth to weariness.

"Ean, don't you even think about it."

As Ean approached her with measured steps, the shovel head and what it was carrying resting off to his side, the Yulari began to back up.

"Ean, don't you dare. Just because you have to stink of that stuff doesn't mean I have to as well."

Ean stayed quiet, closing the distance between the two of them. When he felt he was close enough, he launched the dung at Azalea. He considered it a good shot as it sailed directly at her.

With a squeak, Azalea twisted out of the way, letting the dung fly past her. She stalked directly up to Ean, ripping the shovel from his hands and raising it as if to strike him. Ean stood his ground.

He didn't think she would actually hit him. Hoped she wouldn't at least.

Their eyes locked. Her illusion gave way for an instant, revealing her dark red eyes. Just as quickly, though, the illusion snapped back into place and she pushed the shovel back into his hands.

"Clearly," she growled, "you would prefer to shovel alone. That's fine by me. I'm tired of being around your stink anyway."

With a sniff, she shouldered past him, almost spinning him around with the force. Ean watched her move back towards the front of the caravan, not sure how he felt about the whole exchange. On the one hand, she deserved to be taken down a peg or two. What she had done to that boy, completely messing with his life, and how she had dragged those secrets out of those men was wrong. Unless she planned on turning those men in, he didn't care if she knew about their dirty little secrets.

On the other hand, all of them, minus the boy of course, were fairly terrible. Ean had been surprised to hear about how horrible those men really were, even if he didn't actually know which men in the caravan were which. Killing your brother because a girl liked him more? Bran wasn't even family and Ean couldn't imagine hurting him just for the chance to be with Jaslen.

Bran and Jaslen. He hadn't thought about them the past few days. Should he even bother? They had made it clear how they really felt about him before Azalea had chased them off. Ean was better off without them and their false kindness towards him. He would return home, powerful enough to kill Rottwealth's monster, and show them he had worth. Even with his anger towards them, a part of him deep down inside hoped that they were okay.

Shaking his head, he turned his thoughts back to Azalea. They had to figure out some way to get along or they would kill each other. Literally. No, he wouldn't kill her, but he would send her back to the Abyss, which sounded like it was worse. He couldn't imagine how to fix things. Clearly he was not good at ignoring her. He spent the rest of his morning shoveling dung and thinking about this problem.

By the time the sun was well overhead, a supervisor--thankfully not Gaiden--and another worker came and relieved him for the day. Free of his duties, Ean walked off to the side of the road and sat down. It was nice to be off his feet for a little bit, and Wil's wagon was well behind where he had been shoveling. He took advantage of the break and sat in the grass, watching the wagons loaded with stone amble by, their wheels creaking under all of the weight.

CHAPTER 8

WORLDLY LESSONS

WIL'S WAGON ENDED UP being the second to last of the wagons hauling stone, his large form easy to make out on the driver's seat. The man gave him a friendly wave as the wagon approached, and Lyde reached down to haul Ean up onto the seat next to him. As Ean took a seat, he waved at Baird and Phil who were moving about in the back, securing lines and talking quietly.

"Well," Wil said, his eyes watching the road ahead. "How did you like your first day of shoveling?"

"It wasn't that bad. I didn't get any more than I could handle, and it never got hot enough to really get the stuff to smell."

"That's good. My brothers and I started as shovelers for this caravan. It's honest work and if you save your money, one day you'll be able to afford your own wagon like me. Wagon driving is much better money and very little physical work. Plus the Hawkpurse family that hires you covers most of your expenses. It's a good life. If you're interested, I could probably get you assigned as a shoveler behind my wagons."

Ean grimaced at the thought of shoveling dung for years on end, then immediately regretted it as his eyes caught Wil's eyes.

"I really do appreciate the offer," Ean said quickly. "It's just that I already have a profession. I'm a Healer."

"Mmhmm," was the only reply he got.

"Honest. I know all about plants, at least the ones that can be used as medicine, and I can set bones and stitch wounds."

"That true? Well, that is a good skill to have, but you'll still need some money to get your own place all set up. I'm guessing from the fact that you had to work to pay your way that you don't have a great deal of money. A few years of working for the caravan would put you right on your way to owning your own place."

"Thank you. I will certainly keep that in mind."

Ean tried to sound as sincere as possible, but the look he got from Wil told him he hadn't been that convincing. He needed to change the subject before he found himself walking.

"I've been meaning to ask...who buys all of this stone that you're carrying, and what do they use it for? I've never seen more than a few buildings made out of stone in the villages I've visited."

"Then I suppose you haven't been to Lurthalan yet, lad." The man's tone was cold as he kept his attention on the road. "More and more buildings are being made of stone, at least along Merchant's Circle. The temples have been funding the construction of a wall to protect the city as well."

"The temples fund the building of the walls? Why is that?"

"You really don't know that much about what you're getting yourself into, do you?" Wil gave him a hard look, then let out a sigh. "I guess I best educate you then. That way I can have a clear conscience and won't worry so much about you and your sister. Here Lyde, take the reins so I can give the boy my full attention. It's about time for your turn to take over steering anyway."

Why did everyone insist on calling him "boy?" If it wasn't for the fact that Ean completely agreed with the man about not knowing anything about the capitol, he would have given him a piece of his mind. Instead he held his tongue and waited for Wil to educate him.

"I've already talked to you about the Hawkpurse families and how dangerous they can be, but the High Priests and temples of the gods are even more powerful. They practically own the capitol and make every single decision regarding what goes on in the city. Thankfully they always seem to be at odds with each other, so that keeps many of them from gaining too much power. They usually don't bother with average folk like us, so as long as you're careful not to anger anyone, especially the followers of Alistar, you'll be fine."

Memories like nightmares flooded Ean's thoughts. A thick man, a beautiful woman, and a dangerous looking man standing around an older gentleman. The glimmer of the thick man's blade right before it pierced the old man's chest. A chase through the woods. The dangerous man nearly killing Ean, Bran, and Jaslen. Seekers.

"Yes, I know about the Seekers." Ean didn't even bother to hide the disgust in his voice. "I've seen what they do to innocent people."

"Hush boy!" Wil growled, taking a quick look around. There was no one other than his brothers and future stepson of course, but Wil still gestured for Ean to lower his voice. "It's dangerous to talk about the Seekers in such a tone. You never know who is a devoted follower of Alistar. All it takes is the wrong words in front of the wrong person, and you'll be snatched up and taken to the temple. Most people that are taken there by force never leave. Branded as followers of Ze'an, locked up, and forgotten. Best not even to mention the Lord of the Abyss in the city either. That's another way to get carted off to the temple."

"If the followers of Alistar are so bad," Ean said, keeping his voice low for Wil's sake more than his own fears. "Why do the people put up with them?"

"For the same reason that people flock to the city without possessions or even the promise of a place to sleep. Security, my friend. As much as people may curse the Seekers in private and groan about the laws put in place by the temples, they all know that the city is the safest place in the land. Too large for even the largest bandit parties to raid, and there hasn't been a Scar sighted within a day's walk of the city in years." Leaning in, he lowered his voice again. "Which means that the Seekers are rarely in the city, which of course is an added blessing."

Finally something Ean found interesting. "Scars have never opened up in the city? I would think with how big I've heard the city to be, a Scar would have opened in the area at some point."

"Very true, very true. With all of the stories of small villages having Scars open up nearby and that poor village that was completely destroyed a while back, you would think that a place as large as Lurthalan would have had a Scar open up nearby eventually, but it hasn't happened. Some say it's the gods keeping the area safe, others say it's only a matter of time before a Scar finally appears. It doesn't matter much to me; I enjoy the security just like everyone else."

"A village was completely destroyed by a Scar?" Ean didn't even bother to hide his interest now. A whole village destroyed. It must have taken either a large amount of creatures escaping from the Abyss or one particularly powerful one.

"Yes, a sad story, that. Coriana was a small fishing village that sat on the river flowing south from the city and Lake Melcoi. Every single person torn apart, or so the story goes. I can't imagine what the small trade caravan who found the village that way must have thought. Body parts everywhere, so the rumors say, and not a single survivor." Leaning in again, the man's voice took on his conspiratorial tone. "Except some said there was a survivor, and he's now the head Seeker."

Returning to an upright position, the man shrugged as his tone return to normal. "But of course, it's just rumors. No way to actually prove it as no one would be stupid enough to actually approach the man. Heard he is seven feet tall and wears armor brighter than the sun. Haven't actually seen him before, but that's what I hear."

That was an exaggeration compared to the man Ean had seen in person. He was starting to wonder more and more if Wil actually knew anything or just repeated every little story that he heard in a tavern. It was important to know what to expect in the city, but it was also important not to worry about things that were not true. He would just have to let his own judgment decide the truth from gossip and rumor.

"Anything else you think I should know?" If he got the man on another topic, he could get through his stories faster and hear something that would be useful.

"Plenty, my boy, plenty. It's a good thing we have a few more days until we reach the city. I'll need that long to properly educate you on the different groups and places to see or avoid once we reach Lurthalan. So get yourself comfortable and we'll see how much information I can stuff in your head today before I have to retake the reins."

So they spent the rest of the day talking about the capitol. At one point, Wil tried to retake the reins, but his brother Phil took over instead saying that he should keep educating Ean. By the time the caravan pulled off the side of the road for the night, Ean thought he knew plenty, but Wil said it was just the tip of the mountain. Ean spent a good part of his night with Wil and his family around a fire, although the talk changed to more pleasant things. Once again, when the conversations turned more into a collection of yawns, Ean called it a night and slipped back to his tent.

He didn't find Azalea there, or Zin for that matter. Both were probably off somewhere, up to their own brand of mischief, which was fine by Ean. He had an early day of dung shoveling and didn't mind being able to drift off to sleep.

AND THAT'S HOW THE next three days went: work in the morning, Wil's "education" during the day, and a nice meal and rest around a campfire at night. Zin visited him most mornings, mostly to complain about being bored, while Azalea enjoyed making an appearance whenever Ean was working. She would go on about the different people she met and the horrible things they had done. Ean did his best to ignore it, but eventually he would get frustrated enough to chase the Yulari off. But even she didn't really bother him that much, as he had to admit that he was enjoying his time traveling with the caravan. It was as if nothing else mattered in the world except the journey, and he enjoyed feeling like part of a community.

Which was why, on their fifth day of traveling in the late afternoon, Ean couldn't help but feel bittersweet as they came over a hill, and he finally caught his first sight of Lurthalan. Their trip was almost to an end, and part of him was sorry that it was over. But only a small part. The rest of him was overwhelmed by the enormous city looming on the horizon.

The city, which wrapped around the entire south end of Lake Melcoi, could have fit dozens of Rottwealth villages inside of it. Even from as far away as they were, Ean could make out a dozen large buildings sticking out of the masses of smaller ones spread throughout the city. He also saw the construction of the wall that Wil had mentioned, large stone blocks like the ones in the wagons, four or five blocks high in some places and absent in others. There was a good amount of open land in the area it looked like the wall was going to encircle, which Ean didn't expect. Of course, there were probably a lot of things about the city that he wasn't going to expect, but that just made the wait until the following day that much more exciting.

CHAPTER 9

A WARM WELCOME

THEY MADE CAMP THAT night, which Wil said was due to the fact that most caravans had to be checked and logged when they entered the city so that the temples knew what supplies were coming in. That meant each person, all of the cargo, and even the Vilathos and their owners all had to be recorded. The temples could then appropriate whatever they needed, at a discounted price, before the rest of the materials could be sold off. It all was very official sounding, but it seemed like a giant waste of time to Ean, and Wil agreed.

Getting up early the next day, Ean was surprised to find Trait standing by the wagon where Ean had been retrieving his shovel from each morning. As soon as the man saw Ean coming, he shuffled about in place for a moment and looked as if he was about to walk off, but finally something made him stay in his spot and wave Ean over.

"You did some good work for me, lad," the broad man said, rubbing his hands together. "I didn't receive a single complaint from any of the wagon drivers or the shovelers behind your position. I know you offered to work for your ride, but I never let good work go unrewarded. Here."

Reaching into his pocket, the man pulled out a few coppers and a silver piece. "Now, that's not what a normal worker would make for a few days of service, of course. If you are looking for a job, I could handle hiring you on full time as a shoveler. You would make a great deal more as an actual employee of mine."

"Uh, thanks. I'm a healer in training, but I could use some extra money. Let me think on it a few days," Ean said pocketing the money. With the man finally in front of him, Ean couldn't help but ask about the conversation he had wanted to have with him the first time they met. "Trait, you seemed a bit put off before about the fact that I'm from Rottwealth. Why is that?"

The man looked at him for a few moments, rubbing his hands together faster now. He looked around a few times before putting an arm around Ean's shoulders and drawing him in close. When he spoke, his voice was low.

"Listen lad, I don't know what got you to leave your little village, but out here, things are a lot more dangerous. Especially if you go around telling everyone where you're from. Lots of rumors about Rottwealth, most of them created by the temples, and none of them good. Very few of us know the actual truth, which is far less shocking, but certainly serious since all of the temples are behind it."

"Well," Ean said, letting the frustration show in his voice. "Can you tell me what the big secret is then? I met a few people in Rensen that didn't seem bothered by the fact I came from Rottwealth."

"Sorry, but as a Hawkpurse, I'm sworn to secrecy by my own temple. If I were to break that and anger the deity, Drenks, it could mean the ruin of my entire family. Just listen when I say it's in your best interest not to bring up your village, alright?"

"Fine, thanks, I guess, for the advice."

Not knowing what else to say, Ean started walking him towards the supply wagon. Trait reached out though and caught his arm.

"No need to work today, why don't you just sit and enjoy the view as we make our way down. Now if you'll excuse me, I have a lot to do." Trait walked off, shouting orders as he went. With nothing else to do, Ean headed off towards Wil's wagon.

He found Wil and his family just as they were climbing up and securing the oxen.

"Don't have to shovel today?" Wil called down to him. "That's nice. Nothing beats riding to the edge of the city. You get to appreciate how big it is compared to the lake, and at the same time how small of a city it is compared to the Unyielding Wall."

Gesturing towards the impossibly high wall far in the distance, the older man chuckled lightly to himself.

"It might be a foolish thought, but I would love to head out east some day and actually see the Wall up close. Touch it, you know? Actually experience something so great that it's even supposed to keep the gods out of whatever is on the other side. Can you imagine that?"

Phil reached down and helped Ean up onto the wagon. Wil was still considering what mysteries dwelled beyond the wall as the wagons started to move, prompting Phil to take the reins. Once the wagons reached the road, Wil seemed to shake away whatever thoughts had been taking up his attention.

"Now Ean, you remember everything we've been talking about these past couple of days, correct?"

"Yes, everything," Ean said, nodding to Will. "I'll make sure that my sister doesn't do anything stupid as well." It wasn't likely that he could stop her, but hopefully she would behave for however long they were in the city.

"Good, good. Than instead of bothering you any further, I'll let you enjoy the ride." Leaning back, the man placed both hands behind his head. Ean copied the movement and watched as they approached the city.

This close, and framed by the morning sun, Lurthalan seemed even more impressive than it had the evening before. The first thing you saw as you approached was the construction of the city wall. In some places it looked finished and in others only an outline of its foundation or a few stones marked where it would continue. Where the road met the path of the wall there was a completely constructed gate with two small towers off to each side.

Sitting to the left of the tower and outside the wall was a four-story building constructed of pale unpainted wood. The walls appeared to be covered in a variety of animal skins, making up a patchwork of different colored pelts. No windows or any other identifying marks were visible, only the hide coverings. Scattered around the building were various tents and a large gathering of people moving around them.

Pointing, Ean nudged Wil with his other elbow. "What's that building?"

Following the direction Ean was pointing, Wil grunted.

"That's the temple of Avien'zia, and a place you should avoid."

"Why?"

"The Goddess of the Hunt attracts all kinds of hotheaded followers trying to prove how tough they are to each other."

"Tough?" Ean's ears perked. After all, the purpose of leaving Rottwealth was to find someone tough enough to face the mine monster. "Tough as in Heroes?"

"There's probably a few, but mostly you'll find hunters, sell-swords, and those who think they got something to prove." Wil glanced over at Ean, looking him up and down with slight disapproval. "A fresh-faced kid like you wouldn't last ten minutes in the crowd around Avien'zia's temple, so take my advice and stay away from there."

"I will, thanks." Ean certainly had no desire to get tossed around by a bunch of thugs, so he would happily avoid the temple. He would avoid all of them while he was in the city if he could help it. Let other people spend all their time praying and showing off to the gods. He had no need of them.

As they slowly moved down the hill, Ean was able to see clearly past the wall and into the city. To the left of the entrance were a few larger buildings and many smaller ones. Most of those looked to be made of the same smaller stones that the caravan was hauling. Streets curved and stretched in every direction, the buildings growing more packed together as the roads ran deeper into the city.

Circling the lake on the left side of the river were the docks. Small wooden houses sat clumped together tightly, while a long expanse of wooden piers stretched out over the lake. Almost a dozen small crafts sat in the water--boats were what Wil had called them--or were tied up to the wooden floor. They bobbed slightly in the water, with the boats that were tied closer to the river bouncing more.

Just off the docks, where the lake emptied out into the river, a large stone bridge arched high over the water connecting the two sides. Past the bridge on the right side of the river, three large buildings sat close to the lake's edge with another one larger than even the Sawmill in Rensen or anything Ean had ever seen before.

From the side visible to Ean, it was a huge domed structure made entirely of stone. The dome itself was made of what appeared to be a dark white stone, almost grey in color, while the rest of the building was pitch black. There were no windows or doors anywhere Ean could see, unless the opposite side was different from the rest of the building.

"Wil, how about that building. What is that one?"

"The larger of the two is known as the Endless Tombs. There is a smaller building attached to it on the other side that you can't see. That's the temple of Kaz'ren. The Endless Tombs are the resting place of the dead, where the Soulbearers live. You've seen a Soulbearer before, right?"

"Yes, I saw a procession of them on their way to Rensen after the bandit attack. Even talked with one of them, a man named Kel."

Wil's eyebrows raised and the man turned to better face Ean. "In all my years, I've never heard of a Soulbearer talking to anyone. They stop talking as soon as they put on those robes. Sure you can talk at them and they listen, maybe respond with a nod or shake of their head, but I was always under the impression that they never spoke. You sure he was a Soulbearer and not someone that just happened to be traveling in the same direction?"

"I'm sure. He had on the same outfit and everything. The whole line of them stopped while he talked to us and then started moving again once he was done."

"I see..." Wil was staring at Ean now in a way that made him feel very uncomfortable. It was as if Wil was looking at a snake and trying to determine if it was poisonous or not. "Well," the man finally said, "I've been wrong about things before. If you don't mind, I think I'll relax a bit. Lots of work to do once we get down there, so I should take advantage of my free time now."

Without another word, the older man gave him one more strange look before turning his attention back to the road. Ean, meanwhile, was trying to figure out how he always seemed to put his foot in his own mouth. He continued to ponder this until the wagons came to a jarring stop. They had arrived at the entrance.

Wil told Ean to remain seated, while he and the rest of his family tended to the oxen and basic wagon maintenance. It was going to take a while for the guards to take down the names of all new arrivals, inspect their inventory, and take statements as to the nature of their visit.

Only a quick jog away now, Ean could see that the majority of men and a few women outside the temple were hunters. He noted that they wore animal skin shirts and pants and thick leather boots with padded soles. The majority carried a bow or had one leaning nearby, and each had at least one knife strapped to his or her belt. The tents around the temple also gave the telltale signs of hunters:

skins laid out on drying racks, unskinned animals strung up to drain, and multiple fires cooking nothing but racks of meat.

There were a few people moving about the camps that clearly were not hunters. Ean's attention was immediately captured by a woman with an unusual dark red complexion. She had short black hair streaked with a thick strand of red the same shade as her skin. Standing a head taller than most men, she moved confidently amongst the group. She wore a loose fitting gray shirt and thick leather pants. A variety of small blades hung around her waist.

Ean thought he knew everything possible about the human anatomy, but he had never heard or read anything about humans having crimson skin. There was something slightly off with her mouth as well, but at this distance he couldn't quite make out what it was. The woman was fascinating, something completely new and unexpected, and Ean couldn't help but stare. Until he realized that she was staring back at him. And fingering one of her knives.

Snapping his head quickly back around after being caught staring, he cursed himself for already failing to follow Wil's advice. The man had said that many of Avien'zia's followers tended to take the most innocent gestures as a challenge. Shaking his head, Ean slowly counted to ten before turning to see if the woman was on her way over to give him trouble.

It took a few moments to find her, but she was heading in the opposite direction, her short hair swaying as she moved around the tents. He couldn't see her face, but he watched men take one look at her and quickly get out of her way. Ean couldn't blame them. The stare she had directed at him from so far away had made him flinch. Best to keep his attention off those around the temple of Avien'zia, and just wait until he could enter the city.

That wait turned out to be most of the day. By the time one of the guards or bookkeepers or whatever they were called got to his wagon, the sun was already starting to make its decent into the western horizon. The man that arrived asked him questions that Ean found pointless, and then finally let him go.

Saying his goodbyes quickly to Wil and his family, Ean hopped down off the wagon, eager to explore the large city. He could faintly feel both Zin and Azalea ahead of him, the two already past the construction of the walls and somewhere in the city. Hopefully neither one was getting into any trouble.

Walking around the wagons still waiting to be inspected and those that were moving off to the side to unload the stone, Ean couldn't help but marvel at how much larger the city looked now that he was finally right outside of it. He couldn't even see the lake now with all of the buildings in the way. Quickening his pace, he walked through the open gate and fully entered the city.

He moved quickly past a large building to his left, a fenced in home with armed men lounging around the gate, and rows of homes on his right. Lining the rest of the street were smaller two-story stone buildings, with barely enough room between them to fit a person. They were all built the same--a small door on the right at the front of the house and two windows up on the second floor. The buildings were set a few paces back from the street, allowing room in front for landscaping.

Continuing along the main street, he eventually came to a crossroads. Up on the right corner sat a large building, a sign with a big, white horse swung above a huge set of wooden doors. That must be the High Horse Inn, according to what Wil had told him, and Ean couldn't even afford a meal there, let alone a room.

To his left, the street ran past an open field before entering a highly congested area of both people and buildings. Wil had said that way led to the Merchant's Circle where all kinds of shops and peddlers were set up. The street ran in a circle of stores with the temple of Drenks sitting right in the middle. That was where most of the Hawkpurse families had their stores as well.

To his right the road lead to another residential area, where the individual homes were a mix of wood and stone. Wil had said that was where most of the common workers lived; the wagon crews, shop aides, guards, and anyone else that had been able to put together a little bit of money to own homes of their own

If he followed the road straight ahead, he would eventually reach the Water Market and the Docks. Wil had told him that the poorest of the city lived there, some in shacks, some in less, and some without anything for shelter. It was in that direction he needed to go, as an inn called the Old Barnacle sat close to the water. The rooms there were said to be cheap, or at least cheap enough that Ean could afford a few nights with the little money he had from working with the caravan.

Adjusting the strap of his bag as it hung from his shoulder, Ean made his way past the High Horse Inn towards the Docks. As he crossed in front of the large double doors, he could hear the sound of rowdy patrons and even some music. He was about to move when the doors burst open and Azalea stumbled out, a stupid grin on her face.

"Ean, there you are!" She said, the warmth of her voice throwing Ean off slightly. He was more used to scorn and the occasional sarcasm. "I was wondering when you would finally make your way into the city. I LOOOVE it here."

She slowly made her way over to him, wobbling to the left and right, unable to move straight. As she collapsed into his arms, her eyes were half open and seemed to be glazed over. He did his best to hold her up, but she wasn't helping at all.

"Ean," she stammered into his chest. "You must come inside. There are so many wonderfully horrible people in that inn. I thought I might burst from all of the jealousy and greed and lust that were pouring out of the patrons in there. It was like Ze'an built the place just for me." She pulled back slightly, looking up at him with an expression of glee. Then she hiccupped twice, laughed, and buried her face back into his shirt.

Lifting her out in front of him so he could see her face, still in its flawless and delicate human form, he gave her a gentle shake. "Pull yourself together, Azalea, and come with me to my room."

"Ean," she punched him playfully on the arm. "You'd like that, wouldn't you, you horn dog, you."

Rolling his eyes and losing his patience, he replied, "You know my intentions toward you are completely platonic, pseudo sister of mine. I'm going to rent us a room at the Old Barnacle Inn, where you can sleep this off in peace and quiet."

Grimacing, she pushed him away and almost fell backwards. A smile touched her lips for a moment, but then the scowl returned. "Old Barnacle Inn? That does not sound like a place I would enjoy. Knowing you, it's probably some dirty hole in the ground where the people are boring and old and poor. No, thank you!"

Azalea went to push him again and ended up missing him completely. Ean grabbed her and struggled to keep her from hitting the ground. She flailed about a bit in his arms, but eventually just went limp, burying her face in his chest again.

"Anyway," she mumbled. "I already got us a big room here."

Moving awkwardly to get a better hold of her, Ean almost dropped her at her announcement. "What do you mean you got us a room here? How did you afford...ohhhh. Azalea you didn't."

Before she could answer, a huge man stumbled out of the inn door, his head almost hitting the top of the doorframe as it swung open, looking around for something. He swayed a bit and eventually had to put a hand on the inn wall to steady him. When his gaze landed on Azalea, he smiled for the briefest moment and then scowled as he saw her in Ean's arms.

"Hey!" he yelled, storming over to them as fast as his unsteady feet could move him. "What's going on here?"

The man towered over Ean, who was still shuffling Azalea in his arms, but he wasn't tall enough for Ean to avoid smelling the alcohol wafting out of his mouth. The patched clothing of various animal skins he wore didn't smell too fresh either. If Ean wasn't struggling to hold Azalea up, he would have moved back a few paces from the man just so he could get some fresh air. Instead he had to stand there and hold his breath while the man continued to talk.

"I've been buying this girl drinks all day, and now I catch her with another man? Bal Grogan is not a man you should try and take advantage of, girl!"

"It's not like that--" Ean tried to say, but Azalea of course chose that opportunity to speak.

"I had to take your drinks just so I could handle your smell, you Brayurat-faced pile of dung." She lifted her head enough to sniff at the air then wrinkled her nose. "But I guess I didn't drink enough because you still smell horrible."

Ean had no idea what a Brayurat was, and he doubted this Bal fellow did either, but the man apparently knew an insult when he heard one. Puffing up his chest, the man swung at Ean with a fist twice the size of his own. Ean did his best to dodge the blow, which involved falling backwards with Azalea landing on top of him. Even with her lithe frame, she was all dead weight and knocked a bit of air out of him. She just giggled.

Trying to regain his breath, Ean rolled Azalea off of himself as gently as he could. She rolled arond a bit on the stone road, still giggling. Ean wished he could find the situation as funny. With her weight off of him he tried his best to push himself up, but Bal beat him to it. Grabbing him by the shirt with two large hands, the large man hoisted Ean up and held him dangling in the air.

"So, you and your girl just think this is a joke, do you?" Bal was holding Ean close to his face. The man's breath alone was knocking the wind out of him now. "We'll see how funny you both think it is when I beat my money's worth out of you."

"It's not what you think," Ean tried again, his voice raspy from his struggle to get air. "She is my sister."

The man's face scrunched up in disgust as he removed one hand from Ean's shirt, still easily holding him up with the other one. "You sleep with your own sister? Disgusting!"

"No I didn't mean--" the sudden force of the man's fist driving deep into Ean's stomach cut him off. Two more rapid blows in the same spot almost made him double up in the air. Bal then hit him a fourth time in the stomach before tossing him roughly back down onto the ground.

Landing hard on the stone of the road, Ean struggled to stay conscious. He also struggled with the idea of wanting to stay conscious. It might just be easier on him if he passed out, maybe the large man would leave him alone then. He certainly couldn't try and use his power to defend himself in the city with so many people around. Any thoughts he was having quickly left his head and were replaced by pain as a thick leather boot caught him in the stomach and lifted him off the ground. Ean rolled a few times from the blow and came to rest face up, his breaths coming in shallow wheezes.

Staring straight up at the sky, oddly focusing on how the fading light of the late afternoon was making the sky a dark blue, Ean could hardly move. Why did he let Azalea get him into these situations? It made him angry. Angry was good. Anger might get him moving, help him--

Again he was lifted into the air, the horrible smell coming off Bal shocking him more awake and making him want to throw up at the same time. The man gave Ean a rough shake before laughing at him.

"You must be regretting trying to pull a fast one on Bal now, eh little man?"

The subsequent pain in his jaw woke him up. His face couldn't take much more abuse. A few more hits and he might end up with a broken jaw. Grabbing the man's hand, Ean struggled to get free.

"No escape for you, little rat. I'm going to knock out any thought of you ever trying to take advantage of... arrrrghhhhh!"

Bal let out a yell and dropped him to his feet. Stumbling on impact, Ean fell onto his backside with a grunt, while Bal collapsed to both knees. It took a moment for Ean to realize that Azalea had Bal's arm pinned behind his back. Still half-drunk, she let out a hiccup.

"Excuse me," she said, giggling as if it were the funniest thing in the world.

"I'm glad someone is having fun," Ean retorted, while Bal let out a string of obscenities.

"Let me go, you stupid bimbo. And I'll forget this whole thing every happened."

"I'm sure you'd like to forget getting your ass kicked by a woman," Azalea said. "So how about you apologize to me and my brother before I tear your arm off and beat you over the head with it?"

"Now you best be letting me go, girl," Bal said through clenched teeth. "I won't rough your brother up anymore. But if you keep annoying me--." He cut off with a groan as Azalea twisted his arm almost completely around.

"You'll do what? Moan like a little baby?" She twisted his arm again, getting that exact response out of him. "I think it's you who needs to be taught a lesson, and since I don't have all day to teach you about basic hygiene, I'll have to just focus on teaching you what real pain feels like. Lesson one."

With a sharp jerking motion, she pulled back and up on his arm. A loud popping sound came from his shoulder, immediately followed by a yell out of Bal's mouth. The man's free hand gave out, and Azalea let go of his other arm as he fell face first to the ground. He hit hard and immediately rolled onto his side, at first gripping his head with his uninjured arm and then grabbing at his dislocated shoulder. Ean just watched, his mouth hanging open.

Circling the downed man, Azalea was grinning widely now, every now and then her tongue darting out and licking her lips. "So, what should our second lesson be? A broken bone? A torn off finger? How about a few missing teeth?"

Stopping at his side, Azalea reached over and grabbed the man by his hair and jerked his head back. With her free hand, she grabbed his jaw and forced his mouth open slowly. His eyes opened wide and started to dart about while he tried and failed to speak. All that came out of his mouth was a gurgling sound.

"Oh, you want to say something? Had enough lessons already?" Releasing his mouth and head, Azalea moved around and knelt in front of the man.

"Yes, please, no more." From the sound of Bal's voice, Ean imagined he was using all of his willpower to keep from openly crying. "Just let me go."

Ean watched as Azalea remained quiet. She began tapping her chin with her finger. The longer she went without moving or saying a word, the more nervous the large man seemed to become. Not knowing what the slightly dazed Yulari might do, Ean was growing more and more nervous as well. Finally, after what seemed like an eternity, Azalea nodded.

"You can go. But I don't think I want to see you around this inn. I plan on staying here and don't want my time ruined by your stench. I hear the Old Barnacle has drinks, you should try there." The Yulari smirked in Ean's direction, but he didn't find the situation funny at all.

"Alright, alright, I promise not to come back," the large man whined. His sniveling voice did not fit his macho appearance at all now. "I won't even walk by the High Horse."

Climbing as fast as he could to his feet with one useless arm, the large man stumbled off in the direction of the Docks. Ean wanted to just remain on the ground for a while. His whole body hurt, his jaw felt like it was going to fall off, and he was still trying to figure out how it had all happened. Unfortunately, a crowd had gathered both in the street and in front of the Inn. Ean couldn't exactly just lie in the middle of the road in front of all of those people.

Pushing himself up, Ean's arms wobbled under the strain as his body yelled at him for trying to move. He almost collapsed back down until Azalea caught him, hoisting him up onto his feet and putting one of his arms around her shoulder. For a moment, Ean thought he saw a look of concern on her face, but it was quickly replaced by her usual smirk. It must have just been the pain, messing with his mind. As she steadied him against her, Azalea whispered in his ear.

"You're lucky to have me around, little man. This is the second time I've had to save you. You should be thanking whatever gods you pray to that I happened into your life."

"I'm pretty sure this time it was your fault I was in danger in the first place," he mumbled back.

"Details, details. Let's get you inside. I've been told that the drinks here are good at relaxing the body and making a person forget their troubles. I prefer the sweet taste of emotions, but that won't help you. So let's get you nice and drunk and enjoy the rest of the night."

Looking out at the crowd, Azalea waved them off before moving towards the inn. "Nothing to see here, fight's over. Go about your business." When the crowd refused to move, Azalea stopped and swept a finger pointing to the entire crowd. "Unless someone else wants to limp home with more than a broken ego."

That got the people moving. Most hurried off in different directions, even those that had come out of the inn to watch the excitement. Only a few that appeared to be more drunk than brave wobbled back into the inn ahead of them. Azalea seemed pretty content as she walked Ean up to the door and practically carried him inside.

CHAPTER 10

A NIGHT OF DRINK

THE INTERIOR OF THE High Horse Inn fit its name. The main room was thrice the size of the inn in Rensen with silver trim running around the room and large paintings of horses adorning its walls. The main room was divided into three sections by waist-high dark wood partitions. As you entered the room, a section for circular tables sat to the left, where small groups of families and workers sat peacefully enjoying food and drink. To the right situated in front of a large but empty stage, sat six long tables with large seat benches. Both sections were barely half-filled but were still crowded enough to create a lot of noise. Straight ahead, following a dark red carpet that ran in between the two sections of tables, sat a bar almost half as long as the building. The stools of the bar were all filled with a variety of patrons drinking and talking loudly. The bar ended on the right side into a wall that jutted out into the room, where a little further down a swinging door let out the smells and sounds of a very busy kitchen.

Sensing his discomfort, or more disturbingly tasting it, the Yulari led him over to one of the circular tables and dropped him abruptly into a wooden chair. The jolt made him grimace. Azalea collapsed into a seat next to him, arms and legs splaying out in every direction.

"Whew, what a delicious evening!" she said as her head rolled back and stared at the ceiling. "First a nibble of puppy love, then a nice helping of hatred, ending with the main course of pain and violence. And it's only our first day here!"

Leaning forward, Ean put his elbows down on the table and rested his head in his hands, carefully avoiding putting too much pressure on his aching jaw. "I'm glad you're enjoying yourself. I've barely been inside the city and already I've been beaten up. Not exactly my favorite kind of welcome to a new place."

"Oh, stop being such a crybaby. You're just a little bruised is all, it's not like parts of you are falling off. My older brothers and sisters always told me that it takes a good beating to tell you how strong you really are, and they certainly did their best to prove that point. What you really need is a drink."

Sitting up, Azalea looked around until she spotted a serving girl and waved her over.

"Yes? What would you like?"

"My brother and I would like your finest tasting wine," Azalea said, her voice switching to a haughty tone. "Two glasses. No, on second thought, just bring out the entire bottle."

The waitress gave the two of them--dirty and bruised from the scuffle outside--a quick once-over before replying.

"Our finest tasting wine is twenty silver pieces a glass. An entire bottle would cost three gold coins. Between the two of you, I doubt you could scrape together enough coin for a glass of burnbeer, let alone our best stock."

Seemingly happy with her insult, the serving girl began to turn and walk away, but Azalea shot forward and grabbed her arm, spinning her back around.

"Is that any way to behave towards your inn's most important patron? I doubt your boss would think too highly of you acting snobby to a high paying customer like myself. Why don't you run off and ask him if you should be treating Azalea and Ean with such a dismissive attitude."

Releasing the girl and giving her a little push, Azalea leaned back in her chair and stared at the girl with one raised eyebrow. With a scowl the serving girl hurried off, weaving through the tables and through the door to the kitchen. Azalea let out a little laugh and turned to Ean.

"Watch this, it should be quite entertaining."

Too tired and sore to respond, Ean simply nodded. A few moments later the same serving girl burst out of the kitchen, a dark bottle in one hand and two glasses in another. She came hurrying over, almost knocking over a few patrons in the process, until she halted in front of their table. A smile touched her lips, but her eyes were tear-streaked.

"I am so sorry for the misunderstanding," she blurted out. "I had no idea who you were Ms. Azalea. We get a good deal of riff-raff that just stumble off the street and cause trouble in our fine establishment, and I thought--"

"You thought," Azalea interrupted, her tone cold, "that we looked like riff-raff? Like some poor, pathetic travelers without a coin between us?"

"Yes, I mean no, I mean, I've never seen you before so I figured you were from one of the outlying villages..."

"Oh, so you think that a simple villager would never have any real money? That we don't deserve to stay here?"

"No, it's not like that at all. It's just part of my job to make sure that the patrons here are of higher quality and..."

"You were just being rude. Which is laughable since all you are is a serving wench. You are no better than those you talk down to. I bet if I were to get you fired, you wouldn't last very long in the city."

"Please, please do not!" Dropping to her knees, she carefully placed the bottle and glasses on the ground before taking Azalea's hand in both of hers. "I beg you. I'm the only one that can work right now in my family. My father is sick and my mother ran off a few years ago. Without this job, my father and I will be out on the street in no time, and he won't last long."

"Maybe you should have thought of that before you spoke to us in such a way. I care very little for the well-being of a serving wench and her decrepit father."

"Please," the poor girl was sobbing now. "Forgive me. I'll do anything. Anything you want! Just don't make me lose my job!"

Glancing around, Ean noticed that the girl's sobbing was starting to attract the attention of many of the guests at the inn. He couldn't help but feel bad for the poor girl.

"Enough, Azalea. I'm sure she is sorry. Stop frightening her and let's just enjoy the wine."

"Brother," Azalea said, still sounding a bit haughty. "Weak minded people like her need to be taught a lesson about how they should speak to those better than them. If we let her keep her job, she will have learned nothing."

"No, no, I know I'm wrong," the sobbing girl pleaded. "I've learned my lesson. Honest."

"No, I really don't think you have," Azalea said as she snatched her hand away from the girl. "I think being put out on the streets--"

"Azalea, enough!" Raising his head, Ean slammed a fist down on the table and immediately regretted it as the shock of the impact rattled his jaw. Azalea turned to regard him coldly but he pointed a finger at her anyway. "We will not get this girl fired, and you will stop tormenting her. Do I make myself clear?"

A single eyebrow rose on Azalea's forehead as she looked at Ean for a few moments, and then she shrugged. Lounging back in her chair, she waved away the girl.

"Fine, whatever you say." Azalea reached out and patted the serving girl on the head. "Serve us our wine and be thankful my brother is much kinder than myself. Then get out of our sight until we've at least finished this bottle, understand?"

"Yes, of course!" Jumping to her feet, the serving girl grabbed the bottle and glasses and set them on the table. Ean remained silent as the girl popped the cork off the bottle and poured them two full glasses of the dark red liquid.

"Thank you for your mercy, sir. You have a kind heart." Curtseying slightly to him as she finished pouring, the girl glanced fearfully one last time at Azalea before moving away from their table. Ean watched her go as she swayed about between the tables and disappeared through the kitchen door. Then he turned back to Azalea.

"What was that all about? You didn't have to scare her so badly. She was just doing what the owner trained her to do."

"I don't care what she was told to do. I will not be talked to that way by some lowly human. I can barely stand the way you talk to me sometimes, but I put up with it because of our arrangement. I had no arrangement with that child, so I felt the need to put her in her place."

Leaning forward long enough to grab her glass, Azalea returned to leaning back in the chair and took a small sip. A smile touched her lips for a moment before she continued speaking.

"Besides, the fear coming off of her tasted delicious. Now, why don't you relax and give this wine a try? It does taste rather sweet."

Grumbling to himself, Ean did as the Yulari suggested, not because she had told him to but because he wanted a drink. That was important. As he brought the glass to his lips, the smell of the wine hit his nostrils first, the aroma quite pleasant. Taking a small sip, he immediately agreed with Azalea's evaluation. The wine was quite sweet and tasted wonderful. Ean quickly finished off the glass and poured himself another one. He slowed down on the second one, taking smaller sips and enjoying the flavor.

"Now," he said in between sips. "Why don't you tell me why that girl was scared about displeasing us?"

"Oh, that's such a simple story." Azalea placed her glass down on the table. "As soon as we arrived, I charmed the foolish young guards into letting me into the city ahead of all of you fools standing in line. Oh, and I smelled the stench of imp on my way inside, so your annoying little friend is probably lurking about somewhere." She glanced around, burping loudly as she slammed her glass on the table. "You hear that, Zin. I'm onto you."

Well, that was good to know, the part about Zin at least. Hopefully the imp had a better day than Ean. He took a moment to concentrate and feel for any sign of the imp, but he couldn't even get the slightest feeling where he was.

"So," Azalea continued. "I began walking around, taking in all of the emotions of the people walking by until I found myself slightly tipsy. I focused long enough to ask someone where the best inn was and was quickly led here. From there it was just a matter of getting to meet the owner, charming him as well, and now we find ourselves as guests here in one of the larger rooms of the inn with an unlimited bar tab. I did quite well for us, didn't I?"

He hated to admit it, but after spending so much time with very little shelter, eating small rations of food, and sleeping on dirt and rocks, Ean was looking forward to enjoying everything the inn had to offer. It did make him nervous though, how easily the Yulari could manipulate the people of the city. He could only hope she wouldn't draw too much attention to herself.

"So I'm guessing," Ean said, pausing to take another sip, "that the owner of this inn thinks we're a wealthy family ready to spend large amounts of money in his inn?"

"Actually, he believes I already paid. If he is a good book keeper, eventually he'll figure out that he is missing a substantial amount of coin, but I can keep him charmed until we feel the need to leave." Leaning forward, she smiled broadly at him. "Although I hope that isn't anytime soon. If today was any indication, I'm going to enjoy this little city immensely."

"Yes, well, don't get too comfortable. We're only staying to find out where Zin's old master used to reside, and then we're leaving. So try not to get me in any more trouble. The longer we take, the more damage that creature is doing to my village."

"Fine, but for now, how about you sit back, relax, and enjoy all of the pleasant things I've provided for you."

With the dimming twilight bathing the bar in serene shades of indigo combined with the warm glow of candlelight on each table and the cares of the day weighing him down, sitting back with drink in hand sounded like a good way to salvage the day.

"I think I will, Azalea," he said, leaning back now as well and swirling the liquid in his glass. Taking another sip, he decided it wouldn't hurt to at least be polite to the Yulari. "Thank you, I appreciate the nice things you've done for me today."

She gave him a strange look after his thanks then shrugged uncomfortably. "Whatever, I did it for myself mostly anyway."

"That may be true, but I still appreciate it." Tilting his head back, Ean poured the rest of his wine into his mouth. Leaning forward only long enough to fill his glass, Ean returned to his lounging position and let himself get truly comfortable.

The loud chatter from the other patrons blended together into a sound like the soothing patter of a heavy rain on a roof. Each sweet sip of the wine relaxed his body and mind even further. When they had finished the first bottle, they ordered some food to go along with the next one. A large plate of roasted chicken was quickly placed before them. Just the smell of the food made Ean's mouth water and reminded him of how little he had eaten throughout the day.

They downed another bottle of the wine before they finished their dinner, or to be more accurate, Azalea poured herself another glass while Ean glugged down the rest. The Yulari seemed to enjoy the taste but didn't seem to experience any of the soothing effects Ean was enjoying. Her eyes constantly scanned the room, occasionally falling on Ean before quickly looking away again. Ean thought it was funny, although he didn't know why. The wine was starting to make it difficult to think clearly.

Which was why later in the night, Ean was having trouble keeping even his head up off of the table. His body felt great though, pleasantly numb, although his stomach was beginning to feel a tad bit queasy, until eventually even the smell of the wine made him gag.

Raising his head, which he hadn't even realized had been resting on the table, he was about to ask Azalea where their room was but saw that she wasn't in her seat. When had she gotten up? It certainly hadn't been before they had ordered their fourth bottle. Pushing himself up on shaky legs, Ean glanced about the now much busier room and attempted to find the Yulari. It took him a while, but he eventually found her surrounded by a few men at the corner of the bar.

"Good for her, having some fun," he said to no one in particular. Leaning forward, he let his own weight get him moving and stumbled ahead. Bouncing off a few tables where he quickly slurred apologizes without stopping, he made it to the first partition between himself and the bar. The opening was only a little ways down from him, but it seemed much easier for him to climb over it instead of going around it.

Swinging one leg up and on top of the partition, he grunted slightly as he pushed himself the rest of the way up. Once there, straddling the thick, shoulder-high wall, Ean wasn't quite sure what to do next. The obvious choice was to swing his other leg over and drop down, but he felt that if he did that, it would carry the rest of him over and off the partition as well. Confused, he sat there and tried to come up with a new plan of attack. He might have been making progress, but a waitress came over and spoke to him, sending whatever plans he had been putting together scattering.

"Excuse me, sir, but we don't allow anyone to climb our partitions."

"No, no, of course not," Ean slurred as he tried to focus on the girl's face. "Don't want to mess anything up in this fine...place." Words were becoming much harder to use, it seemed. He couldn't even remember what type of place this was. "I'll get down right away."

Swinging his other leg over, Ean was still surprised when what he had expected to happen, actually happened. The momentum of his leg swinging over the partition dragged his entire body off of it, and he fell crashing to the ground on top of the carpet that ran in between the partitions.

"Well, this is embarrassing," Ean mumbled into the carpet. The smart move would have been to graciously rise. Unfortunately Ean's mind and his body were on two separate paths, and instead of awkwardly rising, he flopped about on the floor like a fish. Meanwhile, the server that had been talking to him had made her way around the partition and stood nearby.

"Do you need some help, sir?" Her tone sounded sympathetic but the look she was giving him was more of annoyance than anything else. Ean worked his way onto his side and stuck a hand out towards her.

"Yes, I would appreciate a little help getting to my feet." At least that's what he had meant to say. By the increasing look of annoyance on her face, what he actually said was probably a bit garbled. She took his hand though, and with a surprising show of strength, lifted him onto his feet.

The girl watched him wobble about for a few moments then sighed as she was called away to serve someone else. Ean placed his hand on the partition and watched her go, his knees continuously failing to support his legs.

"Come on, young one." Azalea's voice caused him to whip his head around, which his body followed only to smack into the partition. It probably should have hurt, but Ean didn't feel a thing. "I think it's about time you get to bed."

Not trusting his mouth to be able to handle actual sentences, Ean simply nodded and held out a hand towards the Yulari. She took it while flashing her usual smirk and wrapped his arm around her shoulder.

"This is the second time today I've had to help you walk," she said, laughing lightly. She did have a pretty laugh. "I have no desire to be your personal crutch, so let's try not to make a habit of this, alright?"

As they rounded the partition near the side doors and the end of the bar, Ean saw a long flight of stairs sitting back in the corner of the room.

There were a lot of stairs.

Azalea seemed undaunted and moved him to the base of the stairs. She took a quick look over her shoulder and then content with what she was looking for, wrapped an arm around Ean's waist and lifted him slightly off the ground.

"I think it would be better," she whispered, "if your feet are not involved at all in this climb. Just make it look like you're walking up the stairs on your own. I'll handle the heavy lifting, but we don't want anyone to realize that I'm carrying you."

He shook his head, his body following the motion. With her arm wrapped around him, he still almost took Azalea off balance. She grunted and gripped him tighter and was somehow able to keep them both from tumbling back down the stairs.

They went up three flights of stairs in total. Possibly. Ean wasn't completely sure, but they went all the way up to the top floor. On either side of the long hallway, a single door sat in the middle of the wall. By the size of the building, the two rooms up on this level must be huge if they took up an entire side. Or Ean's eyes were just playing tricks on him, which was a strong possibility.

Azalea carried him off to the door on the right, inserting a strangely shaped key beneath the handle and unlocking the door with a loud "click." She pushed the door open and moved him inside.

The room was, well, Ean didn't really know how to describe it. It was very dark and he couldn't see much. Or maybe his eyes were closed at this point. He wondered which it could be until he was suddenly dumped face-up on top of something soft and comfortable. A hand gently grabbed the back of his head and lifted it up long enough for something else that was soft to be slid underneath it. Then his head was gently lowered, and the hand patted him twice. Flopping onto his side, Ean curled up into a ball and within moments was fast asleep.

CHAPTER 11

SMALL FISH IN A BIG POND

"YOU SOUND LIKE YOU'RE dying. Are you actually dying? If you are, I need to prepare myself to be sent back to the Abyss."

Zin's muffled voice came from the other side of the door, but even the faintest sound felt like a needle through the brain. Eyes closed, bare knees bent against the cold floor, Ean's head hung over the tub where the contents of last night's over indulgence had come back up. His eyes were closed as he knelt in front of the bathtub with his head hanging over the side. The tub itself was slightly filled with a disgusting mixture of what Ean had consumed the night before.

"Have you learned your lesson yet?" Zin's smug tone made Ean feel even more nauseated, something that seemed impossible a moment before. "You know it's already late in the morning. You're not going to waste the whole morning sounding like you're giving birth to a Crux are you?"

"Go away and let me die in peace." Ean rose and shuffled over to the washbasin and mirror. He checked to make sure there wasn't any vomit on him. Taking one more moment to make sure his stomach could handle movement, he splashed a bit of water on his face and walked out the door. On the other side, he found Zin standing with an obnoxious grin. Ean's immediate reaction was to send a kick the imp's way, but in an effort to treat Zin better, he nudged him out of the way with his foot instead.

Stumbling backward in an obvious overreaction, the imp shook his head as he steadied himself.

"Don't take out your misery on me. Are you functional enough now that we can actually accomplish something today? Or do you need to go moan at the bathtub some more?"

"I'll be fine if you stop talking so loudly. What do you think we should be doing?"

"Finding the lair of my old master, of course. I'm sure it holds a wealth of information about what you're capable of and how to really use your power. It's just a matter of figuring out where it is."

"You really think they would keep records about your master after everything he did?"

Shaking his head, Zin chuckled a few times before replying. "You really don't know that much about your own world do you? Even before Master was killed, the temple of the deity of Knowledge and Wisdom sat at the edge of this lake. Her followers devote their life to writing down everything about anything. If anyone knows where we need to look, it will be them."

"And you honestly think they will just tell me?"

"Probably. They love to show off how much they know, and once they start talking, it's hard to get them to stop."

"Well, I guess it's something. Ni'Aren's followers have to be more tolerant than the Seekers at least."

"Good. I already found their temple last night. All you have to do is take the bridge over the river that runs out of the lake, and it is the huge building at the lake's edge."

"Wait, aren't you coming with me?"

"Of course, but it will look a little strange if you keep getting directions from thin air. This time of day the streets will be packed and you talking to nothing will get us a lot of unwanted attention."

"I didn't think of that."

"Of course you didn't, which is why it's a good thing you have me around."

"What about Azalea?"

"I wouldn't say that's a good thing, more of a--"

"No, I mean, do you know where she is?"

"Oh. No, not really. She let me in this morning and then took off. I think she was slightly annoyed she had to stay in the room the entire night with you."

"Oh." So the Yulari had watched over him all night? That was certainly unlike her. But she had been the one to get him to bed last night and had been fairly gentle about it from what he could remember...

"But enough about the life-sucker," Zin said, cutting into Ean's thoughts. "Get yourself put together, and let's be on our way."

Nodding, Ean set about the room getting ready. He changed into a clean pair of clothes and made sure that his gloves completely covered up his arms. The last thing he needed was a bunch of strangers noticing his arm was glowing. He would have to be more careful in general with anything having to do with Ze'an and the temple of Alistar and the hundreds of followers here. Zin stood and watched him, tapping a foot impatiently.

Once he was situated, Ean grabbed what little money he had and walked over to the door. He opened it but stood to the side, bowing and waving Zin ahead of him grandly.

"After you, good sir." Ean said it with a laugh and earned a glare by the imp for his trouble. Turning invisible, Zin stomped out of the room, making sure to place a well-aimed foot right on Ean's boot. His pointy nails pricked the top of his feet. Ean grimaced but kept his mouth shut.

Making his way out into the hall and down the stairs, Ean was surprised to find the common room still busy for this time of day. It was early afternoon, a time at which he thought most people would be working, but half of the bar stools were full and the circular tables had patrons as well. The inn back in Rottwealth didn't even open until dinner time. It was strange to see all of those people not working, but that thought left him as soon as the smells from the kitchen hit his still-sensitive stomach.

His stomach churned and he had to move out quickly. Directly in front of him was an open field where the wagons that were delivering goods sat. He saw a few from the caravan he had been with but didn't see any sign of Wil. To his right, he saw Zin's glimmering form move towards the Docks and the bridge.

The streets were filled with a variety of people. Many were dressed in typical worker clothes--plain shirts and pants, mostly brown or another dark color to hide the dirt, thick leather boots, and some even wore short-brimmed hats. Sprinkled amongst the workers were Taruun, the tall slender men and woman towering over the rest of the crowd. Others were dressed slightly better, with more colorful shirts and pants, some having strange insignias on them. Many also had someone trailing along behind them, dressed in less impressive attire and usually carrying a few bags or a crate.

Several different groups of temple priests came into view. Ean could tell the various sects apart by the way they dressed. Some wore long robes of dull colors, others dressed in a more colorful array, while still others had robes trimmed in gold. Those in similar colored robes moved about together with the only ones Ean could recognize being the Soulbearers of Kaz'ren.

As Ean walked, he felt like the tide of people was going to wash over and crush him. Moving off to the right side of the road, he took a minute to catch his breath. Maybe settling down here wasn't a good plan for his future if he wasn't able to handle dealing with the mass of people.

A tug on his pants made him look down to find the shimmering outline of Zin standing next to him. Had Zin tried to traverse the sea of people as well, or had he been smart enough to stay off the street from the beginning?

The imp gave one last tug and then began walking along the side of the street. It was much easier to move now that he wasn't in the middle of the mess of people, and it made Ean wonder why so few took a similar course. Were the people here simply used to fighting their way through everyone else? Didn't matter much to Ean. He was happy to be out of that mess.

As they followed the road, it began to curve to the east until the lake sat completely to their left past the small shacks that made up the edge of the Docks area. Up the road, past the bridge and a few enormous buildings, far off into the distance, Ean got another good look at the Unyielding Wall.

Even as far away as it was, its massive size seemed to dwarf everything else. It stretched higher than Ean thought possible, disappearing into the line of clouds that seemed to swallow the top from as far north as he could see to as far south. It managed to take away from the grandness of the enormous temples of the city, including the temple of Kaz'ren and the Endless Tombs.

Turning his attention away from the Unyielding Wall, he focused on the large building sitting in front of the lake on the other side of the bridge.

Not as large as the Temple of Kaz'ren, the Temple of Ni'Aren, Goddess of Knowledge and Wisdom, was equally impressive in its design. Large stone columns ringed the building, holding up the upper floors. Large windows occupied most of the walls while intricate geometric patterns and pictures, mostly of a beautiful woman holding books, covered the remaining space. The most impressive aspect of this temple, though, were the vast gardens that spread out from the building with an assortment of flowers and small trees Ean had never seen before. He wondered how many of the plants he could recognize and how many had not been a part of his education as a Healer.

Getting back on the bridge, Ean forced himself to remain calm as he pushed through the pack of people going in both directions.

There were more priests on this part of the road and a lot more people armed with weapons than the average person. Ean smirked as he noticed the prism around each of their necks, signifying them as Heroes. Before the troubles had started in his village, a single Hero would have made him stop and gawk, but now after seeing the superiority complexes of those that had tried and failed to rid Rottwealth of its monster, seeing a dozen or so as he moved over the bridge hardly phased him.

The Temple of Ni'Aren was immediately to his left as he walked off the bridge, a flower garden circling its side from the lake to a path that led from the temple to the road. The crinkly brown flowers at the front of the temple caught his eye. Not many people knew about nevilswort and how its nectar made a powerful sleep aid and dulled the worst kind of headaches. Unfortunately, they were useless for hangovers. They certainly weren't the most attractive flowers available, which made their choice for the garden framing the path to the temple entrance curious.

Passing the garden, he double-checked Zin's position before he moved up the walkway toward the temple. The imp was moving about the garden in an erratic fashion. Probably caught the smell of a rodent or some other small animal he could munch on. Shrugging, Ean figured the imp would catch up eventually. The path led past the garden to a set of stairs that ran up to the entrance of the temple. Ean climbed the stairs quickly, hoping to finally get some answers. When he reached the top, he found a tall, skinny man waiting for him.

The elderly man was dressed in an extravagant sky blue robe. The robe was covered with swirling lines in the brightest gold, weaving about into patterns almost as complicated as those that covered Ean's arm. His bald head and tightly trimmed beard only added to his intimidating appearance. The way the man was looking at him, with cold, judgmental eyes, made Ean think for a moment that he had been expected. But how could that be?

"Stop right there, lad," the man ordered. "You won't find your answers here, so you just turn right back around."

Ean could only stand there in shock. The man had expected him, and even more surprisingly seemed to already know what he was searching for. As he tried to re-organize his thoughts, the older man made a motion with his hand and two more men appeared, younger but with the same glower for Ean.

"You will leave now," the older man said. "Or I will have these two toss you in the lake." Leaning forward, the old man whispered, "And if you try coming back again, I will make sure the Seekers know where to find you."

Ean quickly backed away, waving his gloved hands in a gesture indicating he didn't want any trouble. Turning, he tried to keep some dignity by moving slowly down the steps, but every fiber of his being was screaming at him to run. He kept a slow, even pace until he reached the bridge, then he took off in a sprint, going past the docks, the High Horse Inn, and skidding to a halt at the opening of the Merchant's Circle.

If the area around the Docks had been crowded, then the Merchant's Circle was a mob scene. It was like a river of people flowing away from the High Horse Inn, past the wagon fields, and then split left and right with the road. The road created a circle that looped around the Temple of Drenks, with rows and rows of shops running along the outside of the circle. The ground around the Temple of Drenks was clear, just large patches of grass where a few people sat and ate lunch or had small blankets set up with items resting on them for sale. Ean pushed his way through the crowd until he reached that area.

Collapsing on the ground in a sitting position, Ean tried to catch his breath and figure out how things had gone so wrong at the temple. Obviously the priests had been told that he was coming, but by who? And why had they been so hostile towards him? Clearly they wanted him gone if they were going to go as far as to threaten him with the Seekers. But if they disliked him so much, why not just alert the Seekers in the first place? So many questions and the only people with the answers had threatened to toss him in the lake.

Zin. Maybe the imp had some idea what had gone wrong. Looking around, he didn't see the telltale blur that was the imp's invisible form, so instead he relaxed and tried to feel the imp out.

It didn't take long to find him. The imp was making his way over to where Ean was, carefully threading through the crowd and probably trying his hardest not to get stepped on. When Zin made it over to him, Ean took a quick look around to make sure no one was close to where he was sitting, then leaned forward towards the imp and pretended to be messing with his boots.

"Zin, any ideas about what happened?" he whispered. "Not only did they know I was coming, they seemed furious by the fact that I was there."

"No idea. From what I remember of Ni'Aren's followers, they are usually quite peaceful and eager to help anyone. The way they reacted to you shocked me. I stuck around for a moment to see if they said anything, but they just stormed back into the temple before I could learn anything.

"Zin, it just doesn't make sense. Who would have such a big sway over the followers of Ni'Aren and know about me?"

A female voice from behind him almost made Ean jump. "Obviously Ni'Aren would be able to sway her own followers to keep you out, boy."

Turning quickly at the sound of the woman's voice, Ean was surprised to see a simply dressed woman of stunning beauty standing directly behind him.

Long blond hair framed a face with petite features, other than her eyes. She had large, light blue eyes that seemed to draw you in, like deep pools of water. Realizing he had been staring, Ean moved his eyes over the rest of the woman. She wore a simple blue shirt and shorts that rested just above her knees, seeming much more plain then he imagined a goddess would appear.

"Um, sorry miss, I'm not quite sure--"

Raising a hand, she cut him off. "No need to deny what you were talking about. Your name is Ean, that smelly creature trying to stay out of sight is Zin, and he is just one of the many things you've pulled out of the Abyss."

Blanching, Ean felt his jaw drop. This was the second time someone had caught him off guard by knowing too much about him. And the things she had said! Glancing quickly around, Ean hoped no one had heard her talk about the Abyss. Thankfully it looked like everyone around them was ignoring them.

"I...uh," Ean managed, trying to unscramble his own thoughts. "How do you know who I am?"

"Simple," the woman said, taking a seat in front of him with her legs crossed. "My name is Kaz'ren."

CHAPTER 12

DEALS WITH A GODDESS

KAZ'REN! THE GODDESS OF the Afterlife? Clearly the woman had to be insane, a Goddess wouldn't just approach him, would she? But she did seem to know an awful lot about him. As she sat in front of him, Ean took a closer look at the woman.

"Fine, fine," she said. "If you don't believe me, I'll show you."

Ean was about to protest, but the woman leaned over and placed a single finger on his forehead.

Colors exploded in his mind then everything went dark. His body slumped, but she held him up with a single finger. A second explosion followed, obliterating all thought. The colors became more intense, pulsating faster and faster, until he felt like a man tossed about in a raging sea. The pounding waves punished his mind and body until Ean thought he would break.

Without warning, the colors began to slow, taking the pain with them. Each individual color began to coalesce. Hundreds of nebulous blobs floated in dead space, each a different color. Before his eyes, they sprouted arms, then legs, and took on familiar human forms.

The first he recognized was that of Lane, the first victim of the Creature that had taken over the mine in Rottwealth. In his current state he looked completely healed, no missing limbs or scars. His expression seemed sad, but he did offer Ean a friendly wave.

The second nameless face was the one he had watched being murdered in Rensen forest. A lot of the other figures seemed upset, but the old man seemed at peace. Ean hadn't understood how the man had been so calm when he was murdered and he certainly didn't understand how he seemed so peaceful now either.

Other faces touched his memories, people that he had been unable to save after the bandit attack in Rensen. The rest could have been anyone, but somehow he knew they were all people that had passed away. Which meant that this person had to be Kaz'ren.

As soon as the thought crossed his mind, the images vanished and he was back in Lurthalan staring at a goddess.

"You're drooling a bit," she said in a pleasant tone. "That sometimes happens, though, so don't feel embarrassed about it."

Wiping his mouth quickly, he leaned back away from her, which ended up making him topple backwards and catch himself on his elbows. Now really looking like a fool, he slowly righted himself back into a sitting position while avoiding eye contact with the deity. Once he had himself completely situated, he brought his head up enough to meet her eyes.

"Why are you talking to me?" he blurted out, then immediately regretted his tone. He was surprised, when instead of destroying him on the spot, she simply laughed.

"Well, you are spirited, aren't you?" She patted him lightly on the cheek. It was all Ean could do to not flinch away. "Good, this would be incredibly awkward for me if you were the type to start bowing and refuse to look at me. We have a great deal to discuss and a short amount of time to do it. So, if you would kindly send your imp away, we can get started."

She did not bother hiding her disgust at the word imp. "He's already in your ear enough, leading you this way and that. I want a little time to talk to you without him lurking about."

Who was Ean to argue with a deity? Turning to Zin, he nodded and gestured with his hand for the imp to leave. The blur that marked Zin's presence hesitated for a moment then melted into the crowd.

"Glad to be rid of the smelly little creature," she said, wrinkling her nose. "I don't know why you keep him around, but I guess I don't understand half the things you do. If dragging an imp around the world wasn't dangerous enough, you decide to keep a Yulari as a pet and let her run all over the place unsupervised as well. Foolish, very foolish."

Shrugging, she moved to her feet and offered him a hand. "It's your decision, of course. I'm not one to judge...much, and it's not the reason I'm here. Come on, it's a nice day and I would prefer to walk about while we talk."

Afraid to refuse, Ean took her hand and she yanked him to his feet so hard that he stumbled forward. In trying to catch his balance, Ean grabbed the nearest thing he could find, which happened to be the goddess's waist. Realizing his transgression, he snatched back his hand, waiting for her to strike him down. Instead she smiled.

"You really think that I offend easily, don't you. Think of it this way: How many times have you offered up a prayer to me?" Ean could probably count that number on one hand. Her smile widened as he remained silent. "Exactly, and yet here I am talking to you, not offended at your lack of devotion in the least. So a little grope isn't more offending than your complete lack of devotion to me."

"I didn't try to grope you!" He hadn't meant for it to come out as a yell, but his mind was racing. Glancing around, he was surprised not to find all of the surrounding people staring at them.

"Oh, don't worry," Kaz'ren said, laughing again. "I've made it so they won't notice us. We can talk about whatever we want, which is good since we're going to be talking about a lot of things that might make other people uncomfortable."

Other people, or humans in general? Ean's nerves were already on edge and this woman, this goddess, kept making him even more nervous. If he could just have a second to process his thoughts maybe he could--wait! She was walking away!

Chasing after her, he thought he might lose her as she entered the crowd of people. Instead, the mob parted around her, not even seeming to notice they were doing so as they crammed themselves together even tighter to give her space. Ean dodged into that space just moments before the mass of people flowed around her.

"Now," she began, looking around and taking everything in as she spoke. "I'm going to start by being honest with you with the hope that it will make our short time together here more productive. Please don't feel rude interrupting if I say anything confusing to you, just try not to stop me every couple of steps. Deal?"

"Yes," was all he could get out.

"Good, so as I said, in being completely honest, I want to start by telling you that I'm going to use you to my own end." That was certainly as straightforward as she could get. "Now, of course, you might benefit from helping me as well, but it's not guaranteed. I just wanted to let you know, because if any of the others had gotten to you first, they probably would have tried to trick you into doing what they wanted. I'd rather keep our relationship an honest one."

"Wait, others? You mean the other deities?"

"Yes, of course, the other deities. They all would use you for one end or another. Well, all of them except Alistar. He would be quite happy to see you dead. I wouldn't go mentioning his name if I were you. You don't want him watching your every move."

"Wait, why would all of you be interested in me?"

"Because of what is under here of course," she said, flicking his right arm. "The last person that wore those same tattoos changed the course of the entire land, first for good and then bad. Like it or not, your existence has the attention of all of us." She flashed him a smile. "You're just lucky that I'm the one that got the chance to interact with you first."

"Why did you get the chance? I'm not complaining of course," Ean said hastily. "I've just rarely prayed to you. I've rarely prayed to any of you, as a matter of fact."

She waved his question a way with a flick of her hand. "Don't worry about that question-- it has to do with how my brothers and sisters interact with each other and the world. Higher being things. Way over your head. Best if we get back to what I would like, yes?"

"Alright," Ean answered, not knowing what else to say. They had crossed the bridge and walked past the temple of Ni'Aren. Ean ducked down in the crowd, not wanting the priests of the temple to see him before realizing that Kaz'ren was doing just that for both of them. He did his best to straighten back up without making it too obvious what he had done. Kaz'ren of course noticed.

"Ah yes, awkward that, when you stopped by her temple. Of course, how could you know that Ni'Aren has been holding a grudge against Ze'an for hundreds of years? As soon as she realized you were going to look for help there, she made a big fuss to her followers about keeping you out."

That certainly explained why the priests had known all about him and the hostility they had shown. But why would a fight between Ze'an and Ni'Aren have anything to do with him? Ean had never prayed to Ze'an before either. It wasn't as if he was running around doing his bidding. As if reading his thoughts, Kaz'ren answered his question for him.

"You wear those tattoos, dear boy, which means you're tied to Ze'an whether you mutter two words to him or not. You do realize what those tattoos represent in the eyes of most people and deities?"

Shaking his head, Ean looked at the ground. "I was told that they would help me grow in strength, be able to summon more powerful creatures." He hoped the tone of his voice didn't show his embarrassment at his ignorance.

"Of course they do that, but it's so much more. As I said, the last person to wear those tattoos caused a great deal of problems for both the people of this land and those they pray too."

"You're talking about the Plague."

"Oh, so you do know something. Did your little imp tell you about that and his former master? That's surprising, although I'm sure he told you after those designs started climbing up your arm. Yes, the look on your face confirms that. I wouldn't completely trust that imp if I were you. Like everyone else, he only has his best interests in mind. You just remember that."

Glancing around, Kaz'ren frowned slightly and grabbed Ean's arm, hurrying him along. Ean looked around trying to see what had caused her sudden haste and felt as if he had been struck in the stomach. To his left, towering over the lake, was a large building made entirely of pure white stone. Very few designs had been placed anywhere on the outside of the building except for one--the half sun with a sword going through it. The same marking the Seekers had worn on their armor.

"Yes, best not to spend any time in front of here. HE can't see you unless you mention his name, but I'm sure he has given his head priest your description and they've passed it around to his other followers. They couldn't see you now, of course, but best not to risk getting his attention." They moved quickly past the building, following the road as it split off to the left and ran around the edge of the lake.

Once they were past the temple, and Ean felt like he could breathe again, what Kaz'ren had just said finally sunk in.

"Wait, none of you can see a person unless we speak your name?" That certainly was a surprise. Ean thought all of the deities could do whatever they wanted. Kaz'ren looked surprised as well, her eyes widening at the question.

"Well, yes we can only find a specific person if they mention us, whether it's in prayer or in idle conversation. Obviously it's not something we like to share, so you just keep that little piece of information to yourself."

She grew quiet, her mood darkening as she kept her eyes on the road ahead. So the deities were not as all-powerful as everyone believed. If Ean learned nothing else today, that undoubtedly was something useful. He would have to take her advice though and make sure Alistar's name never left his mouth again. It was a useful piece of information to have.

Ean found himself smiling now as they walked down the road. It was quiet where they were now. The only building in sight was ahead of them, a three or four story building that had seen better days. Ean wondered what it once had been as they approached.

"Well, this is it," she said, giving the building a good look over. The deity licked her lips as if pushing out a bad taste "This is where you get to help me, and in turn I help you. Although I should count what I've already told you as my side of the deal. Ah well."

Spreading her arms to take in the entire building, the goddess took on a grandiose tone. "I present the Temple of Ze'an, Lord of the Abyss, in all of its glory."

"I don't understand. If everyone hates Ze'an so much, why would they allow a temple to be built to him?"

"Simple. People were not always afraid of Ze'an or the Abyss. There was a time, long, long ago, when Ze'an was worshipped just as openly as any other deity. Then of course, one person had to go and mess everything up for your Lord of the Abyss."

"You're talking about Zin's old master."

"Yes. For a time he was considered a savior to your race. Do you know about the Shadaer Umdaer?"

"No, I've never heard the name."

"Of course you haven't," she said with a sigh. "The Shadaer Umdaer is a strong race of warriors that live to the south, much further than what you call Rensen Forest. They control an amount of land nearly equal in size to Ven Khilada. A long time ago, decades before the Plague, humans and Umdaer met for the first time. With the Umdaer being a race only concerned with fighting and war, they decided that your race and the peaceful Taruun needed to be conquered and made into slaves."

"At this time, your race outnumbered the Umdaer five to one, but that didn't matter as one Umdaer could kill eight or nine well-trained humans on his own. So the Umdaer pushed north, killing or enslaving anyone they came across. Most people at the time still lived in what is now the Plagued Lands, so it only took a matter of weeks for the Umdaer to hold everything south of Lake Melcoi."

She turned and waved a hand, covering the entire lake, temples, and docks that ran along it. "Most of the main temples had been built here at that time, so needless to say, many people and deities were worried about the Umdaer taking this land as well. They had been unsuccessful in even slowing the Umdaer down, so things looked grim. And that is when your imp's former master appeared."

"None of us higher beings knew about him, except for maybe Ze'an himself, but he never really talked to us even back then. As the tribes of the Umdaer marched towards the lake, he came from the Northwest, an army of creatures from the Abyss following him. His forces crushed the Umdaer in a matter of days, which led to the signing of the Treaty of Melcoi. The peace treaty allowed the Umdaer to keep their land to the south and created a wary peace. The man was a hero, and I mean a real Hero, not like the jokers that run around now calling themselves Heroes."

Ean couldn't help being caught up in the story. "What happened afterwards? I mean, why did he suddenly turn against everyone?"

"No one knows for sure, but my guess is that the power went to his head. Power always corrupts, Ean. It's the way of life."

"Even with the gods?" Kaz'ren's face immediately darkened, the edges of her lips twisting downward just as her eyebrows did the same. A tense silence followed. When Ean looked down at his boots, she continued.

"Enough history lessons and pointless questions," she said coldly. "On to why we are here. You want to find that man's old lair. I can not only point you in the right direction but also tell you the most efficient way to travel there. All I ask in return is a little assistance in acquiring one soul that has been out of my reach for too long."

"Wait," Ean's voice went up a notch. "You want me to kill someone?"

"No, no," she replied, her mood lightening slightly. "This soul has already left its body, but it's corrupted in a way that makes it impossible for me to claim."

"And you think I can help you?"

"I HOPE you can help me, but I'm not certain. Let's just call this an experiment. If it fails, I'll still give you the information and you can just owe me some other favor. Deal?"

Ean did not like the idea of "owing" this goddess or any other deity a favor for that matter, but he had little choice. It was doubtful that any regular citizen alive knew where the lair had been, and even if they did, they would hand Ean over to the Seekers if he mentioned anything concerning the Abyss. The Temple of Ni'Aren was a dead end now if the Goddess herself was bent on keeping him out and in the dark. Kaz'ren was his only option.

"You have a deal. What am I supposed to do?"

"Well," she said, her mood becoming slightly cheerful now that he had agreed, "The soul I mentioned is stuck here in Ze'an's old temple. Let's go on in and see what happens."

CHAPTER 13

DISAGREEMENTS WITH A GHOST

THE GODDESS PUSHED OPEN one of the doors, and Ean followed her inside. As he surveyed the dilapidated temple, shivers ran up his spine, but it had nothing to do with the neglected interior. A feeling of dread had settled over him, and he couldn't shake the feeling that he was being watched. Just inside the doors the room opened up into the main place of worship. Cracks ran like spider webs throughout the walls, and the majority of the windows had fist-sized holes punched through them. Moth-eaten and barely-hanging banners were spread out all along the walls, the pictures that had been sewn or dyed into them long faded and indistinguishable. A devastated carpet ran straight from the doors, past rows of mostly rotted out or broken pews, and ended at the foot of a dais. On the dais itself sat an altar in similar disrepair. At one point it had probably been a finely carved work of art, but most of those carvings were either worn down or broken off entirely. Behind the altar were a few doors that likely led to the inner workings of the temple.

The longer Ean stood there with the goddess, the more ill-at-ease he felt, as if some force was making it clear it did not want him there. He stood unsure whether to continue in or flee while Kaz'ren strolled into the building totally at ease. She glanced around a few times and then let out a loud sigh.

"Come on out, Primaren. I do not want to spend all afternoon trying to hunt you down." Turning slightly, she waved Ean to join her in the middle of the room. "It's alright. His presence gives anyone who enters a bad feeling. That's why the temple is still standing and hasn't been torn down. He doesn't let anyone stay here for more than a few moments before scaring them off."

Ean forced himself to stand straight and take the first step towards the goddess. Nothing horrible happened, so he took a few more steps. Feeling a bit more confident, Ean took a few more steps.

And was immediately struck in the back by something small.

"Oww!" he yelled, spinning around and raising his arms in order to defend himself. Instead of finding an attacker, however, he found empty air. A sound caught his attention at his feet and looking down, he found a small piece of stone. Was that what had hit him? "Kaz'ren, I really don't feel comfortable--"

BOOM.

The doors slammed shut so suddenly and with such noise that Ean leapt backwards and fell over one of the pews. He hit his elbow hard on a pew and slammed his shoulder into the stone flooring. Scrambling to his feet, he started to turn slowly, trying his best to keep his eyes out for the next attack.

"Oh, this is so tiring," Kaz'ren said, walking over to stand next to Ean. "He does this to everyone. You would think being trapped here for decades in a place he loves wouldn't have soured his attitude so badly."

Ean grunted, then watched in a mixture of horror and fascination as a larger piece of stone lifted in the air not ten paces away. It hovered there for a few moments and then shot straight at him. Ean didn't even have time to think to put his arms up to defend himself. With a flick of her wrist, Kaz'ren knocked the stone aside, rolling her eyes as she did so.

"I'm not going to let you hurt the boy, Primaren," Kaz'ren said, raising her voice slightly to be heard over the clattering of the stone she had just knocked away. "So how about you stop trying to be a bully and come out where we can see you."

For a moment, the room was deathly silent. Maybe whatever had been causing the problems had left. Ean quickly dismissed that thought as the feeling of dread suddenly spiked to the point where he wanted to run. He stood his ground and watched as something began to take shape in front of them.

It started out as a purplish mist, or maybe a blur, similar to what Zin looked like when he was invisible. Then, it pooled together and the vague outline of a man appeared. A few moments later, the form took on details until a fully clothed man floated just off the ground in front of Ean. He was semi-transparent and completely blue, but Ean could make out even the smallest details.

Depictions of various creatures Ean recognized as being from the Abyss adorned the man's robes. His right hand was opening or closing as if it was used to holding something. The man's face looked young, with a neatly cropped purplish beard and short hair of the same color. Most of his features were average, except for his blazing red eyes, which were staring hatefully at Ean and Kaz'ren.

"See," Kaz'ren said, sounding friendly. "That wasn't so hard was it?"

The man opened his mouth to speak, and what came out was a voice that mimicked the intensity in his eyes. It sounded distant, though, as if he was yelling at them from across the room.

"Foul, slime-faced woman," Primaren said, directing all of his hate towards the goddess. "Why must you continue to bother me? I am free from your touch and will forever remain this way. Why can you not leave me alone and be off watching your band of mutes?"

The smile remained on her face. It was only the slight narrowing of the eyes and hint of steel in her voice that indicated to Ean she was holding back her anger.

"Now, now, no need to be rude. You don't want to make a bad first impression on my friend here. Allow me to make the introductions. Ean, this pleasant fellow is Primaren, former Voice for the temple of Ze'an. Primaren, this is Ean."

"I do not care about the living, and I certainly do not care about you, you wretched excuse for a deity."

"Such a temper. I would watch what you say. You might not be as safe from my control as you think."

"Ha, impotent goddess! My god protects me from your control. I will never join your collection of the dead, so you can just repeatedly go drown yourself in the lake. Maybe that will keep the stench of death off you."

Kaz'ren kept the smiled through the insults, although there was no warmth to it now. Turning to Ean, she placed a hand not so gently on his shoulder.

"This is where you come in, my boy. I cannot claim his soul. He says it's because of some kind of protection from Ze'an, but I'm not so sure. Ze'an was never known to pay much attention to humans."

Scratching his head, Ean alternated between looking from Primaren to Kaz'ren. "What exactly am I supposed to do? I don't know anything about souls. A week or so ago, I didn't know your Soulbearers even existed."

"Let's start by removing your glove." Reaching down she grabbed his right hand. "At the very least, your tattoos might shut him up for a moment."

The spirit let out a laugh. "You really think this over-grown stick of a boy can go against Ze'an's will? You must truly be getting desperate to be rid of me you foul... urk!"

It was a strange sound the spirit made as Ean's glove was removed and his glowing tattoos lit up the area around them.

Primaren simply stood there and stared, well, floated in place and stared, at the softly pulsating glow of the tattoos. Ean was a bit surprised as well, but not from the spirit's reaction.

He could "feel" the spirit now.

It had the feel of a familiar shirt he had worn hundreds of times. Without realizing it, Ean reached out and touched the spirit where it was floating. His hand passed right though, but something was there. Something he could actually touch...

A jolt of energy flashed through Ean's body, and he jerked his hand back. At the same time, Primaren's form seemed to dissipate for a moment before reforming. When he was whole again, Primaren looked at Ean in horror while Ean returned a look of confusion. All the while he could still feel "something" coming from the spirit.

"What is this?!?" Primaren said, the spite and anger in his voice replaced by fear. "What abomination have you brought to do your dirty work, Kaz'ren?"

"Nothing I've created, Primaren." Kaz'ren's voice took on a tone of satisfaction as she addressed the spirit. "The boy is tied to the Abyss and its power."

Pausing to take a seat, Kaz'ren regarded the spirit in the same fashion that Ean might regard a piece of steak after going hungry for a week.

"Tell me, little priest," the goddess continued. "Do you still feel like you can speak to me in such a vile manner?"

For a moment, the spirit looked at the goddess with more contempt then Ean had ever seen. Then those eyes swung around and regarded Ean with a mixture of fear and sadness.

"Whatever she has promised you," the spirit said, his eyes locked on Ean, "you cannot do her bidding. Those marks connect you to Ze'an, not her. As the Voice of the temple of Ze'an, I order you to leave this place, now!"

"Don't you mean former Voice?" Kaz'ren got back up and began walking a slow circle around the spirit, a large smile playing at her lips. "Death strips away all titles. Can you imagine what kind of confusion it would cause if all my former high priests, all of those souls were running around trying to give orders? It would be quite the mess."

The goddess was clearly enjoying herself now, but Ean had no idea why. He had certainly felt something, could still feel something actually, coming from the spirit but he had no idea what it meant or what he was supposed to do about it. Kaz'ren stopped pacing and turned her attention on Ean.

"Well? What are you waiting for?"

"Waiting for? I have no idea what I'm supposed to do."

"You felt something, yes?" The goddess raised her eyebrows questioningly until Ean nodded. "My boy, what you felt is exactly what is keeping me from claiming this soul. This soul, this loyal servant to Ze'an, at some point was infused with energy from the Abyss. That is what is keeping me from claiming him. Now I need you to rid him of it."

"Me? Why don't you do it?"

"Because none of us deities can touch or even feel that energy," she growled.

Where only moments before, Kaz'ren had been smiling and sounding slightly smug, her demeanor now completely changed. Her fists were clenched at her side as she leaned forward slightly towards Ean, her eyes flashing anger. Ean couldn't help but take a step back from the disgust that was flowing out of her.

"Why his god should have access to things that none of the rest of us can even feel is beyond me. As for the priest, I didn't know if having a bit of the energy infused in him was the reason I could not take him because, again, I can't feel it. That's why I need you."

Ean took a few more steps back, risking a glance in the direction of the door. If things turned worse, could he outrun a goddess?

From what little she had let slip, they didn't seem to be as all powerful as everyone made them out to be. He was about to test his luck when the spirit's laughter caught his ear.

"You don't have to be afraid of her, boy," the spirit got out between chuckles. "They can't directly hurt humans. It's one of their rules. It's one of the few things Ze'an told me himself. At best, they can point followers in your direction like those Seekers and pretty much every hunter of Avien'zia, but this little goddess only has a bunch of mutes as her loyal servants."

"It's good to know," Kaz'ren said, some of the smugness returning to her voice, "that there are still a great many things that humans still do not know about us."

"What can I do," Ean asked, "to help release him from being stuck here?"

"You can sense the energy from the Abyss in him," Kaz'ren replied. "Simply reach out and take it. Once you've removed it from him, I will be free to collect him and place him with the rest of the spirits."

"Take it? How can I take it? I don't know--" he stopped suddenly. He did know how to do it, or rather, he knew how to let the energy flow out of his hand. Would it be that much different to take it back in? There was only one way to find out.

Walking over to the spirit, Ean could not help but feel a pang of guilt about what he was about to do. Sure the spirit had assaulted him, and in his condition, it had been stupid of Primaren to insult a goddess. But Ean couldn't imagine what it would be like to be forever trapped as you watched a place you loved fall into ruin. After so many years, it had to have warped his mind a little.

Glancing at Kaz'ren and the smug smile she wore, he knew he had to say something.

"If I do this, if I make it possible for you to collect him, I don't want you to punish him for what he has done in the past. Let's consider this a clean slate for Primaren, and I'm sure he will be more respectful from now on."

Kaz'ren turned a cold stare to Ean, but her eyebrows rose slightly as she looked at him. Tilting her head, she brought a hand to her face and started to tap her chin with a short fingernail.

"You certainly are a bold one, Ean. Why would you care about the spirit of a man you never knew? Are you feeling some sort of loyalty to Ze'an now?"

"No, I just feel sorry for this man, left here by himself for countless years, forced to watch something he loved fall apart and be vandalized. I'm sure you have done your best to taunt him just as much as he has taunted you. I just want what is fair, and that's to let him start over in whatever it is that comes after we die."

"If I do this, if I forget this spirit's past insults, you will owe me. That will mean that you will have to occasionally pray to me so I can always know where you are in case I want you to fulfill your debt. Knowing that, do you still want me to do you this favor?"

"Yes."

The goddess let out a little giggle and clapped her hands in delight. Her behavior was almost childish, but Ean was learning it was best to just keep his mouth shut around the goddess and not let slip what he was thinking.

"Excellent," she said as she calmed down a bit. "Then I promise not to mistreat this soul for any past mistakes he has made." She shot the spirit a hard glare before continuing. "But that does not protect him from anything he says from now on." The spirit simply continued to stare at the floor.

"I understand," Ean said as he took a place in front of the spirit.

Taking a deep breath, he began to gather energy into himself slowly, not from the spirit, but from the Abyss itself. Compared to what he could normally take in, now the amount he let flow into him was the barest trickle. It still caused the tattoos to grow brighter of course.

He could feel the energy intermingled with the spirit now more clearly as he had energy flowing through himself as well. The energy in the spirit seemed to pulse along with the energy that Ean let flow through his own body. Reaching out, Ean placed the palm of his right hand slightly inside the translucent form of Primaren. As the two energies began to mingle, it sent little jolts through Ean's body, but he held his hand still.

"Do not become too indebted to any of the gods or goddesses, boy." Primaren's voice was low and resigned as he spoke, his eyes still locked on the ground. "They are just as spiteful and devious as any man or woman. They are just as spiteful and devious as any man or woman, and they can turn on you without provocation."

"I will," Ean whispered, the conviction in his voice mirroring how he felt inside. "Are you ready?"

"As ready as I'll ever be."

Taking control of the energy, he let it flow out of his hand and become one with the energy resting in the spirit. He let this continue until he could not tell the difference any more between the two separate pools of energy. Then, with a final exertion of his will, Ean pulled all of the energy back into his body.

The force of it almost lifted Ean off his feet. He had known there was energy mixed in with Primaren's spirit, but he had no idea how much until it all came crashing into him. For a moment, as he stood there and wrestled for control of it all, Ean feared he was going to be overwhelmed.

Eventually the surge slowed and he regained control. Sweat dripped down his forehead and back, and his muscles were sore from the strain. Having all of the energy inside him dulled the pain slightly, but he was dreading how he would feel once he let the energy go.

His eyes focused on Primaren, and he was surprised to see the spirit looking more substantial instead of less. Ean had assumed that it was the energy from the Abyss that had given the spirit his strength, but clearly it was something else. Primaren was looking at him as well now, although Ean couldn't read his expression.

Nodding once to Ean, Primaren's spirit turned to Kaz'ren. Floating over to where she was standing, he bowed once and then stood silent. A single eyebrow rose on the goddess's face before she reached out and touched Primaren. His form seemed to grow almost solid for a moment and then just as quickly was gone. Nodding, Kaz'ren walked over to Ean.

"Well done," she said, placing a hand on his shoulder. "You've done me a service, and I won't forget that. Especially now that you'll be praying to me on a regular basis." She winked at him as her hand slowly lead him back in the direction of the door.

"And you'll keep your word?" Ean said, allowing him to be led. "You will not punish him in any way?"

"Ean, of course I'll keep my word. My brothers and sisters and I may focus mostly on our own agendas, but we wouldn't have any followers left if we did not honor agreements we've made. Speaking of which, I owe you some information, don't I?"

As they left the now empty temple, Kaz'ren turned Ean around and placed both hands on his shoulders.

"Before I tell you where the lair of your imp's former master sits, I have something I want to say. I don't know what the imp has told you or why you are following along in his old master's footsteps, and frankly at this moment in time, I do not care. But, if you start causing too many problems for the people of this land, I will start to care and you can be sure my brothers and sisters will as well. We will not put our people through another incident like the Plague, so you can be sure if you start down that path, we will all make it our mission to stop you. Understand?"

It was hard not to understand what she was implying. If he got power hungry, they would put him down like a dog. Thankfully he had no intention of becoming a marauding lord trying to take over the land. All Ean wanted was a peaceful life and to understand what he had done to himself.

"I understand. You have no need to worry about me."

"We'll see," she replied, staring into his eyes. "The place you are seeking lies to the northwest in the mountains behind a village called Ulundkin. The village sits just north of the border into the area affected by the Plague, what is now called the Deadlands."

"The area affected by the Plague?" The shock of the revelation struck him like a hammer. "How can I get there and still live?"

"The Plague acts slowly, infecting people at different rates. Most are fine if they only experience a week or two of exposure. It is safe enough going to Ulundkin. One of the Hawkpurse families takes a caravan of supplies there every few weeks. One of those caravans just happens to be leaving in two days. Getting a ride with them would be your best bet to get where you want to go in a timely manner."

The Deadlands. Ean had only heard bits of pieces from Wil on their ride to Lurthalan. A place where everything was infected by the Plague, from the animals to the very air and earth. Wil had said things that looked like people still lived there, although they were no longer human. He also had said those people were like walking corpses, bits and pieces hanging off, and they disliked anyone human. Why would a caravan want to go to such a place? If it was his best chance of finding out more about his powers, though...

"Alright, I'll go. Which Hawkpurse family is it?"

"Brave boy. You want to look for the Ciantar family. Their stores can be found past the Temple of Drenks, on the west side of the Merchant's Circle. You'll have to figure out how to buy your way with them, but it shouldn't be too difficult."

And if it was, Ean always had Azalea's charm to get them a few seats on the caravan.

"Well," Kaz'ren said, reaching over to pat Ean lightly on the cheek. "I can honestly say it's been interesting to meet you. You have a lot of potential, Ean, both for good and bad, just like your predecessor, but I think as long as you stay true to yourself and not listen to those horrible creatures you keep around, you'll turn out okay. Remember, only mention one of us if you don't mind the god or goddess being able to hear you and know exactly where you are. Unless it's me, of course."

Flashing him a smile and a quick wink, Kaz'ren disappeared in a flash of light, leaving Ean standing in front of the dilapidated temple all alone. Letting the cool breeze that came off the lake wash over him, his mind ran through everything that had just happened. Ean found it almost impossible to believe. Visits from a goddess, putting tormented souls to rest, a quest into a dangerous land...it sounded like a Hero's story.

Ean certainly had no interest in being part of a Hero's story. All he wanted to do was find out more about what he had done to himself and get a little control over his power. Then he could go back and help his village.

He also wanted to learn as much as he could about Zin's old master. That was a new goal, but going by the warnings of spirits and goddesses, an important one. If his tattoos were going to make him power hungry, he needed to learn how to stop it. If Ean found out it was just a weakness of character that made Zin's old master into a tyrant, that would certainly be a relief as well. Either way, he had to find out.

With the energy of the Abyss still flowing through him, Ean was hardly surprised to feel the familiar presence of either Zin or Azalea not too far away. It was probably Zin. The imp certainly wouldn't let Ean too far out of his sight while in the company of a goddess.

Ean saw the blur first, moving along the ground quickly. Crossing his arms, Ean waited for the imp to reach him. A few paces away, the imp became visible and marched right up to Ean. Normally the appearance of the imp in public would have made Ean nervous, but a quick look around showed him that no one was visible on this side of the lake. Probably because of the formerly haunted temple.

"Well, let's hear it," the imp said, his breath coming quickly. "Your pretty little friend whispered in my ear that she was done with you and pointed me in your direction. What exactly did she say and had you do?"

"Have a seat," Ean replied, taking one himself on the bit of grass between the temple and the road. "This is going to take a while."

CHAPTER 14

AROUND TOWN

BY THE TIME EAN had finished his story, the sun was just starting to touch the tips of the mountains to the west. Zin remained silent the whole time, occasionally shifting about or scratching at himself. The imp's expression darkened at a few parts, the worst being when Ean mentioned promising to pray every now and then to Kaz'ren so she could keep an eye on him. With his story finished, Zin shook his head before speaking.

"I don't like this, Ean. I don't like it one bit. At least Kaz'ren," he paused, looking around quickly as if just saying her name would make her appear again. When she didn't, he continued on. "At least that goddess was honest enough to tell you that she was going to use you. That doesn't mean that she was open and honest about everything else. I've been thinking about our, I mean your, situation quite a bit and trying to hunt down my old master's lair isn't the best idea. We've been doing alright so far. Maybe we should just leave well enough alone."

"Zin, saying we've been doing alright is being awfully generous. I turned one bandit into a monster, which he probably deserved, but since he survived, he might be worse now. I almost got myself, Bran, and Jaslen killed twice. Once by the Seekers, which was only partially my fault, and the other time by Azalea, which was absolutely my fault. These are not the actions of someone that is doing alright."

"Ok, ok, so we've hit a few little bumps, but--"

"Little bumps that have gotten us almost killed. Plus, I don't want to end up like your former master, drunk on the power the Abyss can provide and causing death and destruction. If it was this power," he held out his still exposed right hand, the tattoos glowing softly in the late afternoon light, "that turned your master evil, I need to know sooner, rather than later."

"Ean, I'm sure you won't turn into the creature my former master became. I've known you for years now, and as much as you might talk about not trusting or caring about most people, you certainly go out of your way to make sure you don't hurt anyone."

The comment took Ean aback. It was rare for Zin to compliment him. The imp was basically saying that no amount of power would ever go to Ean's head. Zin had no idea about his dreams though...

"Zin, there is something I have to tell you. I've been having dreams, horrible dreams."

The imp shrugged and picked at one of his ears. "Yes, I know. You've told me. You had that one vision of you as a Hound, and another as a Crux. It could have something to do with the tattoos I suppose, but I don't see how that could--"

"Zin, there have been other dreams," Ean interrupted, the words tumbling out of his mouth, "darker dreams where I'm no longer human. Where I'm hurting people I know. Dreams that involve me doing terrible things."

A speck of fear appeared in Zin's watery black eyes. Throughout everything, even when they fought, Zin had never acted afraid of Ean. Ean's chest tightened as he realized that his closest companion, his partner in crime, would now always see a bit of his old master whenever he looked at Ean.

"Zin, I won't become him."

"Never said you would."

"You're looking at me like I'm going to turn into your old master."

"You're imagining things," he said. Zin turned away for a moment and acted like he was looking across the lake. When he turned back around, he seemed like his usual self. "Those dreams of yours, not saying I'm concerned about them, but from here on out you need to tell me whenever you have one."

"Ok."

"And it's very important that you tell me all of the details, no matter how insignificant or how repulsive. What you are doing in the dream, how you're feeling, what you see. Can you do that for me?"

Ean took a deep breath.

"Zin, I'd rather not. Some of the things I've dreamt...they are horrible. I feel like I'm going to throw up sometimes just thinking about them."

"Well we can worry about that the next time you have one." Zin's voice had returned to his normal, sarcastic tone, but the imp still wasn't looking at Ean. "Anyway, we have more important things to focus on, things that we can control. Specifically, getting a ride on that caravan heading into the Deadlands, and we won't accomplish that just standing around this disaster." He gestured at the temple.

"You're right. We need to push on." Ean hoped the despair was gone from his voice. "We still have time before the sun sets. Hopefully, at least one of Ciantar's businesses stay open late and we can find out who to talk to about joining the caravan."

"Then let's not waste any more time." The imp took a few steps down the road before turning and waving Ean on. "Let's go already. If the crowds are just as bad at this time of day as they were earlier, we might not make it in time if we don't hurry."

Ean joined the imp and headed down the road. Try though as he might, he couldn't find an answer to the question stuck in his mind. Was it the power itself that corrupted or was it the weaknesses of the man wielding it? Zin's former master had been able to summon armies of creatures to do his bidding. That kind of power had to be seductive. Of course, Ean couldn't control a single creature at the moment, so it wasn't as if he had anywhere near the same amount of power. That fact didn't make him worry any less though.

Zin wasn't helping his fears either. Every few steps Ean would catch the imp looking at him with contemplative eyes. The imp would quickly look away when he realized Ean caught him at it, but a few steps later, Zin would be looking at him again. Eventually Ean grew tired of it and simply stared at the imp, whether he was looking at Ean or not. When the imp realized what was happening, he laughed nervously.

"Well, going to be people around soon. Best if I'm not seen, huh?"

Disappearing to that bluish blur that only Ean could see--and apparently deities as well--the imp remained at his side. Which made Ean more nervous. The imp could be looking at him with those judgmental eyes and there was nothing he could do about it.

By the time Ean and Zin reached the road leading into the Merchant's Circle, the sun was halfway behind the mountains. The crowd had dropped to a manageable level, letting Ean move down the street without being knocked around. The added freedom let him finally take in how amazing the Merchant's Circle really was.

Brick and stone shops of various sizes, most between two and four stories tall, ran along the street. Windows adorned every floor of those buildings, with brightly colored shutters framing each and one large window on the first floor showing off the stores' wares. Banners hung over the doors of most, brightly colored pieces of fabric that were meant to catch the eye, with detailed pictures of the items sold inside.

An elaborate picture of wheat and bread made the baker's store obvious. Pictures of plants and bottles of different colored liquids were stores of his own profession of Healers. Many of the shop banners showed off different styles of clothing. Practically all of the shops close to the entrance of the circle had wooden placards hanging out, more detailed animals depicted on each. Those were the signs of the Hawkpurse families, so it was just a matter of determining which ones belonged to the Ciantar.

After being flat out ignored by a few people, one older gentleman informed him that the Ciantar family's sigil was that of a bear and that most of their stores could be found further down the street across from the entrance to the Temple of Drenks. Giving the man a quick thanks, Ean began to jog down the street.

Ean glanced at a few of the signs at the end of the street and was surprised to see banners whose meaning he couldn't decipher. One depicted a sword covered in ice crossed with what looked like a gardening hoe with lightning coming out of it while another showed two people connected by wavy blue lines.

Each of those stores had the bear emblem, and each one was closed. Most of the stores with the bear emblem seemed to be closed, but Ean finally found a small one tucked away between two much larger buildings. The banner on the front showed off the hammer and anvil of a blacksmith. Ean found the owner snoring behind the counter. After spending more time than Ean thought necessary trying to wake the man up, he was finally informed of what he was missing-- Caravan passage was booked at the Ciantar family estate and only occurred in the mid-morning hours.

After getting directions to the Ciantar home, Ean decided the best thing to do was to head back to the inn and try to find Azalea. With barely any money, they would need her charms in order to book a passage with the caravan. How quickly he had changed his opinion about the Yulari's skills. It was only days ago that he was frustrated with her manipulation of men, and now he was relying on it.

Loud growls kept escaping from his stomach, reminding him that he hadn't eaten anything all day. A few pieces of bread and a drink, just one drink, would make for a fine end to this exhausting day. Upon reaching the inn, he realized things were not going to be as peaceful inside as he had hoped.

A large group of people were gathered around both entrances to the inn, all of them pushing at each other while two burly thugs kept everyone out. One man tried to push his way past the guards at the front door but received a quick and violent blow and collapsed in a heap. The crowd passed the unconscious man back until he was deposited on his face at the outskirts of the crowd. The side door seemed to be less crowded, so that was the one that Ean walked towards.

By the time he had made it to the side door, his body was sore, both of his feet had been stomped on multiple times, and he had received a few smacks to the back of his head. On top of that, judging by the way the thugs were eyeing him up and down, those might be minor injuries compared to what the brutes guarding the door might do to him.

"Inn's full for the evening, boy," one of the thugs said before Ean could open his mouth. "Children are not allowed in anyway when a Sparkteller is performing, so you might as well just turn right around and get out of here."

"I'm renting a room here," Ean said between clenched teeth. "I'm sure your boss wouldn't want you keeping out a paying customer, especially one with a room on the top floor?"

Ean was hoping that fact would matter, and by the reaction of the thugs, it did. They glanced at each other and then the one to Ean's left stepped inside. Down to one man watching the door, a few of the people on the inside edge decided that now would be a good time to try and rush past. Two quick strokes of the bouncer's cudgel put an end to that. As the two unconscious people were carried out of the crowd, the remaining thug rounded on Ean.

"You're causing me a lot more trouble than I would prefer on a busy night. I actually hope my buddy comes back and tells me you're lying. It'll make what I've done to these other fools seem like a slap on the wrist compared to what I'll do to you."

Ean knew that wouldn't happen, but he still shuffled about nervously. The crowd immediately around him grew quiet, all of their eyes locked on him. Ean had no idea what a Sparkteller was or why all of these people were trying to get in to see him, but those stuck outside now seemed to be interested in a different show. One that involved him getting beaten badly judging by the glare he was receiving from the thug. Ean hoped to disappoint them all.

When the second guard finally returned, the entire crowd grew still. The thug at the door grinned in anticipation of the impending violence.

When his buddy returned he announced, "The kid ain't lying. Let him in."

A collective groan of disappointment escaped the crowd as the first thug reluctantly waved Ean inside.

CHAPTER 15

CATCHING A SHOW

AS SOON AS EAN walked into the High Horse Inn, his senses were assaulted with braying laughter, ashy smoke, and the strong scent of ale. The bar was packed, with the stools full and people standing in-between them. The two areas with tables did not have a single empty seat, with extra chairs placed near the round tables and people crammed into the benches around the longer tables near the stage. Even the path that ran through the middle of the bar was full of people standing and resting their drinks on the partitions.

As he searched in vain for a place to sit, a hand grabbed his arm and spun him around.

"There you are!" Azalea's words were slurred and her eyes were only half open as she swayed slightly in front of him. "I thought you had abandoned me here, which I suppose wouldn't have been the worst thing with all the wonderful people to feed on, but I would have been very mad at you. You wouldn't leave me behind, would you?"

Ean didn't know if it was because she was drunk off of all the people here, but Azalea actually sounded a little sad at the mention of being left behind. Was there a softer side to the Yulari? He almost felt sympathy for the woman, but then her usual smirk appeared.

"Of course you wouldn't leave me behind." Reaching over, she patted him not so gently on the cheek. "You wouldn't survive long without me. Now come on, I've saved us a seat right near the front of the stage. I wanna see why so many people are all worked up over this Sparkteller person."

Azalea dragged Ean into the crowd. The people made way for the two of them, although Ean was sure they had no idea they were doing it. Waves of what seemed like heat emanated from the Yulari, and Ean was sure she was using the same trick she always used to get her way.

"Gentlemen," she said as they reached one of the long tables in front of the stage. "Thank you for holding our seats. You can leave now."

Three imposing men that looked like they would be good in a fight, quickly rose and moved out of the way. One even went as far as to offer Azalea a bow as he shuffled away. With the men gone, Azalea and Ean took a seat on the bench with plenty of space between them. Azalea seemed to like the space and gave anyone that tried to sit with them a look that made them turn right around. Ean decided that now was as good of a time as any to talk to the Yulari about what he had planned.

"Azalea, I need you to do something for me..." Ean said, leaning in so he could be heard over the roar of the crowd.

"Oh, little one," she replied, patting his leg with her hand. "I've decided we're never going to 'do' anything. If you develop feelings for me, which you most certainly will, I'm sure it will just complicate our little arrangement. Don't you agree?"

Ean stared at her. What did she mean? How would doing him a favor make him fall for...

"No, no, I wasn't talking about that," he said hastily. "I mean, I need you to... well... do whatever you do that makes people do whatever you ask. We need to get a ride with another caravan, and with no money, the only way that will happen is if you charm our way onto it again."

Letting out a musical laugh, Azalea patted his leg again as she leaned in closer to him.

"Oh, well that I can certainly handle. I just need to know who to talk to and what demeaning job you would like to perform during the trip this time. Maybe instead of shoveling horse dung, you can help with digging the latrines." Laughing again at her own joke, or what Ean hoped was a joke, she nudged him playfully with her shoulder.

Ean decided to ignore the jab. "I don't know the exact person you need to speak to, but it's the Ciantar family that owns the caravan. They allow booking of passage at their home, which is a little ways down the street past the inn. We have to be at the home sometime during midmorning in order to arrange to ride with them."

"Say no more. I'll take care of everything tomorrow".

"You mean, we will take care of everything tomorrow".

"No. I know I'm a bit giddy at the moment, but I did mean 'I.' You can't help with what I do, and you'll probably go and say something dumb that will make it harder for me to get what we want. Best for you to stay out of my way."

"I still think--" her hand covered his mouth before he could get another word out.

"I said, say no more! Now if you don't mind, I would like to drink in a little more of all this excitement before the man comes out and does his little show." Turning around on the bench so that she could lean back against the table, Azalea took in a long breath and sighed happily. Not knowing what else to do, Ean moved into a similar position and slowly surveyed the surrounding tables.

It seemed that the inn took a first-come, first-served attitude when it came to who had been allowed in for the show. The crowded was an interesting mix; fancily dressed citizens sitting with workers still in their dirty clothes, bakers and cooks still covered in bits of food sitting with hunters and butchers still covered in... other things. It was a unique collection of people, both human and even a few Taruun, making up the crowd, and they all seemed to be getting along, regardless of their profession.

With Azalea ignoring him and nothing else to do, Ean decided it wouldn't hurt to order one mug of beer. Waving a serving girl over he ordered two drinks, one for himself and one for Azalea, which were quickly delivered.

Ean managed to get a single sip out of his drink when the inn staff began moving about the room, lowering the lights. As soon as the last lantern was snuffed, the crowd grew silent in anticipation. When two men stepped out onto the stage, one carrying a drum and the other some kind of flute, the excitement intensified. Were these two the Sparktellers?

A third man walked out, dressed in a red coat with golden designs twirling about the sleeves and running down his blue pants. The crowd erupted into applause. The man moved to the center of the stage and made a few bows towards the crowd. His long gray hair waved about as he bowed and he was forced to move it out of his face each time. After he had finished bowing, he stood there smiling broadly as he surveyed the audience. Chants of "Tremain the Sparkteller" and "Tremain the Amazing" started up amongst the crowd, which only seemed to make the man's grin widen even more.

When the man seemed to have heard enough applause and chants of his own name, he raised his hands, instantly silencing the crowd. When he spoke, his voice boomed as it echoed around the room.

"Greetings, ladies and gentlemen! Thank you for such a prestigious welcome! As much as I love to travel about the land, sharing my stories with all to hear, I never receive as warm of a welcome as I do when I perform here at the High Horse Inn!"

Again the room erupted into applause and chants of the Sparkteller's name. Fists and empty mugs were banged onto table tops, and a few of the women even made some remarks that put a little color into Ean's face. Apparently the man was known for more than just being an excellent Sparkteller. This time Tremain just took everything in and waited for the crowd to die down on its own before speaking again.

"Now, for those few that have the misfortune of never having seen me perform before," he paused as laughter filled the room before continuing. "My name is Tremain Faustman, and I will be your Sparkteller for the evening." Again he paused as applause filled the room.

The man sure likes to receive adulation, Ean thought as he sipped at his drink. Tremain waited for the applause to die down on its own again before continuing.

"Tonight, I intend to amaze you with stories of bravery and action, tug at your heart with stories of love and heartbreak, and terrify you with stories of the most horrendous beasts and monsters. But don't worry, I'll give those that are faint of heart fair warning to leave before I get to those stories."

He winked at the audience, which brought around another round of laughter. The man was effective at controlling the crowd, and as much as Ean wanted to hate his smarmy attitude, he couldn't help but laugh along with everyone else. Taking another sip of his drink, Ean listened as the man continued on.

"Now what story should I begin with?" Another pause as a variety of names were shouted out, none of which Ean had ever heard of before. After a moment, Tremain reached out and seemed to grasp at something in front of him and pull it in. "Ah yes, an excellent suggestion."

Cupping his hands together, he brought them to his face and opened them just enough to peek inside. He glanced quickly at the crowd with a grin and then returned his gaze to what was in his hand. Closing his hands together again, he returned his attention to the crowd.

"Should I show you what story I've caught?" He barely finished his sentence before the crowd yelled out a resounding "Yes!"

"Alright then, here it is... the tale of Dayson and the Beast!"

Throwing his hands out wide, multicolor sparks seemed to shoot out of his fingertips. At first they seemed to be shooting out at random but as more and more of those sparks escaped his fingers, they began to pool together in front of him. Ean's jaw dropped as those sparks began to form the image of two bodies up on the stage.

The first body was clearly a dark skinned man dressed in deep red, leather armor with short hair of a similar color. The image stood almost two heads higher than Tremain and was twice as wide as the thin Sparkteller. He carried a small dagger in each hand, the thin blades on each seeming to writhe in the air. Ean wasn't sure if that effect was on purpose or if whatever Tremain was doing caused it. Most of the image was highly detailed, but the face of the man was a blur of colors and did not have any distinguishable features.

The second body that appeared was certainly not human. Four legs covered in a purplish shell that ended in points where the feet should have been stretched up to a torso that appeared more human than its lower half. Two pairs of arms stuck out of its body, the lower set was shorter and ended in points while the upper set was normal sized but ended in a pair of pinchers. Its head was more insect than human, with four large antennae sticking out of the top.

Ean almost fell out of his chair. It was the same type of creature from his dream, or vision, or whatever it was that he had experienced. The ugly creature, which at the moment was standing face to face with the man that Ean assumed was Dayson, could have come directly from his vision. Ean's first instinct was to get out of his chair and run, but since the other people in the room were all applauding loudly and not running for their lives, Ean stayed cautiously still.

Glancing to his right, he was surprised to see Azalea in a state of near panic. The Yulari was half way on the table, one foot on the bench and the other almost on the table as well. Her mouth had dropped open more than Ean's had, and the effects of her binging on the emotions of the room seemed to have disappeared.

The people immediately around them began to laugh at her reaction until she shot them all a look. Whatever she put into that look made everyone quiet down real quick. Fortunately, the other patrons didn't seem to notice, and the Sparkteller launched into his story.

The story of Dayson focused on the man's quest to kill the beast that had murdered a caravan of traders near some city that no longer existed. The story itself wasn't very interesting, but the Sparkteller was able to bring it to life with his skill in creating images. Ean watched as Tremain recreated the gruesome scene of the creature attacking the caravan, as Dayson tracked the creature's trail of destruction and then the final battle. It was amazing what the Sparkteller could do with what clearly had to be some form of magic. The story had been so entertaining that Ean barely noticed that he had not only finished off his own drink, but also Azalea's.

When the story was finished, the room erupted in applause, most people standing in ovation. Ean was quick to join them and was surprised to see Azalea on her feet clapping as well. He never would have expected the Yulari to be that entertained by a simple story, even one so amazingly portrayed, but she was applauding just as loudly as everyone else.

Tremain seemed to be taking it all in, a giant smile painted on his face as the applause washed over him. Tiny beads of sweat covered his face and he was taking long breaths but the smile never left his lips. Ean's hands were starting to hurt from the length of the applause when Tremain raised both hands to silence the crowd. Most kept applauding a little longer, but the Sparkteller didn't seem to mind. When the last of the applause finally died off, Tremain spoke to the crowd.

"I'm glad you enjoyed my first tale, but I fear I've made a mistake!"

The immediate response of the crowd was a resounding "No!" and chants of "Tremain!" started up. Of course, the Sparkteller allowed it to continue for a bit before raising his hands to silence the crowd once again.

"Yes, yes, despite your confidence in me, I did make a mistake. My mistake was to start off with such a gripping and exciting tale. How could anyone top the story of Dayson and the Beast? I should have started out with a lesser story, maybe the heart-wrenching story of ill-fated lovers Ramone and Isabelle or the darkly humorous tale of The Vengeful Water Spirit."

"I am so sorry, my friends, to have started so strong and not planned ahead. Such a large mistake should not come from a Sparkteller with so many years of experience. I feel like a common storyteller, who, even without my abilities, could have at least planned out their stories to slowly build in excitement over the night. Perhaps this is a sign that I should retire and give the younger Sparktellers a chance to shock and amaze you."

Again, yells of "No!" and "Tremain!" filled the common room. Tremain himself ducked his head, shoulders slumping, and tried to wave them off as he shook his head. To most in the room he probably looked defeated, but being up front Ean got a good view of the man's face. Tremain was wearing an enormous grin. It was all part of the show.

The Sparkteller let the chants go on a little longer and finally raised his head and hands, silencing the crowd once more. The smile was gone from his face, replaced by heavy eyes and downturned lips. Ean couldn't decide if he disliked the man for all of the theatrics or if he enjoyed them.

"Thank you," Tremain continued once the crowd had grown silent. "I have always appreciated the support of the people. For you, I will still continue on this night and give you a show, although it will be a poorer one than you deserve. I simply hope that you still think fondly of me as I retell the fateful story of...Jamirian and the Living Blade!"

The explosion of cheering and applause that erupted from the crowd made Ean jump. Clearly this next story was greater than the first, going by the crowd's reaction. The dejected look, of course, was gone from the Sparkteller, and he lifted his hands as the sparks of multicolor light flew from his fingertips.

This time, a much smaller man appeared, his face a blur, as well. He was clothed in a simple shirt and pants, in a similar fashion to many of the people in the room. What really caught Ean's eye was the sword in his hand. The blade, half as long as the man wielding it, shone with a dark blue light and was more detailed than any of the other images the Sparkteller had created so far. Intricate designs covered the blade itself, its hilt a mesh of twisting yellow lines that could have been gold. The image of the man periodically twirled the blade around as the crowd continued to cheer.

Ean sat back and marveled at the Sparkteller's ability to control the crowd. If Ean could control the creatures he summoned half as well as Tremain could control the people in the room, he would be happy. Taking a sip from his somehow freshly filled mug, Ean couldn't help but smile as the Sparkteller began his second story.

Jamirian had been a farmer who one day was digging in his fields and found a sword. The sword turned out to be magical and imbued with intelligence. Some dark force found out about the blade and this put Jamirian on the run as he tried to learn more about his new companion. The story ended with Jamirian just barely escaping from a cult army and continuing his quest to learn more about his blade.

Jamirian's story was more impressive than the previous one, with a great deal of suspense and quite a few battles. When the story finally came to a close, the crowd again bathed the Sparkteller in applause. Tremain let the crowd applaud for a bit longer than last time, and again began to complain about how he could not top that story. He put on another show of being disappointed in himself before finally revealing the next story, which did end up being even more impressive. This back and forth continued for five more stories, each one more thrilling than the last, until the Sparkteller gave his final bows and left the stage.

CHAPTER 16

FINDING A RIDE

THE CROWD ROSE TO their feet as he left, clapping and yelling out compliments, the women sometimes more vocal than the men. Ean heard quite a few offers from a variety of women that flushed his cheeks. He tried to stand and applaud as well, but ended up becoming dizzy and sitting back down. Maybe it wasn't the brash words that made his face flush.

Glancing behind him at the three empty mugs, Ean tried his best to remember how much he had consumed during the Sparkteller's performance. It had to be more than those three mugs, as he vaguely remembered his cup being refilled a few times while it was still in his hand. Now that he thought about it--as well as he could considering his condition--Azalea had poured her mug into his quite a few times during the night as well. At the time Ean had thought the gesture had been nice coming from the Yulari, but now as his head became heavy and his vision blurry, he wasn't entirely sure.

Looking around, Ean wasn't able to spot the Yulari anywhere in the crowd. Had she left his side before the last story or had she gotten up before the story before that? Shaking his head to try and clear it up a bit, he stretched his senses to see if she was still close by. It took him a while to feel anything, and surprisingly he felt the smaller form of Zin above him first. Feeling out for a bit longer, he finally felt her over in the direction of the bar.

Pushing himself up on wobbly legs, Ean walked his hands along the table as he moved. Once he reached the end of the table, his legs felt strong enough to support him on their own and he carefully began to make his way through the crowd towards the bar. Quite a few of the other patrons Ean passed seemed to be in just as bad of condition as he was, making him feel slightly less embarrassed. He really had to watch how much he drank in the future.

The bar was still packed as Ean reached the end closest to the stage. Most of those sitting at the bar were talking with the people in the immediate vicinity, sharing drinks and a few still having a bite to eat. Down at the end of the bar, though a great deal of people, from common workers to nicely dressed merchants, were all gathered in a circle around one person. Ean would have known that one person was Azalea even if he couldn't feel her.

Moving next to the gathering of people, Ean tried to push his way through but was just as quickly pushed right back.

"You don't have a chance, boy," one man dressed in a fancy looking green coat and pants said as he sneered at Ean.

"You're a little young for this one, I think," another man who could not have had more than a few years on Ean said.

When a third man simply growled at him while placing a hand on his shoulder and shoving him back, Ean had had enough. His head was already half filled with alcohol and now the rest was filled with contempt. Contempt for these weak individuals that were falling all over each other just to get the tiniest bit of attention from Azalea.

Taking in the energy from the Abyss, Ean grabbed the man's hand with a gloved one of his own. Ean's initial instinct was to unleash his energy into the man, forever altering him in some way. That would certainly get the others attention. But that was the alcohol thinking, not his own desires. Deforming the man would probably get him killed by everyone else in the room, and if not, it would certainly bring the Seekers down on him.

So instead, he simply began to squeeze. At first the man just sneered at him, neither intimidated nor impressed. But as Ean applied more and more pressure, the energy of the Abyss increasing his strength, the man's expression changed first to confusion, then fear, and ended with panic and pain as the bones in his hand started to grind together in Ean's grip. Ean kept up the pressure, almost positive that if he tightened even the slightest bit more he would hear the crack of broken bones. When the man's face started to go pale, Ean finally released him, giving the man as cold of a stare as he could manage.

The man, now nursing his hand, quickly got up and moved away without another word. Those around him took one look at his face and cleared a path for him to Azalea as well. Ean had no idea whether it was because they had watched what he had done or because of his expression, but either way he didn't care. He moved quickly through the opening and was not surprised by what he saw.

Azalea was sitting on one man's lap, her hand caressing another man's face while she spoke to a third. All three did not even bother to hide the jealous looks they shot at each other before sending all smiles at the Yulari. Whenever Azalea moved her attention to the rest of the men gathered around her, the three closest would simply glare at the rest, as if their stares alone could make the other men disappear. When she finally noticed Ean pushing his way through, she gave a squeal of delight and hopped off of the man's lap.

"Ean, you're still awake! How wonderful that you chose not to pass out again and have me carry you off to bed. Is my little brother finally able to handle more than one drink?"

Playfully grabbing his side, she smirked at him. Despite himself Ean found a smile starting to touch his lips and quickly tried to squash it. The Yulari had tried to get him drunk, probably so he would be out of her way and wouldn't try to stop her from playing. Her words though were missing their usual scorn and sarcasm...

"Azalea, I think we should probably call it a night," Ean said in as serious a tone as he could muster. "We have to get up early tomorrow and have a lot of planning to do."

"Not at all! By pure luck I met the one person you need to see." Gesturing a hand towards the man that had until recently been her seat, Azalea flashed the older gentleman a smile before returning her attention to Ean. "This happens to be Meganan Ciantar, patriarch of the Ciantar Hawkpurse family. We've been becoming close friends, haven't we, Meg?"

As the man rose to his feet, Ean took a closer look at him. Standing almost a head taller than Ean, Meganan was in his later years with a face that contained more lines and wrinkles than an unmade bed. His white hair was cut short and neat, which matched his closely trimmed eyebrows and small mustache of similar color. His clothing was less impressive than Ean expected for the man who ran one of the most powerful trading families in the land. He wore a simple black tunic and matching pants that had seen better years, and his boots looked as though they had seen their fair share of travels.

The coldness in his eyes was reflected in his voice when he spoke.

"And who is this young gentleman, Azalea? A servant of yours perhaps?"

"No, Meg, you jealous old man," Azalea replied with a short laugh. "This is my older brother, Ean. He'll be joining me on your caravan as well."

"Brother?" Meganan seemed to taste the word at first, then apparently content with it, offered Ean a hand and a slightly warmer smile. "Pleasure to meet you, lad. Your sister is quite the interesting woman, but I'm sure you already know that."

"Yes, well--" Ean started but Meganan just kept talking right over him, the older man's attention back on Azalea.

"Very sneaky of you not mention your brother before. I may have promised you a free ride into the Deadlands, but that same offer doesn't apply to your brother. For him to come, he either has to pay the traveler's fee or work, and going by what you have told me about your family, I doubt you will be able to pay."

"This is true," Azalea replied with a heavy sigh. "With our parents gone and our farm nothing but ashes, we have little money. Thankfully my brother has always worked hard to keep us alive. I'm sure he will be happy to work at whatever job you need filled. Isn't that right, Ean?"

"That's right, whatever I can do to pay OUR way," Ean said through clenched teeth. He shot Azalea a look that hopefully left no doubt about how he felt about the situation. The Yulari probably could have gotten them both a free ride on the caravan, but she just loved to make his life difficult.

"See?" Azalea said, wrapping an arm around Meganan to the chagrin of the other men gathered around. "Everything always works out when I'm around. Now why don't you go get some sleep, brother? We have a long few days ahead of us and you should get plenty of rest. Who knows what fun jobs you'll be performing on the trip?"

"Shouldn't you be going to bed then too, sister?"

"Oh no, not yet," she said, winking at him. "I think there are still a few things that Meg and I need to discuss about the trip. Plus I believe a few of these other gentlemen did promise me a couple of drinks. Isn't that right, boys?"

The resounding "Yes!" from the men around them drowned out Ean's protest. He tried to make a grab for her arm, but the surrounding men quickly moved into the space that had been created and muscled him back to the outside of the crowd. For the briefest moment he considered trying to fight his way back to the center, but he gave up on that idea. If she wanted to stay up and toy with the men here, he might as well let her. There was no real harm in it, as long as no one was found dead the following morning.

With the ale making his eyes heavy, Ean decided that sleep was a good idea. Not because Azalea had suggested it, he was just thinking of how difficult it would be to get up the following morning and make the caravan if he stayed up much later. So with legs still not completely under his control, Ean climbed his way up the back stairs to his room.

Zin was waiting for him as he entered the room, but Ean waved off whatever the imp was trying to say and collapsed onto his bed. He heard Zin mumble something, but the imp eventually grew quiet. With the room silent and his eyes closed, it was only a matter of time before Ean drifted away to a peaceful sleep.

CHAPTER 17

INTERESTING TRAVEL COMPANIONS

EAN STIFLED A YAWN from his seat on one of the dozen or so wagons making their way northwest and away from the city. It had still been dark when Azalea roused him out of bed that morning. Pale yellow light blanketed the local farms as the caravan of wagons rolled over the grass. Ean sat in the back of a wagon that was bumping along somewhere near the middle of the caravan. As he chewed on a tough piece of jerky, a lonely empty feeling invaded his chest. It was a familiar sensation, one he had lived with most of his life. A sensation that had also been missing during most of his journey but had returned with the still of the morning. Zin was off somewhere behind his wagon, up to who knows what. Azalea had probably procured a cushy seat in one of the owners' wagons towards the front, enjoying all of the benefits that came along with getting cozy with the rich and powerful. Ean found himself missing both of their company.

With Lurthalan fading away behind them, the area they were moving through consisted of farmlands and pastures. Tiny houses sat next to massive barns, surrounded by fields of an assortment of different crops. Whenever they passed close to one of the farms, the workers would stop whatever they were doing in the fields to stare or give a quick wave before returning to work.

Even though Ean was curious about the types of food being grown, what really piqued his interest were the flags that flew in front of some of the homes. Grand, solid colored flags wavered on flagpoles, each with a different design. Ean immediately recognized the sigil of the bear on a yellow flag and guessed that the others he did not recognize must be the symbols for the other Hawkpurse families as well.

Ean felt momentarily overwhelmed at how little he knew about the outside world. The Hawkpurse families had their hands in anything that could be sold. The farms they passed without flags were noticeably smaller and clearly not as well taken care of as the Hawkpurse-owned ones. The workers of the Hawkpurse farms were greater in number and seemed to be younger and healthier as well. If Ean had to make a guess, he would say that the older men working on the smaller farms were probably the owners, men just scraping by, compared to the Hawkpurse farms and their ability to hire more workers. The whole situation rubbed Ean the wrong way, but he had no plans of becoming a farmer. Instead of worrying about the influence of the Hawkpurses, he let his mind wander to the journey ahead as the wagons rumbled on through the morning.

When they stopped for lunch, Ean got down and set off to look for a friendlier group. He passed a few of the other wagons as he received the cold shoulder from those drivers. Giving up on the chance to find a more pleasant wagon team, Ean made his way toward the back of the line of wagons. The last three wagons were for passengers that had paid for the chance to travel into the Deadlands, which meant they probably weren't as nervous about the trip as the wagon drivers were.

Reaching the end of the line, Ean took a quick look at the three large wagons that held the paying customers. Painted a dark red that was a sharp contrast to the unpainted brown wood of the other wagons, the travelers' wagons were both wider and taller than the average wagon and had storage boxes attached all along their sides.

Each wagon wall even had a window set right in the middle, although on all three, a curtain blocked the view of the inside.

Around the wagons a few fires had already been started, one for each wagon. The first fire Ean avoided, the men sitting around it were sharpening weapons or checking over armor. It was doubtful that he would be able to have a pleasant conversation with men who were hunters or guards or whatever else required all of those blades. The second fire was more inviting, the few men and women gathered around it were dressed plainly and going about normal chores--cooking, cleaning clothes, checking their supplies. Ean smiled as he approached them, but the smile quickly faded as a woman walked over to him and stuck a hand palm up practically in front of his face.

"He's not doing autographs and has no interest in wagon workers wasting his time. So whatever thoughts you had of asking for a quick show or trick, wipe them straight out of your mind."

Blinking a few times to catch his thoughts, Ean raised his own hands in a soothing gesture. "I don't want to see any tricks. I was simply coming over to--"

"Don't tell me, you want to try and be his apprentice. Let me just dash that dream right here and now, boy. Mr. Faustman does not train Sparktellers, and as far as I know he never will. Now just keep on moving boy, I've already wasted enough time with you."

Without waiting for a response the woman turned her back on Ean and returned to whatever she had been working on. Ean turned and stalked away. The woman had been a whirlwind of words and he wasn't even sure if he should be insulted by her brisk manner. Not that it would matter if he were insulted of course. Trying to brush the experience from his mind, Ean walked over to the last fire.

There were four men gathered around the third fire: a stocky man in a plain brown shirt, vest, and pants; a man that looked to be slightly older than Ean in a similar outfit; a bald, older man wearing a thick red robe, and a younger boy in fancy clothes. The older men were gathered around the fire while the younger boy was lounging slightly away from it. Approaching slowly with no idea how he would be received, Ean seemed to be walking into a heated conversation.

"...don't know why the boy doesn't help with the cooking," the stockier man said with a growl. "Isn't the whole reason his family let him come on this trip to learn what it's like being on the road? That certainly involves cooking his own meals!"

"I think the boy is just acting out, Iacane," the bald man said as he stirred the contents of the pot. "From what he has told me, he has no interest in the trader's life. I would be shocked if this situation had not been forced on him by his parents."

"That's no excuse to be lazy," the one called Iacane replied. "If he didn't want to be here then he should have stood up to his parents. That's what Fredren here did, and he wants to waste his time making maps of the realm." Reaching over, Iacane patted the back of the man that looked to be around Ean's age. "No offense of course, Fredren."

"None taken," the young man replied in a friendly tone, "I don't expect many people to understand the importance of mapping the land. Just give me time though, and my maps will be one of the most sought after items in the realm."

"See?" Iacane said, patting him on the back again. "That's a boy with ambition. I don't see how he will be successful, but my parents said the same thing about me when I told them I wanted to be a traveling Saniteal. Now look at me. I'm probably one of the strongest Saniteals in the land. Not much left that I can't heal. At least as far as I know. Sure, I've heard about a Saniteal down south that can--"

"Oh, hello," the one called Fredren said, the first one to notice Ean had walked up to their fire. Do you need something?"

Three pairs of eyes focused on Ean, making him feel slightly uncomfortable. Shuffling his feet, he waved a hello, felt dumb about doing that, and then finally spoke.

"My name's Ean, I'm working for the caravan to pay my way to see the Deadlands. I was hoping to find a warm fire and some good people to spend the lunch break with before we headed out again."

The one called Iacane was the first to speak. "Why don't you eat with the other workers? I didn't pay all of that money for a ride just so I could eat with the hired help."

"Iacane, that is no way to speak to someone," the bald man said, rising slowly to his feet. "Of course you are welcome here, Ean. My name is Sadiek. This not so polite fellow is--"

"I can introduce myself, thank you very much," the stocky man said, rising as well. "My name is Iacane, although I'm sure you have heard of me before. Many consider me the greatest Saniteal in the entire land of Ven Khilada".

"Self-proclaimed greatest..." the younger man said, his voice low but clear.

"Quiet boy! I am the greatest! No one has my skill or power. Just the other day I was called on to help--"

"I'm joking with you, Iacane. In the short amount of time we have been traveling, we've already heard many of your amazing accomplishments as a Saniteal. I'm just as confident you are as good as you say you are, as I'm confident we will hear many more examples of what you have accomplished on the rest of the trip." Turning his attention to Ean, the younger man stuck out his hand. "My name is Fredren, by the way. Nice to meet you, Ean".

Ean took the offered hand in his own gloved hand and shook it warmly. "It's nice to meet the three of you as well."

"We'll see if you still feel that way after actually spending some time with us," Sadiek chuckled, returning to his seat by the fire. "We've only been traveling half a day and I'm already concerned that we might be at each other's throats before we even cross into the Deadlands."

"Why Sadiek, I did not know you were so humorous," Iacane replied, also returning to his seat by the fire. "Maybe you should abandon your scholarly pursuits and focus instead on entertaining others with your humor. There is probably more money in entertaining than whatever it is you do, and I could follow you around and heal all of those people that come close to dying with laughter."

Ean joined them by the fire, not bothering to hide his smile. This group seemed like they would make the journey enjoyable, at least the three out of the four he had met. Ean glanced over at the boy sitting slightly off by himself, wondering if he would ever meet him.

"That's Creg," Fredren said, talking a seat next to Ean. "He's some distant cousin of the Ciantar family. Apparently his parents forced him to come along so that he could try to get into the family business." Leaning in close, he lowered his voice. "He's been nothing but rude and bitter since we set off. The rest of us have gotten the feeling that this isn't in line with his professional aspirations."

Not knowing how to respond, Ean simply nodded along. It wasn't any of his business what the boy was doing. If the boy were going to be miserable, it would be best if he stayed away. Ean was already starting to warm up to the other three, so there was no need to draw in someone that was going to be in a bad mood the whole trip. Returning his attention back to the rest of the group, Ean had something to ask about.

"Iacane," he began. "You say you're a Saniteal. What is that exactly?"

The stocky man returned such a shocked look, his eyebrows climbing his forehead while his jaw dropped, that Ean turned quickly to make sure nothing was behind him.

"You've never heard of a Saniteal?" Iacane was finally able to get out. "Where are you from, boy, a cave?"

"No, I..." Ean struggled to come up with an answer. He didn't want to mention Rottwealth, not with how that had been poorly received so many times in the past. "I'm from a small fishing village south of Rensen. We don't get many visitors or news from the rest of the realm."

"Oh, I suppose that makes sense," Iacane said, rubbing at his chin. "Most Saniteals tend to stick to where there are a large number of people. Still, I'm surprised you never heard of me..."

"A Saniteal," Sadiek cut in, "is someone that can heal the sick through magical means, usually taking in the pain or disease into their own body, cleansing it, and then releasing it. It's actually a very dangerous practice, with many documented cases of Saniteals killing themselves by trying to heal more than they can handle. It's a testament to both Iacane's skill and intelligence that he is still alive at such an old age."

"Old age?!" Iacane blustered. "I look younger than you, Sadiek, and if I were a betting man, I would wager a large sum of money-- which I have--that you are older than me."

"Now, now, I meant it as a compliment to your ability. I've heard of some of the things you've done, and I doubt any other Saniteal could have accomplished what you have and still live."

"Oh, well then, it is true I've never heard of a Saniteal that's been able to do half of the things I've done in my career either. I have heard a few things about Healers using medicines to cure some of the things I've cured, but that must be all rumors. I mean honestly, to believe a couple of plants could cure blindness or mend a broken bone cleanly? Bunch of charlatans and tricksters, if you ask me. Healers are horrible people that prey on the foolish."

"I'm a Healer," Ean said as calmly as he could.

Ean was surprised at how angry he became at the pompous man's comments. No, on second thought, it wasn't that surprising.

As much as a mean old man Cleff had been most of the time, Ean had always respected his abilities as a Healer. Plus, after everything that had happened at Rensen and all of the people Ean had helped, he would be a fool not to consider himself a full blown Healer by now. So Ean let himself glare at the much older Saniteal with as much anger as he could put into his own expression.

The entire group was silent for a few moments, the only sounds being the low hum of the conversations at the other fires. At first, Iacane returned Ean's stare with a haughty one of his own, but something he saw in Ean's face slowly changed that. When the smug expression had been completely wiped from his face, Iacane looked away and finally spoke.

"I'm sure not all Healers are tricksters. I've seen firsthand what some of your concoctions can do, and they are effective to a degree. They can leave terrible scars though, and bones can heal wrong if not set perfectly. Magical healing eliminates those risks and many other risks associated with medicinal healing techniques."

"You always seem to gloss over the risks to the Saniteal, Iacane," Sadiek said, shooting a glance in Ean's direction before quickly looking away. "For every story you've told, I've heard just as many about other Saniteals that pushed themselves too far and died, often killing the other person in the process as well."

"Bah, bunch of fools. Rushing into healings blindly, trying to take in too much, too fast. Or worse, thinking they can cure what can't be cured. Arrogant idiots, the lot of them, especially since it puts the lives of those they are trying to heal in danger as well."

A crooked smile appeared on Sadiek's face. "Oh, they were all arrogant, were they? And what exactly are your reasons for wanting to travel into the Deadlands?"

"My reasons are none of your business, thank you very much! I could ask the same thing of every one of you, except I'm not that rude. Fredren wants to make his silly maps and Creg was forced to come on this journey, that's obvious. Your reasons and especially this boy's," he said, gesturing to Ean, "are the most mysterious."

Sadiek replied to Iacane's accusatory tone with a laugh. "I'm a scholar of all things, and the least studied area is certainly the Deadlands and its inhabitants. Not many people try to determine the culture of the Living Dead."

"Living dead?!" Ean cut in, rising quickly. "I was never told we were going to a place populated by zombies and ghouls."

The other three burst into laughter, obviously at Ean's expense. So, the talk about zombies had just been Sadiek's attempt at a joke. Fine, fine. Ean could take a joke after all. Sitting down, he joined in their laughter.

"I should have known. Zombies and ghouls are just made up in stories meant to scare little children. They don't really exist. You were just having a joke at the expense of someone from a secluded village. Very funny."

Sadiek stopped his laughing although the other two continued. "No, boy, we are not laughing because they are make-believe. Zombies and ghouls are nasty business, usually raised by Nexmortis. Those types of creatures, though, are called the UnDead".

"The Living Dead," he continued, moving closer so he could be heard over the laughter of the others, "are those that were affected by the Plague. You have at least heard about the Plague, yes?"

"The one that killed off everything in the land?"

"A common misconception. The Plague didn't kill everything; it simply corrupted and twisted the majority of the life in the land before it was halted. Many living beings were corrupted to the point that they are unrecognizable, but others, like many of the people that couldn't escape it, were not changed in a way that is easy to see. Their corruption exists on the inside of their bodies and slowly works its way out."

"So then these 'Living Dead' don't eat other people?" Ean thought it was a legitimate question, but it aroused a whole new wave of laughter from Fredren and Iacane. Even Sadiek looked like he had to struggle to hold back his own laughter.

"No, no. Humans are not on their menu. They mostly eat food grown in their own lands, but that's part their problem. Food grown there is corrupted just like everything else, and it helps speeds up their own body's corruption. Their bodies are slowly dying, you see, the corruption eating away at them while their body fights it. That's the point of these caravans; they bring up non-corrupted food for the Living Dead. Normal food keeps them looking human. Well, as human as possible."

Looking at the long line of wagons, with most of their canvas covers bulging out from what was contained within, Ean began to wonder exactly how much food they were carrying into the Deadlands.

"All of the wagons just contain food? No supplies? No tools? No other goods?"

"No, the Living Dead can make everything else that they need, just like us. The town we are going to, Ulundkin, is actually built right next to a large mine. I've heard that most of the tools used in the Deadlands are made there."

"Then this caravan travels to all of the towns and cities in the Deadlands? Are there actual cities in the Deadlands?"

Sadiek shook his head while rubbing a hand across the top of it as if he had hair left. "This is where your ignorance of the world becomes dangerous, Ean. Ulundkin is the only place close enough to the border of the Deadlands anyone would dare visit. Any other towns or cities, if they exist, are too far into the area affected by the Plague to even attempt to visit."

"Why is that?"

"Ean, you have to know if you chose to come on this trip."

Ean returned the comment with a blank stare. He had heard the Deadlands were dangerous, but Ean felt that Sadiek was referring to something else. The other two had both stopped laughing now and were making a clear effort not to look in Ean's direction.

Placing his face in his hands, Sadiek rubbed them up and down a few times before speaking again.

"Ean, the Plague is still going strong in the Deadlands. Anyone that spends an extended amount of time runs the risk of being corrupted as well. It was only through sheer stupidity by a few merchants that people initially discovered that it was safe to spend some time in the Deadlands and not become affected by the Plague. Others were not so lucky and either ended up corrupted or dead."

Ean couldn't help the shiver that ran up his spine and shook his body. What had he gotten himself into? It must be somewhat safe if this caravan made frequent trips, but the way Sadiek was speaking, clearly, safety was not a guarantee. Had Kaz'ren known about the risks he was taking? Had Zin? Would the Plague even affect the imp?

"Wait, I thought the Plague mainly just corrupted people," Ean was finally able to get out. "How have people died?"

"From not knowing they were corrupted," Iacane cut in, his voice just as somber as Sadiek's voice had been. The usual smarminess was absent. "Sometimes it takes a while before those corrupted can actually feel the effects of the Plague. They think they are fine after spending time in the Deadlands and try to leave. When they cross the border, they usually have just enough time to realize what's happening before they die a horrible death."

Even sitting in the sun next to the cooking fire, Ean felt his whole body go cold. "How do they die?"

"It's the magic," Sadiek said, taking over again. "The magic that was used to stop the spread of the Plague. It stops everything associated with the plague from moving any further south. Anything even barely affected that crosses the border begins to break down and dissolve. When a person crosses..." He gave a little shudder.

"Well, I've never seen it, but from what I've heard, it's a very gruesome way to die."

Sadiek became quiet, his eyes drifting off to look at the ground. The others remained quiet as well. He wanted to vomit. How could he expect to find the lair of Zin's old master knowing that every second increased his chances of becoming a permanent member of the Deadlands? Or worse, if he became corrupted without knowing it and tried to leave? Was trying to increase his control over his power and the creatures he summoned worth the risk? He had to talk to Zin.

The sudden loud clanging of a bell made everyone around the fire jump before they realized what it was. The sound signaled that the break was over. It was time to pack up and continue the journey.

"Bah, now we'll have to eat on the wagon," Iacane grumbled, rising to his feet. "Come on Fredren, help me get the stew into something we can eat out of while bouncing around inside." Turning to Ean, the older man frowned. "Sorry lad, guess you miss out on the meal."

As everyone else rose and started getting things ready to move, Sadiek grabbed Ean's arm and lead him away from the rest of the group.

"You might want to consider leaving the caravan before we cross over, now that you know what you're heading into. The caravan stops at Wethrinter, which sits close to the border. While it's true that we spend very little time in the corruption and that deaths are rare crossing back over, it's still something that can happen. No one would think any less of you for leaving."

"I... have to talk to Azalea and Zi--," Ean stopped, shaking his head. "I mean I have to talk to my sister, and see what she thinks. I doubt she knew how dangerous of a trip this was either."

"Well, you make sure you stress how dangerous it is. I don't know your reasons for wanting to travel into the Deadlands, but the two of you need to decide if it's worth your lives. If it will help, feel free to bring her by our fire tonight if you need help explaining the dangers."

"I will do that. Thank you, Sadiek".

"Of course. Now if you will excuse me, I better help with the loading up. I don't want to listen to Iacane complaining about how he did all the work the entire rest of today's journey."

And with that the older man rejoined the others. Toward the front of the caravan of wagons another bell clanged twice, signaling for an increase in the preparations to get underway. The next time the bell rang the wagons would start to move, whether everyone was ready or not. Ean began to jog up the line. He had to get back to his wagon and receive his work assignment before that third bell.

CHAPTER 18

PUT TO WORK

REACHING HIS WAGON, EAN was immediately pointed in the direction of the third wagon from the front. A large covered wagon like most of the others not meant for carrying people, Ean had originally assumed it was another wagon full of supplies. He was surprised when he climbed up into the back and found a small workshop set up inside.

Various tables were bolted to the waist-high walls of the inside of the wagon, each one having a small lip that stuck up around its edge that kept things from sliding off while the wagon was in motion. In the places where a table was absent, a chest or set of drawers sat latched to the ground, so that the entire inside perimeter was occupied. The crossbeams that held the canvas cover in place were double the width of the other wagons, and each had hooks or tools hanging from them.

In the middle of the mess sat a short man in plain brown clothes and a black apron. His unruly black hair matched the frayed state of his clothing. A belt with a collection of tools hung around his waist. The man was hunched over something, and he did not look up when Ean entered. Standing in the entrance Ean coughed once and, failing to get the man's attention, coughed even louder. It took a loud third cough before the man finally looked up.

"Wha... who are you?" he said in a grizzled voice. Ean could see yellow teeth peeking out from his lips as he spoke. "Oh, please don't tell me you're my assistant for this trip."

"I think I am. My name's--"

Placing something metallic on the ground, the man stood and threw his hands in the air.

"I ask for an apprentice and they give me just any old lad off the streets. Let me guess, you have absolutely no experience in blacksmithing, tinkering, or working on wagons."

Even though it had come out as more of a statement then question, Ean tried to answer. "No, I'm a Healer by trade--"

"Bah! It would be better if you had no experience in anything at all. Healers... if weak people can't handle being sick, then they should just die off, if you ask me. The world is becoming too coddled with medicines and magic making everything easier."

Another person demeaning being a Healer, Ean could barely believe it. Did no one appreciate his profession outside of Rottwealth and Rensen?

"Weak?" Ean couldn't help the anger that laced his voice. "You call someone with a sword or knife wound, bleeding out on the ground, weak? Or someone bitten by a poisonous spider or snake weak?" Looking around for a moment, he pointed to a collection of large metal poles that were hanging lengthwise above them. "If those things fell and crushed your arm or cracked open your skull like an egg, would you consider yourself too weak to let me fix either situation?"

"Those things are replacement axels for the wagons. If you are going to be working with me on this trip you should at least start to learn the names of everything." Looking at Ean, who was still visibly trying to control his anger, the man gave a short laugh. "Well, at least you're passionate about what you do. That makes one redeeming quality that you have. And a backbone makes a second one. Maybe you won't make this entire trip seem like weeks in the Abyss. Come over here, boy."

Biting his tongue, Ean moved over to the man's side. The grizzled man reached down and picked up what he had been examining when Ean had entered. It was a cylindrical piece of metal with two small bumps sticking out of holes in the middle but on opposite sides. When the old man pressed the two bumps they retracted under the pressure but then returned to their position when he released them.

"I don't suppose you know what this is," he said, not bothering to frame it as a question. "This little piece of metal and spring keeps the wagons connected to the horses and ox harnesses. One of these goes and we don't have a replacement, we basically have to leave a wagon behind. A wagon left behind means a loss of money for the family, and can you guess where a good chunk of that money comes from? My wages. So you can understand why this job is so important to me... uh, what did you say your name was again?"

"Ean".

"Well Ean, I'm Graden, by the way, since you were too rude to ask, and like I said I don't tolerate any mistakes. You will do what I say, when I say it, without question. Do we understand each other?"

Ean barely had enough time to nod before the older man grabbed his arm and pulled him down to a squatting position next to him. Launching into a mix of lecturing and insults, Graden began to explain the complexities of the little piece of metal that he was holding.

The rest of the day was a blur of activity as Graden moved from one job to the next, dragging Ean around their tight quarters. The Tinkerer, as he called himself, didn't slow down the entire day. He was constantly explaining the uses of different items or tools or showing Ean how to fix them. Not once did he allow Ean to fix or even handle a tool or piece of equipment on his own. Instead, he kept the younger man's attention focused on his explanations or work, even going as far as jabbing Ean in the ribs with a thin finger whenever Ean's attention started to wander.

As the light from the outside grew dim and the wagons rolled to a halt, Ean felt physically exhausted. Which was strange since he had done absolutely no work the entire afternoon. With the wagons stopped, Graden started going about lighting lamps that he then hung from some of the hooks screwed in the beams overhead.

"You're done, boy," the older man said, not bothering to stop his movements about the wagon or even glance in Ean's direction. "Go on and get something to eat, but no drinking! I want you to start here early in the morning tomorrow instead of the afternoon, and I don't want you getting hung over and throwing up all over the place. Do you understand?"

"Yes, of course."

"Good, now get out of here so I can actually get some work done without you being in the way all the time".

Which is how Ean found himself standing outside of the wagon, squinting in the light from the low hanging sun. The afternoon had been such a whirlwind of activity that he hadn't even had the chance to think about what he had learned about the Deadlands. His conversation with Sadiek came back to him in a rush, along with the nervousness and dread that it had initially caused. He didn't want to waste any more time, he needed to figure things out and that meant he had to find Zin and Azalea.

Closing his eyes, he focused on trying to feel the general direction of where the imp and Yulari were in the camp...

And practically jumped as he realized Zin was standing right next to him. Lowering down to one knee, Ean pretended to adjust the laces on his boots.

"And what have you been doing all day?" he whispered.

"Keeping an eye on the Yulari, of course. Making sure she doesn't get us into any trouble".

"For being the person that suggested we bring her along, you certainly have very little faith in her."

"I said she had her uses," he growled, "but that doesn't mean we can trust her."

"She's already done some things that I would consider fairly loyal, even if I don't always agree with how she does them."

Ean almost tipped over as an invisible claw suddenly grabbed the front of his shirt and pulled him down lower.

"Do not let her get to you, Ean." The imp's voice was cold and more serious sounding then Ean was accustomed to, coming from his friend. "We're both lucky her abilities don't seem to have any effect on you, but that doesn't mean she can't charm you all the same. A Yulari only cares about one thing--herself. For whatever reasons you or I think she is helping us, they are probably wrong."

"You're probably right. If she was completely on my side, she would have kept me from getting such annoying jobs the two times she's gotten us onto a caravan."

"Oh, she's just making you uncomfortable for a laugh," the imp joked, the seriousness suddenly gone from his voice. "If I was in her position, I probably would have done the same thing. Actually if I was in her position, I would have made sure you were shoveling dung again this entire trip."

"Well, whatever," Ean said softly between chuckles. "The three of us need to talk, and since you're here and I trust you, we'll talk just the two of us first. Let's head to my tent."

Rising, Ean grimaced as he noticed two workers staring at him from a few paces away. By the looks they were giving him, they had obviously noticed him talking and laughing to himself. Nothing he could do about that now. Dropping his head to look at the ground, Ean walked off quickly towards the area that was designated for his tent.

When Ean reached his spot, he was happy to see that a tent had already been put into place and a fire was started nearby for those on his wagon. The looks he received from those gathered around the fire, however, made it clear that they would prefer he didn't take a seat. Which was fine with Ean. He wanted to talk to Zin alone, try and figure some things out, then either find Azalea or just go straight to where Sadiek and the others would be camped out and get some dinner.

Pushing the tent flaps aside, Ean entered slowly enough to let Zin scoot in past him. The tent itself was smaller than the one he had slept in with the other caravan, but the material used to make it seemed thicker and kept out more of the elements while providing slightly more privacy. It also kept out most of the light, which kept the inside of the tent shrouded in darkness. Taking a seat towards the middle, Ean waited until he felt the imp settled into place before he spoke.

"I have some concerns," Ean began, letting some of the fear that he had been feeling creep into his voice. "Concerns about our trip into the Deadlands. Did you know that the curse is still alive and strong?"

Silence. Silence that clearly indicated that the imp had known.

"Zin, these are the types of things you need to tell me about! Finding relics of your former master won't exactly help me understand and control my abilities if I turn into some undead--"

"Living dead," the imp interrupted. "They are the Living Dead. Much different than the creatures known as the undea--"

"I know the difference!" Well, he had just learned the difference today, but that fact didn't matter. "I don't want to be stuck in the Deadlands like those other cursed people. Or worse, try to leave and wind up dead as I cross the border. I'm seriously considering giving this whole trip up, as soon as we reach Wethrintir".

"You can't!" the imp yelled with such ferocity that Ean leaned away from him. "We've come so far already. I promise you having access to my previous master's old things will be well worth the risks involved."

Ean let Zin's comments sink in for a few moments. What could be worth the risk of possibly dying or, in Ean's mind a worse scenario, becoming one of these Living Dead? Like a Sparkteller's images, Ean's future flashed through his mind. He had two choices of where he could go.

The safe road meant leaving the caravan at Wethrintir and trying to make a name for himself as a Healer. He could try and find his way back to Rottwealth, but that wouldn't solve the problem with the monster in the mine. Rottwealth wouldn't survive without someone taking care of it, and for all he knew Bran and Jaslen were lost for good.

The second road meant continuing on, entering the Deadlands, and risking his life. Risking the chance of being stuck in a land that, according to everyone Ean had talked to so far, said was both horrible and dangerous. And for what? What was the possible rewards? Insight into how to use his power? Better control over the creatures he summoned from the Abyss? Or something else entirely new? Even Zin didn't know and he was the one pushing for it.

And what if it was one of those perks or even all of them? What would Ean do with that kind of power? Could he use them in a way that could be helpful? Probably not with the fear and hatred associated with Ze'an and anything that came from the Abyss. He couldn't imagine becoming a monster like Zin's old master, but if he continued down this path, would he even have that choice? Would he even be able to stop himself from becoming a monster, if he gave up using his power now?

Too many questions and no one but the gods to give him answers, and they weren't offering any. Except Kaz'ren, but she made it clear that there was a price for receiving any help from the gods. Best to keep them out of his life whenever possible. Which meant that he had to make the decision on his own, without any idea what the future might hold.

While Ean struggled with himself, Zin remained surprisingly quiet, his small arms folded across his chest as he watched Ean closely.

"Fine, we keep going, at least for now," Ean finally blurted out. "But if we get to Wethrintir and I decide that we are not pushing forward, I don't want to hear any arguments, understood?"

"Yes, yes, fine. But you are making the right decision, Ean. This is the best way to make sure none of your nightmares come true."

"Don't you dare use those to keep me on this path! You know I'm already worried about that enou--"

"Hello?" a voice said from the tent flaps and was immediately followed by Sadiek's bald head sticking through the opening.

Ean froze.

Unfortunately, so did Zin.

CHAPTER 19

SECRETS

"WHAT IN THE ABYSS..."

Sadiek's expression went from squinting in the low levels of light to pure shock. The older man looked at the imp. Zin looked at the man. Ean looked at them both. What felt like an eternity passed. Then, without warning, Zin disappeared in a flash. This made Sadiek's eyes almost bulge out of his head, and Ean quickly grabbed the old man by his robe and pulled him completely into the tent. The man let Ean drag him in without putting up a fight and collapsed into a sitting position inside.

"Sadiek," Ean began, not exactly sure what to say. "I can explain what you saw. It was an illusion, a...trick. You know, like what a Sparkteller can do." Ean's lie was off and running. "I don't tell many people about it because I'm just learning. That's why the image disappeared so quickly when you came in, you startled me and I lost..."

Ean trailed off as the old man began shaking his head. "Ean, we both know that wasn't a Sparkteller illusion." The man's words came out slowly, as if each one was being carefully thought over and placed before Ean. "That creature reacted to me the same way I reacted to it. I've never seen anything like it. Was that a creature from the Abyss?"

Ean sat in silence. How many years had he kept Zin a secret? How careful had he always been before? Ean's mind was reeling.

"I'll take that as a yes," Sadiek continued. "I don't know what I find more shocking-- something from the Abyss free in the world or the fact that he is obviously your slave. Or is it companion?"

"Uhhhhh...." was all Ean could manage.

"Doesn't much matter, I suppose. What matters is whether you found it or if you brought it out of the Abyss yourself."

"I...found him a long time ago. His name is Zin, and he certainly is not my slave."

"It has a name? Most curious." Sadiek's expression had changed again, his eyes slightly squinted and a small smile forming on his lips. "I must say, Ean, I had thought seeing the Deadlands was going to be the most interesting part about this trip, but clearly I was mistaken."

"Interesting? Does that mean you're not scared of him? Scared of me? You're not going to turn me over to the Seekers?"

Sadiek laughed, which startled Ean at first but then relaxed as a broad smile appeared on the older man's face.

"Scared?" Sadiek got out eventually between laughs. "Of what? That little creature? Or you having a tie to the Abyss? Ean, my young lad, I'm a scholar. I'm not your typical villager scared by old stories and superstition. I seek out knowledge about things that most people shy away from, and the Abyss is one of those things."

"You have to promise me you won't tell anyone, Sadiek. I've already had a run-in with people that would kill me because of my connection to the Abyss. I'm glad you can accept it, but I would rather not risk trusting anyone else."

"I promise, Ean, I promise." Leaning forward, an almost hungry expression appeared on the man's face. "But you must tell me everything. Any recorded information about the Abyss and Ze'an has been lost or destroyed for decades. Whatever knowledge I can learn from you would be the envy of any scholar."

"Uh sure, I guess." The man's intense interest made Ean nervous, but he could keep back whatever information he wanted and the man would never know. "I guess there is no point in Zin hiding anymore. Come on out, Zin."

The imp appeared reluctantly from behind Ean, completely visible again, inching his way out and sitting as close as he could to Ean without touching him. Flashing Ean a look of pure annoyance, Zin settled in and folded his arms across his chest.

"Amazing," Sadiek said. "An actual creature from the Abyss. Does it do any tricks? Other than turning invisible, I mean. Like I said, so very little is known about--"

"I really think this is a bad idea, Ean," Zin interrupted, turning his back to Sadiek. "How much do we really know about this guy? For all you know he could be a devoted follower of you-know-who. What if he is just trying to get as much information out of you as he can before running off to the Seekers."

"It can talk!" Sadiek exclaimed, his hands going to his face.

"Yes, I can talk. Yes, I'm standing right here and can hear you, and yes I have razor sharp teeth," Zin growled. "Best that you remember that, old man."

"Zin, easy," Ean cut in. "He's just curious, is all. We have to trust him at this point, he already knows you exist. He might be able to help us, especially since he knows so much about the Deadlands."

"I would feel easier if he stopped looking at me like some prize to be dissected."

"Zin..."

"Fine, fine. Whatever you say." Pointing a clawed finger at Sadiek, Zin narrowed his eyes as he spoke. "I'll be keeping an eye on you, though. You never know when I might be around either. Keep that in mind."

For the briefest moment Ean thought he saw Sadiek's eyes grow cold as the imp addressed him, but they returned to wide-eyed interest so quickly that Ean thought he might have imagined it. It was hard to see much detail in the tent, after all.

"Well," Sadiek said. "What else can you tell me about the Abyss?"

"How Ean first started summoning creatures is none--"

Turning slightly to the imp, Ean put a hand on his back to cut him off before Zin gave too much away.

"Wait, you summoned this creature?" Sadiek leaned forward. A hungry look painted his face. "Is this true? Do you have magical powers as well?"

"I found a book, Sadiek," Ean replied. He raised his hands in a soothing manner when the man leaned in further. "But I lost it. What little I was able to get from it allowed me to summon Zin."

"Truly a shame. A book like that would be priceless. There has never been a book found that has any connection to the Abyss since after the Plague. They all were burned to ash."

"Well, it was written in the actual language of the Abyss, something that neither Zin nor I could translate very well. When we lost the book, we both simply gave up trying."

Leaning forward, Sadiek was nearly salivating. When he spoke, his voice was low and slightly commanding. "I might be able to help you, Ean. I am knowledgeable about all known languages in Ven Khilada. I can speak Taruun, Umdaer, and even a little of the language of the missing Aelcrane people. I'm sure with my ability to break down and decipher languages, I could help you figure out the language of the Abyss."

"Like I said, the book was lost. I don't know what you could--"

"You must remember something!"

Ean was caught off guard by the intensity of Sadiek's words. "A few words, a paragraph from the book...at the very least whatever you used to summon the imp." The older man rounded on Zin. "Or you must remember something. Ean said you knew some of the words. If you could write them down for me, maybe I could start to put together something, maybe rebuild the language."

Sadiek was smiling at Ean again, but for some reason now it seemed slightly off.

"We...um, might be able to come up with something. Between the two of us." Ean said, which earned him a "humph" from Zin. "Maybe given some time alone we could put something together."

"Excellent, excellent. Do you have paper? Something to write with?"

"No."

"Not a problem. I always travel with a bevy of writing supplies. I'll be right back."

And with that he was gone.

"Well," Zin said after a few moments of silence. "At least you weren't stupid enough to tell him about Azalea as well. Everything else on the other hand..."

"Zin, he saw you. I did my best to try and cover it up, but he wasn't even close to believing anything I said. Giving him a little bit of information made it easier to hide the more important bits."

"But to tell him about the book--"

"Which I said we lost."

"But we're giving him access to the language of the Abyss--"

"Zin, even with the book, it took a good deal of experimentation until I could even summon you. Do you really think he can do anything with a few dozen words?"

"Yeah, I suppose that's true."

"And just think what we can accomplish if he can come up with a key for the language. No more guessing at what kind of creature I'm summoning. No more fumbling blindly with my powers. By the Abyss, there could be pages of information about the tattoos. These things," he pulled back his glove to reveal the tattoos on his arm, "are slowly expanding over the entire right side of my body. I'd be lying if I said it wasn't making me nervous."

"Ok, ok. But we still don't know the man. Can we at least agree to keep as much secret from him as possible? At the very least he doesn't need to know about your tattoos."

"Agreed."

"And we should keep your 'sister' a secret as well. If this man does end up turning on us, it will be good to have Azalea as a secret weapon."

"I think you're being a bit overly paranoid, but if it will make you feel a little better, I can agree to that. I'll try to keep all of his focus on what scraps we give him and deciphering the language. I promise".

"Well, I guess that's something at least." Zin sounded less than thrilled, but he lay back on his elbows and seemed a little less tense. "But I am going to keep my eyes on him as much as possible. There is just something about him that I don't--"

"I'm back!" Sadiek said, rushing into the tent.

Zin shot back up, his lips pursing in a frown that showed off some of his teeth. Ean was surprised as well at the old man's speed. The travelers' wagons were parked quite some way from where Ean's tent had been set up. The old man must have sprinted the entire way to get back so quickly.

"Now," Sadiek said, either ignoring or not noticing their surprise. "Let's get to it."

Taking a seat, Sadiek pulled out a few pieces of paper, a few quills, and an inkwell from his robe. He passed a piece of paper and quill to both Zin and Ean, then stared at them expectantly.

"Start with words you know the meanings of, especially if you know both the human definition and the Abyss one."

"Well, I don't know exact translations..." Ean began.

"It's hard to match human words and those from the Abyss," Zin said over top of him. "Many words have similar meanings but not an exact translation."

"I'm sure you will do your best." Sadiek gestured towards the paper in each of their hands. "Best to get started."

Glancing at Zin for a moment, Ean got to the task at hand. He could think of maybe a dozen or so words off of the top of his head. The word for imp was an easy one. Zin's name, which meant "hope" in the Abysmal language, was one of the first he had learned. How Zin had come by it when he said every other imp in the Abyss was nameless was another one of his friend's secrets. The one time he had asked about it, Zin had tried to brush him off with his usual sarcasm, but Ean had seen the pain in those dark, beady eyes. He didn't push then and wouldn't any time in the future. Zin would either tell him when he was ready or he would hold on to that secret forever.

Glancing at his friend, he noticed that Zin had written more than twice as many words as Ean. Sadiek was staring at both lists as if they were well-cooked steaks.

"Is that it? Neither of you can think of more?"

"It's late, Sadiek." Ean handed over his list. Zin did the same. "Give us time. During the trip I'm sure we can come up with more."

"Hmmmph."

Sadiek pulled out a piece of paper and began to write. His attention went back and forth between what he was jotting down and the notes Ean and Zin had written. His penmanship was extremely neat and orderly, but none of what he was writing down made any sense to Ean.

"Is that a different language?" Zin asked.

"It's my own shorthand," Sadiek replied, not bothering to look up. "Makes taking notes easier and quicker. Once I start making some progress, I'll be sure to translate my notes into something you can read."

"Wonderful," Zin mumbled loud enough for everyone to hear. Sadiek seemed so caught up in what he was doing though that he missed the imp's sarcasm.

"Zin," Ean said in a soothing tone. "I'm sure that--"

"If you do not mind," Sadiek cut in crisply. "I can be easily distracted. If you could sit quietly, it would be greatly appreciated."

Both Ean and Zin stared at the man for a few moments. Turning to Zin, Ean shrugged, which of course earned him a roll of the imp's eyes, before leaning back on his sleeping pallet and letting the old man work. After all, if he could come up with a way for Ean to read the Abysmal Tome with ease, then any shortness or bother the man caused would certainly be worth it.

CHAPTER 20

DINNER CONVERSATIONS

THE NEXT FEW DAYS flew by. His mornings consisted of working in the Tinker's wagon, fixing pieces of equipment, and learning a great deal about wagon maintenance. As grumpy as Graden was to work with, he reminded Ean of Cleff, which made Ean homesick. Ean had never thought he would miss that place at all once he had left, so the aching for Rottwealth was unexpected.

When he had finished working for Graden and the wagons had stopped for lunch, he would always find Sadiek waiting for him. The old man wanted more words to work with and would practically drag Ean back to his wagon and try to coax some more information out of him. The man barely let him free the rest of the afternoon and was always pressuring him to make Zin join them. Ean would remind the man that Zin was a friend, not a slave, which always earned him a frown. They would remain behind the curtain that kept Sadiek's area of the wagon private. When the wagons eventually rolled to a halt, Sadiek would let him free with a grunt, and they would have dinner with Iacane, Fredren, and Creg.

Out of those three, Ean found Fredren to be the only one that he really was comfortable talking with. The young man was overly friendly, but not in an annoying sort of way, and Ean found his desire to map out the land very interesting. The maps that he had already created were finely detailed, from the tiny trees representing Rensen Forest to the individual streets and buildings of Lurthalan. The current map Fredren was working on, the one detailing the path they were taking from Lurthalan to the Deadlands, was updated each time Fredren showed it to him.

Unfortunately, Iacane was always close at hand and always joined them. The longer they traveled together, the more pompous and arrogant the man appeared to Ean. The man would find any connection to what they were talking about to launch into a longwinded story about some amazing feat of healing he had performed or someone interesting and powerful that he had saved. And every time, Ean and Fredren would just look at each other and roll their eyes.

Iacane was tolerable in small doses though, and sometimes the man could be funny, on the rare occasion he let himself relax a bit. Creg, on the other hand, was never pleasant. The boy would grumble under his breath and push his way past someone even when there was plenty of room in the wagon or outside to easily go around. Mercifully, he stayed in his small, secluded spot most of the time the wagons were moving and kept to himself outside once the wagons had stopped for the night. His very presence always seemed to rub everyone the wrong way. And with the Deadlands quickly approaching, everyone was already on edge.

The conversation leaned more and more towards the Deadlands. Ean couldn't tell if talking about it helped people feel better or worse. It certainly didn't help that each day when they awoke, people were missing. It started small, a wagon driver missing the first morning when everyone had awoken. Most people just chalked it up to nerves, saying that the pressure of going into the Deadlands had gotten to him. Ean could understand, having decided to carry on and enter the Deadlands, his nerves grew worse every day.

On the second day, though, three more drivers were missing, and every single person on the caravan became noticeably jumpier. On the third, five more workers were gone, meaning some of the loaders had to take over as drivers. Even Graden was forced to take over a driving shift on one of the wagons. That didn't improve the man's mood, and he certainly let Ean know what he thought about the whole situation. Needless to say, the third night had everyone nervous as they sat around the fire outside of the travelers' wagons.

"Well, are we going to talk about it or not?" Iacane said, breaking the silence that had covered their group since stopping for the night.

"Talk about what?" Fredren replied. The fact that he kept his eyes on the ground let the others know full well he knew what Iacane was getting at.

"The disappearances, of course! I've heard of people abandoning this trip, but nine? Most of which, according to the people I've talked to, have been regulars on this trip for years. I think something much more sinister is going on here than a couple of nervous drivers not wanting to face the Deadlands."

"Sinister?" Sadiek laughed. "Iacane, I think you are jumping to conclusions. Or, are you hoping to uncover some mysterious plot and add to your repertoire of amazing stories?"

"Joke all you want, but all of the workers I've talked to have said it's very strange to have nine abandon their jobs. Four or five before we reach the edge of the Deadlands, maybe. But nine?"

"All of the workers you've talked to? You mean the two men in charge of driving our wagon, don't you? I wouldn't exactly call that a lot of people." Raising his hands to cut off a response, Sadiek continued on. "Let's look at the facts, shall we?"

"One, men abandoning their jobs is common place on this caravan. Everyone agrees that to be true."

"Two, all of the men's possessions are gone. Did the two men you talk to mention that, Iacane? Because the dozen or so I asked made sure to mention it."

"Three, all of the workers sleep close together during the night and there are guards patrolling. It would be much simpler for a man to sneak out of the camp than for something to sneak in, take these men AND their belongings, and sneak back out. Especially five in one night."

"Four, there is already a great deal of trepidation about going into the Deadlands. Add to the fact some people," Sadiek blatantly stared at Iacane for a moment, "are talking about sinister plans making people disappear, and of course it becomes more likely for a larger number of people to want to leave. I believe," Sadiek finished up, "that if you connect all of those facts together it becomes clear that all we have are nine men that decided whatever they were getting paid was not enough for the risks involved. I am sure that if, after this trip, we went to the families of all the men that disappeared, we would find them safely at home."

"Your facts and theories are all well and good," Iacane growled, "but I will still be sleeping lightly the rest of this trip".

"Feel free," Sadiek said, shaking his head. "Tomorrow we'll reach Wethrinter where I'm sure even more will decide to abandon their jobs. And as usual, according to those that I have spoken to, men from Wethrinter will be hired to finish out the rest of the journey. Apparently it happens every time, and I don't plan on losing any sleep over it."

"And if you're wrong?"

"Then you can come and rescue me great, Saniteal, and repeatedly tell me 'I told you so' until I can't take it anymore."

"Keep joking," Iacane grumbled, getting up and turning to walk away. "We'll see if I even bother trying to rescue you if you disappear." And with that he stormed off and entered their wagon, slamming the door behind him.

"You didn't have to mock him," Fredren said after the Saniteal had gone inside. "You have to admit, nine people disappearing..."

Sadiek waved the younger man off like he was shooing away a fly. "Don't you buy into all that 'sinister plot' drivel. You know as well as Ean and I, that man will look for any excuse to find something he can fix."

"Don't bring me into this," Ean finally chimed in. He could see the merits of both the scholar's and the Saniteal's opinions. The men Ean had talked with over the past few days had said that the men's possessions were gone, but they were still nervous about so many leaving, just as Iacane was. Even Graden thought that nine men gone before they even reached Wethrinter was a little suspicious. Of course on the other hand, Sadiek was a fairly intelligent man and Ean trusted him. Had to trust him of course, but trusted him all the same.

Rounding on Ean, Sadiek shook his head sadly. "Come on, my boy, don't you buy into it too. I'll admit on any other trip even a few people suddenly gone would be highly suspicious. But this is a trip into the Deadlands, a trip that could very well infect any one of us with the Plague. A person would have to be a fool to not be at least a little afraid of that. Honestly I'm surprised more people don't run off."

"Sadiek is right," Fredren said, sounding more like he was trying to convince himself than Ean. "The closer we get, the more I want to give up as well. Luckily I have our little group to keep me confident that everything will be ok. I don't want to start freaking myself out more because less than a dozen guys got cold feet."

"Fine, fine." Ean could see the other young man's point. No need to upset them more than the thought of going into the Deadlands was already doing. It wasn't like Ean could do anything about the missing men anyway. What could he do, summon his Abysmal Hound to try and sniff the men out? Anyway, if anything ever came when he was sleeping, Zin would warn him. The imp slept very little to begin with and was a fairly light sleeper at that.

"Good," Sadiek said as he rose to stir the pot of stew that would eventually be their dinner. "Then let's move on to happier topics."

But there was very little talk from that point on. They sat around in silence, ate in silence, and all wandered off to bed in silence. Even Zin was quiet, sitting in the corner of their tent and chewing on some small animal carcass. By the time the imp had finished his meal, Ean was already under the blankets and just starting to drift off to sleep.

"We need to talk," Zin said, interrupting Ean's attempt to fall asleep. "Tomorrow we'll be at Wethrinter and then it's into the Deadlands".

"Mmhmm."

"I think all this time spent with Sadiek needs to stop, and you need to return to learning more from the Abysmal Tome on your own."

Turning his head sideways, he could barely make the imp out now in the tiny level of light that peaked through the tent flaps. "Why? From what he's said, he is close to figuring out at least what some of the individual symbols mean and could start making a key as early as tomorrow night. Wouldn't that be better than the two of us grasping in the dark for the meanings of individual characters and symbols?"

"I don't trust him, Ean. I've been keeping my eyes on him and something does not feel right. He talks to himself you know. I haven't been able to get close enough to hear what he says, but I've heard him mumbling to himself plenty of times."

"He's probably just trying to work things out in his head. Old Cleff used to do that all the time, remember, and he is as sharp as a knife."

"I'm telling you, something about him rubs me the wrong way. It's a gut feeling that I just can't shake."

"It's probably just a bit of paranoia, because he knows some of our secrets. The old guy seems harmless, and he is sharp enough not to let anything slip."

"All the same, humor me. Tomorrow, once we've settled into the village for the night, let's work on learning from the Tome together without Sadiek."

Turning over on his side, Ean grunted. "Fine, fine. Sadiek can handle just working off of his notes for one night. Now can I go to bed?"

"Of course. You should be as rested as possible. We have no idea what we'll find in the Deadlands, and especially what is in my old master's lair if we can find it. Best to start resting up now."

"Mmhmm," was all Ean felt the need to reply as he closed his eyes. It only took a matter of moments before he was fast asleep.

CHAPTER 21

A STROLL AROUND TOWN

IT ONLY TOOK HALF of the morning before Wethrinter came into sight.

Sitting out in the middle of an open plain, the village of Wethrinter was similar in size to Rottwealth, built in what seemed to be an ever-growing circle. Farmlands dotted the landscape all around the village, each with dozens of workers out in the fields. One main dirt road started outside of the village and ran right through the middle of it, effectively dividing the village in half. The wagons of the caravan passed right through town and stopped on the northern outskirts, letting Ean get a good view of the town in the process. Graden had to take over driving another wagon, which left Ean free that morning to observe the town as they passed through.

While similar in size to Rottwealth, the buildings of Wethrinter more closely resembled the more modern ones found in Lurthalan. Medium-sized two story buildings stacking up against each other lined the main road. The buildings themselves were a mixture of stone and wood, similar in build but each one vastly different in color and design. Most of the first floors, for instance, consisted of a single front door on the far left or right side and two windows spaced evenly on the other side. Each door was painted a different color, however, not one repeated until at least a few buildings down, and the windows varied from shutters to drapes to nothing at all in the buildings that were clearly stores.

Narrow alleys that ran deeper into town ran between a few of the houses. Larger streets appeared every now and then, but they also quickly turned off from the main road and were lost behind other buildings. Fredren would have his work cut out for him if he was going to map the town.

Where Lurthalan had a section of the city cordoned off for the sale of goods and services, Wethrinter's business fronts were randomly intermingled among the houses. Glancing down the larger side streets showed a similar lack of organization, as shop signs hung randomly in between regular houses.

When the wagons finally came to a stop in a flat area of earth and weeds to the north of town, Ean thought briefly about finding his traveling companions or the new people he met on this trip, but knowing they each had plans of their own, he decided to go exploring instead. The only one that might be available was Sadiek, but Ean would rather be alone than be grilled by the overly inquisitive man. Better to put off seeing the man until evening and hope that he did not run into Sadiek somewhere in town.

He navigated through workers loading and unloading wagons until he found himself at the edge of town. After wandering the dusty streets for a while, he finally found the inn, The Last Stop, at the center of Wethrinter. A little further south, across from a row of shuttered homes, he spied the mortar and pestle sign of a Healer's shop. With two options before him--grab a well-cooked meal and something to drink or converse about the healing trade with the store owner--Ean decided to do a bit more exploring before making a decision.

He was about to start moving again when an arm wrapped around his neck.

"There is my little brother!" Azalea said playfully, pulling him close.

Ean's face rubbed against the brown fabric of her robe as she pulled him in, or at least the illusion of it. Whatever magic she used to conceal her true form certainly worked well. In reality his face was rubbing against her skin, probably right against...

With a start he pulled away quickly, which just earned him a laugh from Azalea. Ean could only imagine how red his face must look. Why did she always insist on messing with him?

"Oh, brother, how I've missed your innocence. The men I've been spending my time with are, well, let's just say, not innocent." She let out another laugh before patting him on the back. "But now that we have some down time, I wanted to spend some time together. Make sure you don't think I'm too rotten of a 'person.'"

She winked at him then, and despite everything, Ean had to fight to hold back a smile. Even without her powers to manipulate him, she was charming enough on her own. But he wasn't about to let her get too confident. Without knowing it, she had helped him decide what to do next.

"Well, I'm about to head to the local Healer to see what kind of supplies he has, maybe see if he knows any remedies that I might not have learned. I'm sure it won't be that interesting to you."

"Splendid!" she replied. "You've tried talking to me in the past about what you can do and have almost put me to sleep. Maybe if I can actually see these plants it would spark my interest." She gave him a quick jab with her elbow. "Probably not, but it's worth a try."

"Really, that's ok. I'm sure you would find much more entertainment in the inn--"

"I've had plenty of entertainment on the road here," she replied, winking at him again. "That's why you haven't seen me at night. I've been having too much fun."

A thought crashed into Ean's mind. All of those missing men... Could Azalea...

His facial expressions must have matched the dark thoughts, as Azalea untangled her arm from his and slightly pushed him away. "It wasn't me!" Her lower lip curled into an indignant pout. "We made a deal, Ean, and I stick to my deals. I've been having my fun," she leaned in closer and lowered her voice, "but no one has died. Honest, I've been good. Well, maybe not good, but I haven't taken a life since that farm."

Azalea actually looked on the verge of crying. Was it all an act? Could the Yulari even shed tears? Or was she so used to manipulating people that the actions came naturally to her? But something made him believe her, something that Azalea probably had no idea that she had even done. Her eyes, those magnificent dark red pools, had flashed through her disguise for the briefest moment. Ean locked that observation away; it would certainly come in handy.

"Fine, fine," he said, lifting his hands in a calming gesture. "I believe you. But has anyone you've been around said anything about the disappearances?"

"Yes, yes," she said quickly. "Meganan was ranting about it all last night. He was infuriated that so many men, some that had been with him for countless years, had decided to 'chicken out' on this trip. All of his little followers and servants found it strange and a little frightening, but Meganan has been too angry to view what has been happening as anything but the men being cowards."

"And what do you think about the missing men?"

Shrugging, she took his arm again and pulled him close. "I only know what my kind would do in this situation. An intelligent creature like myself certainly wouldn't have taken so many men. It's too noticeable, and as you've seen, makes most people paranoid and nervous. Not a very good idea if you want to keep unnoticed. In my opinion, if something is taking these men, then it's either not very intelligent or its too hungry or driven by something else to care about the fear it is causing."

So either hardened men that had been to the Deadlands countless times had gotten spooked or some sinister creature had snatched them away against their will in the middle of the night. Neither option bode well for Ean.

"But not to worry," Azalea said, reaching over with her free hand and messing with his hair. "You have me to look after you. I'll make sure to stick by you more once we enter these Deadlands. That should help you feel better!"

"I appreciate that, Azalea, I really do."

"You better!" she said, bumping him slightly with her hip. "Now let's go see this ever so exciting store of plants. Maybe at the very least there will be a pretty flower you can buy me to wear in my hair."

"We'll see."

The Healer's store sat just south of the inn, a small alleyway separating the two buildings. Hanging racks of assorted plants hung out front, some of which Ean had never seen. Through the window he saw enough plants to fill a greenhouse. Potted plants covered the sill, while vines coiled around the many shelves. It made Ean think of his home and the myriad of plants that Cleff grew throughout the house. So as he reached for the door, he couldn't help feeling a mixture of nostalgia and excitement...

And was immediately disappointed to find it locked.

After knocking a few times, Ean detached himself from Azalea's arm and moved over to a window. There was no sign stating that the store was closed, but everything else seemed to indicate as much. Peering inside, he was disappointed to see a dark storeroom, the outlines of different plants barely visible. Tapping on the window, Ean couldn't help but show a little of the frustration he was feeling. Azalea, on the other hand, didn't bother hiding her relief.

"Ah well, I guess fondling plants and boring ourselves to death talking about them is not in the cards for today." She punched him playfully in the arm in what Ean imagined was an attempt to take some of the harshness out of her words. "So now it's my turn to decide what we do, and I say we walk into that inn, grab ourselves a table, and have some fun."

"I haven't exactly had the best experiences with drinking, Azalea."

"Yes, I've seen, and I do take partial responsibility for the nights I've been around." Her face scrunched up slightly and she shook her head. "I might have been trying to get you drunk so you wouldn't stop me from having some fun."

Ean opened his mouth, but she quickly cut him off with raised hands.

"Not that I would have, you know..." she paused for a moment, dragging a finger across her throat, "but I thought you would stop me from even using my charms to mess with all of the gentlemen gathered. I promise though, this time will be different. Fun in moderation."

Ean wanted to yell at her, but what good would it do? Azalea was a Yulari just being a Yulari. Ean would have as much impact yelling at a dog for stealing food off a table. It was just her nature, and Ean had to get used to it--to a degree.

"Fine," he said, trying to sound at least a little angry, but his heart wasn't in it. "Let's go have your version of fun. We have the rest of the day to kill anyway. At the very least I heard some music coming from inside. That should be entertaining."

"Good!" Clapping her hands together, she jumped up and down in happiness. "But I promise the people inside will be more entertaining than the music. You just wait and see."

CHAPTER 22

A DRINK AMONGST FRIENDS

"TWO GLASSES OF YOUR house ale," Azalea said, smiling at the serving girl from their table. They had only been seated in the inn for a few moments before the waitress had walked up. Turning to Ean, she tilted her head slightly. "Are you hungry? We could order food too. I don't usually eat...bar food...but I could share something with you if you're hungry."

"No, uh, I'm fine, thanks."

"Suit yourself. Alright, just the two drinks, please."

"Two drinks will be fourteen coppers," the waitress replied. Before he could pull any money out from his meager supply, Azalea sprinkled about a dozen silver coins onto the table.

"This will cover us, at least for the first part of the afternoon I think." Grabbing one off the table, she tossed it a bit forcefully at the girl. "Now why don't you run off and get our drinks?"

Fumbling with the coin for a moment, the girl bowed slightly to Azalea and hurried off. Letting out a low growl, Azalea leaned back in her chair and watched the girl weave her way through the crowd for a moment before turning to Ean. "Money, money, money. That's all most of you humans care about. You all seem to think power comes from money, but power comes from so many other things."

"That's not what I think."

She looked him up and down in the same way the serving girl had. "Clearly not, or else you wouldn't always be wearing the same beat up clothes." She laughed a bit as a frown appeared on Ean's face. "Oh, I'm just teasing. Well, slightly teasing at least. You really could try something new every once in a while, you know."

"My gloves are kind of a permanent accessory now. They don't really go with fancier clothes. It doesn't leave me with too many other options."

"True," she nodded, then shot him a wink. "But you won't always have to have those arms covered up, my boy."

"What does that mean? I'll always have these tattoos on the one arm and ugly scars on the other. The scars I'm not that self-conscious about any more, but glowing tattoos could certainly get me the wrong type of attention."

Reaching over, she patted him on the cheek. "Don't you worry about that."

The waitress appeared at that point, stopping Ean from pressing the question. She placed the two cups of ale carefully in front of them and deposited six copper pieces into the pile of coins on the table. "Is there anything else I can get you at the moment?" Her tone was slightly less haughty, but her eyes were filled with contempt whenever they passed over Azalea.

"No, but why don't you keep the drinks coming when our mugs get low. At least for a few more rounds," she winked at Ean. "We'll probably slow down a bit after the fourth. Or maybe the third. My brother has trouble handling his drink sometimes."

"As you wish," the serving girl said curtly, then turned and stalked off. Azalea watched her go again, giving Ean the opportunity to try and continue his line of questioning.

"You didn't answer me. What did you mean when you said I wouldn't have to always hide my tattoos?"

Appearing to ignore his question, Azalea let out a short laugh as she kept her attention focused on the serving girl.

"Azalea, I want--"

"Want to know why the girl is so snobby? Or at least what I think is the reason?"

"That's not exactly something I'm going to lose sleep--"

"She has waves of jealousy mixed with lust wafting off of her. I can feel it from all the way across the room. The jealousy picks up whenever she passes that one woman leaning near the entrance to the kitchen, and the lust increases whenever she passes that man that's been moving about talking to all of the tables. I would bet two imps and a Hound that the man is the owner, the woman his wife, and the serving girl is sleeping with the owner."

"You got all of that just by tasting the emotions coming off of them and watching them for a few moments?"

"It's just a guess, but an educated guess. I could charm the serving girl and have her tell us if I'm right."

"No. No need for that."

"You sure? I like knowing whether I'm right or wrong. Think of it as a way to make sure I understand humans, because if I have to pass as one, I should be able to figure things like that out."

"Not necessary," he said quickly. "Let's just assume you're right".

"Fine, fine. I'm more interested in this pompous man walking towards us anyway. The pride radiating off him could feed a family of Yulari for a week, and my kind have VERY large families."

Cringing slightly, Ean had an idea who she was talking about even before a hand clasped down on his shoulder and a familiar voice boomed over the crowd noise and music.

"Ean, my boy!" Iacane's voice had the slight slur of a man that was already a few drinks down. Moving around Ean, he sat down in between Ean and Azalea and let his eyes scan over the Yulari. "If this is your sister, I feel slighted that you have been hiding away such a beautiful creature. And if it's not, then good job to you, my boy. I didn't think you were this much of a ladies man."

"Azalea, this is Iacane" Ean grumbled. "Iacane, this is my sister, Azalea."

"Sister! Excellent! Pleasure to meet you, of course." Iacane slid his chair slightly closer to the Yulari. "Let me properly introduce myself. My name is Iacane Brill, the greatest Saniteal in Ven Khilada."

"Pleasure, I'm sure," Azalea said dryly.

"Ean hasn't told me or my companions much about you. You would think the boy was ashamed to have such a stunning girl for a sister."

"That is not true, I just--"

"It's quite alright, brother," Azalea said, cutting Ean off. "I understand. My brother and I don't always agree on things, and it's caused problems in the past. I'm trying to fix things now though."

"Disagree with you?" the Saniteal scoffed. "Must simply be sibling rivalry making him speak against you."

"No, no, it's true. I'm quite difficult to live with. I always seem to be getting in trouble." Leaning forward, the Yulari batted her eyes towards the man and her voice dropped to a low purr. "Most other people don't seem to mind the trouble I get in, though. I'm sure the two of us could--"

"Enough Azalea." Ean had to cut in. "I thought we were going to relax and enjoy ourselves."

"Of course, you're right, brother." Leaning back, Azalea's entire demeanor changed. The smokiness left her voice and she relaxed back into her chair. She snatched her mug off the table and downed the rest of her drink in one big gulp before she slammed it back down. "To relaxing!"

The men stared at her for a moment, both equally caught off guard by her sudden change in personality.

"Erm, yes..." Iacane replied. "To relaxing and having a bit of fun. The gods know we need it now, before we enter the Deadlands." Taking his own mug, he tilted it back for a moment before carefully placing it back down.

"So tell me," Iacane continued. "Why is a beauty like yourself making such a risky trip into the Deadlands? Your brother here has been tight-lipped on his reasons, but surely your own must not be that secretive."

"Oh, but my reason is a terrible secret. The truth would actually scramble your mind, it's so dark and terrifying. You see, I'm not even human, I'm actually--"

"Ok, that's enough fun," Ean cut in quickly. "Enough jokes, Azalea. Tomorrow is going to be stressful enough as it is without making up stories. I'm sure all three of us would benefit from talking about happier subjects."

"Hush, Ean," Iacane leaned closer to Azalea, a small smile touching his lips. "I'm a grown man, and I think I can handle whatever little story your sister wants to tell."

"Exactly," Azalea said, sticking out her tongue briefly at Ean before leaning closer to Iacane. "Now, before my brother rudely interrupted, I was about to tell you my dark secret. You see, I'm actually a soul-sucking creature from the Abyss, and Ean is my Master."

"Oh, really? How intriguing! And what evil plot have you both come up with that involves going into the Deadlands?"

"Simple. We plan to enter the old lair of the creator of the Plague, take any remaining items or knowledge that we can find, and raise Ean up to conquer the world."

"Brilliant!" Iacane exclaimed, clapping his hands together. "For a moment there I almost believed you. You seemed so serious. And talking about such taboo subjects like the Abyss and the Plague. If I had let you keep going, you would have mentioned Ze'an himself, I think."

"No, I've never met the Lord of the Abyss myself. I don't like to drop names of people I've never even seen. I'm not that prideful of a creature."

"Ean my boy, you have the most interesting sister I have ever met," Iacane said, clapping Ean roughly on the back. "Most people, especially women, would shy away from talking about such things. Why, I've heard of people flat out disappearing in Lurthalan for speaking too much about the Abyss and Ze'an."

"Yes," Ean grumbled, "my sister certainly does not have much tact when it comes to certain topics and a vivid imagination to boot." Turning to Azalea, he tried giving her his most intense stare. "I'm just a simple Healer after all. I haven't the slightest interest in fame or glory. And taking over the world sounds like more trouble than it's worth."

"That's my brother for you, can't even pretend to be ambitious. If Ean even got the smallest amount of power, he would have no idea what to do with it. Thankfully, what he lacks in ambition he more than makes up for with his ability to keep me entertained. Why just the other night he had a bit too much to drink and I had to practically carry him up to his bed."

Iacane leaned back and let out a deep, bellowing laugh. Ean had never seen the man this jovial before. The sudden change must surely have originated from the bottom of his mug.

"Ean, my poor boy," the Saniteal said in-between bouts of laughter. "You certainly don't get a break from your sister, do you?"

"No, not even a little one," Ean growled.

Azalea moved quickly around the table and wrapped her arms around Ean's shoulder in a tight hug.

"Oh, you know I'm only teasing." Moving her hands up to cover Ean's ears, she pretended to whisper to Iacane, "Don't tell my brother, but I'm quite fond of him. Flaws and all. What he really needs is a little guidance every now and then, which is why it's a good thing he has me around."

"Yes, I'm quite lucky, because you've spent so much time with me this trip."

Azalea placed a hand over her heart. "Ean! Does that mean you've missed me?" Reaching down she gave him another hug. "Well, don't you worry. Like I've said, I'll be around you much, much more from this point on."

"And I will make sure to look out for you both," Iacane cut in quickly. His attention, however, was entirely on Azalea. "To make sure nothing bad happens to you while we are in the Deadlands."

Azalea shot the Saniteal a smile and slowly returned to her seat. On the way she paused long enough to pat Iacane on the head. "That is most generous of you, and greatly appreciated."

"And unnecessary," Ean grumbled, but seemed to be ignored by the other two.

Falling back into her chair, Azalea grabbed her empty mug and used it to pound the table a few times. "Now, I don't know about you gentlemen, but I came here to drink and have some fun. All I need at the moment is for that surly waitress to get back here and fill my mug."

Iacane grabbed his own mug and drained the contents before slamming it down as well.

"Agreed!" he said, his voice sounding even more slurred. "To a night of fun!"

Despite himself, Ean slowly began to have some fun as the night wore on. Azalea continued to drink like each mug was her last, but she never showed any signs of the alcohol affecting her. She lessened the jabs she took at Ean as well, instead turning her insults on those around the table. The Yulari still made comments every now and then about Ean having no direction or idea what he was really doing, but each comment was accompanied by a genuine smile or wink.

Iacane on the other hand, who had already been slightly drunk when he sat down, continued to spiral down as he finished off more and more mugs. At first it was entertaining, as the usually serious man was more relaxed and less conceited. But as the afternoon turned to dusk and dusk turned to night, the boastful and arrogant Iacane made a reappearance.

The Saniteal dominated the conversation during the late night hours with stories that Ean had mostly heard already, except embellished even more. Whenever he would start one, Ean would immediately zone out and stare down into his mug. Azalea seemed interested at first, but she too slowly got tired of listening to the man speak about himself. While Ean pretended to listen, Azalea made a show of NOT listening; yawning loudly, turning to talk to the people seated around them, even going so far as to try speaking directly over what Iacane was saying.

But the Saniteal continued, the amount of drinks he had in him either making him not realize what she was doing or not caring. It finally took the man placing his head down on the table and passing out for him to quiet down, but even in his sleep he continued to mumble as if he was continuing his stories. That was the signal that the three of them should call it a night.

Leaving Iacane in the capable and stronger hands of some of the caravan workers to get him back to his tent, Ean and Azalea headed back to the collection of wagons. By this point Ean was a bit wobbly and happy to accept Azalea's help in making their way back. At the beginning of their walk, they kept silent, with Ean's arm draped around the Yulari's shoulder, but some thoughts that had always been swirling around in Ean's mind finally slipped out of his mouth.

"Azalea," Ean said, trying his best not to slur his words. "Why are you sticking around? What did you and Zin agree on?"

"What can I say," the Yulari laughed, keeping her attention straight ahead. "I'm a fan of the corruption and greed that exists in this world. It's an unending supply of nourishment and tastes much sweeter than the creatures I feed off of in the Abyss."

"That's not all of it, and you know it."

She was silent for a time, trudging with him past the flickering light of the few lamps lit on the main street. The tiny flames did little to illuminate much past the building walls they were attached to and sent shadows running around inside of the windows and down the alleys. When Azalea finally answered, her voice was lower and had an inflection that Ean had never heard from her before.

"Do you know what the Abyss is really like, Ean?"

"I pictured it as a place where all of the creatures created by Ze'an are running around together. Zin said it's divided into different levels, and some creatures control those levels. He also said it's a horrible place for his kind."

"Your imp friend is right, but it's much more than that, even if you are a more powerful creature. Unless you are at the top of the food chain, it's a constant battle for survival. It's a fight to control those weaker than you, so that you in turn can use them and not become controlled by those stronger than you. It's a battle to not become someone's possession, used up and tossed aside on a whim. And that's not just by other creatures stronger than you, it's by your own kind as well. I'm considered young for my kind, which means the majority of the older and stronger members of my race could easily snatch me away and use me for whatever they wished. There is no peace in the Abyss, no safety."

Azalea paused for a moment, making Ean stop as well. Turning to him, Ean could actually see pain in her slightly squinted eyes and downturned lips. And although the alcohol might be playing a part in his thoughts, he actually believed it to be a genuine emotion from the Yulari.

"This, Ean," she said, waving a hand that took in the two of them and then the rest of the world, "is peace. This is freedom."

Hoisting Ean into a better position, she turned away and started them moving again. Through the fog of his ale-laden mind, Ean tried to process what the Yulari had said.

"But you're not free," he finally got out. "You're tied to me just as tightly I'm sure as you would have been to some strong creature in the Abyss."

"And a creature in the Abyss would have used my mind, body, and spirit in any way they wanted. Do you plan on using me in the same way?"

"Of course not!" Ean said quickly.

"And that, my boy, is why I consider our relationship as being free." A small smile touched the corner of her lip. "I can handle the rules you put in place because to survive in this world undetected, I would probably have to follow those rules anyway. Plus, I find your own inner conflicts interesting."

"My own inner conflicts? What do--"

"Enough questions, my little human. I feel like we just had a moment, you and I. Let's just enjoy it in silence for a moment, yes?"

Ean complied. Instead of talking, he concentrated on putting one foot in front of the other, which was getting more difficult by the minute. Back in the tent, she helped him ease onto the cot before taking a step towards the exit.

"Azalea, wait."

"Yes?"

"I trust you, Azalea. I just wanted you to know that."

She stood there, facing him, her face barely visible in the low level of light peaking in from the outside. Ean strained to catch her expression, but the combination of moonlight and the alcohol made it impossible. When the Yulari finally responded, her voice was low and serious.

"You probably shouldn't...but thank you."

Without another word she was gone, the tent flaps closing behind her, leaving him in darkness.

CHAPTER 23

ENTERING THE DEADLANDS

IN THE DARKNESS BEFORE dawn, the caravan workers loaded the wagons. By first light, the wagons set off to the north with Ean bobbing along in the back of one with an apple in his hand. An unseasonably cold wind began to howl out over the lake and follow them as they moved past it. It was as if the air itself was trying to warn the caravan about their destination.

When the sun reached its peak, the wagons began to slow down. The animals began to act restless, crying out and digging in their hooves, refusing to move for no apparent reason. Even their owners seemed on edge. Men yelled out orders in crackling voices. The usual chatter that accompanied the squeaking of the wheels had died off. Peeking out the back and around the wagons in front of him at what was ahead, Ean immediately began to get a feeling of dread.

The lead wagon was the first to disappear into a wall of dense fog that stretched from east to west as far as the Ean's eye could see, as if they had come to a point in the world where the gods had run out of material and light. The sight of it sent a chill up Ean's spine, which grew to a frost the closer they got to that wall. As they drew closer, something else mixed in with the dread. Something was reaching for him. Pulling at him. Something familiar...

"Cover up, brother."

Ean jumped as he felt Azalea's hand tugging at his right glove while her other hand pulled his sleeve down. He hadn't felt her coming or heard her climb up into the wagon. She took a seat next to him in the back, her hands still resting on his arm.

"Azalea, you almost gave me a heart attack. Do you not see what we're riding into? Now is not the time for surprises."

"For one, yes, I did see what we're riding into, which is why I came back here to be with you. I told you I was going to stick with you from this point on. And it's a good thing I did. You clearly didn't even notice your arm."

"My arm? What do you mean..." Looking down he saw a small amount of his arm between his glove and sleeve still exposed. The tattoos were glowing as brightly as if he was full of as much energy from the Abyss as he could hold. For a moment Ean thought he had taken in the power, maybe out of reflex at being nervous. But not a single drop of the power flowed through his body. He wanted it, though. Almost like he needed it.

Snatching his arm from Azalea's grip, he covered his skin by tucking its edges into the glove. The move blocked off the light, but it didn't get rid of the dread or the hunger. Part of him desired to fill his body with the energy of the Abyss. Become intoxicated with its power. His rational side, however, feared that desire. Feared what he could become if he so easily gave in to his hunger.

"Oh, calm down," Azalea said, apparently seeing the angst in his expression. "I thought you would have expected something like this. After all, from what I've heard, this whole Plague or whatever it's called, originated from the Abysmal energy released when Zin's previous master died. It's only natural that it should still exist in one form or another."

"Except this feels wrong...or at least off." He took a quick glance towards the front of the caravan. The wall of fog was only three wagons ahead of his now. "I was worried about the Plague making me a Living Dead. But what if the fog interacts with my body differently because of my tattoos?"

A variety of scenarios took form in his head. Two taking prominence:

-An unstoppable amount of energy rushing into him until his body couldn't hold anymore and he exploded;

-The Plague working on his body at an accelerated rate, rotting off his skin and corrupting his mind, turning him into a horrible monster...

Every thought made him want to leave before he reached that fog. What was he trying to find anyway? Power? Knowledge? Healing is my trade, Ean reminded himself. If he had any sense left, he'd jump out of the wagon and run back to Rottwealth. Why should he let curiosity potentially end his life, or worse, change him into something resembling Zin's old master?

Curiosity was the force behind him stealing the book in the first place. It was what drove him to experiment with the runes he had found between the pages and summon Zin, then later Azalea. After all this time, as he trekked toward the Deadlands, he wondered if this insatiable curiosity would finally lead him to his doom.

Zin and Azalea.

Ean trusted them more than most of the humans he had ever met. An imp and a Yulari. Both still hid things from him, he was almost positive of that, but they had shown more loyalty than most humans in his life. Was it that he gave them their freedom from the Abyss that elicited their loyalty, or was he growing on them just as much as they had grown on him? He hoped it was the latter, at least for Azalea. Zin, he trusted with his life. As much as he had liked to blame the imp anytime they both got in trouble, more often than not it was Ean that had gotten them in trouble in the first place. Well, Zin had said that he should be alright, so--

A blow that felt like a hammer the size of a wagon nearly knocked him out of the back of the wagon. Azalea grabbed him as he began to roll over the back, saving him from a painful tumble to the ground.

Her face had gone pale and she was shaking slightly as she wrapped her arms around her body. Ean tried to ask her what happened, but another invisible hammer seemed to strike his very being. Then the blows began to fall like rain. He tried to move to Azalea's side, tried to call out, but all he seemed to control was his vision. Everything was taking on a purplish hue, as if someone had placed a thin curtain over his eyes...

Not a curtain. It was the fog.

They had passed into the Deadlands.

CHAPTER 24

A WELCOME AND A WARNING

"THIS IS HORRIBLE," AZALEA whimpered, holding herself tighter. "I didn't think I would be able to feel the Plague. It's like someone filled my mouth and stomach with bile."

Ean wished that was all he was feeling at the moment. What had started out as hammer blows, now felt like drills boring into his bones...as if the Plague was trying to eat its way to his very core. Was this what everyone felt or was it only unique to him?

"Azalea... I..." The pain made it practically impossible to string words together. "Too much...can't..."

A vicious blow doubled him over. He fought the darkness with every ounce of willpower he could muster. If he passed out, there was no telling what might happen. The Plague might overwhelm him. But it was becoming a more and more difficult battle as the Plague seemed to suck the energy right out of him while at the same time trying to drill into his body. He needed more strength to hold the plague off.

Strength.

Without another thought, he opened himself to his connection with the Abyss.

The energy flooded into him, filling him to the brink in an instant. His shirt scarcely contained the glow of the tattoos covering his right hand and arm, a strong outline blazed through the bland brown of his clothes. The power felt good, like soaking in a hot bath on a cold night. It had been a while since he had opened up to the Abyss, and he had almost forgotten what a rush it was to have all of that energy inside of him.

Just as quickly as the energy filled him, the pain was gone. The pressure was still there, trying to squeeze in on him like a hoard of ants, but he no longer felt like it was trying to pierce his entire body. He lifted his head and the resistance made him feel like he was underwater. It was uncomfortable and strange, but it was much more preferable.

Looking over at Azalea, she seemed to be adjusting too, although not as well. The illusion she adopted still looked healthy, but the way she was holding her body made it seem like she was about to be sick up in the wagon. Her body still shook, her arms trembling as she pulled her knees against her body. Her eyes were locked on Ean, though. Was that concern painted across her face?

"You seem to be doing better," she said, her expression quickly changing to that of annoyance. Had Ean imagined the concern? "I feel like I've digested a month's worth of mud."

"For a moment there, I felt like I was going to die."

"You looked like it, too. Why the sudden turn-around?"

Shrugging, which again felt weird against the pressure pushing down on him, Ean inched closer to Azalea. "I needed strength not to pass out, so I took in as much energy from the Abyss as I could. That stopped the pain, but I guess I have to hold onto it for as long as we're here to keep the pain out."

It was the Yulari's turn to shrug. "So?"

"I'm just not comfortable with having the power inside me more than necessary. It's...strange"

Letting out a small laugh that seemed somewhat forced, Azalea scooted her way the rest of the distance between them and leaned her head on his shoulder. She smelled nice, like the sweet Javaran flowers that people used to freshen up their homes. Ean wondered if that was natural or just another part of her illusion.

"You should embrace your power, Ean." Although Azalea seemed to relax against him, her voice was still strained. "Enjoy the power you can control."

"Let's talk about something else. Something pleasant or funny."

"Alright. You're a funny boy, Ean," she said, adjusting her head slightly on his shoulder. "Even without my charms, most men would be very interested in the illusion of the girl I appear to be. Not you, though. I can only taste the barest hint of lust coming off of you."

"What? I don't feel that way..."

Giggling, which was something he had never heard her do before, she entwined one of her arms in his. "I said it was just a tiny amount, you prude. Relax."

"Oh, well, ok then. I'm probably not attracted to you, because I know what you really are."

"Oh."

Ean was the farthest thing from an expert in women, but even he couldn't miss the hurt in that one word. "I mean, I know we are just partners, I guess. Companions. I wasn't implying what you really are isn't attractive."

His stuttering words were met with another laugh and she pulled herself closer. "Just shut up, you silly boy. I feel too sick to talk anyway. Let me take a nap. Hopefully I can sleep the rest of the trip to this village. Maybe by then my body will have adjusted to whatever it is that infects this part of the world."

"Alright."

With Azalea cozying up against him, Ean turned his attention to what lay outside of the wagon. The fog still hung thick in the air, hiding the rest of the world from his view. But as the wagons rumbled on, the fog lessened, allowing him to see a small distance into the haze. What lay outside the wagon could have been a completely different world.

The ground itself was mostly dirt, black dirt like what was left after a fire had ravaged the ground. Random patches of grass grew, but it was thicker than normal grass and was a dark blue instead of green. Off to either side of the wagon he would occasionally glimpse at what looked like tree branches sticking through the fog, although he never caught site of the actual tree trunk. The branches seemed weird, bare of any leaves natutal for this time of year, and the bark was a dark purplish color. It was eerily quiet as well, the sounds of the wagons the only thing he could hear. There was no wind, no chirping of birds. It was as if the wagons were the only things moving in the world.

Nothing new came into view as the wagons trudged along, even after the fog had thinned even more. Ean spent the rest of the morning thinking about what other oddities this land could hold. The pressure of the Plague continued to press down on him, but at the most it was a minor annoyance. Azalea also accomplished her goal, staying asleep on his shoulder and only occasionally shifting around against him. He envied her. Sleep would have been a welcome relief, but he didn't even close his eyes as they rolled along. The power rushing through him might be protecting him from the Plague, but he didn't trust it. Didn't trust his unconscious self with it either.

After what seemed like an eternity, the wagons began to slow. Azalea stirred and opened her eyes but kept her head on his shoulder.

"Are we there?"

"I think so," Ean said, smiling at the small splotch of drool that dampened his shirt. "We're slowing down at least."

"Good, I want to get up and move around. Hopefully that will help my stomach settle."

Pulling her arm out from around his, Azalea climbed to her feet...and almost fell over again when the wagon came to a sudden stop. Glancing out the back, Ean saw that they had come to rest on a barren patch of earth. Even more interesting was now that the fog was thinned, he could see a dirt road he hadn't noticed before. He had almost forgotten they were supposedly going to a civilized area with how badly the Plague had affected him. Seeing something as common as a road made the Deadlands less intimidating to him.

"Well, come on already," Azalea said, pushing him out of the way so she could start to climb out. "I told you I would stick by you but that doesn't mean I'm going to sit around in this wagon when there is so much fear and dread floating around just outside."

Azalea got out first and offered Ean a hand. He accepted it, and when he tried to step over the side, he stumbled out into her arms.

"Sorry. The pressure is messing with my balance."

She rolled her eyes and pushed him away with a grunt. Using the wagon for balance, he moved around from the back of the wagon and got his first look at the village of Ulundkin.

Past the patch of land where the wagons were all now sitting was a village of a few dozen houses, most two stories and made of a blackish stone. They were spaced out at random, with large spots of beaten down grass all around them. A road paved with the same stone as the houses ran right down the middle, although very few buildings actually sat on the road. To the west of town, the mountains ran north and south, the climbing peaks the only thing that seemed untouched by the Plague.

Directly attached to the wagon area was a large building that stood out amongst the rest, three times as large as any of the other buildings and made of the same material. A single set of large wooden doors sat in the middle of the wall facing the wagons with a lone man standing in front of it. In sharp contrast to the black stones of the building, the man dressed all in red guarded the double doors.

All of the members of the caravan were making their way towards an opening in the middle of the wagons. Meganan was standing on a small box looking around impatiently while some of the wagon leaders waved everyone closer. By the time Ean and Azalea reached the clearing, nearly everyone was gathered around Meganan.

"Welcome to Ulundkin," the older man shouted, and immediately the crowd grew silent. "Those of you who have made this trip before already know what I'm about to say, but this doesn't make my words any less important. For those that have made the trip for the first time, heed my words."

"The Ciantar family has been trading with the people of Ulundkin for over a decade, both by the blessing of our patron deity, Drenks, and by our relationship with the good citizens that live here. To keep up our excellent relationship, there are a few rules set forth by the Mayor that must be followed. Understand that I take these rules extremely seriously, and breaking any of them will lead to a forfeit of wages from any of my employees. For those not under my employ, you will be punished based on the rules of the village, which can include time spent in their jail. Such a punishment combined with the Plague would probably lead to you becoming a permanent citizen in the Deadlands."

The tall man grew quiet for a few moments as he let that thought set in. The crowd remained silent. Looking around and seeming content with what he saw, Meganan continued.

"The rules are as follows, and I list them in terms of importance and strictness in punishment:

"One: no one is to go near the path leading into the mountains and the mine. Trespassing there is punishable by death, regardless of whether you are an employee or not."

Again he allowed his words to settle into the crowd before continuing.

"Two: those with free time are permitted on the main road and may stop in the general store or The Shade Inn if they are open. It should go without saying, though, that you should refrain from buying anything here, especially food or drink."

"Three: most citizens of this town feel uncomfortable with their appearance when compared to our own. If you do come in contact with anyone here, it is considered impolite to focus on their 'differences.' Please refrain from staring, pointing, and especially making any comments. Remember, we are their guests."

"With that being said, Loaders and Handlers, you are to get right to work transferring the goods into the warehouse." He gestured to the large buildings behind him. "Everyone else is free to their own devices. Again, remember the rules."

Giving one last look over the entire crowd, Meganan stepped down from the box and started making his way towards the warehouse. The rest of the crowd quickly dispersed as well, many of them with jobs to do. Ean glanced around until he saw the familiar wide frame of Iacane and the mostly bald head of Sadiek. Motioning Azalea with his head, they both made their way over to the two men.

CHAPTER 25

SNOOPING AROUND

"A VERY INTIMIDATING SPEECH," Sadiek said as he and the rest of his fellow travelers approached. "I did not know things were so serious here."

"Well, what did you expect?" Iacane was looking about with a frown, his hands clenching and unclenching nervously. "Of course the people here do not want too much interaction with us. They probably feel embarrassed with pieces of them falling off or missing."

"Iacane," Sadiek said, sighing loudly. "That is exactly the type of talk we have been warned against. You don't want to insult these poor people."

"Do you see any of them around?"

"No, but I've read that the Plague gives them slightly heightened senses. For all we know they could be on the other side of the village and hear you talking like a fool."

The comment earned a "hhrrrummph" from Iacane but the man nodded in agreement. "Well, I hope that they don't all stay in hiding while we are here. Otherwise the whole trip will have been a waste for me. Now if you will excuse me."

As soon as the rotund man left, Sadiek rounded on Ean.

"And where were you last night?" The frustration in his voice was clear. "I came by your tent twice and you weren't there. I thought we had an agreement."

"Oh yes, well..." Ean mumbled, avoiding the man's gaze.

"I'm sorry, I don't think we've met," Azalea jumped in, extending a hand towards the man. "I'm Azalea, Ean's sister."

His angry gaze instantly softened when it fell on Azalea's pretty face.

"Pleasure to meet you, finally. My name is Sadiek."

It was barely noticeable, but a bit of confusion flashed across her eyes as they shook hands. When she spoke, it was with all of her usual charm.

"Will you be accompanying us as we look around, Sadiek?"

"Yes, that would be lovely."

"Excellent, then, if you gentlemen would be so kind as to escort me into town?" Hooking both of her arms, she waited until Sadiek entwined one of his arms around hers as Ean took the other one. Then all three of them made their way out of the group of wagons and onto the main street.

"So," Sadiek said as they started slowly walking up the street, "if you don't mind me asking, why did you want to make the trip with your brother?"

"To look after Ean, of course." Azalea's eyes were darting around, taking in everything as they walked down the street. "He has a knack for getting himself into trouble. Plus, I need to make sure he follows through with the task at hand."

"And what is the task at hand?"

"Find the lair of the man that caused the Plague, poke around a bit. Get into some trouble. I'm here to make sure he doesn't chicken out." She let out a laugh, which quickly faded as she caught Sadiek's cold stare.

"I am only kidding, of course," she said quickly. Sadiek ignored her, however, and turned his attention to Ean.

"Is this true? Are you really looking for the Plague-bringer's old lair? When you told me you knew some of the language from the Abyss, I thought that your connection to it was more of a curiosity than anything else. But if you are actually trying to find the lair of the monster behind the Plague..."

"Ean?" Azalea cut in. "What does this man know?" She slowly released her hold on Sadiek, but Ean didn't like the way she was eyeing the man up.

"It's ok, Azalea. He found me talking to Zin. At that point there was no way to keep MY secret any longer." He hoped she caught the emphasis he put on the word 'my'.

"That stupid, little imp," Azalea growled, but stopped eyeing Sadiek. "The fool is more trouble than he is worth." She poked a finger none too lightly into Sadiek's chest.

"Since Ean is foolish enough to trust someone he's just met, I suppose I have to accept it. But you make sure you understand that I meant what I said about protecting my brother. If I even think that you could put him in danger..."

The Yulari trailed off as she looked at the older man. Sadiek was angled toward Azalea as they continued to walk, so Ean couldn't tell what he looked like at that moment, but something made her shrink back from the old man. Ean began to tense.

"Listen here...girl." Sadiek's voice was as cold as the Chill season. When Ean finally caught a glimpse of the old man's face, the expression he found there was a barely controlled rage. "You will never threaten me again, and more importantly, you will not touch me either. Do I make myself clear?"

Azalea stood up straight and returned his stare with one of her own.

"If you think I'm going to let some human try and intimidate me..."

Moving quickly, Ean stepped in-between the two before they came to blows. He made sure not to touch Sadiek as he did so.

"That's enough," he said, his attention more on Azalea. "We don't need to do anything stupid here, like fight. I'm sure we can calm down and just forget--"

"Excuse me," Sadiek cut in. "I think I need some time alone." Pushing past Ean, the older man headed back towards the wagons.

Azalea and Ean both watched him go for a few moments before rounding on each other.

"If you could just stop from trying to joke about why we are here..."

"Why don't you just tell everyone about who you really are..."

They stared each other down for a few moments, but surprisingly it was Azalea that was the first to look away. Looking back towards the wagons, Azalea grunted.

"There is something not quite right about that man. Even if he didn't know so much about you, I would tell you to be careful around him. He doesn't taste...right."

"What does that mean?" Ean said, also looking back towards the wagons for a moment before returning his attention to Azalea.

"I don't know. His emotions just taste different. And he felt less lust towards me than you do, and I have been using my tricks on him since we walked up to him. He just feels very wrong."

"He is just a little eccentric, I think. Plus, he has been trying to decipher the language of the Abyss for me, which would be a great help, so I would prefer to stay on his good side."

"Wait, wait, wait. You didn't actually give him your book did you?"

"Of course not. I've written notes for him to look at and work with. I've never let the Abysmal Tome out of my sight."

"Alright good. I was hoping you weren't stupid enough to let a stranger have your book alone. And no, I'm not saying you're stupid in general, so don't give me that look."

"Let's just forget about him then, ok? Like you said earlier, we are here for a reason. Kaz'ren said the Plague-bringer's lair is nearby, so let's see if we can figure out where without angering anyone else around here."

"Well, that part's easy. There is only one place it could be." When he just stared back at her, Azalea sighed. "The mine. The one place that if you go, it's punishable by death?"

A knot of stress started to build in his stomach. The one place it was probably impossible to reach.

Smiling at Ean, Azalea reached over and patted his arm. "Sometimes it takes a while for things to sink into that thick skull. Come on, let's go see what we are up against. No use worrying about things until we see what we have to deal with."

Grabbing his arm she began leading him down the street. Her eyes darted about while Ean kept his on the stones in front of his feet. It made sense that getting into the Plague-bringer's lair was going to be dangerous. Why wouldn't it be? Ean mentally kicked himself for even having the hope that things would be easy as soon as they got to Ulundkin. A warning from Kaz'ren would have been nice. He could always send a prayer her way and see if she responded...

"There!" Azalea whispered excitedly into his ear.

Ean trained his gaze in the direction she was pointing and caught sight of a small path worn into the ground that wrapped around a well and then a few of the buildings off the road.

"How do you know?"

The Yulari shrugged. "I don't, but it looks like that path has been used a lot. Let's see, and if it's nothing, we'll come back to the road."

"Fine."

They began walking off the road, following the path past the well. The mountain loomed over the few houses, stretching up into the fog and barely visible past the rooftops. Ean hadn't realized how close the mountains were when he had first gotten out of the wagon. It made sense that a path into the mine, and hopefully the Plague-bringer's old lair, would be so close to the village.

They passed two houses along the path with only one more in the distance. It was eerie moving around the village without a soul around, the only sounds the distant shouts of the men working near the wagons. The houses they passed were dark and appeared abandoned although in good condition. Were the people here out performing their jobs? Or were they hiding from the caravan? Ean would like to at least meet one--

A sudden blow to the back of both of his legs knocked him to the ground. Face down in the dirt, he heard Azalea hiss somewhere above him.

"Don't move!"

Ean didn't recognize the voice and quickly rolled over onto his back. Looking up he saw two men in red outfits like the one in front of the warehouse, each one pointing a thin black blade at Azalea. The Yulari had her hands spread wide, her expression clearly showing her intentions.

"Azalea, stop!"

The Yulari looked down at him, then back at the men, then at Ean again, before relaxing slightly. She folded her arms across her chest and glared at the two men. They kept their swords raised although the one closest to Ean had turned his attention away from Azalea towards him.

Raising his hands, Ean tried to put on his most innocent looking expression.

"What seems to be the problem?"

The one closest to Ean snarled at him, although Ean couldn't see his face. Taking a closer look, Ean realized that the two men weren't wearing red outfits. It was actually dark red armor.

The armor, made from what looked like fist-sized plates, covered the men from head to toe. The way the plates overlapped made it look like one solid piece, but when the men bent their arms or legs, Ean could see the gaps that separated the different pieces. The armor even covered the man's entire head, with two small openings for the eyes, the only perceivable openings in the entire outfit. It was considerably different from the armor he had seen the Seekers wearing.

"Humans are not allowed here," the one closest finally said. His voice was cold, and slightly muffled by his helmet. "You should have been told that."

Moving slowly into a sitting position, Ean kept his hands raised. "We were told that we were not allowed near the mine."

"Exactly." What Ean assumed to be a guard, gestured back over his shoulder. Ean's eyes followed the path as it ran up towards the mountains. "That is the mine."

"We didn't know. We were told not to go near the mine, but we weren't told where it was located. We simply saw this path and decided to follow it."

The guard swung his sword around and leveled it close to Ean's face. He heard Azalea take in a sharp breath and hoped the Yulari wouldn't do anything foolish.

"Ignorance is no excuse. We are in our rights to detain you for execution if we wish."

"Try it," Azalea growled. Again both swords were pointed in her direction, and her face darkened.

"There is no need for that," Ean said, talking both to Azalea and the guards. "I'm sure we haven't gotten so close to the mines that you absolutely have to take such drastic steps."

"It is within our right..."

"Enough, Naren," the other guard said, speaking for the first time. "They're only kids. We've scared them enough."

"I wasn't trying to scare them. We are in line with the law to--"

"They didn't even make it to the base of the mountain. Threatening them with execution is pushing--"

"Enough. Fine." Grumbling, the guard closest to Ean lowered his sword, his partner mirroring his action. "Both of you return to the wagons. If I catch word that you've gone anywhere off the main road again, I won't be as generous next time."

Rising, Ean nodded slightly. "Thank you, we appreciate it. Come on, Azalea."

The Yulari let out another low growl at the two men, but let Ean linked arms with her and led her back towards the road. Once he got back to the road, he didn't slow down until he had dragged Azalea most of the way back to the wagons. Members of the caravan now littered the road, walking with no real direction. They seemed to just be taking everything in. Ean noticed a few tried the door to the general store and found it locked.

"You should have just let me kill them," Azalea growled, catching the attention of two wagon drivers that Ean had seen before. He waved them off with a smile and dragged Azalea further down the road.

"Quiet! Do you want to get us in more trouble?"

When she spoke again it was in more hushed tones. "I'm just saying, two men--"

"Two armed and heavily armored men."

"Two heavily armored men would have been simple even without my skills."

"And you could have taken care of them quietly?"

"Well...no, probably not..."

"And do you know how many more might have been waiting up by the mine? Or even in that house we were next to, or the other ones close by?"

Azalea's face scrunched up as the point behind Ean's questions began to sink in. "Fine, fine, mister know-it-all. What's your big plan then?"

Surprisingly, a plan was starting to come together in Ean's mind. Nothing overly dramatic or exciting, but more subtle than he thought he was capable of. A safe plan. Well, safe-ish. Closing his eyes for a moment, he tried to ignore the weight pushing in on him and started feeling out for energy from the Abyss...

And was nearly crushed by the enormity of what he found...

The energy was EVERYWHERE. He had simply been trying to find Zin, but that was impossible. He felt the energy in the grass, the buildings, even the air. He could even feel the people, for the most part hiding away in their houses, the guard by the warehouse, the two closer to the entrance of the mine.

And the mine itself...it pulsed like a heartbeat, the strength of each beat hammering against him. The energy coming out of it had the power of a dozen Scars. So much energy...

But something was off about it; it wasn't quite right. He could feel the difference between the energy he held inside his own body and the energy all around him. The energy inside of him was like running his hand through a raging stream--raw power and completely pure. The energy around him--the energy that had soaked into everything in the Deadlands--was like running his hand through a viscous bog. Its stagnant funk had settled into everything. Ean didn't know how energy could feel dirty, but it was the only way he could describe it.

How could this Plague-bringer have corrupted the power this badly and have it spread out to the lands in the south.

Closing himself off from the outside energy and its filth, Ean turned to Azalea. "Would you be able to find Zin? I'm...having trouble feeling where he is."

Ean expected some kind of argument about how they didn't need the imp but was surprised when she simply nodded.

"I can find the imp. Nothing else around here smells as bad as he does." She sniffed at the air three times and in three different directions before nodding again. "He's in town. You wait by the wagons, I'll go get him and bring him back."

The Yulari walked off at a brisk pace. Ean watched her go, smiling slightly every time he saw her lift her nose slightly in the air. When she was a decent way down the street, he shook his head and turned back towards the wagons. It didn't take him long to walk the rest of the way back, and what he found was a flurry of activity.

Wagon drivers and loaders alike had formed human chains to carry large sealed crates off the wagons and into the warehouse. Off to the side of the doors sat three people: the guard Ean had seen earlier, Meganan, and a new person that Ean had never seen before.

The newcomer was dressed in old-fashioned fancy clothes. He wore a broad-collared, light-blue coat that hung down to his knees, with golden embroidery and large gold buttons holding it closed. His pants were solid black and neatly pressed without a single wrinkle. The color of his boots matched his coat, with red-dyed laces running up their fronts. Finishing off the outfit, a dark red sash covered the lower part of his mouth, tied tightly around his face and neck.

From far away, the outfit looked very impressive, but as Ean got closer, he could see the wear that could only come from dozens of years of use. Patches of the coat were darker in color, making it clear that the coat had once been a dark blue but had faded over time. Both coat and pants had a variety of stitches in different places, well done as to not be obvious, but it was clear those clothes had been used well past their intended lifetime. Even the boots looked worn, the fabric barely holding at some places, the laces frayed.

The man held a clipboard in his hands, his eyes darting from it to the people carrying the crates and back. Each time his eyes returned to the clipboard, he made a mark on it, in sync with each crate that was carried inside. Occasionally he would make a comment to Meganan, who then would say something to one of his men. The man then walked into the warehouse and returned carrying a red crate different from the ones being carried inside.

The man then took the crate to the nearest wagon, dropped it off, and returned to wait nearby.

Ean was very curious about what could be in those red crates. Everyone had made it very clear that most things in the Deadlands contained at least some residue of the Plague. That meant that as soon as it crossed whatever magical barrier separated the Deadlands and Ven Khilada, it would dissolve. The Ciantar family apparently kept it very quiet what they were able to acquire from the people in the Deadlands. It would be interesting to see what could make it out of this land.

But Ean had more important things to worry about, namely getting up the path and into that mine without having a few of those thin swords the guards were carrying run through his body. Once inside, Zin should hopefully remember enough to take him to where he needed to go. And that was the third thing Ean was going to have the imp do. The first thing was going to scout out the path so they knew exactly how many guards they had to deal with and if there were any other surprises waiting for them. The second was going to be to cause a distraction so they could get into the mine.

Between the three of them, Ean knew they could come up with something. Their real problem was going to be time. Ean wanted to wait until nightfall, as that would give them the best chance of sneaking up to the mine. Unfortunately, he had no idea how long the unloading and loading of goods was going to take or how long they would need to spend in the Plague-bearer's old lair. One more thing he would have to ask Zin when the imp returned.

Deep in thought, Ean almost jumped as a hand slapped down on his shoulder.

"Complete waste of time, this was," Iacane's deep voice was filled with disgust. "I come all this way to spend a day studying the condition of the people here and not a single one is available. The only ones I've seen are those in the funny red armor and the one by the warehouse, but no chance of interacting with them. This place is practically a ghost town."

"So that's why you wanted to come. The great Iacane wanted to cure the Plague."

Iacane smiled, clearly missing the sarcasm in Ean's voice. Maybe the man didn't know what sarcasm was. "Thank you for the vote of confidence, lad, but I doubt I could completely wipe it out. I was just hoping that I could cure individuals of the infliction, or at the very least find a way to determine if someone had passed the point of no return."

"And you don't think if it was possible, someone else would have figured it out by now?"

"No."

"But you can?"

"Given the chance to examine a few citizens here and some of the men on the caravan that haven't been corrupted? Yes, I believe I could."

Ean just had to laugh at the man's confidence. If you could cure things on pure self-confidence alone, Ean could believe the man could cure death. But no, Ean highly doubted it was as easy as he thought. It would probably take someone with the ability to--

"Anyway, I wanted to ask you if you had seen Fredren. The boy said he was off to map the village. I haven't seen him since, and I've been wandering around the main street most of the day."

"No, and I've been doing a little exploring myself and I haven't seen him either."

Shrugging, Iacane looked around slowly. "I'm sure he is fine. He's a smart boy. Oh look, here comes your sister."

Sure enough, Ean caught sight of Azalea strolling towards them, a smile already on her face for Iacane. While the Saniteal was happy to see the beautiful illusion of the Yulari, Ean was happy to see the shimmer at her feet that marked Zin.

"If you'll excuse me, Iacane," he said quickly. "My sister and I have some things to discuss. Family matters. You understand."

Ean heard the man start to grumble as he moved away. Clearly, Iacane wanted to flirt with Azalea some more, but Ean didn't have time for that. They had plans to discuss, and judging by how close the sun was to the mountains in the west, not a whole lot of time.

Reaching Azalea, he gently grabbed her arm and began leading her further toward the wagon grounds. She batted her eyelashes at Iacane as they passed by the man. Ean gave her a small shake in annoyance and received a smile in return.

"What?" she said. "I don't want to get out of practice charming the men."

"I highly doubt that's possible."

"Oh, you are such a flatterer."

Ignoring the comment, Ean took them to a nice, secluded spot in between two wagons. After checking inside both for workers, he sat down and motioned for Azalea and Zin to join him. They sat close, Zin still completely invisible.

"Alright, here is where we stand," Ean began. "We know where the mine is and how to get there. We also know that they take trespassing there very seriously, which makes me think that they know what it really is. We've seen two guards, but there could be more up the path."

"Six." Even after years of hearing Zin's voice float up from seemingly nothing, it was still strange.

"Six what?"

"Six guards. There are six guards sitting at the entrance to what they are calling the mine. That's where I was, scouting it out."

"Oh, uh, well...good. That's one question answered. The next thing we have to think about then is how we can distract those guards long enough to sneak inside."

He looked at each of them expectantly. Azalea just returned a blank look and eventually shrugged.

"Clearly, they aren't affected by my tricks so I can't help there. I might be able to take the two guards at the bottom of the path and then the six at the top, but not without attracting the attention of the entire village. And then who knows how many more of the Living Dead would come after us."

Ean knew, he had felt them earlier. There were probably over a hundred in this small village, and even if only half of them could fight, it would be too many for them to handle.

"Alright, well, obviously the direct approach is out. Any ideas, Zin?"

"We could set a few houses on fire."

"WHAT?"

"That might actually work," Azalea chimed in. "That one near the base of the path and then a few houses leading away from it. The guards would leave their posts to handle a bunch of house fires."

"Wait a minute, we can't just go around lighting buildings on fire. People could get hurt or killed." Azalea looked at him blankly again, and Ean could feel Zin's gaze. "Listen, there has to be another way. Maybe we should come back to that. Zin, how much time do you think we will need to really explore your master's old lair?"

"I don't know," Zin replied. "It's been a long time since I've been in there. I *think* I know the general layout, but I'm not certain. A lot can change in however many years it's been."

"That's not exactly helpful," Ean grunted.

"Once we're inside, things will be easier. There is a way to find what we are looking for."

"And what way is that?"

"I'll let you know when we get there. It's hard to explain."

"Do you even know what we should be looking for?"

"I know the names of some rooms where we might find something interesting or helpful." The imp sighed as the blur shifted again. "Listen, much of this will be easier for you to find, as opposed to having me try to explain it poorly. Let's just get inside and see what we can find."

"Fine, then that leads us back to how we are actually going to get inside."

"I still like the fire idea," Azalea chimed back in.

"You could just summon a fire spirit and see what happens," Zin agreed.

"Yes, yes! A fire spirit!" Azalea clapped. "They are so cute and small in the Abyss, but with so much here for one to feed on, it would grow quickly. I would love to see one fully grown."

"No fires!" That earned Ean a stuck-out tongue from Azalea, which he ignored. "If we start destroying the village, obviously the first people they are going to blame are the outsiders. It's enough that we are putting ourselves in serious danger here, but I don't want to drag the entire caravan with us."

The other two grew silent. Ean hoped it was because they agreed with him but knew it was probably the opposite. There had to be some way to get all of the guards away from the mine long enough for them to get in. But how?

A yell broke his chain of thought, and he swung his head about trying to determine where it came from. A moment later, a few men went running past, followed by a few more. Then another yell. Glancing at Azalea for a moment, Ean climbed to his feet and took off after the men. As he rounded the side of one wagon, he saw the majority of people moving in the direction of the warehouse. Ean followed the rest of the workers with Azalea close behind him.

CHAPTER 26

RELEASE

TWO SEPARATE CROWDS HAD gathered. The one closer to Ean was composed of all the workers and other members of the caravan. They seemed to be highly agitated about something. The second crowd stood near the warehouse and were a sharp contrast to the first. Under the red light of the fading sun, their dark blue skin took on the hue of a mottled purplish bruise. They all wore clothes of similar design and condition to the man Ean had seen early with the clipboard.

These were the Living Dead of the village, no longer in hiding. It was hard to see much else of them from his spot behind the crowd of workers, but not a single person looked like a decaying rotted corpse. They looked normal, if you could overlook the old clothes and their skin color. They stood completely still, watching something that was happening between the two groups.

Wanting to get a better look and hear what was going on, Ean began to weave his way through the crowd. This was where being thin and lanky had its benefits as he made his way towards the front. He got a few grumbles and even more elbows as he maneuvered through, but he soon found himself at the front.

In the open space between the two crowds, four men and two guards in red armor stood around a lone man who was down on his knees. Meganan was arguing with the man with the clipboard, one of his guards standing right behind him. The strange man with the clipboard wore a stoic expression as he listened to Meganan's words. The man down on his knees was Fredren.

"...doesn't have to be this way," Meganan growled, pointing down at the cowering Fredren. "He's just a stupid boy."

"It is the law," Clipboard man said. His voice was flat, emotionless, and had a small scratchiness to it. He still had the scarf around his face. "He was caught up by the mine. The punishment is death."

Fredren let out a little whimper. Bruises were starting to appear on his face, and there was a small cut above his right eye. He was as pale as a ghost.

"Now, wait a minute, Ulften," Meganan said, addressing the man with the clipboard. "I've been making this run for close to fifteen years now. Not once in the dozens of trips I've made all those years has a person broken your laws. Don't you think you can be a little lenient for this one boy?"

"No."

"Ulften, I--"

"It begins with a little leniency," Ulften cut in. "Then I have to start being lenient with my people. From that point, the rules of the village start breaking down. This village falls to chaos and then it spreads to the other villages. The chaos reaches all the way to the Eternal King. And who will he blame? Humans from the south? No, he will blame lenient Ulften. There will be no leniency while I am in charge here."

"Take his life now!" shouted someone in the opposite crowd.

"Spare him, you monsters!" said another man somewhere over Ean's left shoulder.

Both sides took to yelling, the combined voices like a rumble of thunder. Fredren was openly weeping now, his face in his hands and his body shaking. Ulften was staring at him, like a man staring at a rabid dog that needed to be put down. At the same time, Meganan was motioning for the men on either side to quiet down, although his efforts were having no effect on the Living Dead or the humans.

Ulften looked up to scan the bystanders with his cold eyes, singling out the most vocal with a gaze like sharp daggers. A hush fell over the crowd, until only the heart-wrenching sobs of Fredren remained.

"The laws for humans were made before the first caravan came here by the Eternal King. You agreed to those laws, did you not?"

"Yes," Meganan sighed in defeat.

Fredren lifted his head. A wild look, like an animal cornered in a cage, shined in his eyes. "I'm just making maps. Maps! I didn't mean any harm. Oh, someone help me. Deities save me!"

Ean cringed when Fredren's eyes settled directly on him. Not wanting any attention, he tried to melt back into the crowd. Unfortunately, they had tightened into an impenetrable wall, forcing him to remain up front.

"Ean!" The boy pointed right at him. "Tell them, Ean! I just make maps!"

Every eye, it seemed, shifted from Fredren onto Ean. He made one last vain attempt to push his way back into the crowd and then gave up with a sigh. With nothing else to do, he met Fredren's eyes. He at least owed the boy that.

"Ean, please..." Young Fredren's pleas ripped at his heart.

"Hey, wait a second, I know that one," one of the guards by Fredren said, pointing with a gauntleted finger. "I saw that one near the path to the mines, as well."

Ulften let out a sigh and gestured towards Ean. The guard that had pointed him out drew his sword and started to walk over. Cursing Fredren under his breath, Ean took a step towards the guard... and suddenly found a few of the wagon drivers standing in front of him.

"You're not taking another one of ours, rot face," one of the men growled. "You like to threaten little boys, let's see how you fair against a man."

As much as Ean hated being called a boy, he was more surprised by this sudden show of support by a complete stranger. Whether the man was standing up for him on principle or simply hated the Living Dead, at this point Ean didn't care.

"Boyd! Traiz!" Meganan yelled. "Do not interfere!"

Both men stood their ground for a moment, then with a glance back at Ean, stepped aside.

Taking a quick glance to the horizon, Ean saw the bottom of the sun just starting to touch the peaks to the west. If Ulften even suspected Ean, he would have no chance of ever reaching the mine.

The guard sheathed his sword as he approached, then grabbed Ean by the arm. Immediately Ean felt the power inside of him surge. He felt like a pitcher of water, full to the brim, being carried around by a drunk. It was all he could do to contain the energy inside of him, to the point where as soon as the guard started pulling him along, Ean tripped and almost fell.

"You've already made me regret letting you go," the guard growled quietly. "Stay on your feet and stop trying to make me look like a fool."

But Ean couldn't get his limbs to work properly. His power was reacting to something, and he had no idea what it was. Just like the Plague had been trying to bore into him, now his power was straining to burst out. Gathering all of his will power, Ean attempted to steady himself. He gripped the guard's hand tightly...

...and the runes on his arm burst into a blazing light.

His glove and half of his shirt were gone, leaving his right arm, shoulder, and side completely exposed. The tattoos that he thoght had only extended to his shoulder had made their way down his torso. They now covered his entire right side and even stretched out to part of his chest and stomach. But Ean had no time to examine the radical change.

The guard screamed as the power rushed out of Ean and into him, the light of it flowing into every hole of his armor. Ean closed his eyes tightly as he felt the power stretch forth from his own body like a million little hands. Mystical fingers of power took hold of the guard's body, covered him like a blanket, and seeped into his pores until it fused with mortal flesh. At first, Ean had no idea what the energy was doing. It was a force of nature, unstoppable. The more it surrounded and infused the terrified guard, though, the more familiar it seemed...

He knew when the power had felt like this before. Back in an old forgotten temple. Back when he had been in the presence of a goddess. Back when he had pulled the energies of the Abyss right out of the ghost of the old priest. Ean's eyes shot open at the realization of what was happening.

The unbridled energy of the Abyss latched onto the plague-infected energy in the guard. The latter energy resisted the former, but it was like a trickle of water trying to hold back a raging river. The pure energy that was flowing through him overwhelmed the corruption, burning it clean. All that was left behind in the guard was the same pure energy that flowed through Ean.

And then all of that energy, both Ean's and the guard's, flowed back into him.

The guard let out a blood-curdling scream. Ean watched in horror as the guard's scream quickly turned to a gurgle, and then a gasp as the guard's body went limp and collapsed to the ground. At least, it looked like he collapsed, until the armor rattled on the ground and each section came apart. The guard's entire body was simply gone. All that was left was the dark red armor, with piles of what looked like sand and dust pouring out of the edges.

Complete silence fell over the Deadlands.

Slowly glancing around, he saw everyone staring at him. Mouths hung open. Some people were huddled together, frozen in place. Others were still covering their ears as if the guard's screams were still echoing down the street. However, all eyes, including Fredren's, were dead-centered on Ean. Their expressions ranged from horror, to bewilderment, to anger--as if they were gazing at a murderous demon that had just crawled up from the depths of the Abyss. And the worst part was wondering if maybe they were right.

"I didn't mean to--"

The village erupted into chaos.

CHAPTER 27

CHAOS

"GET UP!"

A woman was yelling at him. When Ean opened his eyes, he was on his back staring up into a hazy mist. How did he get on his back?

"Get up, you idiot!"

Hands grasped what was left of his shirt. The right half was completely gone. That seemed strange. The crisscrossing runes on his right side were glowing faintly, casting light around him.

When the hands forced him to sit up, a flash of pain went through his head, scattering his thoughts. He brought his hand to his temple and felt wetness. Was it raining? When he lowered his hand, it came back red. Was rain in the Deadlands a dark red? His head felt all muddled.

So many questions...Ean tried to grasp for at least one but was rattled more as he was lifted up onto his feet.

"If I have to carry you, I swear by the Abyss, I will never let you live it down."

That voice. Azalea. She was helping him up. That was nice of her. There were other sounds too. People yelling. Should he be worried? His muscles tightened as fear gripped him. There were blurs of things moving all around. Actually, a particularly red blur was coming straight at him.

"Wonderful."

Ean was about to ask what was wonderful when he suddenly found himself face down on the ground. Turning to his side, all he could see were a pair of red-plated boots and the brown sandals that Azalea always wore. The four feet were dancing around each other, sometimes close together, other times far apart. Then the red boots were gone for a moment, and all he saw were Azalea's feet.

The man in red armor hit the ground next to him with a clatter, his helmet flying off. The man's head was face up and yet the rest of his body was face down. His neck didn't look right either. Or his face for that matter, which was completely missing its lower jaw. But by far the thing that struck Ean the most peculiarly was when the man started to push himself back up off the ground. His head flopped about on a neck that no longer provided any support. The sight was horrific.

Again he was grabbed and hoisted over someone's shoulder. The horror of the previous scene had cleared his mind, and going by the plain brown robe and how they smelled of lilies, Ean guessed it was Azalea.

"Hold on, Ean," she yelled. "I'll get you out of this yet."

Azalea had no trouble running with him draped over her shoulder. All Ean could do was hold on as the ground passed in a blur beneath him. Every now and then he would see an arm or a leg lying motionless on the ground, some having the pale purple skin of the Living Dead, other times the fleshy tone of a human. And all the while, the sounds of yelling and fighting surrounded him.

"So much for sneaking around," Azalea yelled as she leapt over a body. "If we're lucky, all the guards will be done in the melee, and we will have easy access to the mine."

She barked a laugh. "If we make it there alive."

With his wits slowly returning, Ean lifted his head to try and get his bearings. The dusk light mixed with the shallow glow coming

off his tattoos cast shadows everywhere. They were moving around different buildings, currently in a spot free of the fighting. The pulse coming off the mine mirrored the pulse in his body. It seemed to be coming from ahead and to the left, which meant they had somehow gotten to the north side of the village and were making their way south.

"You can put me down now," Ean managed to get out as he was being bounced around. "I can walk."

"Not yet, little one. We're still being followed, I think." She reached up and patted his backside. "You just be a good little lantern up there and let me handle things for now."

Ean gave her a scowl as a reply, which felt all the more stupid since she couldn't see it. So he contented himself with holding on while she ran toward the sunset. They skirted around houses, Azalea sometimes getting closer to the shadowy mountains and other times heading back towards the main road. She doubled back on herself a few times, all the while Ean kept a look out for any pursuers. By the time night had settled in, Ean's tattoos were providing more light then the three moons. Huffing only slightly, after a journey that would have killed lesser creatures, Azaelea finally stopped. She carefully set Ean down on his feet, keeping a tight hold on his shoulders.

"You ok? Test out your legs. Do you feel comfortable standing on your own?"

Standing on one leg and then the other, Ean nodded. "Yeah, I feel much better. What happened back there?"

"Someone, not sure from which side, threw a rock at your head."

"And then the people from the caravan came to my aid?"

She shook her head. "No, I think most of those humans were scared of you at that point, which is why I don't know who threw the rock. I did see a few stones get thrown into the crowd of Living Dead though, and I heard some not-so-nice words aimed at them as well. I think some of the men hate the Living Dead and just used this as an opportunity to start something. And start something, they did."

Just that moment, the sounds of shouting reached them, quickly followed by the clash of weapons.

"What about Fredren? Did you see him get away?"

"I didn't see him dead. So anything is possible."

"How about Zin?"

"I'm sure the imp is fine. I bet he is already waiting for us at the entrance to the mines. Speaking of which..."

She gestured behind her at a path that led up into the mountains. The ground was crushed flat and looked old and heavily trodden, following a nearly straight and steep line up into the mountain.

"Let's get going," Azalea said, giving him a gentle push towards the path. "I think I lost the mob, but we certainly don't want to just stand out here in the open waiting for them to find us."

"Good point. Hopefully the guards Zin saw earlier came down to help with the riot."

"Probably. Well, Ean, you wanted a distraction and you certainly got one."

"True," was Ean's only reply as he started up the path with a sigh. Azalea stayed back a bit and kept watch behind them.

A distraction. Ean had seen enough bodies on the ground as Azalea had carried him to know what his distraction had cost. The sounds of yelling and fighting coming from the village told him that the price was still climbing. It might have been Fredren's curiosity that started the ball rolling for the events tonight, but Ean certainly felt just as responsible for those that wouldn't make it back to Ven Khilada.

Trying to push thoughts of death and dying out of his head, Ean forged on. The path rose to a steep incline, higher and higher, zig zagging into the mountain as it cut a deep path into its side. Ean wondered if the armies of Zin's former master had cut the path or if the citizens that lived down in the village had made it.

Upward and onward they climbed, Ean looking back every now and then to take in the view and check on Azalea. The view left much to be desired, the fog and mist making it hard to see very far. Ean could barely see the top of the houses below or anyone pursuing them. Hopefully, they were high enough that the constant fog of the Deadlands put them out of sight from those below.

Azalea seemed to be faring well. She marched on with a smile on her face, which grew slightly each time Ean looked back. The Yulari was handling the situation well, but of course why wouldn't she? She lived off of emotions like pain and suffering, which there must be plenty of down below. And yet at the same time, with everything she could be feeding on, Azalea didn't have that drunken stupor she usually got after overfeeding. Was she abstaining?

Not paying attention to the path, Ean tripped and fell face first onto the ground. Instead of feeling the slope of the mountain beneath him as expected, the surface was a level plane. Barely catching himself with his hands, he gave a grunt as the hard stone ground scraped his palms. He expected to hear Azalea laughing at him, but he met with only silence.

When he rolled to his side and saw what he had tripped over, vomit rose in his throat. It was a severed arm encased in red armor. Sinew and bone were splayed out from where it used to be attached to some poor man's shoulder. The blood was still watery and fresh, so whoever or whatever had done this might still be nearby.

Jumping to his feet, Ean scanned the area for any sign of what had caused the carnage. They had reached a flat portion of the path, roughly the size of one of the houses below. There was a large opening cut into the mountain not too far from where Ean was standing with two lit torches framing it.

And littered around the clearing were bodies. Or pieces of bodies. All wearing the same red-plated armor.

Ean wanted to flee back down the mountain, but he couldn't move. His own fear had gripped him tighter than the strongest bonds. All he could do while he tried to keep from dry heaving was survey all of the damage done. Not only were most of the body's limbs torn apart, even the armor had deep rents in it. Whatever had done this was more of a monster than anything he could bring out of the Abyss.

Azalea, of course, was unaffected, strolling between body parts and guts as if they were nothing. She stopped at a few, looking down at the bodies and nudging them with a foot before moving on. While Ean felt like he was going to pass out, Azalea looked as if this was as common as a stroll in the woods.

"Eight, at least I think. These were the guards Zin had seen earlier."

"Do you think the fighting down below spread up here?" Ean managed to get out before gripping his mouth and holding back the bile that wanted to escape.

"No," Zin said, suddenly appearing near the mine entrance. "I came right up here as soon as the fighting started and found them already like this."

"Such a brave imp," Azalea said with a dark laugh, "to go running off and leaving your poor friend behind."

"I figured you could take care of him," Zin growled, "and it wasn't like I could do much against a mob of people and the Living Dead. And look, here you both are safe and sound, so I guess I was right."

"Yes, luckily for Ean I was there to take care of him."

"Enough!" Ean yelled, and immediately had to fight down another urge to retch. "We have enough to worry about now without fighting amongst ourselves. Zin, do you have any idea if whatever did this went into the mines or down to the village?"

The imp shrugged nervously, its eyes focused on the ground. "I can't be certain, but there is a trail of blood leading into the mine."

"Wonderful. We have something that can tear armored men apart in the mine and a mob down below that would love to string us up."

"I can handle whatever is in the mine," Azalea said a bit flippantly. "So let's just--"

"Really?" Ean cut in. "Could you have done this? Torn into these men like this?"

"Well, no but..."

"Azalea. We can't just rush in there without knowing what we are up against. What if it's a pack of...monsters...that did this? Do you think you could protect me and fight off a pack of anything?"

"It would be tricky..."

"It would be impossible and you know it. We need help."

"Now wait a minute." This time it was Zin's turn to jump in. "You're not suggesting summoning something else are you?"

"I am."

"But you can't even control a Hound!" the imp yelled, and then seemed to calm himself. "Ean, there is nothing you have summoned so far that you control. That Hound you are so fond of almost came after you and your friends last time. And a Cruxlum, well they can sometimes be pointed in the right direction like you saw, but I wouldn't count on one right now for a guard."

"Zin, we are out of options, and have very little time. I'm not asking your permission."

Before the imp could reply, Ean knelt down on an open patch of rock and placed his bare right hand on the ground. With a thought, a summoning rune began spreading out from his hand, one he had done a few times before. Ean heard the imp hiss behind him as the rune took shape. Clearly he recognized it.

Ean couldn't help but smile. So much easier than drawing the complicated rune by hand. Now if controlling the creature could be just as simple...

A few shouts and the scraping of stone behind him made Ean lose his concentration for just a moment before he quickly regained his focus. Out of the corner of his eye he saw Azalea move back towards the path down the mountain. Hopefully it was nothing. He had enough to worry about with whatever had killed all of these guards, but if there was something coming up, human or Living Dead, they would be better off with four in their group than three.

"Company is coming!" Azalea shouted from behind Ean.

The rune flared once and then sank into the ground, creating a hole the size of a barrel top. A blue and purple mist filled the opening, making it impossible to see much past the surface. Ean always wondered if that mist was the Abyss itself or just part of the gateway between the two worlds. A question for another time. Bracing himself, Ean mentally prepare for the pain that came from a summoning.

But the pain never came. Ean watched in surprise as a clawed paw reach out and clamp onto the stone ground. The claws dug into the stone like it was dirt, raking marks as thick as fingers. Another paw quickly followed, and then his hound's massive head poked through the opening. It took a quick look around for a moment and then pulled the rest of its enormous oily black frame free. And the entire time, the only thing Ean felt was the pressure of the Plague. Standing, Ean couldn't help but smile with relief. Was he rid of the pain of summoning forever?

"I hope you know what you are doing," Zin murmured. The imp was suddenly standing right behind Ean's legs. "Wait, shouldn't you be wriggling around in pain?"

"Yes, I should. Zin, I don't feel a thing."

"Well, that's great and all, but we can celebrate some other time when there isn't a killer animal staring at the two of us."

Ean nodded, turning his full attention to the Hound. The beast was looking around, its nose sniffing at the air every now and then. Glancing at Azalea, it paid a considerable amount of attention to Zin before finally resting its gaze on Ean. Despite the animal's relaxed posture, Ean couldn't help but feel it was just moments away from springing at him and Zin.

"Here, boy," Ean said softly, frowning at his own timid voice. "Come here." This time there was a bit more authority in it. A small amount.

The Hound looked at him for a moment longer, then walked over to the nearest corpse and began to gnaw on its leg.

"I would laugh if I wasn't scared for my life," Zin said dryly, moving slightly out from behind Ean.

"Yes, well, give me a chance here."

"I would get a grip on the Hound fast," Azalea shouted over to them. "Those blurs are getting closer. And there are a lot of them. And most look red."

"Right," Ean said, moving away from Zin and towards the Hound. He got within a few paces of the beast before it looked up at him. Ean froze. The Hound didn't growl or show its teeth, but Ean distinctly got the impression that he shouldn't get any closer. The Hound watched him for another moment as he stood there before returning to its meal. It seemed to be having a bit of trouble with the armor, which seemed to be too tough for the hound's teeth and acidic saliva.

"Uh, stop eating and come here...now." Pathetic. If the roles were reversed, Ean didn't think he would even listen to such a wimpy command.

"There, see?" Zin said, sounding a mixture of annoyed and worried. "Doesn't listen to you. Best to either send it back or just leave it here for those coming out the mountain to deal with."

"Maybe..."

"The rune..."

Turning slightly so Ean could keep an eye on the Hound and look at Zin, he frowned at the imp. "What did you say?"

"I said to send it back or..."

"No, after that. About the rune."

Zin cocked his head and gave Ean a weird look. "I didn't say anything about the rune. What are you talking about?"

"I could have sworn you said something about--"

"The rune...absorb...into yourself..."

Ean froze. That voice certainly wasn't Zin's voice. It was much higher pitched, almost feminine, and very faint. Ean risked taking his eyes off of the Hound for a moment to look around the entire clearing. Azalea was still watching the slope, her foot tapping lightly on the ground. Although Ean was sure Azalea could change her voice just as easily as her appearance, he doubted it had been her that he had heard.

Turning his attention to Zin, he found the imp staring at him intently. "You feeling alright, boss?"

"Yeah, I just keep hearing this voice..."

"Ean, now is not the time to come unhinged. Why don't you focus your attention on the giant eating machine behind you?"

Ean found that the Hound had moved on to another body part, this time the torso. He was eating out of the armor like dried meat from a dog bowl. That was fine with him. As long as the Hound was eating, it was probably happy.

"Take the rune...part of yourself..."

The voice was so faint that Ean could almost believe he was imagining it.

"Zin, if I said 'take the rune into myself,' what would you think I meant?"

Again the imp stared at him funny for a few moments before responding. "Well, Ean, don't you know if you are the one saying it?"

"Humor me. Did you ever see your old master do something like that? Absorb a rune or transfer a rune?"

"No, but he rarely let anyone see what he was doing unless it involved torture or death."

Frowning, Ean walked over to the summoning rune. It glowed faintly on the stones, the light barely fighting back the evening darkness. Kneeling down, he looked at the rune with no idea what to do.

Am I really listening to some voice in my head?

He placed his hand on the rune. As soon as he did, he heard a low growl to his left.

"I'm not sending you home," he said, turning to look at the Hound quickly. The Hound was staring at him, its jaw dripping with pieces of meat. It looked at him a few moments longer, then either understanding or not caring, returned to its meal.

"Alright," Ean mumbled to himself. "Take it in. I want to take it in." Nothing happened. Staring at the runes for a few moments longer, he began to laugh. Of course nothing was happening. Why would something he heard from a voice in his head work? He really must be going crazy to think that he could just absorb--

The runes on his body came to life, glowing brightly and casting their dark azure light on the area. The summoning runes on the floor responded in kind, the light coming off of them just as bright as those on his arm. Ean felt something too, a connection between the runes on the ground and the ones on his arms. No, not just a connection. The runes on his arms were pulling at the summoning rune.

The rune on the ground gave one last bright flash and disappeared. No, not gone. It was resting on the back of his right hand, much smaller, overlying the tattoos that were already there. Ean watched in wonder as it flashed a few times and then began to move. Over his wrist, up his forearm, across his elbow. It shimmered as it moved on its own, weaving in front of and behind his tattoos. Once it reached the top of his bicep it stopped, as if waiting. On cue, the tattoos that were already there began to shift and writhe, slowly clearing a space for the summoning rune to fit. Once a space was cleared, the summoning rune settled in, and Ean's other runes began intertwining back into it.

By the time the tattoos had stopped moving, the summoning rune looked like it had always belonged there. It wasn't just a cosmetic addition to the design. Ean felt...stronger. Stronger than what small boost holding the energy from the Abyss provided. He felt more energized, like he could run for days. His sense of smell was heightened as well...and with all of the dead bodies lying around, that was a perk he did not particularly appreciate.

There was more, though. He could feel the Hound. Not just the sense of the Abyss that clung to everything that came from that world. He could feel the Hound's satiety as it filled its stomach. Feel its desire to hunt and stalk prey. Feel its attention now move away from its meal and focus squarely on him.

The Hound tilting its big head as if it had the intelligence to study him. Its dark purple eyes were almost invisible behind the black of its fur, but even at this distance, Ean could make out the red slits of its irises. A small bit of something hung from its mouth, which it continued to chew slowly. Ean felt a wave of curiosity wash over him through their new bond.

"Here, boy," Ean managed to get out, waving the Hound over. It came without hesitation, padding over lightly to stand in front of him.

"Watch him," Zin said, clutching at Ean's leg. The imp's claws dug into Ean's skin to the point where he was sure the slightest bit more pressure would probably break the skin. "Just because you've done something new doesn't mean it's safe."

Ean nodded, keeping his attention on the Hound.

"Sit."

The Hound sat.

"Down."

The Hound lay down.

"Roll over."

Ean didn't actually expect the last command to work, but sure enough the Hound did one roll and then remained on the ground. Laughing, he reached down and patted Zin's back. The imp released his hold, but still remained behind Ean.

"Come on, Zin, isn't this great? The Hound is finally listening to me."

"Right... so you have complete control over it now?" The imp sounded less than convinced.

"Well..."

Control wasn't the right word. Ean could feel the Hound think about each command for an instant before following his directions. It certainly felt more compliant. But if Ean told it to go take a leap off the mountain, he highly doubted the Hound would follow. It was more like they had come to an understanding.

"He won't have you as a meal, I think I can promise that." Was that disappointment he suddenly felt coming off the Hound? Best not to mention that to Zin.

"You think? That's reassuring..." Zin mumbled, moving away from Ean while still keeping one eye on the massive beast in front of them.

"If you two are finished playing with your new pet," Azalea shouted from her spot looking down the path, "you might want to think about what we are doing next. There is a large group of those blue freaks getting closer, and they look heavily armed."

Azalea quickly took a step to the side, an arrow glancing off the stone where she had been standing a moment later. "And I don't think they are coming to apologize."

Decision time. Stay here and face the mob or venture into the mine and risk running into whatever it was that had torn these guards apart. It really wasn't much of a decision, but Ean felt a little better heading into the mine with at least one more ally.

"Let's go, hopefully we can lose them in the mine."

"Easily," Zin said, starting for the mine entrance. "It might have been a long time since I've been here, but I used to know these caverns and pathways like the back of my clawed hand."

Azalea pushed past Ean, moving towards the mine as well. "Unless of course they've already explored the entire mine and dug new paths of their own."

Ean started after them, then paused and glanced back to the Hound. "Come on, then."

The Hound looked at him, and then swept its gaze around at all of the bodies still lying around. Ean felt its reluctance at leaving so many easy meals behind. He wasn't positive, but Ean thought that if the Hound's belly hadn't already felt full, it might have ignored him. Thankfully it complied, and they both hurried towards the mine entrance.

CHAPTER 28

COMING HOME

"ANYONE HAVE A LANTERN handy?" Ean asked as he peered into the mine. He had been the last to get to the entrance, following the hound to walk up to where Azalea and Zin were standing around, staring into the dark depths of the mine.

"The three of us don't exactly need one," Zin said, shrugging. "But yes, we do have one." He gestured at the runes glowing dimly on Ean's body.

"Oh, right." With some effort, Ean let the energy he was holding back flow through his body, lighting up the runes on his right side. The glow was strong enough to penetrate the darkness, but it also cast shadows everywhere. The effect made the sharply descending mine even creepier.

Azalea grabbed Ean's hand and started pulling him down the slope of the mine. "Best get started so we can figure out how to lose the crowd behind us."

So down they went into the mine, Azalea dragging him along, with the imp and hound close behind. They walked along quickly, the noise of their feet stepping on the stone floor making the only sound. They had yet to come to any branching paths or side tunnels. He had the eerie feeling that they were being watched by eyes sitting just behind the curtain of darkness ahead and behind them.

He couldn't tell what the Yulari or imp was feeling, but the hound seemed completely relaxed. It loped along casually, sniffing at the air and occasionally looking back behind them. Every time it looked back, Ean felt a small pang of disappointment. Probably missing all of those easy meals. It seemed content to follow along, though, which was all that really mattered.

After a brief walk down the same rocky path, they came to their first junction. Two paths opened up to their right and left, running perpendicular to the main tunnel. The group slowed as they approached the openings, everyone except Ean who sniffed at the air. The hound sniffed a few times at the path to the right, then the one to the left, and returned to Ean's side. Ean got the distinct feeling that the hound smelled something, but whatever it was did not cause the beast any anxiety.

"Humans have been down here very recently," Azalea whispered, a small frown touching her lips. "More than a few. They were in a great deal of pain as well."

"How do you know?" Ean whispered back.

"Their body odor is faint, but the emotions they left behind remain strong. It's a confusing mixture of pain and pleasure. It tastes...wrong."

The Yulari seemed to lose herself in her thoughts, so Ean turned his attention to Zin. "Which way should we go?"

"Straight. These two side paths are new. The Living Dead must have dug them out sometime after my old master died. The first real sections of my master's old lair start much, much deeper down."

"Alright then, let's keep going."

"The humans went straight..." Azalea said, still sounding a bit off.

Ean shrugged and started down the path, this time pulling Azalea along behind him. Zin fell behind for a moment until he realized he was close enough to touch the hound, then quickly jogged up past both Ean and Azalea. Ean would have laughed if he wasn't so nervous.

They continued on, passing more junctions with a single path to either side or two like the one they had passed. Each time the paths ran perpendicular and away from the main one, vanishing into darkness. They paused at each for only a moment, Zin instructing them to continue on each time. Azalea kept a slightly confused look to her face as Ean dragged her on, but it lessened at each junction. Either the tastes were fading or she was getting used to them.

When they finally reached two branching paths running diagonally in either direction, Zin called the group to halt.

"Home, sweet home," the imp announced. "This is where my old master's domain truly starts. The tunnel to the left goes down to where the kennels and Carnslug hatchery used to be. Straight ahead leads to the quarters where the various hordes of creatures he controlled used to live. Finally, this way," he pointed to the right, "leads to my old master's throne room and personal lodgings. All of the paths eventually connect, of course, but the path to the right is the most straightforward way to where we should look first."

"Wait," Ean said, releasing Azalea and moving closer to the imp. "If it's so easy to get to, wouldn't it be likely that the people in the village below would have looted everything there already?"

"They might have found some trinkets or statues, but I doubt they would have been able to enter his inner sanctuary. That was magically locked behind stone doors."

"But we'll be able to get in?"

Pointing at Ean's glowing arm and side, the imp smiled. "With those tattoo lamps we will. I'm sure of it."

"Then let's press on," Azalea said, her mouth twisted in a frown. "I'm really starting to not like this place. Plus, we do still have that angry mob somewhere behind us. By now they've probably found the remains of their friends, so I'm sure they want young Ean's blood more than ever."

"Good point," Zin said and immediately began walking down the path to the right. The others followed along quickly.

As they moved down the path, Ean began to notice that the walls down this path were slightly different. Still consisting of the black rock of the mountains, the walls of this path were much smoother. Moving a bit closer, Ean thought he could even see a few designs running down the walls. It made him more excited about exploring the lair.

The path began to snake in one direction and then the other. It made a sharp turn to the left, followed by a sharp right turn, then another abrupt left. At every sharp turn they would move ahead slowly, being careful just in case something jumped out at them. By the fourth sharp turn with nothing around the corner they began to relax. Unfortunately at the fifth sharp turn, they found that the pathway was completely caved in.

"Well, this is just wonderful," Azalea mumbled.

"How was I supposed to know this section had a cave-in?" Zon shot back. "It's not like I've been here recently."

"One excuse after another. You're no better than every other insignificant speck of your kind. If anything, you are more annoying than the average imp because you can talk."

"I can bite, too, you ugly Brayurat. I don't know why I agreed to convince Ean to let you come along in the first place. You'll probably turn on us the first chance you get."

"Yes, I really showed my disloyalty when I saved Ean's life TWICE so far. And don't even try to act like you are completely on his side. You really don't want to go there, imp."

Striding in-between the two, Ean raised his hands to signal calm. "Enough, both of you."

The Yulari and imp continued to glare at each other but remained quiet. After a few moments, Zin threw his hands in the air in disgust and stormed back to the corner. Azalea stuck her tongue out at the imp as he went then turned her attention to Ean.

"You really don't need the imp around, you know. The two of us and your mutt would be fine without him."

"Zin has always been with me. He is the most loyal person I know." Ean raised his hands quickly in a calming fashion as he saw Azalea's eyebrows rise. "That's not saying I don't trust you. I appreciate everything you've done for me. But Zin is part of our group, and you two have to try to get along. At least until we get out of here."

"But that little stain..."

"Azalea, please, at a minimum, try not to push his buttons as much?"

"Fine, fine. I'll leave the imp alone, for as long as we are down here and in danger."

"Thank you. That's all I ask."

"If you two are done," Zin said from his spot by the corner. "We should probably get back to the main junction. The next quickest path will be past the living quarters and the kitchen. Hopefully, that mob has not reached the first junction yet or gone off in another direction."

"That sounds like an excellent idea!" Azalea exclaimed with a bit too much enthusiasm. "We will certainly follow your lead since you know this area the best."

Zin just stared at her, his mouth slightly open. Shaking his head, Ean walked away from them and was the first to head back. The two of them were eventually going to drive him insane--if his powers didn't corrupt him first.

Moving along at a brisk pace, Ean tried not to think about that possibility. The others followed along behind him, and they began to make their way back to the main junction. They reached the last major curve before the beginning of the lair. Ean slowed down and waved the hound to come up next to him. The hound trotted up to his side.

"Is there anything up ahead?" Ean asked the hound and got a blank stare in return. Scratching at his head, he tried to figure out the right words or thoughts. He had never had a pet before; not many people in the village had pets either. So his experience with intelligent animals was limited.

"Danger?" he pointed ahead of them. He tried to project the feelings of fear and caution through the bond that he shared with the hound. The dog immediately tensed, its attention focused ahead of them. Taking a few steps, it sniffed at the air then waited. Then it took a few more steps and repeated the action. It did this a few times then looked back at Ean. A wave of confusion washed over Ean through the bond.

"Nothing, huh?" That made Ean relax just a bit. Maybe the mob wasn't going to be as big a concern as he had thought. Ean was glad to have something to be happy about. Trusting the hound's sense of smell, Ean continued on at a faster pace, the hound at his side and his other two companions behind him. Glancing back he smiled slightly at the two of them, which earned him a smirk from Azalea and a frown from Zin.

It also made him miss seeing the armored man come striding into the junction at the exact same moment he did.

The two of them collided with a thud, the man's red armor absorbing most of the impact for him while Ean was knocked squarely off his feet. He fell back with a grunt, bouncing twice before coming to a stop a pace or two from the wall.

Azalea was at his side in an instant, grabbing him by the arm and lifting him up. Her eyes were on the path that lead back out of the mountain. A low snarl came out of her mouth that Ean would have expected more from the hound than the Yulari. Once Ean was finally on his feet and got some of the air back in his lungs, he was able to look up at what Azalea was staring at.

Ten, red armored men stood at the opening to the path back, each one holding a long wooden pole with a nasty spiked blade on the end. Behind those men and the ten spears all pointed directly at Ean, looked to be the entire town. Men and women of various size and all manner of clothing stretched back as far as Ean could see, each blue face staring at him with a mixture of hate and fear.

"Do not move," said a familiar voice from behind the guards. Two of the red clad guards moved to the side, and the man named Ulften stepped between them. "Surround them."

As a single unit, eight guards circled around Ean and Azalea, separating them from the hound and the now missing Zin. The two remaining guards placed themselves in front of the hound. Ean wanted to try to figure out where the imp had gone already, but the guards put the tips of their spears practically in his face. Once they were properly surrounded, Ulften stepped forward into the ring of guards.

"I'm not one to waste time on words," he said, addressing Ean. "I want to know how you killed one of our people, where you found that monstrosity," he pointed to the hound, "and I want to know how you came to wear those runes on your body."

Ean remained quiet, letting a few wheezing breathes of air back into his body. He shot the hound a look through the guards, sending the feeling of danger through their bond. The dog tilted his head and returned the feeling of confusion. It didn't consider any of those surrounding them as dangerous. No wonder it hadn't given any warning. What *did* a creature as big and potentially vicious as a hound consider dangerous?

"My name is Ean. I'm just a simple Healer--"

"Maybe I didn't make myself clear," Ulften said, cutting him off. "I don't care who you are or where you are from. I want the answers to the three questions I asked. Now."

"I don't really know how I killed your man. It was an accident." Ean drew out every word, trying to think. "He grabbed me and then, well, you saw what happened next."

"Yes, I saw a man I've known for close to two hundred years, a man that has been with me almost since the founding of our town, reduced to dust in less time than it took you to answer just one of the questions I asked. And a poor answer it was."

"Kill the girl," he said as casually as if he was telling his men to fetch him lunch.

"Now wait a minute," Ean said, pulling himself out of Azalea's grip and standing in front of her. "There is no need--"

"You had your chance to talk," Ulften said, cutting him off again. "Now, you get to see how serious I really am. I hope after she dies, you--"

A loud moan from behind Ean interrupted Ulften. Every eye turned to the middle tunnel behind Ean, the one that was supposed to lead towards the living quarters. Ean glanced quickly at Azalea and saw that same confused look on her face. She seemed slightly tense but not overly worried.

"What was that?" Ulften said, his voice not hiding his annoyance. "Who else is with you?"

Another moan, quickly followed by another higher-sounding one filled the junction. A third joined it, then a fourth and more and more until it sounded like a pack of creatures in pain. Straining his eyes, Ean thought he could make out movement on the edge of the darkness down the tunnel.

"What other things have you brought into our mines?" Ulften was at Ean's side now, the man clearly not afraid of him or what he had done to his friend.

"Whatever it is, I had nothing to do with it."

Ulften seemed to consider this for a few moments and then motioned to the guards. The majority moved into the opening to the corridor leading to the living quarters with only the two guarding the hound remaining in place. Even as tall as he was, Ean had to stretch slightly to see past the line of guards. And all the while the moaning grew louder.

CHAPTER 29

MONSTERS

SOMETHING SHUFFLED OUT OF the darkness. Ean's eyes were immediately drawn to its face. The familiar face of one of the men snatched from the caravan in the middle of the night stared back at him. Ean's jaw slowly dropped. The face was the only thing that still looked even remotely human.

Attached to that human head was a body bloated and scarred with boney spikes sticking out randomly over its entire torso. Tan human shoulders extended into grey arms, two to each shoulder. Where those grey arms reached the elbow, the flesh seemed to be torn apart. From those wounds extended one singular bone claw from each elbow, twice the length of an average man's forearm, as if the bone had shot out and torn through where the hands used to be. Its legs looked like they were put on backwards, the knees bending towards its back, while stumpy feet faced forward.

The man, or what had been a man, was a nightmare, the likes of which Ean had never seen, and judging by the few steps back the guards had taken, it was a new sight for them as well.

"By the gods..." Ulften breathed, a hand going to his mouth. He made a gagging noise, which was surprising coming from a man who had casually ordered two separate deaths earlier this night.

More monstrosities started to shuffle into the light, each just as horrible to behold and groaning loudly. They were grossly distorted human beings, each unique and grotesque in its own way, with boney projections sticking out like pins in a cushion or long blades, the flesh hanging off in shreds. They shambled along on their backward legs, slowly making their way towards where Ean's group and the Living Dead were all gathered.

Though their bodies were no longer recognizable as human, the faces on each abomination remained untouched. In a way that was worse, because he was able to attach a name to each face of the men that had disappeared from the caravan. They all wore the same expression, a mixture of pain and ecstasy. That was probably what Azalea had been smelling the whole time, what these poor souls were feeling as they shuffled around.

Ean counted seven now, two less than the total that had gone missing, which meant either the other two had left the caravan like everyone thought, or they were walking around somewhere deeper in the lair. Ean couldn't pull his gaze away from these monstrosities, but thankfully Ulften was more in control of his wits.

"Men, line up," he said, his voice strained. "Those monsters must be put down. We can deal with this murderer afterwards."

He almost felt bad for the monsters that had at one time been men. Did they even realize what they had become? Or were they just mindless creatures? And most importantly, who or what had done this to them?

"Spears at the ready..." Ulften said, his eyes locked on the creatures.

They were only a dozen or so paces away now. Ean could clearly see their eyes, vacant and staring off into space.

"Aim straight for their heads." Ulften sounded more confident now. As grotesque as the creatures were, they moved slowly and would make easy targets for the men. Ean continued looking at those poor faces as they moaned away.

The creatures moved slowly, their vacant eyes seemingly devoid of all thought. But in the blink of an eye, the look changed from blank to unbridled fury. With surprising speed, they burst into action, sprinting across the mine to crash into the line of guards. Which is why he was probably the only one that saw the eyes of the creature closest to them snap forward and focus on the guards. Caught flat-footed, the majority of the guards went down, the creatures on top of them. Those sharp protruding bones stabbed and slashed at their armor, but were turned away by the red plated armor. The guards that were still on their feet tried to adjust their spears into play, but there just wasn't room with the creatures right on top of them.

Ean backed away quickly from the melee but couldn't tear his eyes away from it.

"Help them, you fools!" Ulften's voice cut through the clatter of bone on armor. He was gesturing wildly now towards the two remaining guards that were guarding the hound.

The two men took one look at the hound then moved to join in the fray. With more space, the two men began jabbing their spears into the creatures wrestling with their fellow guards. The spear tips went into the beasts easily, slicing through the skin. Each time they were pulled back out, the barbs on the blades tore the gashes wider, pulling off bits and chunks of flesh.

Rounding on the men still standing, the fleshy monsters seemed to ignore the wounds they were receiving and pushed past the spears to engage the men. Bone hooks and claws slashed and poked at the men's armor, each deflected blow evoking an annoyed moan from the recipient. Most of the men had discarded their spears now and had pulled smaller blades from belts. The daggers slid into the unprotected bodies just as easily as the spears, with the frantic stabs of the guards doing more damage than they would have if they had tried to be more precise.

While the brawl raged, neither side seemed to gain an advantage. The monsters' bone blades were unable to cause any damage to the guards' armor, while the fair amount of damage the guards were causing with their blades did not seem to slow the monsters down in the slightest. In fact, many of the wounds on their bodies stopped bleeding soon after they were created. It seemed as if the two groups would be locked in battle until one side simply ran out of energy.

But then one of the creatures was able to get its sharp bones into the small divide between a guard's chest plate and leg grieves.

The guard stiffened as the bone blade slid into the armor and pierced the poor man's stomach. A gasp of pain escaped from underneath the armored helmet he wore while a moan of triumph accompanied the limp grin that spread across the creature's face. Sensing the weakness, the creature's other three bone spikes flicked into the same space as the original one. The spikes slipped in between the armor easily directly into flesh and lifted him completely off the ground. The guard flailed for a few moments, suspended in the air, until with a sickening crunch the creature pulled its four bone protrusions apart.

Effectively ripping the guard in half.

The two pieces of the man fell to the floor, his legs still kicking while his upper half hit the floor, landing on his back with a clatter. He flailed his arms around like an overturned turtle, trying unsuccessfully to right himself. The whole thing might have been comical if the man's insides weren't starting to leak out of the bottom of the armor.

Ean had to turn away, barely able to contain the bile rising in his throat. It had been one thing to see the aftermath of the attack of these creatures outside of the mine. It was totally different to see the process in person.

A second guard had been taken down, this one missing an entire arm. The remaining guards were starting to become overwhelmed by the creatures, spending more energy keeping those blades from finding the holes in their armor than actually doing any damage against them. Ean wasn't any kind of fighter, but even he could tell the red-clad guards were fighting a losing battle.

A few of the Living Dead began pushing their way back towards the exit, while some of the women and even a couple of the men began screaming in terror as they tried to get out as quickly as possible. A few frantically pushing citizens quickly turned into dozens, and it only took a few moments before the way out was completely blocked with fallen or struggling soldiers.

Not all of the villagers went running however. More than a dozen men and women ran into the fighting instead of away from it, each one carrying some kind of makeshift weapon or small blade, and all of them not wearing a bit of protection. Most went to help the guards while a couple tried their best to pull the wounded away.

Not encumbered by any armor, most were nimble enough to dodge the attacks of the flesh and bone beasts. While unable to do any major damage, they kept the beasts from killing more of the guards. It seemed like they were going to be forced into another stalemate until one of the unarmored men got inside of one of the creature's reaches and planted a knife hilt deep right between the thing's eyes.

The creature immediately dropped its gruesome arms and legs, creating a clatter as it struck the stone floor. The man that had killed the monster stood over it, Ean easily able to see the shock on his face.

The death of one of their fellow monsters sent the other beasts into a frenzy. With a collective moan they started lashing out in every direction. The unarmored men were forced back, those not getting out of the way quickly enough receiving deep gashes to their arms and bodies. The beasts didn't stop there, though. Where before, they had stayed in the tunnel leading towards the living quarters, now they started to push towards the wider space of the junction. With danger surging towards him, Ean had to move.

Ulften was still standing next to Ean, the man's already pale blue face turning paler by the moment. If anyone could get the people calm enough to march out of here, it was him.

"Ulften. Your people..."

The man rounded on him faster than Ean expected, a small, curved blade suddenly in his hands. His face was twisted, the mouth snarling and his eyes glaring but with a slightly vacant look.

"This is your fault! Those things are your doing, and you led us all in here to die!"

Before Ean could even respond, the man thrust the blade straight at Ean's chest. Just as quickly, Azalea was there, her hand grabbing the man's wrist before the blade even got close to Ean. But it wasn't Azalea, the tan, pretty girl with blond hair that stood next to Ean, glaring at his attacker. It was Azalea the Yulari, her blue skin amplified the light coming off Ean's tattoos while her dark purple hair seemed to absorb it. Her leathery wings were folded closely behind her body, twitching slightly as she stared down Ulften.

A small smile spread across Azalea's lips, showing off her perfect teeth and two small fangs. She sniffed a few times at Ulften and her smile widened.

"You know what I am!" she said, a mix of surprise and pleasure in her voice. "You are emanating so much fear right now it's delicious, but it's more towards me than at those ugly beasts."

"I know what you are, temptress," Ulften replied, not bothering to mask the disgust in his voice. "Just another monster. I thought we were rid of your kind forever when the previous owner of these mines died." He finished his sentence by spitting at her feet.

"Not very polite, trying to kill my friend and now spitting at me." Her face twitched, and a crunching sound came from Ulften's wrist. The blade dropped from his hand, clattering to the ground, while he quickly pulled his hand back. The hand was limp and the wrist bone looked broken to Ean's trained eye.

"Azalea, we don't have time for this..." Ean began, but Azalea spoke right over him.

"I just saved you from receiving a knife to the stomach. Don't even try to lecture me on how I go about--"

Four separate yells resonated over the already deafening noise of the fighting and screams of those trying to flee. As all three of them turned together, Ean's eyes went wide as he watched three of the flesh beasts finish taking down four of the unarmored defenders at the same time, opening up a clear path right to where Ean, Azalea, and Ulften were standing. With a triumphant moan, the three beasts charged towards them.

As Ulften let out a terrified yell, Ean braced himself for the worst, but again Azalea moved right into action.

Wrapping Ean up in a bear hug, she lifted him off the ground. Her wings wrapped around both of them, shutting them off from the rest of the world just as the flesh beasts were about to reach them. Held by Azalea, Ean felt the impacts as the creatures crashed into the wings. To Ean's surprise, the creatures did not tear right through the wings. Instead, Ean heard dull thuds beat against the leather. The Yulari's wings were much sturdier than Ean had expected.

Azalea began to move sideways, taking Ean with her as the muffled sounds of battle continued outside of protective wings.

"Fourth time I'm saving your life," she whispered to him. Held this close, with most of his shirt missing and the little amount of clothes she wore in her natural form, he could feel the warmth of her body against his. It was a strange, comforting feeling that was the complete opposite of what he should be feeling at the moment.

"Thank you," he said back, feeling a bit awkward for some reason.

Laughing, she squeezed him a little tighter for a moment. "Such a polite boy. Well then, I'll be polite too. Sorry."

"Sorry for whaa--" he began, but his words turned into a yell as her wings opened up and she tossed him a dozen paces away from her. He bounced a few times on the stone before rolling and coming to a stop on his side, facing Azalea. Taking a quick look around, Ean found himself down an empty tunnel. Behind Azalea, Ean could see the junction and the battle still going on.

Azalea flashed him a quick smile and a wink before turning just in time to meet the rush of two flesh creatures. Her wings folded against her back as she nimbly dodged the bladed arms of her attackers, stepping under their hasty strikes. It looked like a graceful dance the way she weaved in and out of the eight separate arms of the two creatures. Occasionally she would lash out with a foot, the long nails on her toes raking into the skin of the creature and forcing it back. Ean watched in amazement, marveling at the Yulari's power combined with unnatural grace and speed.

After a few moments of dipping and dodging, Azalea increased her attacks. She lashed out with a foot at one of the flesh monsters, sending it backwards then grabbed the bone blade of another with both hands at a spot that was slightly past where it jutted out of the creature's fleshy elbow. With a loud crack, she broke the blade off as easily as Ean would snap a twig, tossing the large piece of bone to the ground. The monster attacked with another of his three remaining blades, but Azalea was too quick. Repeating the same action, she broke off a second bone. By the time the other monster had rejoined the battle, Azalea had broken off three of the monster's bone blades. All in a matter of a few heartbeats, smiling the entire time.

Just as quickly, though, two more of the creatures appeared out of the crowd behind Azalea, joining in on the attack. They must have either realized who was the greater danger or had simply finished off most of the remaining guards. Either way, the three creatures and their one wounded brother surrounded Azalea, each one lashing out and trying to catch her unaware.

Azalea's wings lifted slightly, protecting the back of her head from any attack she couldn't see coming. She still dodged and weaved, escaping the blows of almost twice as many bone blades now. Azalea didn't seem to pick up speed as she ducked under one blade then dodged to the right to avoid another, but the smile was certainly gone from her mouth now. Not taking her eyes off her attackers, she yelled out to Ean.

"Get out of here, now. If one slips by me, I don't know if I'd be able to stop him from getting to you." She ducked under another blade and then let a different blow graze off her wings.

"I'm not leaving you!" Ean shouted back, taking a step towards the Yulari. When he tried to take another, it felt like his leg was caught on something. Looking down, he found the blur of the imp wrapped around his leg.

"Zin, let go! We have to help!"

"Help how? By dying?" the imp's voice sounded desperate. "She can handle herself. We would just get in the way. We need to go."

"No chance!" Ean tried to move back towards the fighting, but it was difficult to walk without tripping with the imp on his leg.

"Ean, if we try to help, she'll get distracted watching out for you, and we'll all die. If we go now, once we've gotten far enough away she can get away as well."

Ean grimaced, knowing that the imp was right but still not wanting to leave a friend behind. He took another step towards her.

Glancing back at him, the Yulari frowned as she dodged two bone blades at once.

"Get out of here now!" She yelled before sending a kick that snapped the leg of one of the monsters. The creature dropped like a stone, but even from the ground its bladed arms tried to catch Azalea. Snatching one of the blades in her hands, she broke off the edge, spun out of the way of two other blades meant to impale her, and launched the piece of bone she held in her hand at Ean.

The tip struck him squarely in the chest, with just enough force to break the skin. With a wince he took a step back then nodded as his eyes met Azalea's for the briefest of moments. Then she was spinning away again, always on the move, keeping each of the creatures around her occupied.

"Fine," Ean said, although the word burned his tongue. As soon as it was out of his mouth, Zin detached himself from Ean's leg. "Let's go."

Something else tugged at him then, and he looked down at Zin once more before realizing it was the connection to his hound. Ean felt boredom from the beast. Of course. He had told the animal to stay and surprisingly, it had listened, not bothering to even move after the chaos ensued.

Ean sent what he hoped was an order for the hound to join him. He received a sense of relief back, and in moments the hound came barreling through the crowd, knocking over both Living Dead and flesh beast alike as they crowded in the junction. The hound even managed to knock down two of the flesh beasts that were engaged with Azalea on his way to Ean's side. The Yulari took the opportunity to lure the two standing away from the opening to the tunnel back towards the middle of the junction. Ean watched as she disappeared into the crowd of bodies and beasts, all four of the flesh beasts she had been fighting giving chase for a moment, then changing their targets to the more easily overcome townsfolk.

Straining his eyes one last moment to try and catch sight of her, Ean sighed and turned his back to the carnage. He immediately began to jog down the tunnel, not waiting to see if Zin or the hound followed, letting the tattoos on his arm dim so that the light and everything around him was barely visible. No point lighting the way for those creatures to follow them. So, on he jogged in silence, into the darkness, leaving a piece of himself back with the Yulari that was fighting for him.

CHAPTER 30

SHARED STRENGTH

"NOT THAT WAY," ZIN says after they stumbled along for a while. "If we keep following that tunnel, we will run into the kennels and a dead end. Head right."

Ean stopped at the imp's words, staring ahead towards the kennels. He hadn't been jogging for long, but it felt like it had been days since he left Azalea. He had been lost in his own thoughts, moving ahead without really paying attention to the bends and sharp turns of this tunnel. Zin had remained quiet up until this point, Ean's breath and the panting of the hound the only sound echoing in the corridor.

"Where does the other path lead?" he asked quietly.

"Back through the two Carnslug hatcheries and then the kitchen." The imp's voice sounded odd, lacking its usual sarcastic tone. Clearly, he recognized the gravity of the situation. "The kitchen connects to the dining hall and back towards the living quarters one way, the library and then the throne room the other way."

"Fine."

Ean paused to stare back down the way they had come. Taking a moment to better attune himself to the energy flowing within him, he mystically reached out in an attempt to try and feel where Azalea was in the mines.

It was useless, of course. The entire mine hummed with the energy of the Abyss, growing stronger in the direction Zin was leading them. He couldn't even distinguish Zin or the hound in all of that energy, and they were standing only a few paces away. All he could do was hope for the best...

...or he could be a man and go back and try and help her...

"She wouldn't want you to do that," Zin said as if he had read Ean's thoughts. "She purposefully drew the beasts off so we could get away and continue on. Let's not waste that effort."

"You're happy to see her gone," Ean growled. "You never trusted her, even though it was your idea to have her come along in the first place." Disgust laced his words. A part of him knew that the disgust was more for himself, but he couldn't help directing it at the imp. "Now you don't have to worry about her anymore."

"Ean..." the imp began, but Ean cut him off with a raised hand.

"I know... I know..."

Leaning back against the wall, Ean let himself slide down into a sitting position. What kind of a man was he? First he had no problem letting Bran and Jaslen run off into the woods, abandoning them to who knows what. He had barely even thought about them since that night. For all he knew, they could have died in those woods, lost and starving or attacked by animals. He should have gone after them.

And now he was doing the same thing to Azalea, leaving her on her own. Except those monsters were far worse than anything Bran and Jaslen could have run into in the forest. Sure, she might have been able to hold her own against four of them, but could she survive more than that? Ean by himself wouldn't last a few moments against one of those creatures, but the hound could help...

An image flashed through his mind--Azalea pinned to the ground by dozens of bone blades, his hound being ripped apart, Zin impaled on the blade of another monster...

It was one thing to know that moving on was the right decision, but it certainly didn't make it any easier.

"Ean, we have to go," Zin said softly.

"You're right." Pushing himself back to his feet, he nodded. "We still have things to do."

So they pushed on, neither speaking a word, the hound slightly behind them. Ean tried his best to not dwell on things, but every now and then, the image of Azalea's smirking face flashed in his mind. He needed to keep his mind on the task at hand. But first...

"Zin," Ean finally said, growing tired of the silence. "I'm sorry."

Glancing down at the imp, Ean caught Zin give a slight shrug. "It's fine. Like you said, I supported bringing her along. I thought we could use her and then didn't like it when the two of you started getting all buddy-buddy."

"Jealous?" Ean tried to force a laugh after the word, but he couldn't put any emotion into it.

"No, not jealous. I was worried that she was manipulating you, turning you into one of her playthings."

"But her tricks don't work on me."

That got a laugh out of the imp. "You might be immune to her Yulari tricks, but she has the same set of tricks as all beautiful girls. Did I ever tell you that a beautiful human woman, not all that different from how the Yulari looked, led to my former master's downfall?

Ean's ears perked up. "Uh, no. Go on."

"Well, like I've said, by the end, my master was a harsh and cruel man set on taking over the entire land. He did things that give me the shivers. But through it all, there was one constant thing that could occasionally bring out his old, more compassionate side. A girl named Adara.

Now, I won't bother you with their entire history, but Adara was supposedly at my master's side from the beginning. She was there back when he was, well, whatever he was before he came into power. She stuck by his side as his power grew and even supported him when he started down a darker path. From what I remember of the two of them, anytime she was around, all of my master's minions relaxed just the slightest bit. If Adara was in the room, you felt the slightest bit safer."

"But you said she led to his downfall?"

"From what I've overheard. Remember, I wasn't there when he died, and in the chaos that ensued after his death, it was hard to get any straight answers. Most of his minions were worrying about when they would be dragged back down to the Abyss, and most wouldn't waste the time talking to an imp in even the best circumstances."

"So then what did you hear happened?"

"She betrayed him, which led to his death. Other than that, I have no idea. I overheard some Cruxlum raging about how Adara had been the one to deliver the killing blow. A pair of Mangoli mentioned that she had simply distracted him long enough for someone else to make the deadly strike." Zin shrugged, his face scrunching up slightly. "I'm sure someone knows, but they are probably still stuck down in the Abyss. If they are still alive after this long."

"So, you thought Azalea would bring about the same fate for me."

"In one way or another. Of course, I thought she was a completely selfish creature as well. She certainly proved me wrong today. Believe it or not, I do hope that we round one of these corners and find her smirking at us. Just hopefully not with any of those horrible creatures close behind her."

"Hopefully," Ean replied, and they continued on in silence.

After a dozen more twists and turns, they came upon a large pair of stone doors standing open. Stepping through the opening, the tunnel opened up into a huge cavern. Stalagmites and small pockets in the stone littered the room, which was three times the size of the average barn. Ean took in more of the energy of the Abyss, letting the tattoos on his body flare up and illuminate the large room even more. Shadows danced everywhere as the light coming off of him grew in intensity, made even creepier by the silence all around them.

"Carnslug hatchery," Zin said quietly, his eyes darting around.

"Expecting something dangerous to leap out at us?"

"No. Just looking for a left over meal. Carnslugs are pretty hardy, and I thought a few might have survived. I haven't had anything to eat in a while."

Ean shook his head as he began walking around the room. "I can't imagine how something with 'slug' in its name could be that appetizing."

"You say that now, but if you tried one you would like it. They taste like chicken, but with a bit more flavor."

"Mmhmm."

"I don't think there are any in here. Best if we move on. We still have to pass through the second hatchery before we reach the kitchens."

"Fine with me."

Glancing around, Ean found another set of open doors with a tunnel behind them. When Ean nodded in its direction, Zin returned the nod, and they both made their way towards the doors. The hound had its back to them, its head down low to the ground as it sniffed around.

"Looks like the hound has picked up a scent. You sure there couldn't be any of these Carnslugs left around?"

"I guess there could be. They eat the fungus and dirt off of cave walls, so in theory they could live down here forever. They multiply like crazy though, which is why they are such a good source for food, and they simply split apart to breed. If there was even one left a few days ago we would have found dozens today."

Ean urged the hound to follow through the bond they shared. It looked up at him, sniffed at the air a few times and trotted over. Ean felt boredom coming though their bond. What did a hound do for fun anyway?

The hound looked over at Zin. Licking its lips a few times, the hound's mouth opened up into a toothy smile. Zin caught the look and began to shift about nervously.

"Don't even think about it," Ean said, shaking a finger at the hound.

Annoyance was all Ean received through the bond, the hound's mouth closing as it pushed its way past Ean. The beast almost knocked him over as it went past, not making any effort to go around him. It took a few steps past the door and then turned its head and looked back.

"Did I mention before how nervous that hound makes me?" Zin said, walking up to Ean's side.

"Yes, many times. But I'm almost positive that it will listen to my commands and not turn you into a meal."

"So reassuring." Gesturing with a clawed hand towards the tunnel ahead, the imp made a mock bow. "After you."

Rolling his eyes at the imp, Ean walked up and past the hound. The tunnel stretched ahead of him into darkness, a sharp turn barely visible at the edge of his vision. He kept the energy of the Abyss flowing through him, the tattoos on his arms lighting up the tunnel as brightly as any torch. They had been walking long enough to make him think that they had left those monsters behind for good.

The faint sound of a moan echoing far behind them sent a shiver down his spine.

Zin rubbed his hands together nervously. "You need to close the doors."

Ean hurried over to the big stone doors and gave one of them a push. He might as well have been pushing the wall. Bracing himself, he put all of his strength into trying to move one of the doors. Again, nothing. Across the empty hatchery he could hear the moan growing louder.

Ean was about to try and wedge himself between the door and the wall when Zin tugged at his pants.

"They are too heavy for you."

"Yes, I realize that now," Ean grunted, still pushing on the door. "If you knew it was too heavy, why did you tell me to close it in the first place?"

"My old master used to be able to shut the doors using his power. Something about the runes. I figured you might be able to find a way to close them the same way".

"You should have said that right away!" he growled, then immediately regretted it. The moans coming from the opposite tunnel paused for a few moments before starting up again, much louder than they had been before. Ean looked down at the imp.

"What do I do?"

Zin frowned, his shoulders rising and falling. "I'm not completely sure. He would place his hands on the doors, runes would light up, and the doors would swing closed."

Ean looked at the bare stone doors, bereft of any markings. Moving around to the front of them, he tried his best to find the slightest etch in the stone. They were completely blank.

"There is nothing here. The doors are completely bare. How can I activate runes that have worn away over time?"

"I don't know."

A flicker of movement caught Ean's attention and he turned around. Just starting to walk through the opposite doorway was one of the monstrosities, its body covered in slashes with one of its bone blades completely broken off. As Ean's eyes met the creature's, it let out a long moan and began shuffling towards him.

Both surprised and thankful that the thing hadn't broken out into a sprint at the sight of him, Ean turned his attention back to the door.

"Zin, tell me if that thing starts moving faster or if any more of them show up."

"Absolutely." The imp ran up next to him, his small body tensed.

Running his hands over the smooth surface of the door, Ean tried to think. Zin's old master had just placed his hand over the door, no magic words, no tracing new runes on top of the surface.

"Two more just came through the doorway." Zin's voice was low, as if the creatures didn't already know they were there.

Placing his right palm on the door, Ean tried to concentrate. He let his senses reach out through the energy of the Abyss. Immediately he felt the thrumming of Abysmal energy running through the place. The energy saturated the lair, making it feel alive in the same way it felt in Ean's body. Maybe that was the key...

"The closest one is about halfway across the room. We might want to think about leaving..."

No, not leaving yet. He was on to something.

The energy, it was in everything. Did that mean whatever magic or runes had been inscribed were still there? Carefully, Ean let a small amount of the energy inside of him flow out from his hands and into the door. The two energies merged as if reunited. Hundreds of different runes suddenly rushed through his mind, less than a dozen of which he knew.

"We're just about out of time..."

Glancing back, Ean saw that Zin was right. The closest flesh monster was almost on top of them. This close, Ean could see the drool coming out of its mouth and the trickling of blood from its dozens of wounds. The whole sight filled him with dread. If only they had a little more time...

A black blur darted past him, causing Zin to jump out of its way. Ean watched in shock as the hound sped towards the closest monster, its legs pumping faster than Ean had seen before. Its nails sounded like chisels as they stabbed into the rock, propelling its body along the floor.

The flesh monster stopped for a moment, as if considering what to do. Then it, too, started sprinting forward. In only a moment, the two creatures were right on top of each other. The monster's four arms and their protruding blades went wide in anticipation while the hound went low, looking like it was about to launch itself up onto its opponent.

The creature's four blades stabbed as one, directly at the hound, but the hound was smarter. Instead of launching itself at the flesh monster and into its waiting blades, the hound threw itself at its feet, smashing into its legs and launching the monster into the air. It came down hard with a thud as its bone blades and protrusions hit the stone floor, its face smashing into the ground.

The hound was back on its feet, spinning around with its mouth open wide. It leapt onto the back of the monster and bit down hard into a fleshy arm. Even from a decent distance away, Ean could hear the hiss as the hound's saliva began eating away at the flesh. He clenched his left hand slightly. He knew the damage that saliva could do all too well.

Coming to its senses, the monster tried to buck the hound off its back, trying and failing to get its bone blades around to stab at the beast. It rolled left and right, arching its back, but the hound hung on. The area began to reek of burning skin as the hound's saliva did its work.

"Ean, the door! The other two are almost to the hound!"

Zin's voice brought him back and he returned his attention to where it should have been all along. The hound was out there buying him time, and he had been wasting it like a fool. Focusing on the door again made the multitude of symbols flash through his mind.

"Zin, what is the symbol for 'closed'?"

"It's, uh...well, it looks kind of like, I guess, like two doors closing."

Frowning, Ean searched the library running through his mind until he thought he found what he was looking for. At least, it did look like two doors closing. Focusing on that rune, Ean tried to picture it on the door.

Sure enough, right on the center of the smooth surface of the stone door, the rune appeared. With a groan the two doors, which had probably remained immobile for hundreds of years, began to swing slowly shut. With a yell of triumph, Ean stepped through the doorway.

His yell quickly turned to one of agony as a sudden sharp pain pierced his side. Falling to the ground, he tried to roll so he could see his attacker. What he found instead was Zin staring at him with a confused look on his face. Looking past the imp, through the slowly closing doors, he gasped at what he saw.

The other two flesh beasts had reached their fallen partner. One had the hound pinned to the ground, its bone pike piercing the hound's side. The hound was squirming around, trying its best to bite the arm that was holding it down. The other flesh monster was moving in, two bone blades raised high and ready to strike.

Ignoring the pain in his side, Ean pushed himself up and scrambled towards his fallen hound.

"What are you doing?!" Zin screamed, standing in his way.

"I'm not losing anyone else," he grunted, taking another step.

It was hopeless, though. Ean couldn't move fast enough, and even if he could there wasn't anything he could do. Those monsters would tear him apart easier than they had the Living Dead. It tore at Ean's heart as he watched the doors close...

"Give it your strength..."

That voice again, like a whisper in his mind. This time Ean didn't bother questioning it. He reached into the bond, feeling the pain and worry of the hound and pushed all of himself into it. All his anger, his strength, every bit of energy that his connection to the Abyss was providing him.

The hound quivered for a moment and leapt up, dragging the monster's arm and the rest with it. It dodged out of the way of a second flesh monster, all while still impaled by the other beast. After bounding away a few steps and dragging the one monster with it, the hound was finally able to dislodge itself. Instead of rushing to Ean's side though, the hound rounded on the three monsters.

Ean's strength gave out and he fell forward. His outstretched arms kept his face and body from smacking into the ground, but just barely. The impact of his knees hitting the floor sent a burst of pain up his body. His arms felt only slightly stronger than his non-functioning legs. Every bit of his strength was going into the hound. Ean's chest felt heavy, each breath becoming more and more difficult. All the while, the doors continued to swing slowly shut.

The hound on the other hand was sending feelings of excitement and hunger through the bond. Eagerness and the desire to kill rushed over Ean, with the slightest hint of joy. If the hound kept attacking though, the strain of what Ean was doing might kill him, and at the very least, the doors would shut and trap the hound on the other side. Not wanting either option to come about, Ean sent a strong desire for the hound to return to his side. He received anger and defiance in return, the desire to kill rising in the animal. Fighting to keep himself from completely falling over, Ean sent his desperation and fear through.

One of the two seemed to work, as the hound looked over quickly and then took off in his direction. It dodged a few attacks on the way but quickly covered the distance and entered the diminishing gap between the doors. As the hound reached Ean, it stopped and placed itself between him and the door. Ean looked past it, allowing himself a smile as he saw the flesh beasts moving too slowly to get to the door before it closed. He still watched until the doors closed completely before he let himself relax and stop feeding his energy into the hound.

Both collapsed then, Ean with a grunt and the hound with a whimper. Zin came running up to both of them and looked down at Ean.

"What in the darkest reaches of the Abyss was that?"

"I gave the hound..." Ean panted, "some of my energy. Most...most of my energy."

"What? How did you know you could even do that? Or that it wouldn't kill you?"

"The voice told me."

"What?" The imp started getting even more agitated. "What voice?"

"The same voice that told me how to take the hound's rune onto my body." Ean's strength was slowly starting to return, which was good since Zin looked like he was about to murder someone.

"That's just great," Zin said, pacing away from him, and away from the hound, who was still collapsed on the ground with his legs splayed out in every direction. It was still conscious and watching them both. "You start hearing things, and of course your first instinct is to listen to the voice. Which could just be you going insane."

Before Ean could say anything, Zin waved him off and continued on. "You're probably not going insane. My previous master wasn't insane; he just became power-hungry and evil. He also wasn't stupid enough that he would just blindly listen to some voice in his head. How do you know that's not just one of the gods messing with you? You know the Goddess of the Soul already has some sort of an agenda concerning you. What's to say the others don't as well?"

"Zin, I know the sound of Kaz'ren's voices, and this wasn't..."

"Don't say her name! You said that makes it a million times easier for them to find you."

"Zin, I really don't think it was her."

"Fine, fine, then who was it? I don't like this, Ean. First I have to worry about Azalea, then the gods themselves, and now this mystery voice. I'm telling you, every one of them has an agenda."

Ean reached up and grabbed the imp without thinking. The fact that he caught him at all, let alone at his weakest, made both of their mouths gape. Relaxing his grip some, Ean held on to the anger he was feeling.

"Don't lump Azalea in with the gods. We've already gone over this; she has more than proven her loyalty. As for the voice, we can figure that out later." Releasing Zin, Ean slowly got to a kneeling position. Not quite trusting his legs, he crawled over to check on his hound.

The hound watched him come, its body rising and falling heavily with each breath. The only feelings Ean got from it were exhaustion, but surprisingly no pain. His own side didn't hurt either. Had the previous pain been from the hound or something different? That was something he would unfortunately have to just wait and see if it happened again.

Reaching the hound, he was even more surprised to find that there wasn't a single wound in the side of the beast that he had seen impaled. He even ran his hand over the hound's body to make sure. Thankfully the hound let him and didn't try to bite him like it had done in the past. Had he not only strengthened the hound but healed him as well?

Placing his hands on the ground, Ean slowly pushed himself to his feet and immediately regretted it. His head grew light, dark spots started swimming in his vision and his legs wobbled. He began to fall...and found the hound standing, braced to catch him. His hands dug into the hound's fur, the hair course and oily against his skin. Ean's arms shook but he was able to keep himself up. The hound hadn't wavered under his weight. Apparently it was recovering a lot faster than he was. Ean let himself take a few moments to gather his strength as he leaned on the hound before trying to stand again. This time it was a success, but he kept one hand on the hound, petting it lightly.

"I think you've earned the right to a name," he said, looking down at the hound. It looked back up at him, confusion and curiosity rolling across their bond. "It has to be a good name, of course, something fitting." Thinking for a few moments, Ean smiled. "I've got it. Yaeger."

"Yaeger?" Zin said, wrinkling his nose. "That doesn't sound very tough."

"It's Crux," Ean replied, still not understanding how he knew the race's entire language. "It means 'to devour.' At least I think it does, I'm not entirely sure I understand the language completely."

"Well, you apparently know it better than I do." Flashing a sarcastic smile, the imp pointed a thumb over his shoulder. "Now if this big show of affection is over, can we move on? We still have a ways to go before we reach the throne room."

"Sounds good to me." Actually it didn't sound that good. His legs were still wobbly, and he felt like he needed a week's worth of sleep. He removed his hands from the hound's back and took a few tentative steps.

"Alright, you lead the way, Zin."

"Sounds good. Hopefully there is a Carnslug or two left in the next hatchery. I'm famished."

CHAPTER 31

POWERS DARK AND OLD

IT WAS A FAIRLY straight shot to the next hatchery, with only a few twists and turns and not incredibly long. Unfortunately a new problem presented itself upon their arrival. The enormous stone doors were shut.

"Well," Zin said. "Open them up."

"Hold on, it's not that simple. For one, I don't know the symbol for open..."

"It's the same as the symbol for closed, except there is a space in-between."

"And second," he cut back in, letting a touch of annoyance enter his voice. "We don't know what's on the other side."

"Hopefully it's a pack of Carnslugs, all fat and juicy from years of growth without anyone to eat them."

"Or it could be a pack of those monsters."

"Doubtful," Zin replied, walking over to the doors. "Just open it up."

Ean walked up to the doors and placed his right palm on the smooth stone. Letting some of the energy he held flow into the door, Ean pictured what he figured was the symbol for 'open.' It was the same as the symbol for closed, two door-shaped runes spread apart instead of opened. There was also a circle around the 'open' rune that wasn't around the closed rune, but Ean dismissed that fact as the rune came to life on the door.

With a groan the door began to open, the loud sound of stone scraping on stone filling the corridor. There was another sound too, one even louder than the opening door. At first, Ean thought it was the sound of running water, a loud sloshing sound that reminded him of heavy rain running down the side of Cleff's house. Peering in through the small opening the doors had made so far, Ean squinted his eyes to see with what little light his runes were providing.

Movement. Lots and lots of movement.

With a start, Ean reached out for the door, intent on closing it quickly.

"No!" Zin yelled, a toothy grin spreading across his face. "No danger there. Just food."

Ean frowned at him but stayed his hand. He didn't need to feel the eagerness of the hound coming through the bond to know that Yaeger was excited about what was on the other side of those doors as well. The hound's mouth was open wide, its tongue lolling out, even its short, stubby tail was wagging slightly. Clearly, it was anticipating catching something in there, and it wasn't dangerous. If both Zin and Yaeger thought it was safe, he trusted their judgment.

When the door had opened up enough to let them through, Ean stared in wonder at what he found inside. The floors and walls were covered with small, red and gold creatures about the size of two fists placed together, looking more like blobs of color than an actual living thing. Two thin eyestalks were the only discernable feature on the creature, the stalks waving about as the Carnslugs moved slowly about the room. While Ean took in the sight, both the imp and hound pushed past him.

Entering the room behind them, Ean noticed a pair of doors on the other side of the chamber settling into an open position as well.

Had both pairs of doors in the previous chamber closed at the same time? In the commotion and danger, Ean couldn't remember. It would certainly have been helpful if they had closed, trapping those three flesh beasts inside.

Both Zin and Yaeger were running around like children in a store full of sweets. Zin was herding packs of Carnslugs around before finally snatching one up and biting into its head while Yaeger was scooping them up into his mouth two at a time as he ran.

Part of Ean wanted to rein them in and get moving, but a smile crept onto his face at the unexpected levity of his two companions. They still had a ways to go, Azalea was still missing, and those flesh monsters were still out there somewhere. But seeing both the hound and imp running around, having fun while they enjoyed their feast, helped Ean relax, if only for a brief moment. With the horrors they had seen and the trouble that they might still face in the near future, a small respite would be beneficial to all three of them.

"Ean!" Zin waved him over with one hand, a Carnslug wiggling around in his other. "Come over and try one. I know you humans are peculiar in what you will and will not eat, but I promise Carnslugs are rather tasty, even raw." For emphasis he bit into the one he was holding, then began chewing away at it with a closed but wide smile on his face.

"I don't think so," Ean replied, carefully stepping over and around the Carnslugs that littered the floor until he reached the imp's side. "I don't think I could just bite into something that looked so slimy, especially while it was still squirming around and looking back at me."

The imp let out a 'harrumph' then finished chewing and swallowed what was in his mouth.

"Oh, too fancy now, your majesty?" It had been a long time since the imp had spoken to him this sarcastically. It felt good to hear Zin being his old self. "Well, I'm sure I could help make it a bit more appetizing."

Snatching up another slug, the imp held it up in front of Ean then stabbed a long nail right between the slug's eyestalks. The slug shuddered once and went limp. Zin offered up the dead slug to Ean, but seeing the look of disgust that crossed his face, the imp let out a laugh and sat down. Using a clawed finger he sliced into the back end of the slug, cutting off a bite-sized piece.

"Here, you baby," the imp said, holding up the small piece of slug. "Try something new for once in your life, so I can laugh at you when you admit that it tastes good."

"Fine, fine." Snatching up the piece of slug and expecting the worst, Ean popped it into his mouth. Trying not to let the slimy piece even touch his tongue, he chewed it as quickly as possible. Surprisingly, the little piece of slug, skin, slime and all did taste pretty good. It was better, in fact than the goat meat that he had often ate growing up in Rottwealth. Shaking his head in disbelief, he stared down at what was left of the slug. His stomach growled at the tease of nourishing food.

Zin looked him over and began to laugh. "I told you they were good. Now, do I have to cut up the rest of this one for you, or can you manage getting your hands a little messy and just eat the rest of it on your own?"

Taking up the challenge, Ean reached down and grabbed the slug. Holding it in his hands for a moment, he sighed once before sticking a large piece in his mouth and bit down into it. His teeth cut through the skin and meat of the slug easily, like it was a fresh loaf of bread, and he pulled back the rest of the slug while he began chewing what was in his mouth. Again, he was surprised at how tasty the slug actually was. If they had time to cook one he probably wouldn't be able to tell the difference between it and a well-seasoned piece of chicken.

"Mmmm," Ean said between chews. "You know, I hate to admit it, but you are right, Zin. These things are pretty tasty. I could probably live off of them for--"

BOOOOOOM.

A shockwave of sound reverberated throughout the entire room. The ground shook with the force of it, almost knocking Ean off his feet. The force of it also shook dozens of slugs from the walls and ceilings. They fell like a gold and red shower, hitting the ground and then continuing on like nothing had happened. A few bounced off Ean's back and shoulders harmlessly, dampening what was left of his shirt with their slime. It felt like small pillows filled with porridge were attacking him. Getting his bearings, Ean glanced down at the imp.

"What in the Abyss was that?" He was not immediately reassured by the look of fear he found on Zin's face.

"I'm... I'm not sure..." The imps eyes darted around, looking everywhere except at Ean.

"Zin, if you have an id--"

BOOOOOOOOM.

This time Ean fell hard, landing on a pack of Carnslugs. They squeezed out from underneath him and continued on as before. Glancing over, he found Zin and Yaeger also off their feet. The hound looked more confused than anything, which was the exact emotion it was sending through their bond. Zin, on the other hand, looked like he had been told he only had moments left to live.

"It can't still be alive..." the imp was muttering, "not after all these years..."

"Zin..." Ean said, making his tone as serious as possible. "What are you talking about?" But the imp didn't seem to hear him.

"Of course... the armor they wore... how could I be so stupid..."

"Zin."

"He couldn't possibly hold a grudge against me...we talked all the time...he had to know I couldn't do anything to set him free..."

"Zin!" Reaching over, Ean not so gently smacked the imp in the face. The fact that he was able to do that without Zin dodging the blow told him how serious the situation was.

"Ean, this could be really bad," the imp said, finally snapping out of his daze. "My old master kept something locked up, a creature of immense power and ruthless intellect. No one knows where they came from or how many of them exist, but they have the ability to cause vast destruction and should be feared. All the creature was to my master, though, was a prize, a trophy he used to show off his power.

"But if it's alive and free..." Zin began, then turned to Ean, his eyes going wide. "Ean, I wasn't paying attention," he glanced guiltily at the Carnslugs around him, "but the rune you used to open the door. It was exactly like the one you used to close it except the two runes that looked like doors were slightly open, right?"

"Right, basically two open doors." Ean said, shrugging. "Oh, and they had a circle around them."

"No, no, no, no, no..." Zin said, climbing to his feet. "You should have used a rune without a circle! Do you have any idea what you've done?"

"Obviously not!" Ean yelled back, also getting up.

"You've opened everything! Every door, every lock, everything!"

"How was I supposed to know, it looked exactly like you said. I had no idea the extra circle wasn't supposed to be there! After all...wait you said everything is open now, right?"

"Yes, everything," the imp replied with a sneer. "And if Lav'zernathar is free and roaming around down here, my suggestion would be that we get out of here as quickly as possible. At least until he has gone."

As if to accentuate his point, another loud boom shook the room, almost taking them off their feet again. What kind of creature could shake an entire mountain?

A low moan, followed by another one broke Ean out of his thoughts and returned his attention back to Zin.

"Zin, if all of the doors are open, that means..."

"That those things that used to be people are probably almost here..." Glancing at the doors ahead of them and the doors they had passed through to enter the room, the imp looked at a loss. "I don't know which way we should go..."

"You have to be kidding me!" Ean said, starting to walk towards the doors leading away from the flesh creatures. "As horrible as you make that other creature out to be, we know we can't face one of those flesh beasts, let alone three. We have to take our chances and hope we simply won't run into this Laz...whatever".

"It's Lav'zernathar, and that's just its name. I don't know what kind of a creature it is, it wouldn't tell me...Maybe we could try sneaking past those flesh beasts..."

"Down a hallway without any other turnoffs? Zin, there is no way. Come on, maybe once we get to the kitchen and dining hall, we can double back past them, but there is no way I'm going back that way."

More moans came out of the doorway leading to the other hatchery. Yaeger crouched slightly, growling in the direction the moans were coming from. That seemed to get Zin moving. With a whimper, he joined Ean's side and they began moving quickly to the opposite edge of the room. Yaeger joined soon after, easily catching up as they reached the opposite doors.

Reaching his hand toward the doors, Ean was about to make them close when Zin grabbed at the bottom of his pants.

"What are you doing? We can't close the door! If Lav is this way, we'll have to run back and fast."

"Zin, you keep forgetting those monsters behind us. If we don't close the door, they will just keep following us until they catch us. You don't even know where this other creature is or if it even has a grudge against you".

"You just don't get it," Zin said, the frustration clear in his voice. "First off, this thing was locked up for hundreds of years. Hundreds! I can only imagine how big of a grudge it is holding. Plus at his core, Lav' is--"

"What am I, imp?" A voice boomed from down the hall. The sound carried like a dozen men and reminded Ean of the noise that had shaken the entire room.

"Oh no..." Zin whispered, slowly backing away from the door.

Ean glanced at the imp and saw a look of utter terror dominate his features, his mouth clamped shut and his eyes wide. Just from his expression alone, Ean tensed, taking in as much energy from the Abyss as he could hold. His runes flared to life, the light stronger than he had ever seen before. It illuminated the corridor ahead, revealing the faint outline of something walking towards them. Something that looked human...

"Go on, imp," the voice said, loud enough to ring in Ean's ears. "Tell your master what I am. Tell him the horrible things I am capable of doing to you both."

Stepping into the light was a man taller than Ean by almost two heads and twice as broad. He wore an intricate suit of armor similar to what he had seen the Living Dead wear, except this one only covered the man's torso and had crisscrossing etched into it that Ean had never seen before. In stark contrast to his crimson armor, his pants were a dark grey, the same kind of pants Ean would see the average farmer wear out in the fields. Rings adorned the man's fingers, green and blue and red gems gleaming from each, reflecting back Ean's light in strange colors.

The man's face was the most striking, wearing a smile that held little warmth framed by a tightly trimmed red beard. His nose was pointed like a beak, slightly hooked and sticking out in front of a pair of deep-set eyes. Shaggy dark red eyebrows topped those eyes, the same color as the man's hair, which was wavy and reached down just above his shoulders. Those eyes, though...they flared red from inside the deep recession of his eye sockets, slitted and certainly not human.

"Lav', you have to understand--" Zin started, but was quickly cut off by the man's raised hand.

"I allowed you to butcher my name while I was held captive, imp," the man growled, "because I wanted you comfortable around me. I hoped to learn as much as I could about your master and possibly even get you to somehow set me free. Now, I no longer need that information or your help. You will address me by my full name, or I will strike you down before you can even blink. Do I make myself clear?"

"Yes of course, Lav'zernathar. I'm sorry, it will not happen again." The imp actually bowed as he said it. "If I may just say..."

"No, I don't want to hear your voice at the moment. You can speak if I decide to ask you a question." Turning to Ean, those glowing red eyes looked him up and down before the man started to walk towards him. "You. You are not this creature's first master. Because of that, I won't kill you yet. You do however wear many of the same or similar markings. How did you come to wear those on your skin? Explain yourself. Now."

Ean's mind raced. The weight of that stare was like a dozen hammer blows. By the time the man was only a few paces away, Ean had barely been able to open his mouth, which now hung slightly open. If he hadn't been so intimidated, Ean certainly would have been embarrassed.

"I...uh..." he tried to get out.

"The truth!" Zin hissed at him. "Just tell him the truth, all of it."

That heavy stare shot to Zin for a moment, making the imp cower, before returning to Ean.

Steeling himself, Ean did exactly as Zin had said. He told the truth. He began with finding the book that had started this all, summoning Zin, the years of practice and failures in trying to use and understand the book. He talked about the threat to his village, leaving with his friends, how quickly they found out about his secret. He glossed over his time in Rensen, fleeing and being lost in Rensen woods, only spending a brief time on how he pushed Bran and Jaslen away and Azalea joining him. That part was more painful than he realized as he recounted it. Ean talked about meeting with Kaz'ren, being directed here, the caravan and the missing men. Finally, he ended with the battle in the village below, the flight into the mines and Zin's old home, and the battle and separation from Azalea.

The entire time Lav'zernathar kept that heavy gaze on Ean. Even when Ean finally finished talking, the man-creature just stared at him for a time. Ean felt like he was being judged, and that a poor judgment would lead to a quick death. If only Ean knew what the man...what the creature wanted. Ean risked a glance at Zin, but the imp was staring at Lav, the imp's body hunched over. The imp wouldn't be any help at the moment. When Ean returned his gaze to the man in front of him, their eyes met for a moment, and before Ean even knew what was happening, he was being lifted into the air by a large, gauntleted hand wrapped around his throat.

Lav brought them face-to-face, those red eyes like drills into his soul, probing. The pressure on his throat increased, making him grab the gauntleted arm with both hands. Behind him he heard his hound start to growl, but he sent reassurance through their bond. If the hound attacked, things would definitely get worse, and by the way Zin was behaving, Ean doubted the hound could help him anyway.

Again the grip tightened, making it almost impossible to breathe now. Well, just because he didn't want the hound to attack didn't mean that he was just going to let this Lav' creature crush the life out of him. With no other option, Ean let all of the energy surge out of him through his right hand and into the gauntlet that held him. For a moment, it felt like all of that energy hit a wall...

Then an explosion of force launched him backwards through the air, over both Zin and Yaeger's head. When he landed, he hit the stone ground hard, rolling a few times, the wind knocked clean from his body. Not knowing what happened, nor caring at this moment, Ean sucked in a large breath of air. Then another. On his fifth, he felt strong enough to push himself to his knees.

Lav'zernathar was there waiting for him.

Grabbing Ean by what was left of his shirt this time, Lav held Ean out in front of him. Lav was smiling slightly, although those slitted red eyes were still as intense as ever.

"You have some fight in you. This could be both good and bad for me. For the moment, though, you are less of a threat than the company you keep. Maybe in the future you will prove to be as ruthless and ambitious as your imp's old master. If that is so, know that if you come for me and try to make me some 'prize' as he did, I will destroy you to your very core. Understand?"

Ean nodded quickly.

"Good, I'm glad we have an understanding. Now," he said, looking past Ean, "do those things belong to you as well?"

Turning as best as he could while still in Lav's grip, Ean's eyes went wide as he saw three of the flesh monsters emerge from the opposite door. "No, no, they've been trying to kill us."

"Really?" Lav said, laughing. "So young and already you have enemies? Maybe you are more dangerous than I thought."

With a flick of his wrist, Lav casually tossed Ean to the side. Caught by surprise by the move, Ean was barely able to land on his feet, stumbling as he tried to keep from falling over. Once his feet were firmly planted beneath him, Ean watched as Lav casually walked towards the slowly shuffling flesh monsters. The monsters seemed to get excited as he approached, their arms and those deadly bone blades waving around in anticipation. When the closest one reached Lav, it lashed out with its upper right and lower left blades, a triumphant moan escaping its mouth.

Without the slightest bit of emotion or effort, Lav grabbed both blades in his gauntleted hands. Before the creature could bring his other arms around, Lav kicked the creature directly in the stomach, leaving his foot pressed against the monster's torso. Then, with a horrible ripping sound, Lav tore both of the arms he was holding from their sockets. Where Ean expected fountains of blood, only trickles came out of the monster's gapping wounds.

Lav didn't stop there. While the creature was still reeling from the damage, Lav took a few steps in, grabbed the creature by its face with one hand, its shoulder with his other hand, and just as easily as if he were plucking fruit from a tree tore the creature's head from its body.

Before the lifeless corpse hit the ground, the other two flesh beasts were running towards Lav at full speed. He calmly stood his ground, taking up an almost uninterested posture. Ean couldn't see his face, but he had no doubt that whatever Lav was, he probably was bored.

The remaining two monsters reached Lav at the same time, neither one stopping their charge. Instead they tried to ram him, using their bone blades as spears.

Again, with what seemed to be little effort, Lav dodged them both, taking a big step to the right and leaning out of the way from a pair of bone blades. In a blur, a red gauntleted fist grabbed the head of the closest beast, yanked it off its feet, and smashed its skull down into the hard stone floor. The sound it made as the skull was crushed made Ean nauseous.

Lav took a moment to kneel and wipe his hand off on the body of the dead monster while the last remaining flesh beast was still turning around to face him. Again the monster came at him at full speed, its moans deep and guttural now.

Not even bothering to stand, Lav lifted his right hand, palm out towards the beast. There was a loud "POP" and the creature was suddenly engulfed in flames. All Ean could see of it was a faint outline in the bright red fire that consumed it. An outline that thrashed about at first, then slumped to the ground and grew smaller and smaller until all that was left was the flame.

Getting to his feet, Lav waved casually at the fire and it disappeared. The monster was gone, not even ash remained. The only sign that anything had been there at all was the scorch marks on the stone where it had fallen. There wasn't even a burnt smell to mark the creature's death. Not bothering to look back, Lav started casually strolling towards the opposite door.

"Wait!" Ean called after him. Wincing, he looked down and found Zin with one of his clawed hands pressing into his leg. He ignored the imp.

"Lav'zernathar. We could really use your help. There are more of those things out there, and we wouldn't stand much of a chance against more than one of them."

Lav leaned back and let out a loud laugh that filled the room. When the man... creature... finally stopped laughing he turned, a large smirk on his face.

"I destroyed those three things," he said, gesturing to the two corpses, "because they were in my way. And ugly to look at. But I have no desire to run around this cave looking for the rest of them. I have spent far too long down here in the dark, and I have a grudge to settle. Since your imp's old master is dead, I'm going to take out my anger on the next best thing, those wretches that live outside and have been harvesting my scales."

"The people below? And what scales..."

Lav laughed again, this time shaking his head. "You really know so little. This," he took a moment to spread his hands and motion towards himself, "is just a form I take to better fit in and move about without frightening you primitive creatures. My real form is much grander, and I was stuck in it while I was chained to this place. Those cursed souls that live outside took advantage of that fact and took my scales, sometimes just picking them up as they fell off, other times tearing them off my body."

He paused, a sneer erasing the smirk he had been wearing for a moment.

"And all the while I had to sit and let them pick away at me while chained to this place. Their leader had the Master Key and could have released me, but instead used me just as the imp's master used me. So as I said, since I can't punish my original captor, I can at least take out my centuries of rage on the next best thing."

Lav took a few steps away from them, then stopped again.

"If I see any more of those creatures on my way out," he said, not bothering to turn around to look in Ean's direction, "I'll destroy them. Consider it a thank you present for setting me free. Even if it was accidentally."

Returning to his exit march, the man almost reached the doors before a thought struck Ean and he called out one last time.

"We have one more companion with us, a beautiful girl with wings, if you see her please don't harm her and point her in our direction?"

Without breaking stride, Lav raised a hand and waved them off.

"The Yulari?" he said, his voice still loud enough to carry across the room. "I saw her either unconscious or dead and being dragged by a human--not one of those deformed ones--in the direction of the throne room. Neither was any concern of mine, so I left them alone. If the Yulari is your friend, I would hurry after them. There was something not quite right with the man, and he had the faint smell of those flesh beasts on him. My guess is whatever he has planned for the Yulari will certainly not be pleasant."

And with that, Lav disappeared through the doorway, leaving Ean with a cold knot deep in his stomach.

CHAPTER 32

UNTOUCHED KNOWLEDGE

THE TUNNELS SEEMED TO stretch forever as Ean ran, a straight line encased in stone with nothing ahead but darkness. It had only been moments since he had taken off out of the second hatchery and into the tunnel that lead to the kitchens, but his fear increased with each moment. Not for himself, but for the Yulari. For Azalea.

The hound was at his side, effortlessly keeping up. Ean felt the warm sensation of enjoyment coming through the bond as the hound ran along beside him. Glancing back, Ean caught sight of the imp only a few paces behind doing his best to keep up. Zin was fast on his feet in tight spaces, but his short strides were no match for Ean's over-long distances. Zin would have to try harder. Ean was determined to save Azalea, with or without Zin by his side.

Ean skidded to a halt in front of a set of open wooden doors, stopping at the edge of the threshold. Yaeger stopped at his left and sniffed the air while Zin caught up with them.

The light emanating from Ean cast the dim room in a faint blue light. Large stone tables took up most of the space, sitting next to large square or dome stone constructions that Ean had never seen before. Glancing around and not detecting any movement, Ean slowly moved into the room.

"The kitchen," Zin said. "Hundreds of meals were prepared here in those ovens," he gestured to the large stone constructions. "Every day for the creatures that dwelled in the lair. Human slaves were used to cook the meals, as not too many creatures from the Abyss waste their time learning to cook."

"I don't care, Zin," Ean replied, not bothering to hide his impatience. "Which way?"

"Straight through the kitchen there is an exit to the tunnels closest to the library and then the throne room. If we went right, that would take us--"

"Fine. Straight. Let's go."

Ean began making his way through the kitchen. It was a slow process, the room seemed to be set up more like a maze. More than once he found himself stuck between tables and the ovens and had to backtrack a bit. The floor was littered with debris and rubble from collapsed tables and ovens as well, just waiting to catch Ean's foot and trip him up. By the time he reached the door on the opposite side, he was considerably annoyed.

Out of the room, he continued on, returning to a jog. All he could think about was Azalea and this mystery person that had taken her. If the man had been able to take Azalea, what chance did *he* have...

No! You will not be a coward this time.

He would figure something out. Maybe the man had gotten lucky. Maybe she had passed out after killing a bunch of those flesh monsters and had been easy prey. Maybe he would suddenly know how to use all of this power he supposedly had to defend someone he cared about. If that voice that seemed to know so much would talk to him more...

He couldn't help but laugh bitterly as he hurried on. Hoping a voice in his head would save him. What Ean needed to do was think things through, come up with a plan, and make his own decisions. Of course that realization came at the same time that he reached a

T-junction, the tunnel he was in stopped and stretched left and right into darkness.

"Which way, Zin?" he said with a sigh, then frowned as he was met with silence.

Turning around, he found the hound just catching up to him. How fast had he moved down the tunnel that he had even outpaced the hound? Not terribly far behind the hound was Zin, sprinting at full speed. When the imp reached Ean, he was panting and bent over slightly, his hands on his knees.

"Which way, Zin?" The imp shot him a glare, but Ean didn't care. He didn't have time to be polite. "Now, Zin."

"Left."

With the briefest of nods, Ean took off again, following the left path down a long but fairly straight tunnel. All he could think about was Azalea at the mercy of that man. If he turned her into one of those monsters...

Just that thought drove him on. His legs started to ache. His lungs were starting to burn. It reminded him of his flight with Bran and Jaslen through the woods, trying to get away from the Seekers. In the end, he had lost Bran and Jaslen, not because of some outside threat, but because of his foolishness and weakness.

He would NOT lose Azalea.

His foot struck something and he tripped, his momentum carrying him a small distance in the air before he struck the ground. Not giving himself time to recover, Ean pushed himself up to a kneeling position. And realized his hands were not on bare stone.

Looking down he found some kind of carpet underneath his hands, the fabric worn and frayed, and the color a light red faded with age. Carpets were something he had yet to see in the lair. Getting to his knees, he looked back at what he had tripped over.

A book. Or to be more specific, a pile of books.

Glancing around he realized he wasn't in the tunnel anymore, but was actually in a room. A room twice as high as the hatcheries with row upon row of bookcases reaching all the way up to the ceiling. The bookcases were everywhere, blocking his sight of most of the walls and making it difficult to figure out how wide the room actually was. Each one was almost completely filled with books of all colors and sizes, more books than Ean thought existed. The ground was littered with books as well, unorganized piles here and there, just like the one he had tripped over.

For a moment, it was all a little overwhelming. All of that knowledge on who knows what just sitting there waiting to be explored. How many books were about the Abyss? Or Healing? Or the Deities? Or contained the histories of the land before the Plague? Ean's curiosity took over his mind for a moment and he forgot everything else.

But only for a moment.

Azalea.

He rose to his feet. If this was the library, then the throne room was just ahead. Azalea and her captor were within reach. He needed to push on. Even if he didn't have a plan...

Yaeger was suddenly at his side, giving him courage. Glancing back, he waited a moment to see if Zin was catching up, but clearly the imp had fallen behind. That was ok, there wasn't much Zin could do to help, and if Ean was running into a situation that he had no chance of surviving, better for his friend not to be there. If Ean died, Zin would return to the Abyss. Probably not the imp's first choice in where to go, but certainly it was better than dying. Ean even considered getting the hound to stay behind for a moment, but knew without Yaeger, he wouldn't have a chance against those flesh monsters.

"Let's go," he said to the hound. It jogged along at his side as Ean took off again, this time making sure to pace himself. The last thing he wanted was to go stumbling into a group of those flesh beasts just like he had stumbled into the library. He might not have a plan, but he certainly wasn't going to just throw himself into danger.

Ean and the hound passed more than a dozen bookshelves as they moved straight ahead, with Ean catching glimpses of even more rows behind the ones he passed. If they somehow did survive this, Ean could spend weeks searching through the books just to find the ones that would peak his interest. But that was the future, which wasn't looking too bright at the moment. Best to focus on the present.

They passed through another set of double doors and into another tunnel that looked exactly the same as all of the other ones. They were close now. According to Zin this one would open up right into the throne room. It was interesting how in such a short amount of time Ean's goals had changed. When they had first entered the lair, they were focused on getting to the throne room in order to find something Ean could use. Now he was trying to get there in order to save a friend.

Before Ean knew it, a set of open, stone doors appeared down the hall in front of him. He slowed to a walk, approaching the door carefully, his senses straining to hear or smell anything. There was light coming from the throne room, although a large pillar of stone a few paces in blocked his view of most of the room. Ean released some of the energy he held, the light coming off his tattooed body dampening to the point that it was hardly noticeable compared to the light coming out from the throne room.

Reaching the door, he sent a command through the bond with his hound, telling it to stay. When he received the feeling of acceptance back, he moved ahead, crouching low. He poked his head through the doorway first, glancing to his left and right. Not finding any immediate threat, he moved ahead to the pillar, pressing against it and freezing in place. He heard something now. A sound he had heard many times as a Healer.

The sound of a blade cutting into flesh.

CHAPTER 33

IN THE PRESENCE OF A MADMAN

HIS HEART IN HIS throat, Ean moved around the pillar to get a good look at the room.

Enormous was the first word that came to mind. The room was larger than any he'd ever seen, four or five times larger than the hatcheries. A dozen pillars went around the semicircle-shaped room. Torches hung from those pillars, some of them lit, which explained the light he'd previously seen streaming out of the entrance. Neglected tapestries and paintings, some of them shredded from who knows what, hung from the walls. The back wall was the flat part of the semicircle, with a huge dais that held a large throne in its center. In the middle of the room was a black stone sphere the size of a wagon, its surface cracked and charred. Short flagpoles with varying geometric designs circled it, indicating that the sphere used to be an object of importance.

But Ean wasn't interested in spheres. All he cared about was finding Azalea.

Sitting off to the left side of the sphere, a figure was hunched over something, its back to Ean and its arms moving feverishly. All Ean could tell from his position was that it was wearing some sort of robe. Whatever it was, it was not Azalea or one of those flesh monsters. Ean was about to move forward when the figure stood, its robe dropping away.

The figure was a man, shorter than Ean with a mostly bald head. A fit body, covered in red markings, dressed now in only a small loin cloth, standing completely erect. For a moment his hands were out of view, but then he spread them wide. In each hand the man held something that made Ean's blood burn with a hundred fires.

Wings. Familiar black leathery wings. And they were dripping with blue liquid. The color of Yulari blood.

A thousand needles of despair stabbed at Ean's chest as he watched the man place the edges of the wings on his back. The markings on his body glowed faintly and the edges of the wings seemed to sink into his body. His skin writhed and pulled as the wings sunk in, covering and fusing in a matter of moments. When the skin stopped moving, the runes died off and disappeared, leaving the figure's skin bare.

The man stretched out his arms, the wings following suit. Whatever the figure was, he was now the owner of a new set of wings. Azalea's wings.

The energy of the Abyss, mingled with his outrage, flowed through Ean like a raging river. He reacted before he could think, throwing himself at Azalea's assailant like a wild beast.

And he was smacked down by a backhand that he didn't see coming.

The pain from the blow scattered his thoughts as his body was knocked across the room. A moment later his face smacked against the stone floor. It was only the energy running through him that kept him conscious. When Ean tried to rise, pain shot up his left side, the force of it flipping him onto his back with a groan.

When he landed, his head rolled to the side and he found himself staring into Azalea's dark red eyes.

The Yulari's eyes were glazed over and her mouth hung open. Ean watched as her chest rose and fell slowly with each breath. Her back was a wreck; long vertical slices where her wings had been ripped off oozed viscous blue blood, flowing freely over her back and down her side.

She was alive, but barely. He had to do something.

"Ean, my boy. I didn't know it was you. My apologies."

The voice hit him like a bucket full of ice water. It couldn't be...

"You really shouldn't just run at someone. A person might get the wrong idea," Sadiek said, staring down at him with a condescending smile. "Of course, you couldn't have known it was me with my new addition."

The man's wings--Azalea's wings--fully extended for a moment before Sadiek brought them back in.

"Wondrous, are they not? Very fortunate to come across such a creature here--"

"Azalea is not some creature!" Ean was surprised at the strength in his voice, and by the look on Sadiek's face, so was he.

"This is your sister?" he said, a hand going to his chin. "Well, I suppose she can't be your sister technically, as you are human and she clearly is not, but you were passing her off as your sister. So I assume, then, she is something else from the Abyss? Like your imp?"

"What did you do to her?"

Tilting his head to the side, Sadiek flashed Ean a frown. "I took her wings obviously. They have such strength and make a fine addition to my body. They will be very useful in the coming years. I have such wondrous plans, and the ability to fly will certainly help."

"But you've practically killed her!"

Again, that slightly confused frown. "An acceptable loss. You can always summon another one after all, if she comes from the Abyss..." He passed a hand over his head, his fingers running over it as through hair that was no longer there. "Does this specific one mean something to you?"

"Yes," Ean growled. With the energy flowing through him, he was getting his senses back, but his mind was still foggy as he struggled to think up a plan.

"Oh," Sadiek said with a shrug. "Well, that is unfortunate. I had planned on asking you to join me in my mission, but that will be difficult now, yes? If you are the type to hold grudges, of course. If not, then we have so much we can accomplish together."

"What mission?"

"To change the world, my boy!" Laughing, Sadiek began to pace around. Ean took the opportunity to inch his way closer to Azalea while the man went on a rant.

"The people in this land, the Deadlands, Ven Khilada, and the lands to the south that those savage Umdaer hold, have made countless mistakes. The Plague being the most recent, but there was an even more devastating mistake before that. Cast out, the people of this land were, sent to this land from one a hundred times better, all because of the actions of their deities.

"Selfish gods, that's what the people here worship, what I used to worship. I followed the Goddess of Knowledge for the longest time, studying and learning as much as I could. But now I know the truth, know how both their actions and inactions continue to bring all of the races that acknowledge them down." Sadiek threw his hands in the air, his wings expanding again.

"They must be brought down, and only I have been told the way to do it."

Ean had made his way over to Azalea's side by that point and reached out a hand to her. Grasping her shoulder, he shuddered at how cold her skin felt.

"So," Sadiek said, turning his attention back to Ean. "Will you join me?"

Stall. What he was stalling for, Ean had no idea. Other than the hound waiting just outside, he had no one else to help him and no plan. And every passing moment, Azalea was that much closer to death. He needed time to think.

"Those monsters, the things that used to be men that went missing from the caravan, did you do that?"

"Yes!" A wide grin spread across the older man's face. "Magnificent, are they not? Just a little change to their bodies and they became so much more than simple wagon drivers and loaders. They are the future of humankind!" He waved a hand at nothing, laughing sheepishly. "Well, the first steps, at least. I am still working out what I can do with the human body."

Ean had to keep him talking. The moment the man realized Ean wasn't going to join him, he was probably dead. He had to help Azalea, no matter what, that had to be the first priority. She might not have much time left.

"So, the whole land is going to be a bunch of mindless monsters?"

"No, no. I just said they were the first step. Experimentation, that's the key. Unfortunately those that I used could not handle such a drastic change and at such a quick pace. It broke their minds. The next group, I will make sure to change slowly, a few pieces at a time. Maybe not as dramatically as well." He let out a short laugh. "I have to admit, I got a little excited at the possibilities once I started changing the first man."

"I don't think I really like the idea of being changed," Ean said carefully. Clearly the man was unhinged and dangerous, best not to make him angry. "Would it be possible for me to join you and not end up like them?"

Sadiek scratched at himself as he considered the question, giving Ean time to think. He had to help Azalea. Rottwealth powder and some Flashseal could close and heal the wounds but he had neither and doubted Sadiek would allow him to apply them anyway....

The bond.

If he could form the same magical bound that he had with the hound, he could give her some of his strength and get her back into the fight. At the very least he could keep her alive. Then maybe the two of them and the hound would have a chance.

"No, trust me my boy, the change will be good. You will be stronger, a better person on top of the skills you already have. After all, as you are, you are physically weak. It would be for the best, I think, to improve your body to match your growing abilities."

Reaching his right hand underneath his torn shirt, he searched around until he found the small piece of bark hanging from his neck that bore Azalea's summoning rune. Closing his eyes, he pictured the rune becoming part of the others that now covered most of his upper body.

The designs on his body flared to life, the dark blue light slightly overwhelming the torch light and covering the room in a dark blue hue. Sadiek quickly took a few steps back, eyeing Ean wearily.

"What are you doing?" The old man said, confusion mixing with annoyance in his voice.

"Saving my friend," Ean grunted in reply as the magic took hold. Both Sadiek and Ean watched as Azalea's summoning rune suddenly appeared on Ean's exposed arm. It rode the rest of Ean's tattoos like a current, rising and dipping as it moved up his arm, over his shoulder, and then coming to rest on the right side of his chest. Just as the hound's rune had done, Azalea's rune settled into place and quickly began to merge with the designs already there. In a matter of moments it was completely integrated with the rest of his body. The bond was there too, sending him Azalea's torment and sadness.

And that's when the pain came.

If felt like two jagged blades were jabbed into his back just below both of his shoulder bones. The pain came so suddenly, Ean was caught off guard and writhed in agony, both hands reaching back to grab at blades and wounds that were not there. Trying his best to block out the pain, Ean took in as much energy as he could to dull the pain through the bond. It worked enough, diminishing to feeling like a sore back than two stab wounds. Catching his breath, Ean did his best to focus on Azalea's emotions and not so much on her pain. Sadness, fear, and a small amount of acceptance. She knew she was dying.

"That did not look like you provided much help," Sadiek said, cautiously moving closer to where Ean was laying. "But whatever you did to cause yourself such pain, it is a good sign. I'm afraid you have a lot more pain to come as you change into a better you. And you will be better off without your friend here anyway."

"I'm not done with her yet," Ean growled, and poured everything he had into the bond between himself and the Yulari.

Ean's attention was on Sadiek, but he heard Azalea gasp and start to cough behind him. He let himself feel her agony again, a small smile touching his lips as he felt the wounds on her back start to lessen in pain. Risking a glance back, he let his smile grow as he watched the wounds on her back slowly close. It had worked.

"What did you do?" Sadiek said, his voice slightly strained. "How are you doing this?" Walking over, the old man reached down and grabbed Azalea by the hair and lifted her off the ground. She gave a low whimper as she was dragged up and suspended in the air, her hands weakly began to claw at the hand that held her suspended. Her nails barely left scratch marks.

Turning her to the left and the right, he watched as the last bits of bruising and cuts disappeared from her body, leaving two long, thin scars running down her upper back. As the last of her wounds disappeared, Ean lessened the amount of his own energy he sent over. She still seemed weak, but he couldn't give her much more if he wanted to have any chance of defending himself as well.

Giving Azalea one last look over, Sadiek let her go and turned towards Ean. Before Azalea even hit the ground, her body folded up on top of legs too weak to hold her up, Sadiek had a firm grasp on what was left of Ean's shirt. Lifting him up so that they were face to face, Sadiek licked his lips as he regarded Ean. The stale smell of rotted meat washed over Ean every time the man opened his mouth.

"There is still so much I do not know about what you can do," Sadiek said, looking Ean over like he was a piece of meat. "You are quite the puzzle, and I do like figuring out puzzles..."

Sadiek's eyes started to drift off to the side, his attention seeming to go elsewhere for a moment. Ean took the moment to glace down at Azalea. The Yulari was on her hands and knees, but she was struggling to sit up. Ean felt nothing but determination through their new bond. If they weren't in such a bad situation, Ean would have complimented Azalea on her refusal to give up. Instead he settled on sending pride through their bond.

"Don't look away from me while I'm talking to you!" Sadiek was suddenly shaking Ean, small specks of spittle coming out of his mouth. "It is quite rude after all!"

Ean's attention snapped back to the man. "Sorry," Ean managed to get out before the man shook him any harder. Thankfully it was enough to calm him down. Not enough to get him to put Ean down however, leaving Ean still stuck in front of the man's foul smelling breath. Or was it the man himself that smelled...off...

"As I was saying..." Sadiek blinked a few times and paused, then shook his head and continued. "You are a puzzle, but a dangerous puzzle. Since I don't know exactly what you can do, or how many other creatures you have summoned," He waved at Azalea. "Or what I can do will mix or reject whatever is happening to your body already, it creates quite the list of problems."

"Which would be a good reason why you shouldn't try to--"

Pain exploded on the right side of his face as Sadiek backhanded him. Ean again didn't even see the blow coming. Black spots raced across his vision, fading in and out for a moment.

"Do not interrupt. If I decide to keep you around, you must learn to only speak when spoken to or say to others what I have given you permission to say. Our numbers are small, especially since your pet girl killed four of my new creations and none of the other ones have returned. If they are all dead, that would just leave the two of us to continue on with my mission. As powerful as I am and as you might be, I fear most of the people in both the Deadlands and back in Ven Khilada are not ready for what I have planned and would try to stop us. So it is best, I think, if you don't speak once we leave here."

"I completely understand." *That you are crazy.* "I can keep quiet." *Until I figure out how to escape.*

"Good." The older man set him down much gentler than he had Azalea. "Now, let us see how good you are at following more orders. Kill her." He gestured at Azalea like he had just told Ean to kill a gnat.

Why was he pandering to this lunatic? If he had to face the man and die, he might as well get it over with.

"No."

"Ean, Ean, Ean," Sadiek said, shaking his head. "For a moment there I thought you understood your situation. I suppose you need a few more lessons first." Ean tensed as Sadiek took a slow, deliberate step in Ean's direction. This was it.

A loud growl emanated from Ean's right, stopping Sadiek in his tracks. They both turned to look and found Yaeger slowly walking towards them both, his head low and his teeth bared. Ean had been so focused on his bond with Azalea that he had forgotten the hound. The huge beast moved slowly, its eyes locked on Sadiek as it took deliberate steps towards him. The older man watched the hound warily, a frown marking his face.

"If that is your animal, Ean, you better call it off," he said through clenched teeth. "I promise you things will get much worse if I have to put that creature, as well as your girl, down."

"I don't think so," Ean said, his tattoos glowing brightly as he took in even more energy. "I'm not going to let you hurt either of them."

CHAPTER 34

SACRAFICE

"NOT GOING TO LET me? Interesting. I'm going to kill them both, and you as well now, and I promise the process will hurt a great deal."

Before the words were even completely out of his mouth, Sadiek took two quick steps towards Ean. The hound responded, covering the remaining distance between itself and Sadiek by the time the older man was taking his third step. Yaeger leapt at Sadiek, its teeth bared wide.

But the older man was fast, faster than even the hound. He sidestepped Yaeger's attack, the hound's teeth biting down and just missing Sadiek's chest. As the hound sailed past, Sadiek thrust out both palms, catching the hound in the side and sending him spinning off course. Instead of landing straight on his paws, the force of the blow sent the hound hitting the ground on its side, its head smacking into the smooth stone floor.

But Yaeger was up in an instant, turning around and facing Sadiek with squinting purple eyes. It growled loudly again, drool dripping from its open mouth. Steam rose as its slobber hit the ground, sizzling as it landed. If the hound could just land a bite or even get some of that drool on Sadiek's skin, it might distract him enough that they would have a chance. Ean would have to help.

This time when Yaeger charged, Ean went running in as well. Being faster, the hound reached Sadiek first, making a move as if it was going to leap at the man's chest again, then changing at the last moment and sticking to the ground, its mouth going for the man's legs instead.

Again Sadiek was just fast enough, leap-frogging the hound and barely avoiding its gaping jaws. Not a drop of saliva hit the man, but he was still on his way down when Ean reached him.

Not slowing down, Ean ducked his shoulders and plowed into Sadiek, wrapping his arms around the man and taking them both down to the ground. To Ean it felt like he was tackling a tree, his shoulder ached from the impact, but he heard the satisfying whoosh of air escape from the man's mouth as the breath was knocked out of him.

They skidded along the ground a pace or two before coming to a stop, Ean quickly getting to his knees. Hovering over the dazed man, Ean began raining down blows with his fists. He only had experience receiving blows instead of delivering them, so he focused on landing as many blows as he could instead of going for one knockout blow. His fists found their mark, splitting the man's lip and bloodying his nose.

Sadiek curled into a ball for a moment then lashed out with his legs, kicking Ean squarely in the chest, the force sending him tumbling backwards. He stopped rolling and got instantly back onto his knees but Sadiek was already on the attack, this time tackling Ean the rest of the way down.

Now it was Sadiek's turn to hover over Ean and rain down blows. Ean brought his arms up to protect himself, but the older man simply varied where he was punching. If Ean blocked his face, Sadiek would land a blow to his chest or stomach, if Ean moved to protect his body, Sadiek would get in two or three blows to his face before Ean could change his guard. Sadiek was quickly wearing Ean down.

A loud thud was all Ean heard before the blows suddenly stopped. Quickly looking around, he found Sadiek and the hound a few paces away rolling along the ground. Sadiek's hands were somehow keeping the hound's mouth away from his own throat. Despite not being able to reach the man, Yaeger's mouth kept snapping at him, drops of drool landing to the left and right of the man and setting off little wisps of smoke when they hit the stone.

Ean tried to get to his feet but was still feeling woozy from the pummeling he just received. Unable to stand on wobbly legs, Ean instead began moving on his hands and knees towards the melee.

While Ean was moving, a scream erupted from Sadiek as some of the hound's saliva finally started hitting his arms and chest. With as close as Ean had gotten, he could see the man's skin start to peel and burn away as each drop made contact.

But the pain seemed to add to Sadiek's strength instead of sap it. With a great heave he rolled on top of the hound. Freeing his right hand, Sadiek raised it back preparing to strike, his fingers held together and pointing at the hound's exposed belly. Ean watched in horror as the older man's skin peeled away from his finger tips and exposed bone. Four small, pointed fingertips glistened with the man's own blood. Extending twice as long as they had been right before the change, Sadiek gave a triumphant yell and drove them into the hound's stomach.

The hound whined in pain as the small bony daggers pierced his stomach. The pain of it coming through the bond almost brought Ean the rest of the way to the ground. But if he went down, Sadiek would surely finish the hound off.

Using the pain to drive him as well, Ean scrambled a few paces more until he was close enough to launch himself again at the older man. He grabbed Sadiek's arm, his momentum pulling that dangerous hand out of the hound and taking them rolling away. They both landed on their sides, Ean's left hand locked on Sadiek's right wrist, his full attention on those bone blade fingers now covered in the hound's blood. Which left Sadiek's other hand free to grab Ean's throat.

Ean's eyes went wide as he was suddenly cut off from air. His free right hand went instinctively to grab at the hand around his throat, but the man's grip was iron tight. If he used both hands he might be able to free himself, but that would free up Sadiek's dangerous bone blades. Ean did his best to try and buck around on the ground, hoping to loosen the man's grip enough that he could get some air. It failed.

His vision started going spotty. He had to try wrenching the hand off his throat with both hands before he lost the strength. If he passed out, those bone-bladed fingers would be free to finish him anyway. Releasing the man's right wrist, Ean grabbed at the man's left wrist with both hands now and tried to pull him off.

But Ean had waited too long. He could not pull even the slightest bit. As the edges of his vision started to go dark, he saw a look of triumph pass over Sadiek's face. Casually, taking his time now that he was completely in control, Sadiek raised his right hand and pointed two of those pointed fingers directly at Ean's eyes.

This was it. The end.

A light blue hand grabbed that wrist before it could descend, four purple nails digging into the man's skin and pulling it back. Air suddenly rushed into Ean as Sadiek released his throat and attempted to rise. A small blue foot caught the man in the face as he rose, spinning him around. Sadiek landed face down, his hands catching him from hitting face first. He rolled quickly away and got to his knees, his eyes blinking quickly as he shook his head.

"Get up," Azalea said, grabbing Ean by his shirt and putting him on his feet. "I couldn't take this monster alone when I was completely healthy, which I certainly am not right now."

"Yaeger can..."

"You're hound is dying, boy," Azalea said, her words short. Risking a glance back he saw that the Yulari was right.

Yaeger hadn't moved and was lying on his side, blood pouring out of the savage wound in his stomach. Each breath by the hound was accompanied by a small gurgle and extra spurt of blood from the wound. The hound's eyes were locked on Ean as its head lay on its side, and actual fear accompanied the pain that Ean felt through their bond.

Turning his attention back to Sadiek, he found the man slowly rising. Azalea's kick must have really done some damage to slow the stronger man down this much. Even so, Ean didn't like their chances as they were. But if he was going to die, he was going to make sure his companions at least had a chance.

As Sadiek started advancing towards them, Azalea tensed and readied herself. Ean on the other hand sent everything he had through the bonds to both Azalea and Yaeger. All of the energy from the Abyss, all of his own strength, and more went to both of his companions. He felt it all go to them both as his legs started to give.

With a roar Sadiek charged them, his eyes clear now and filled with rage. Ean knew he wouldn't be any help in the fight anyway, so instead of bracing himself like Azalea was doing, he tried something he hoped Sadiek wouldn't expect. Knowing his body was about to give out, Ean pushed off Azalea and tumbled forward. Ean watched Sadiek's expression as he fell and would have laughed if he had the energy. The older man's face turned from rage to confusion and then surprise as Ean fell directly at his legs. Moving quickly, Sadiek had no chance to dodge around Ean's body as it fell.

Sadiek's thigh smacked into Ean's face and spun him to the side before he finished falling. Sadiek also left his feet as he tripped over Ean's body, falling forward. Ean didn't see him land, as without any strength left, he wasn't able to even catch himself as he fell. All he was able to do was turn his head to the side right before he hit the ground, saving himself from breaking his nose and losing some teeth. He was able to hear the sound of the other man hitting the ground shortly after he did.

Lying on his stomach, Ean continued to pour everything he had into his two friends through their bonds. He could feel Azalea rapidly gaining in strength, a mixture of determination and anger flowing back to him through the bond. From the hound, Ean felt the fear and pain lessen. He hoped he was saving the hound's life, if not getting him back into the fight.

Unable to move, Ean could only stare ahead at one of the pillars while he listened as somewhere behind him Azalea and Sadiek began to battle. It started with the patter of feet moving around quickly, Ean feeling Azalea's focus through the bond. Then the sound of grunts and the thuds of fists and feet hitting their targets. A tearing sound at one point accompanied by a slashing pain to Ean's right shoulder told him that Sadiek had landed a blow. As time slowly moved on, he could tell that even with all of the energy he was giving Azalea, she was wearing down. Ean had to get back into the fight.

Ean let himself feel the hound through their bond. The animal was still in pain, but not as much as before, and a sense of relief floated along to him from the animal. Ean hoped the animal's relief came from being healed and not from its body just giving up. Either way he needed some of his energy back if he was going to help Azalea. Stopping the flow of his own strength through the bond, Ean kept a sliver of the energy from the Abyss feeding into the hound.

Feeling slowly returned to his body and he started to push himself up. A slashing pain to his left thigh--Azalea's--almost brought him back down but he worked through the pain. Once he was on his knees, he turned around and got a real view of what was taking place. Many of the nearby small flagstaffs were completely knocked over or leaning against the strange black rock that sat in the middle of the room. Drops of both red and blue were scattered about the ground and nearby pillars as well.

Azalea and Sadiek were circling each other, their eyes locked and their hands held out defensively in front of them. Azalea's shoulder and left leg was scratched and the beginning of dozens of bruises covered her body. She limped slightly as she circled, breathing heavily as she gave her opponent a cold stare. Ean could feel through the bond that her strength, even with what extra energy he was providing, was waning.

Sadiek's body looked slightly worse, claw marks covering a great deal of his exposed body, most of which were bleeding. The fingers on his hands now ended in those sharp bone blades, most covered in either the hound or Azalea's blood. As he circled around and faced toward Ean, the damage of the hound's saliva was clearly visible. A good deal of skin around the man's right shoulder was black, pieces of it hanging off his body. All of the wounds didn't seem to bother the man though, as he moved just as easily as he had before. Azalea's wings still clung to his back like a protective shield and his face was twisted into a horrible scowl, which worsened as he noticed Ean back on his feet.

Gritting his teeth, Ean began making his way towards his enemy. Sadiek stopped circling around as Ean began to move, backing up slightly instead and keeping both Ean and Azalea in front of him. As he moved back, Sadiek's eyes flickered occasionally to the hound before returning to watch Azalea and Ean.

Good, keep part of your attention on Yaeger.

Ean could tell through the bond that the hound didn't have the strength to roll over, let alone return to the fight. But Sadiek didn't need to know that. Let the man worry about the beast, Ean would take any advantage he could get.

Moving in to Azalea's left, he gave her the briefest nod before returning his attention to Sadiek. The older man's eyes were flitting back and forth now between Azalea and himself. When the man's arms dropped slightly, Ean braced himself, expecting the man to rush them.

Instead he was greeted by the sickening sound of ripping flesh accompanied by the grinding sound of bone on bone. Ean watched in horror as the rest of the skin covering Sadiek's hands tore itself away, leaving only the bone beneath. Those skeletal hands quickly changed, the bones seeming to fuse together until all that was left was one large blade extending out of what was left of each of Sadiek's arms. They looked exactly the same as the arms on those flesh monsters. It all happened in a matter of moments, and while Ean was still trying to comprehend what had just happened, that was when Sadiek charged.

The man, or whatever he was now, made straight for Azalea. Bracing herself for the charge, Azalea let out a grunt of surprise as Sadiek suddenly changed directions and ran straight at Ean. Only a few paces away, Sadiek raised his right arm as he ran, a look of agony and anger painting his face.

Ean dropped down just in time as Sadiek went past him, the bone blade protruding from his arm slicing through the air where Ean's neck had been just a fraction of a moment before. Ean rolled to a crouching position, mostly because he wasn't sure he could stand right away and turned to face Sadiek. He found the man already charging towards him, his right blade held high and ready to swing down.

But Azalea got there before Ean could react, grabbing Sadiek's arm at the elbow with both hands. Her nails dug in deep as she held the arm in place, and she growled with the effort it was taking her to hold the arm off.

Sadiek brought his other arm back, his attention now on Azalea, but Ean was already on the move. He launched himself up, wrapping his arms around the skin of the man's left arm and pulling it back as much as he could behind Sadiek's body. It took all of his strength to keep the arm immobile.

Azalea let go of Sadiek's arm to step to the side, letting the tip of the blade crash down into the stone floor. Ducking down, she grabbed the bone near the tip with her right hand, then delivered a palm strike with her left just above her other hand.

Ean felt the force of the impact as it traveled through Sadiek's body, shaking them both. With a loud cracking sound, the bone broke, leaving the sharp tip sticking straight down into the stone.

Ean expected that to slow down Sadiek, but the man seemed unstoppable as he lashed out to strike Azalea across the stomach. The broken edge of Sadiek's bone tore into her skin. Azalea clutched at her new injury and tumbled backwards.

As Azalea rolled away, Ean aimed a kick at Sadiek's knee. Big mistake. The shift in balance gave Sadiek a chance to yank his arm free. The next thing Ean knew, he was being tossed into the air. He landed just a pace or two away on his side, the pain of the impact numbing his arm.

Before Sadiek could move, Azalea was back, this time leaping in-between Sadiek's wings and digging her nails right above where the wings had only recently connected.

"Give them back!" she screamed, clawing at the man's back.

Sadiek spun around, trying in vain to impale her with his bone blade arms. When that failed, he threw his entire body backwards. Towards the floor. Azalea tried to leap off in time but got caught up in the wings and went down as well. With a loud thud, Azalea smacked into the ground right before Sadiek's body slammed into her, pinning her arms underneath the wings.

As Ean got to his feet, he watched as Sadiek slammed the back of his head into Azalea face. Unable to defend herself or even move, Azalea let out a weaker and weaker cry each time Sadiek's head was brought down against her face. After the fifth blow, Sadiek rose and turned to face her leaving his back towards Ean. He stomped a foot down hard into her chest, pinning the barely conscious Yulari to the ground again.

Knowing Azalea had little time left, Ean rushed to her aid. Spying the piece of blade Azalea had broken off lying on the floor, he scooped it up as he ran past it.

Raising both his broken bone and full bone blades above his head, Sadiek let out a maniacal laugh. "Die, you wretched beast!"

Ean rammed into Sadiek's back, driving the blade in his hand deep into the lower left side of the man. The momentum took Sadiek off Azalea and sent both him and Ean tumbling to the ground, with Sadiek letting out a cry as he fell. As soon as they hit, Ean pushed himself off Sadiek's back and rolled away, forcing his legs to push him into barely a standing position. He risked a glance over at Azalea and found her still prone, although her eyes were blinking slowly. He needed her to recover quickly otherwise he was in a lot of trouble. The only weapon he had ever held was still sticking out of Sadiek's back, and he barely had the energy to stand, let alone dodge the man's remaining blade.

With a groan, Sadiek began to push himself up. If the man got to his feet, Ean wouldn't have much of a chance. Even with the blade still stuck in his opponent's back.

His legs wobbled as he charged Sadiek this time. He just needed them to last a few more paces before giving out. Miraculously, they did not let him down and he threw himself on top of Sadiek, landing on the man's wings and forcing him back to the floor. Sadiek began moving his wings, trying to shake Ean off. Ean was able to hold on with just one hand, freeing up his other one to try and grab the bone blade sticking out of Sadiek's back.

Realizing the wings were not getting the job done, Sadiek pushed himself over with surprising strength. Ean had only a moment to react before he would be crushed like Azalea. He used the man's own momentum to launch himself off the wings.

Leaping off Sadiek's back, he somehow landed on his feet a few paces away. And then his legs gave out. Letting out a surprised yelp,

Ean fell over on his side. He didn't hit the ground hard, but he struggled to get back on his feet.

At the same time, thankfully, Sadiek was having an even more difficult time at getting up. He was down on one knee, trying to push himself up with both hands and very shaky arms. While he struggled, he kept his eyes locked on Ean, the look on his face clearly showing his rage.

Ean glanced around quickly for anything he could use as a weapon, knowing he only had a brief amount of time before Sadiek came at him again. Unfortunately the room was mostly bare. The stone throne sat up on the dais, but Ean had no chance of reaching it and probably couldn't have moved it if he did. The flagstaffs that had been broken littered the ground, but they were all behind Sadiek at the moment. He was completely on his own.

The thought froze him. He was on his own and he was going to die. If he died, Zin, Azalea, and Yaeger would surely share the same fate soon after. Or they would get sucked back to the Abyss. All of their struggles, everything he had accomplished and how he had grown would be for nothing. And worst of all, he would have failed everyone.

Ean watched, paralyzed by his own fear, as Sadiek got to his feet. The older man took a quick glance at Ean's companions and a wicked smile spread across his face. He knew. He knew Ean was all alone. Ean, the least threatening of the three. The one with little strength. No speed or fighting abilities. Not even a weapon to defend himself.

With a short laugh, Sadiek turned his back on Ean and began advancing on Azalea.

Anger returned, filling Ean, burning away his aches and pains, scorching his fear in its inferno. How dare this monster dismiss him as nothing? How dare Sadiek try to murder his only friends, thinking Ean would just stand there and watch? Ean would probably die, but by the Abyss, he was going to make Sadiek regret underestimating him.

With a yell, Ean charged Sadiek one last time, filling himself with as much energy from the Abyss as he could, more than he had ever held before. He took on more than he knew he could handle, not caring anymore if it killed him. The energy charged his body, tore at it, but gave him one last burst of strength. He stopped funneling some of it to the hound, taking in that energy as well. His body hummed with power, the runes on his body blazing and overtaking the torch light. He charged ahead, a blazing light of rage and desperation.

Sadiek turned as he heard Ean yell, his body hunkering lower as it braced itself for the attack. Both of his arms went wide, like the teeth of a trap ready to snap shut as soon as Ean got in their range.

But Ean wasn't all emotion at this point. Just as he was about to reach Sadiek, he ducked low. The monster's blades swept above him, missing as Ean drove his shoulder into Sadiek's midsection. The blow rattled Ean's entire body, but he ignored the pain and brought even more energy from the Abyss to wash over it. He held so much now it felt like he was all energy, his body burning, overwhelming him. But he wasn't finished yet.

Not pausing, Ean began to unleash a flurry of blows to Sadiek's torso. The runes on his right hand blazed as he drove it repeatedly into the man's stomach. The satisfying sound of grunts from Sadiek accompanied every blow as the force of his fists lifted the man slightly into the air.

One of Sadiek's knees rose to strike Ean, but he simply punched it as well. He punched or swung his arms at any part of Sadiek that moved. Keeping this close, Ean realized that the man could not bend his arms to bring those deadly blades into play. So he stayed close, trying to make each blow count, maybe wear his opponent down, cause any kind of permanent damage before he burnt himself out completely.

A knee got past his defenses, slamming into his side, the pain almost doubling him over, but he kept swinging.

An elbow caught Ean on the side of his head, slightly blurring his vision, but he continued to throw everything he had.

An explosion of pain on the top of his head finally staggered him.

A kick to his chest caused Ean to stumble back a few steps.

And then, while Ean was attempting to recover...

Sadiek's full, unbroken right blade slide straight into Ean's chest.

CHAPTER 35

INSINCERE GOODBYES

THE POWER OF THE Abyss left Ean as the blade sliced through him. Pain took its place, the burning of overworked muscles, the stings of small cuts covering his body, and shockwaves flowing out like spiderwebs to his entire body from where he was skewered. Ean wasn't sure why he hadn't already passed out, but he wished he could. All he could do was reach down with both hands to grip the blade and hold himself up to keep from sliding down the blade further.

Since he was still conscious, he kept himself from looking down at what he knew was a mortal wound. Instead, he locked gazes with Sadiek, giving the man his best glare. If Ean was about to die, he wasn't going to give the man the satisfaction of seeing him afraid.

All he got in return for his effort was a smirk from the other man.

"It didn't have to end like this, my boy," Sadiek said. "You could have worked with me, been part of something amazing. Instead you let your fear and loyalty to a bunch of beasts cause your downfall. Pity."

"Someone...will stop you..." Ean got the words out through gritted teeth. "The people...or the Seekers will..." A coughing fit interrupted him, and he almost lost his grip on the blade. A small trickle of saliva ran out of the corner of his mouth. At least, he told himself it was saliva.

"The people? The people of this land are sheep, following the wills of deities that only talk to a handful of them. Even a blind man could tell that the high priests of the temples have their own agendas. But the 'people' follow along blindly anyway, moving about their mundane lives with no real purpose. I will give them a purpose, and they will thank me for it."

"And as for your Seekers, they are the worst of everyone. Blindly trying to hunt down anything connected to the Abyss, they won't bother with me or my creations. At least not until it's too late. By then, what good will three highly trained warriors be against a legion of my creations, creations that will be ten times as deadly as the ones you've seen. No, the Seekers won't be any trouble at all. No one will be any trouble."

"You're insane."

Those simple words seemed to strike a nerve.

With a snarl, Sadiek lifted Ean into the air by the blade in his chest. If Ean had thought the pain was excruciating before, the edges digging and cutting even more on his insides as his weight tried to pull him back down was beyond description. It took every last scrap of strength he had remaining to keep himself from sliding forward down the blade.

"Insane?! INSANE?! This world is insane. I am not the one that is insane." Spittle flew from Sadiek's mouth as he raged, contradicting his statement. "It is a shame you will not be alive to see my Master's return. To see how he sets this world right. When he is done, the way the world seems now will look insane. And if the people of this world fight the change too much and refuse to become a part of a better future, my Master will wipe them from this world, and we will start anew."

"The gods..." Each word was painful, but Ean wanted to keep pushing the man. It was the only act of defiance he had left. "Will never...let that..."

"The gods are impotent!" Sadiek screamed. "They are worthless and petty. The gods will be brought down just as easilllluuurrrkkkkk!"

A sharp pain pierced Ean's right leg just as a gurgling sound escaped Sadiek's mouth. It was nothing compared to the constant explosion of pain in his chest, but it was strong enough for him to notice. Looking down while trying his best not to see the damage still being done to his body, Ean's eyes went wide as he saw the top of one of the wooden flag staffs sticking into his leg.

Even more surprising was that the rest of the staff seemed to be coming right out of the middle of Sadiek's chest.

The pain in Ean's chest magnified as Sadiek suddenly threw out his arm, effectively dislodging Ean from the blade and sending him tumbling away. Ean was only in the air a moment before he crashed to the ground, hitting the stone floor hard. It probably would have hurt if the pain in his chest wasn't making the rest of his body feel numb. Coming to rest on his right side, Ean had the perfect view of Sadiek.

Standing behind the grotesque man, Azalea had both of her hands wrapped around the bottom of the flagstaff, a grim look of determination on her face. Even through slightly dimming eyes, Ean could see Azalea's legs wobble as she held herself up by the staff she had rammed through the back of Sadiek. Ean couldn't feel her through their bond but just by looking at how hunched over she was and how her body trembled, he guessed she was barely conscious as well.

Sadiek suddenly spun, the pole through his chest spinning with him and sending Azalea tumbling to the side. The Yulari didn't hit the ground that hard, but when she stopped rolling she didn't get up.

Sadiek did not seem to have any intention of going after her or Ean with a long pole sticking through his body. Letting out another gurgle, Sadiek stumbled away, heading in the direction of an exit out of the room. As he moved, the blades that used to be his forearms and hands began to shift. By the time the man was through one of the doorways, Ean could just make out the beginning of finger bones growing back into place.

With the main threat gone, Ean tilted his head slightly enough so that he was able to see the hound. It was still lying on the ground, breathing heavily but also seemed more relaxed. The wound in its stomach appeared to be healed although the fur was gone and a large, jagged scar was still visible. But it looked at least like the hound would live. Happiness for small victories.

The knowledge that the hound, and probably Azalea, would survive the day helped Ean relax. As much as the pain would allow. He kept his sight locked on the hound, having no desire to watch as life literally bled out of him.

It was strange for Ean, knowing he was going to die. What little energy he had left he funneled into a rage. He glanced down at his right arm, which was spread out in front of him, and at the runes covering it. They no longer glowed, the energy of the Abyss completely gone. Getting that tattoo had effectively sealed his fate. It had been the driving force behind every choice since he got it and ended in his journey here. No, the day he had summoned Zin for the first time had been what led him here. The imp, always convincing him to do foolish things, always getting him in trouble. If anything was to blame for Ean's death, it was that cursed imp. He wasn't even here to say goodbye. Better that he wasn't, he would probably spit in the imp's face...

No. It's not Zin's fault.

Ean let the anger drain out of him. No one was to blame, especially not Zin. Any trouble Ean had gotten into because of the imp had always been minor, a minor punishment from Cleff, a short beating from a bully. The other villagers had already looked down on him even before the imp had arrived. No, if anything Zin had been the reason he had lasted as long as he had in Rottwealth. Having Zin around had kept him sane, kept him from going down a darker path. He had certainly kept Ean from summoning anything that would have razed the entire village.

Zin truly was his best friend.

"Sorry I can't keep you from the Abyss..." Ean murmured.

"That doesn't look too good."

Speak of a friend, and he will come.

Walking into view, Zin's attention was completely on Ean's stomach. By his wide, downturned eyes and sad frown, Ean could tell the imp knew how bad things really were. He sat down a pace or two away from Ean's face, although his gaze remained on the wound for a few moments more.

"I'm sorry I couldn't help. I got here in the middle of the fight..."

"It's ok, Zin...."

"I tried to get close, bite him, claw a leg, but you both were moving so fast..."

"Nothing you could have done..."

Zin opened his mouth as if he was about to say more, then closed his eyes and sighed. When he opened them again, they returned to Ean's wound.

"That's not something you can just walk off, is it..."

"No..."

"What if we found some medicine, wrapped the wound, and did something..." There wasn't a drop of hope in the imp's voice. "There could still be something around here that hasn't been looted that you could use."

"It's fine...Zin...I know..."

Hanging his head, the imp looked down at his hands. They were clasped together instead of his usual nervous trait of rubbing them together. Ean and Zin sat there in silence for a few moments before Zin finally raised his head.

"So, I guess we should say our goodbyes then."

"Yes."

Silence.

"Well, this is horrible."

"Zin... you don't..."

"No, no, I do have something I want to say."

The imp stood, glancing quickly at Ean's wound, and then looking away just as fast. Shaking his head, Zin made an obvious effort to look Ean in the eyes.

"Alright. Since that first time you brought me back into this world, I know we haven't always seen eye to eye..."

Ean grunted.

"Let me finish!" Zin growled. "Now, like I was saying. We haven't always seen eye to eye but I have always respected you. The way you tolerated how you were treated in Rottwealth. Well, it reminded me of how all of my kind are treated in the Abyss. Like the lowest form of life. And you stayed strong, just like I stayed strong during my years of captivity."

Zin began to pace as he continued.

"I never talked about the more than one hundred years I was enslaved to one of the Nar'Grim, and this moment certainly isn't the time to start. But seeing what you went through in Rottwealth and how strong you stayed was like looking into a mirror. Well, a broken one at least that distorts your appearance. Anyway, that's how I knew I could trust you. And how I knew that eventually I could show you how to apply those tattoos."

"They didn't...help much..." Ean was able to get out weakly.

"Right..." Zin paused a moment, then continued on. "Anyway. It's important that you know that I trusted you completely even though you didn't always trust me. I have always tried to act in your best interests."

"I know."

"Good. That's important."

The imp stopped moving, but kept his gaze ahead leaving the room mostly silent again. Besides Ean's own labored breaths and the sounds of the Yaeger's heavier breathing. The flames in the torches hanging from the walls seemed to dance around silently as they bathed the room in light. How peaceful. He could close his eyes for just a few moments...

"Anyway, hey, HEY!" Two small hands started shaking Ean and he opened his eyes. They were so terribly heavy and the stone floor was so cold, maybe Zin could find him some straw or something else he could use to cushion his head...

"Stay with me for just a moment longer." Zin was right in his face now, his legs crossed as he sat near Ean's hand. The imp's hands were clutched together almost as if the imp was in prayer. "I just want to say that I know you would never become the monster that used to call this place home. You are a stubborn and difficult person, but you also have shown how much you care for the people in your life, even if they are not human. Your acceptance of Azalea and me, and even that stupid hound, shows what kind of a person you are deep down. And that person would never turn into the monster that was my former master in this world."

"Thanks...Zin..."

"Yes, well, enough of this mushy stuff, I think. Best to say our goodbyes while you still can." His voice took on a nervous edge, which Ean barely noticed. It was hard for him to focus on anything at the moment. He just wanted to sleep. "How do you humans say goodbye? Shaking hands? Can you manage that?"

"Sure." His arm didn't respond at first. It felt asleep. Probably because of how he was lying. After a bit of a struggle, he was finally able to lift his right hand up slightly off the ground and hold it out to Zin.

"Goodbye, Ean." The imp grasped his hand tightly and gave it a good couple of shakes. Even with his entire arm and hand mostly numb Ean felt a sharp pain. Had the foolish imp grabbed him too tightly and sunk his nails into Ean's hand? No, the pain was on Ean's palm.

Zin let go of Ean's hand and it dropped to the ground. Ean simply did not have the energy to keep it up. It smacked on the stone floor, Ean's palm opening face up. Something was resting in his hand. Trying his best to focus, Ean saw what looked like a small piece of stone sitting in his hand. It was black and scarred, just like the sphere in the center of the room. Strange. Why had the imp--

A flash of white light, brighter than anything Ean had ever seen seared his eyes. Seared his brain. Seared his soul. White fire engulfed him. His mouth opened to scream, but the fire took him, burning him away to nothing.

CHAPTER 36

FULL CIRCLE
END OF THE WARMTH, 184 A.P.

THE CROWD LET OUT another cheer as Bran was lifted into the air. Men and women alike boosted him up, while those around them pushed tables and chairs out of the way to get closer to him. Every single villager of Rottwealth was crammed into the Golden Coin to celebrate their hero. The monster that had plagued their small village for an entire season was finally dead, its head hanging over the bar as a monument to Bran's accomplishment. The sound of the cheering crowd floated out of the open windows of the inn and echoed off the mountains surrounding the small village.

Bran let out a laugh as the crowd began to pass him around, although it sounded forced to anyone that was paying attention. No one was. Many of the villagers had started celebrating early in the morning when the news of Bran's victory began to spread. Even though the monster had been slain the night before, Bran's father had made sure that he had all day to plan the true celebration for his son's victory. He also wanted to make sure his son was as healed up as possible, and practically had him bathed in a Rottwealth salve. He had used most of what his wife had been able to salvage from Cleff's destroyed home, although she had left Cleff's body under the rubble where she had found it.

Branston the First was behind the bar, making sure the drinks were flowing and the money was coming in. His wife mingled with the crowd, saying repeatedly, "That's my son. The boy I raised to be a Hero."

"What a fine job you've done with him," one of the other mothers would say."

"You should be so proud," another man added.

She wore the biggest grin, puffing out her already ample chest even more. Both of Bran's parents' smiles grew as the crowd began to yell out in praise of Bran.

"To Bran! The slayer of beasts!"

"To the Savior of the Village!"

"Bran for Mayor! Bran for Mayor!"

The last chant quickly wiped the smile from Branston the First's face. Apparently the elder Branston wasn't ready to hand over his power to his son quite yet.

Eventually the crowd let the hero down and the back slapping by the men and cheek-kissing by the women began. Bran was passed around more than a newborn baby, a fake smile painted across his face the entire time. More than one girl swooned in his presence. A couple of cheeky older women whispered suggestively in his ear, bringing a blush to his cheeks. They all seemed ready to take advantage of Jaslen's absence. The men on the other hand all wanted to see his blade, a strange sword made of stone that weighed less than a handful of flowers. No one seemed to be talking about the two companions that had left with Bran at the beginning of the season and were absent now. No one even seemed to notice.

Well, no one except Zin.

Zin could see it all from his spot on one of the window ledges. See the fake smiles and insincere congratulations. Sure, many were happy to be free of the beast, but Zin saw a lot of jealousy in the faces of many of the men. If Azalea was here, Zin was sure she would be drinking deeply of all of the unpleasant feelings that were drifting around the room.

Azalea. That girl was even more trouble now than she had been before. Zin knew that having her wings ripped from her body had to be the most traumatizing experience for her, but a Yulari that was afraid to be in a crowd? It was like finding a hound that didn't want to eat. And the hound. That creature had been almost impossible to herd along back to Rottwealth. Zin had wanted to just leave it behind, but oh no. Azalea wanted it for protection. Like she couldn't rip apart most humans with her bare hands.

Zin let out a grunt of disgust. A patron that was sitting near the window turned to look around, glaring at the window and out into the night but didn't see the invisible imp. With a shrug, the man turned back to the excitement inside the inn. Zin had almost hoped the man had seen him. Biting one of these humans might improve his mood a bit. Instead he was left to simply shake his head at the whole affair inside before he climbed out the window and landed easily on the dirt below.

With the entire village packed into the inn, the streets of Rottwealth were completely empty. Even the small torches that sat in front of each home on the edge of the main road were dark, making the light of the moons the only thing lighting his way. Not that he needed even the moonlight. His eyes were well adjusted for the dark. But he should be off, things to do tonight after all.

Zin casually strolled down the street, thinking about what this night could mean while keeping his eyes open for a stray meal. One or two rats would be perfectly filling, and with the village so dark at the moment, they should be brave enough to be out and scurrying around. It wasn't until he had reached the south edge of the town square before he finally caught sight of one. It led him on a merry chase but eventually Zin caught it and sat for a few moments to enjoy his meal before continuing on.

The blue moon hovered in the northern sky, while the green one climbed into the eastern skyscape opposite the red moon just starting to rise in the west. Still quite a bit of time before midnight. Not that midnight had any significance other than the fact that the partying villagers would be too sloshed to notice a Yulari and an imp strolling through town.

Zin paused as he reached the ruins of Ean's old home, feeling slightly nostalgic. It had been his old home too after all, maybe not for as long as it had been Ean's but still for many years. From what he could gather from eavesdropping on the villagers, something had set the lizard creature off one night and Cleff's home had simply been the first thing it reached. A shame really, both in Cleff's death and how little respect he received.

Zin had been there to watch as Bran's mother sifted through the rubble like a vulture, picking up whatever she had thought was useful and not giving Cleff's body a second glance. Zin knew Ean would have been heartbroken to see what had happened. The boy seemed to respect the older man, if not love him like a father. To have Cleff left like that in his makeshift tomb instead of properly buried surely would have angered Ean to say the least.

"Oh, well," Zin said aloud. Ean wasn't here to see it. No point worrying about the past, the future was going to be difficult enough to worry about.

Leaving the ruined house behind him, Zin followed the path to the marsh, and then followed the edge of the marsh to the mine and the cabin where the foreman used to work before the madness of the lizard creature began. Walking up to the door, he knocked on it a few times, trying not to get angry at the fact that the door knob was placed high enough that it was out of his reach.

"Who is it?" Came a reply from inside, the feminine voice trembling with each word.

"Obviously it's me, Azalea. Open the door and get out here. All of the villagers are far too busy to come down here tonight."

The door opened slightly, a purple eye appearing in the gap and took a quick look around. Seemingly satisfied with what she saw, Azalea opened the door the rest of the way. She had shed the appearance of the common girl that she had been using for most of the trip and looked her full Yulari self, minus her missing wings.

"What, you think I would bring a bunch of people here just to mess with you?" Zin said, slightly annoyed.

"You mean like how you tricked me into entering that 'abandoned' house in Wethrintir and I found myself walking into the middle of a gathering of housewives?"

Zin couldn't help but laugh. The Yulari had run cowering from the building and right out of town. It had taken him the rest of the night to find her.

"Ok fine, but do you honestly think I would mess with you on a night like tonight?"

"Yes," she replied in a pouty voice.

"Stop being a baby and let's go." Glancing around, he frowned. "Where is the hound?"

"I let him go explore the mine. He was growing restless in the cabin here and was starting to gnaw on some of the table legs."

"Whatever." Turning his back on the Yulari, Zin walked towards the mine. He could feel the Yulari's eyes on his back, but was not surprised when she came jogging up and fell in at his side. They both stayed quiet as they walked into the pitch black opening of the mine, the gravity of what they were about to do hanging heavily on Zin. The Yulari's mood had been impossible to predict ever since her mutilation. She now behaved differently than any Yulari he had ever met. In some ways he found her more pleasant, but mostly she made him more wary than ever.

"Do you really think this will work?" the Yulari asked quietly, her voice breaking the silence. They were deep enough into the mine now that the entrance was barely visible.

"I would hope so, or else the trip here was a waste of time."

"Well, I had suggested we stay at your master's old lair. With the village below it completely wiped out by Lav'zernathar, we wouldn't have been bothered. I don't like having Ean's old village and all its people sitting right outside."

They had found Ulundkin completely destroyed once they had healed up enough to head outside. Lav'zernathar hadn't been lying when he said he was going to pay the villagers back for whatever they had done to him. Every single house had lay in smoking ruins or was still on fire when they had left. Zin couldn't help but shudder knowing that Lav was out there somewhere, completely free to do whatever he wished.

"Did you really want to stay in that cursed land?" Zin asked. "I don't know about you, but the Plague twisted my stomach. I had no desire to stay in a place that constantly made me feel sick."

"Maybe..."

Did the Yulari actually fear humans now that much that she would rather constantly feel sick than live in a place this close to them, even when they were a constant source of food for her? The girl was more messed up than Zin had realized. He almost felt bad now for his little prank in Wethrintir. Almost.

They continued on in silence after that, following the gently downward sloping path deeper into the mine. They began to pass random bones lying about, leftovers from the lizard creature's meals, no doubt. When the sound of ripping and the occasional growl reached them, coming from somewhere ahead, they slowed in unison.

"That has to be the hound, right?" Zin said, hoping he was right.

"I'm sure it is. That lizard thing is dead."

Zin found it humorous that the Yulari was terrified of humans, but disregarded anything else that might be a threat.

"And the villagers didn't mention anything else being down here. But what could he possibly be eating?"

At the back of the mine they found where the lizard creature had made its home. Large collections of bones and torn clothes lay scattered about, even a few decaying pieces of villagers here and there, adding a rotten smell to the air. In the middle lay what was left of the lizard creature, minus its head. Yeager had his jaws sunk into one of its legs. Bran must have left it where it fell, and now the hound was getting a meal out of its carcass.

"You want to do this here?" Azalea wrinkled her nose in disgust. "It stinks in here."

"We can clean it out after we've done what we need to do."

"Well, how long will that take?"

"I have no idea."

Throwing her hands in the air, the Yulari stalked a few paces away before sitting down on the ground with her back up against the stone wall. Pulling her knees in close to her chest, Azalea wrapped her arms around her legs and rested the side of her head on her knees so that she was still watching Zin.

With a sigh, Zin began kicking aside various bones, rocks, and other things that he would rather not know what they had been. The hound lifted his head once when a random bone struck him in the nose, letting out a small growl before returning to his meal. He seemed to be struggling with the lizard's scales, but was slowly making progress with the help of his saliva. Zin was just glad the hound was keeping itself occupied.

When a suitable space had been cleared to Zin's liking, he sat down in the center and glanced over at Azalea. "Can you toss me the stone?"

Azalea sat up long enough to throw a black stone the size of the imp's palm to him, and then curled herself back up into a ball. She truly looked pathetic compared to her former self. Zin was starting to hope this worked just so that the Yulari might get some confidence back. Or she would just end up hiding down in the mine the rest of her long, long life. Didn't much matter to Zin either way. At least that's what he told himself.

Taking the stone, he drew the one symbol he needed into the ground. The symbol for the Abyss.

"Here goes nothing," he said, and then dropped the stone onto the symbol before leaping back to watch the light show.

CHAPTER 37

EPILOGUE

WHITE LIGHT. FLOATING, DRIFTING along in nothingness. No pain, no fear, no memories. Ean had never been so at peace. A thousand seconds versus a thousand years--they were all the same here--in this state of perfection.

And then the light flared, ruining everything.

Memories washed over him like a flood, each one eliciting emotion. Happiness, pain, love, disappointment, joy, loss, determination. Each memory filled him with the emotions that had been missing, each one making him feel more alive. And making him question if he wanted to be.

Physical sensations came next, and unfortunately the only thing he felt was a burning pain everywhere. He tried to scream, but nothing came out, or nothing was there to make the scream. He had no idea. There was just the pain and the memories.

The light grew in intensity, the pain growing with it. Another sensation slowly started to surface amidst the pain as well. It was cold, a chill, that originated from his hands and legs until it coated his entire body, mixing in with the pain. Except he had no body, no arms or legs. All that existed was the light.

No, that wasn't true. He felt more than cold, the rough feeling of stone, pressing against his palms. He tried moving his fingers and the tips brush against the surface, one finger even moving a small object. So his hands did exist. But all he could still see was the light. And feel the pain. It was intense, scouring his mind, making it difficult to think.

"Calm. Find calm. It's almost done."

That voice. He had heard that voice before. He tried to search his memories. The pain made it difficult. That all of his memories had only moments before returned in a jumble of pictures and emotions made it impossible.

Something else was out there in the light. Something familiar. He tried reaching for it and immediately regretted it as the pain tripled in intensity. But every time he was able to block out some of the pain and focus his mind, he felt that familiar presence. It felt so close and comforting, like a warm fire after a cold day spent in the marshes of Rottwealth. If he could just touch it...

Instead of reaching out for it with his hand, he reached with his mind. With his soul. He grasped it, and the energy of the Abyss trickled into him.

Pain tore through his body and he threw his head back, his arms flung out wide as he tried to scream again. It started as a gurgle, at least having some sound now, and then grew into an actual yell. Colors filled his vision for the briefest moment before eyelids slammed shut, bringing darkness but not an escape from the pain. It felt like he was being torn apart into the tiniest of pieces and then slammed back together, over and over again. His voice became hoarse as he continued to yell.

And then the pain was gone and the energy of the Abyss rushed into him like a flood. It almost overwhelmed him, but he somehow wrestled it under control. It filled his being, gave him strength and comfort, made him feel alive. He and the energy felt one and the same.

Bright spots were all Ean saw at first as he opened his eyes, little round balls that danced around his vision and mingled with a faint blue light. Ean increased the flow of energy again into his body and the light increased. The spots faded away and Ean stood, then immediately regretted it as black spots raced across his vision, his head suddenly going light. Falling to his knees, he winced as they smashed into the hard ground and then immediately fell forward onto his hands before emptying his stomach. At least his body tried to empty his stomach, but all that came out was bile. When he was finished, he remained on his hands and knees, taking a moment to catch his breath and get his bearings. Clearly his body had yet to really recover from...whatever it was that had happened.

"Well, that was gross."

Zin. Turning his head slightly to the right, Ean found the imp leaning up against a stone wall. His small arms were crossed in front of his chest and he wore a satisfied smirk, the right edge of his mouth showing off the tiniest bit of teeth.

"What happened..." Even talking made Ean's stomach gurgle at him and he returned to looking at the ground. The floor was like the wall Zin was leaning against, nothing but stone and rock, but roughly cut unlike the smooth stone paths of the lair of Zin's old master.

"Well," Zin replied, pushing himself away from the wall and moving closer. "You were going to die, and I had put way too much time and effort into you to let that happen."

"Zin..."

"Ok, ok. So maybe it had been part of my plan all along. Well, not the part where you almost died. You didn't need to be on the verge of death for it to work."

Taking a deep breath, Ean sat up straight. His head grew light again but he fought off the nausea. "Zin, start from--"

A pair of arms and legs suddenly wrapped around him. The impact would have knocked him over had he not tensed up immediately, thinking he was under attack. But the smell of lavender or lilies quickly made him realize it was Azalea even before she spoke.

"I thought you were gone forever." She sobbed, which alone almost made Ean fall over. Azalea was not one to sob. Or even tear up for that matter. "I'm so glad you are alive."

"Yes, well..." Ean had no idea how to react to this side of Azalea. The fact that she was squeezing him tighter and tighter wasn't helping either. "Azalea, you need to lighten up a little, it's getting hard to breath."

"Oh, sorry." She stopped squeezing as tightly but made no move to detangle herself from around him. Instead she rested her head on his shoulder. Even in his weakened state, Ean couldn't help but enjoy her touch.

A cough brought his attention back to his surroundings. He shot Zin an annoyed look. "You were about to tell me exactly what your plan had been?"

"Yes, um, right." The imp moved around until he was in front of Ean then took a seat. "Well, to sum it up, the plan was to get those tattoos on your body, have you use your power as often as possible so they spread, and then get you to my master's old lair to complete the process."

"Complete the process?" He shifted around into a more comfortable sitting position, Azalea moving with him, before he continued. "What process, Zin?"

"Well, to keep with telling you the summarized version, to make you immortal like my old master."

"What?!"

"I said, to make you--"

"Yes, I heard you, I heard you. I'm immortal? Wait, your master was killed..." Ean considered himself fairly intelligent, but he was completely lost now.

"Ok, well, it's mostly immortal. Your life is tied to that."

Ean followed the imp's pointing finger to the side of the room, past where his hound was apparently snacking on something with scales, and found a small white orb floating just a small ways off the ground. It was a perfect sphere, rotating slowly in the air and giving off a faint light. A closer look revealed that the orb looked almost translucent with small clouds floating along inside of it. Now that he realized it was there, he could feel it in the same way that he could feel Azalea and the hound through their bonds.

"What is that?"

I am Auz.

That voice! It was the same--

"Think of that as your heart," Zin said, interrupting his thoughts. "From what I could figure out, it keeps you alive even when you receive wounds that would kill even the strongest person. It also connects you to the Abyss somehow." The imp shrugged. "To be honest, my master never talked about it, but I knew it was important. When my master was alive, he acted like it was more important than anything. It was also much, much larger which makes me think yours will grow as well."

A flash of a memory raced through Ean's mind. Sitting in the center of the throne room of Zin's old master had been a huge sphere, its surface scorched and cracked. It had seemed unimportant at the time, just a piece of art or something to fill the room. Was that what Zin was talking about?

Yes, that was corpse of Auz. Now, I am Auz.

The voice was confusing Ean. "The sphere?"

Yes.

"Yes," Zin replied, then tilted his head slightly as he regarded Ean. "Are you alright? You look strange. Besides just coming back from being nothing a few moments ago and having a Yulari wrapped around your body, of course."

"I'm just getting used to the thing speaking in my head".

Zin blinked rapidly. "What?"

"The sphere, it's talking to me."

Not an It. Auz.

"Fine, fine," Ean said, looking over at the sphere. "Your name is Auz." A feeling of satisfaction flowed back to him from the little sphere.

"Oh, right. Talking to the orb..." Zin said slowly.

"You didn't know it was alive!"

"Listen, like I said, my old master didn't tell me anything about the orb. I just knew it was somehow connected to his power and we would need at least a piece of it to create the same thing for you."

"So, that's what you put in my hand when I was about to die."

"Yes." Getting up, Zin walked a few paces over to the orb, leaning over it to take a closer look. "I had no idea exactly how it worked. I just knew that touching it to those runes on your body would start...well, whatever it is that connects the two of you. The plan wasn't for you to be mortally wounded when we tried to make the connection though. I was worried, but thankfully, it worked."

"Otherwise, I would be dead." Ean winced slightly as Azalea squeezed him a little tighter.

"Yes, pretty much."

"And so it took my body, and then did what? Why did it bring me back here? Where are we anyway?"

The imp shrugged, rubbing his hands together. "I know as much as you do about it. As for where we are, I brought you back home. We're in the mine at Rottwealth."

"Home?" A dozen thoughts ran through Ean's head and just as quickly poured from his mouth. "But what about the monster?" A quick look at what the hound was chewing on quickly answered that question. "What killed it? Was it the hound? Or did Bran and Jaslen return with some way to kill it. Have you seen them? Have you seen Old Cleff?"

Turning away, Zin shrugged again. "You were gone for over thirty days. That's how long it took for the three of us to get back here. The lizard thing was killed by Bran the night before we got back. Everything else, we can catch up later. We have more important things to discuss."

The absence of news about both Cleff and Jaslen was obvious. "Zin, tell me--"

"Ean, I really haven't heard much in the short amount of time we've been back. Bran killed the monster with some weapon he was given or found sometime after he left us. Jaslen didn't come back with him, and since she snuck away, most of the village thinks she became one of the monster's victims."

"But we know that's not true. Bran must have some idea--"

"We can discuss that later, too. At the very least, the first thing you need to do is get some clothing. It's making me uncomfortable having to talk to you while you are naked."

His eyes going wide, Ean looked down and saw that the imp was telling the truth. He wasn't wearing a single piece of clothing. The only reason he probably wasn't shivering from the cold was because Azalea was providing him with plenty of warmth. Heat certainly was filling his cheeks.

"I can't walk into town naked..." Ean mumbled trying his best to ignore the feel of Azalea against his body. "Someone needs to go get me some clothes. And figure out what's been happening since I've been gone. Maybe Azalea could go get me some clothes and use her charms to--"

He cut off as she squeezed him tight. "Don't make me go alone. There are so many people. I couldn't stand it."

"Couldn't stand it?" Turning his head, which was all he could move at this point, Ean shot Zin a confused look. "What's going on?"

"Nothing. She just has some fear of humans now. No big deal."

Sighing, Ean began to carefully unwrap Azalea from his body. She made a small whining sound but otherwise let him.

"I guess I could sneak into the village and try to steal some clothes. Shouldn't be too difficult at night."

No. Impossible.

"What?" The voice in his head had sounded very serious.

Cannot leave. Must stay close. Rule.

"What rule? What are you talking about?" Both Azalea and Zin were looking at Ean now, faces completely blank. "It's the orb. It's telling me--"

Auz. Name is Auz.

"Fine, *Auz* is telling me I have to stay close to it."

Zin walked back over to stare at the sphere. "Maybe it's got attachment issues. Or maybe Azalea has already rubbed off on it."

"Go and rot, you stupid imp!" Azalea lunged for him, but Zin was too quick. He leapt away from Azalea and right into the side of the hound. That earned the imp a growl and he moved away, finally ending at the path back out of the mine. When Azalea made to lunge again, Ean rose and stood in front of her, cutting her off. He expected to have to struggle to rise, but he felt surprising strong now.

"Enough. I have enough to deal with right now without having to keep the two of you from each other's throats."

"Fine." They both said in unison, and then shot each other similar dark looks.

"Good. Now, I'm going into town. I'll be right back."

Cannot go.

"I'll be right back, Auz."

Ean turned and began walking away, passing Zin and moving further out of the mine.

CANNOT GO.

Ignoring the booming voice in his head, Ean continued on. Until he hit a wall. At least that's what it felt like, his nose pressing against his face, his knee smacking up painfully against some invisible barrier. Raising his hands, Ean could actually feel a smooth surface preventing him from going further. It covered the entire opening, effectively blocking off the only way out of the mine. Making it impossible to leave.

Spinning around, he stormed back to where everyone was gathered.

"Did you do that?" It felt somewhat weird yelling at a small floating orb, but it also made him feel better.

Cannot go.

Throwing his hands in the air, Ean began to pace around. Almost killed, ripped apart, and then brought back. Naked. A Yulari that was afraid of people, an imp that had given him the gift of immortality without knowing any of the details, and a hound that listened when it felt like it. And now a sentient orb with a control problem. Rounding on the orb, and feeling stupid for what he was about to do, Ean glared at it while pointing a finger.

"You can't keep me here. I need clothes, food, I want to see..." Well, he had no one really to see in the village except Old Cleff. "I can't stay down here."

Not Auz fault. Is rule.

"What rule? What are you talking about?" He didn't care anymore how stupid he looked arguing naked with the sphere.

Rule five.

"And what is rule five?"

Master can go as far as connection allows.

That didn't sound promising. "And will the connection allow me to go further?"

"When Auz grows, connection grows."

"And when will that be?"

When Auz grows.

Giving up, Ean collapsed to the ground. He immediately regretted the dramatic move as his bare bottom smacked against the cold, hard, and not so smooth mine floor. Placing his chin in his hands, he let out an exasperated sigh.

"So I'm stuck here, with nothing".

"Well, not exactly," Zin said, moving next to him. "Azalea?"

The Yulari moved over to the side of the mine and picked up a pack that had been sitting there. Untying the string that kept it closed, she opened the bag and dumped its entire contents on the ground. The Carnslugs, over a dozen of them, hit the floor with a squishing sound and then immediately began to crawl around.

"See?" Zin said, "Not a completely horrible start. At least we have an unlimited supply of food now."

Without making a sound, Ean buried his face in his hands. Immortality was going to be a long and painful experience.

THIS ENDS THE TALE OF EAN THE HEALER,
ADOPTED SON OF CLEFF.

THIS BEGINS THE TALE OF EAN THE IMMORTAL,
MASTER OF BEASTS AND FOREVER
BOUND TO THE ABYSS.

T H E   E N D

ABOUT JAMES

JAMES VERNON was born and lives in eastern Pennsylvania. He enjoys reading, writing, most types of music, and anything in the fantasy and sci-fi realm. Often stuck in long commutes for his job, James's imagination was free to create new worlds and stories. Through the assistance of family, friends, and some generous backers, James has been able to pursue his dream to spread his stories to more then just his own mind.

For more information about James and the Three Moons Realm, visit us at jamesrvernon.com!

THE FOLLOWING IS A LIST OF MY VERY, VERY GENEROUS
KICKSTARTER BACKERS.
IT'S THANKS TO THEM THAT THIS STORY IS
SEEING THE LIGHT OF DAY.

My Strath Haven Family: Tara Flynn, Pat Walsh, Chris Buhler, Kate Woodruff, Megan Shell, Vanessa von Hagen, Maureen

Rob and Angel Logan, Mary and Michael Hahn, Amanda Johnson, Sarah K. Greybeck, Jennifer L. Pierce, Eric Camil Jr., Nathan Briley, Robbie, Alexandra N. Walters, Laura Stephenson

Christopher J. Markus, Brent Day, Keith Hall, Christopher Sneeringer, Silence in the Library Publishing, Nick Tyler, D-Rock, Kate Scott, Daniel Engstrom, Robby Thrasher, Butch Shomph, Edward Earl Duggan, Don, Beth, and Meghan Ferris, SwordFire, Benjamin Abbott, Vanessa Chalub, Bob Whitely, Stephen Cheng, Paul D., Paulina Stefanek, Pamela Wayne